S0-BKV-335

SEASON
1946-47

EDITED BY
DANIEL BLUM
NORMAN MACDONALD
ASSOCIATE

DANIEL BLUM, Editor and Publisher
NORMAN MACDONALD, Associate Editor
VIOLA KRUENER, Executive Secretary
GEORGE FREEDLEY, WILLIAM LEONARD,
TORBEN PRESTHOLDT—Feature Writers
CONSTANTINE—Staff Photographer

ABOUT THEATRE WORLD . . .

This is the Third Volume of THEATRE WORLD, the complete pictorial and statistical yearbook of the 1946-47 New York Theatrical Season.

THEATRE WORLD is published annually.

THEATRE WORLD is gaining international popularity because its profusion of illustrations speaks a universal language and offers an unparalleled visual panorama of the theatrical activity in America.

Readers will find this comprehensive compendium will afford great enjoyment as well as prove to be a ready reference.

THE EDITORS

CONTENTS

The editors wish to thank the Broadway Theatrical Press Representatives, the Theatre Collection of the New York Public Library and Celebrity Service, Inc., for valuable assistance.

Published Yearly
Printed by The Stuyvesant Press Corp. Engravings by Western Photo Engraving Co.
To obtain copies of Volume I or II or any information concerning this publication—write to Norman Macdonald, Theatre World, 105 West 43rd Street, New York 18, N. Y.

HELEN HAYES in "HAPPY BIRTHDAY"

THE NEW YORK SEASON

The 1946-47 season will be remembered as a season of revivals. Nearly one third of all the productions to reach Broadway were revivals. There were twenty-six of them, as against thirteen last year.

Excluding experimental productions and City Center return engagements, eighty-one attractions arrived on the Broadway scene. Among the new plays achieving success were: "Finian's Rainbow," "Joan of Lorraine," "Brigadoon," "Happy Birthday," "All My Sons," "Icetime," "John Loves Mary," "The Medium," "Years Ago," "The Fatal Weakness," "Present Laughter," "Another Part of the Forest," and "The Iceman Cometh."

The revivals that found favor critically or financially included "Lady Windermere's Fan," "Burlesque," "Cyrano de Bergerac," "Sweethearts," "The Importance of Being Earnest," "Alice in Wonderland," the musical version of "Street Scene," "Volpone," and "Androcles and the Lion."

The calibre of the new straight plays was decidedly mediocre; not one of them would be worthy of joining a list of revivals in future seasons. The musicals, however, were in most cases distinctive. "Finian's Rainbow," "Street Scene," "Brigadoon," and "The Medium," could more than hold their own in any season.

In many ways it was a quiet year. The producers, the playwrights and the press were all very friendly. Maxwell Anderson loved all the critics, and the critics, with one exception, loved Maxwell Anderson. Orson Welles kept his distance on the West Coast, and Irwin Shaw had no play ready for production and therefore had nothing to complain about. All was peaceful and calm save for one little ripple. Margaret Webster, from a lecture platform, hinted that the critics ate and drank too well before going to work. The Critics' Circle, with a new system of voting (making a selection mandatory), labeled "All My Sons" the best play of the season. This is more than can be said of the Pulitzer Prize Committee. They didn't think any play this year worthy of an award and said so.

Among the events of the season to be remembered were the failure of the highly publicized American Repertory Theatre; the interest taken in the Experimental Theatre and its aims; the establishing of the Lunts' long run record with "O, Mistress Mine"; the return of Eugene O'Neill with "The Iceman Cometh,"—his first play to reach Broadway in twelve years; the failure of Donald Wolfit's Repertory Company to duplicate last season's success of the Old Vic Company; the triumph of Hollywood's Ingrid Bergman on the legitimate stage in "Joan of Lorraine"; the successful return of Ina Claire after too long an absence; the now famous one word ("No") Robert Garland review of "Heads or Tails"; and the return of European plays to the New York Stage.

Broadway Calendar

June 1, 1946
to
June 1, 1947

BARRYMORE THEATRE

Opened Monday, June 3, 1946.**
Ruth Chatterton and John Huntington present:

SECOND BEST BED†

By N. Richard Nash; Staged by Miss Chatterton and Mr. Nash; Setting and Costumes by Motley; The Song, "Would You Win The World's Acclaim" composed by Richard Dyer-Bennet.

Cast of Characters

Ballad Seller........Richard Dyer-Bennet
Nell Garris........Elizabeth Eustis
Fenny Brushell........Peter Boyne
Yorick........Ralph Cullinan
Anne Hathaway Shakespeare Ruth Chatterton
Lewis Poggs........Ralph Forbes
Squire Simon Lummle........Howard Fischer*
The Beadle........Max Stamm
Will Shakespeare........Barry Thomson
Master Yarrow........John McKee
Farmer Legge........Jefferson Coates
Michael, The Tavern Keeper......Ralph Sumpter
Harelip Ben........John Gay

A Comedy in three acts. The entire action of the play takes place in the combination "Main Room" and "Parlor" in Anne Hathaway's Cottage, Shottery, parish of old Stratford-on-Avon, Warwickshire, at the beginning of the Seventeenth Century.

Company Manager, SAM NIXON
Press Representative, VINCE MCKNIGHT
Stage Manager, LILLIAN UDVARDY

†Title taken from the only mention made by William Shakespeare of his wife, Anne Hathaway in his last will and testament: *"Item: I Gyve unto my wief my second best bed."*
*Played by Richard Temple during tour.
**Closed June 8, 1946. (8 performances)

Ruth Chatterton Barry Thomson
Encircled: Ruth Chatterton

Ruth Chatterton—Howard Fischer—Peter Boyne—Elizabeth Eustis—Barry Thomson—Ralph Cullinan—Richard Dyer-Bennet—John McKee—Max Stamm—Jefferson Coates—Ralph Forbes—John Gay—Ralph Sumpter

Colin Keith-Johnston—Luis Von Rooten—Helen Flint

Luis Von Rooten Edgar Kent

BILTMORE THEATRE

Opened Wednesday, June 5, 1946.**
George Abbott presents:

THE DANCER

By Milton Lewis and Julian Funt; Staged by Everett Sloane; Music by Paul Bowles; Designed by Motley.

Cast of Characters
(in order of appearance)

Henry Wilkins .... Edgar Kent
Aubrey Stewart .... Colin Keith-Johnston
The Inspector .... Luis Van Rooten
Sergei Krainine .... Anton Dolin*
Madeline Krainine .... Bethel Leslie
Catherine Krainine .... Helen Flint

A Murder Mystery in three acts. The entire action takes place between 8:30 and 11 P.M., in the living-room of Aubrey Stewart's house in present day Paris.

General Manager, CHARLES HARRIS
Press, RICHARD MANEY, ANNE WOLL
Production Manager, ROBERT GRIFFITH
Stage Manager, EMERY BATTIS

*Played during tryout tour by Leon Fokine.
**Closed June 8, 1946. (5 performances)

Bethel Leslie Colin Keith-Johnston

CENTER THEATRE

Opened Thursday, June 20, 1946.***
Sonja Henie and Arthur M. Wirtz present:

ICETIME

Production by Sonart Productions; production director, William H. Burke; Lyrics and Music by James Littlefield and John Fortis; Staging and Choreography by Catherine Littlefield; Settings by Edward Gilbert; Costumes by Lou Eisele and Billy Livingston; Assistant Choreographer Dorothie Littlefield; Lighting by Eugene Braun; Skating Direction by May Judels; Musical arrangements by Paul Van Loan; Conductor, David Mendoza.

Featuring

Joan Hyldoft — Freddie Trenkler*

The Bruises:
Monty Stott, Geoffe Stevens, Sid Spalding
Helga and Inge Brandt
Florence and Robert Ballard
Buster Grace and Charles Slagle
Evelyn and James Kenny**

James Caesar	Ann Michel
Helen Carter	Sharlee Munster
James Carter	Berenice Odell
Paul Castle	Buck Pennington
Charles Cavanaugh	Ragna Ray
Grace Church	Jack Reese
Jinx Clark	Jerry Rehfield
Kay Corcoran	Lucille Risch
Claire Dalton	Jean Sakovich
Fritz Dietl	Joe Shillen
Helen Dutcher	Jimmie Sisk
Walli Hackman	Bing Stott
John Kasper	Sally Tepley
Patrick Kazda	Eileen Thompson
Marion Lulling	Cissy Trenholm
Edward McDonald	John Walsh

Vocals: Jay Martin, Denise Briault, Shirley Weber, Richard Craig

Songs: 'Song of the Silver Blades,' 'Mary, Mary,' 'Ole King Cole,' 'Mandy,' 'Cuddle Up,' 'Shine On Harvest Moon,' 'Lovable You.'

Production Numbers: Overture, Winter Holiday, Ski Lesson, Mary, Mary Quite Contrary, Setting The Pace, Higher and Higher, Ole King Cole, Light and Shadow, Sherwood Forest, The Nutcracker, The Bruises, When The Minstrels Come To Town, Entr'acte, Cossack Lore, Divertisement, Lovable You, Zouaves, Double Vision, Garden of Versailles, Those Good Old Days, Precision Plus, The Dream Waltz, Bouncing Ball of the Ice, Finale.

Fourth Edition of the frosted spectacle in two acts, twenty-four scenes.

Company Manager, JOHN BERGER
Press, J. L. ROBERTS, S. J. BRODY
Stage Director, BURTON MCEVILLY

*During Mr. Trenkler's absence Skippy Baxter was featured.
**Replaced by Jack Millikan and Grace Church.
***Closed April 12, 1947. (405 performances)

The Bruises: Monte Stott—Sid Spalding—Geoffe Stev
At the Top: Claire Dalton and John Walsh
Below: "Cossack Lore"

Jack Diamond—Josephine Boyer—Joey Faye

Lee Trent Joshua Shelley
Above: Miranda and Josef Marais

PLYMOUTH THEATRE

Opened Monday, July 8, 1946.**
Arthur Klein in association with Henry Schumer presents The Youth Theatre:

TIDBITS OF 1946†

Sketches written and directed by Sam Locke; Orchestra directed by Phil Romano; Supervised by Arthur Klein.

Featuring

Joey Faye	Muriel Gaines
Lee Trent	Josephine Boyer
Jack Diamond	Eddy Manson
Robert Marshall	Joshua Shelley
Candido	Sherry Simmons
Mack Triplets	The Debonairs

Josef Marais & Miranda
Carmen & Rolando

Musical Numbers: "On The Way To Sloppy Joe's"; "Hi, Havana"; "Harmonica Days"; "On the Veld"; "So It Goes At The Met"; "I'm The Belle Of The Ballet"; "Step This Way"; "Capetown Capers"; "Never Kill Your Mother On Mother's Day"*; "The Lass With The Delicate Air."
Sketches: The Man Who Came To Heaven, Psychiatry In Technicolor, In A Jeep, Meet Me On Flugle Street.

An intimate Musical Review in two acts, eighteen scenes.

Company Manager, SAM HANDELSMAN
Press Representative, KARL BERNSTEIN
Stage Manager, ROBERT SHARRON

†This material was tried out during the week of May 20, 1946 at the Barbizon Plaza Theatre.
*Written by Mel Tokin.
**Closed July 13, 1946. (8 performances)

BELASCO THEATRE

Opened Monday, July 15, 1946.**
Jules Pfeiffer presents:

MAID IN THE OZARKS†

By Claire Parrish.

Cast of Characters

(In order of appearance)

Gram Calhoun	Ervil Hart*1
Thad Calhoun	Larry Sherman
Mohawk	Jack Mathiesen
Bart Calvert	John Ladd
Lydia Tolliver	Johnee Williams*2
Temple Calhoun	Jon Dawson
Frances Tolliver	Gloria Humphreys
Cypress Young	Burman Bodel
Amy Young	Evelyn Wells Fargo*3
Daisy Belle	Cecile De Lucas*4
Miss Bleeker	Marcelle Gaudel

A Hill-Billy Burlesque in three acts, four scenes. The action takes place in the Kitchen of the Calhoun Home in the Ozark Mountains in Northwestern Arkansas.

General Manager, ADOLPH ADLER
Publicity, J. M. MCKECHNIE
Stage Director, LES MCLEOD

†This play was first presented in the fall of 1940 at the Footlight Theatre in Hollywood, and was called "Blue Mountain." On January 21, 1941 H. F. and Charles R. Woolever, printers, opened it under its present title at the Alcazar in San Francisco. Legend has it —they printed the tickets and inherited the play. Mr. Pfeiffer presents it by special arrangement with the Woolevers. It played 86 weeks in Los Angeles, 62 in Chicago, 12 in San Francisco, 9 in Detroit, 6 in St. Louis, etc. Although advertised by its producer as "the worst play ever to hit Broadway," he excused its presence by saying "It had no place else to go."

*Replacements: 1 Myrtle Ferguson, 2 Princess Manoa, 3 Elsie Kerbin, 4 Carmelita Pope.

**Closed September 29, 1946. (102 performances, many of which were Saturday midnight showings and morning milkmaid matinees.)

Gloria Humphreys

Gloria Humphreys Jon Dawson

Jack Mathiesen Cecile De Lucas

ROYALE THEATRE

Opened Wednesday, September 4, 1946.*
Hunt Stromberg Jr. and Thomas Spengler present:

THE FRONT PAGE†

By Ben Hecht and Charles MacArthur; Staged by Mr. MacArthur; Designed by Nat Karson; Costuming by Irene Aronson.

Cast of Characters
(in order of appearance)

Wilson, American	Roger Clark
Endicott, Post	Jack Arnold
Murphy, Journal	Bruce MacFarlane
McCue, City News Bureau	Benny Baker
Schwartz, Daily News	Ray Walston
Kruger, Journal of Commerce	Pat Harrington
Bensinger, Tribune	Rolly Beck
Mrs. Schlosser	Isabel Bonner
"Woodenshoes" Eichorn	Curtis Karpe
Diamond Louie	Joseph De Santis
Hildy Johnson, Herald-Examiner	Lew Parker
Jennie	Blanche Lytell
Mollie Malloy	Olive Deering
Sheriff Hartman	William Lynn
Peggy Grant	Pat McClarney
Mrs. Grant	Cora Witherspoon
The Mayor	Edward H. Robins
Mr. Pincus	Harold Grau
Earl Williams	George Lyons
Walter Burns	Arnold Moss
Tony	Leonard Yorr
Carl	Fred Bemis
Frank	Vic Whitlock

Policemen, Citizens, Hangmen, etc.

A Revival of the Comedy-Drama about Chicago politicians and news reporters in three acts. The entire action takes place one Friday night in the press room of the Criminal Courts Building in Chicago, some years ago.

General Manager, Tom Elwell
Company Manager, Ralph Kravette
Press Representative, Bernard Simon
Stage Manager, Henri Caubisens

†First produced on Broadway by Jed Harris. Opened August 14, 1928 at the Times Square Theatre, with the late Osgood Perkins as Walter Burns, Lee Tracy as Hildy Johnson, and Dorothy Stickney as Mollie Malloy. It ran for 276 performances.

*Closed November 9, 1946. (78 performances)

**Roger Clark—Jack Arnold—Ray Walston—Olive Deering—Bruce MacFarlane.
Above: Arnold Moss—Lew Parker**

George Lyons **Lew Parker**

SHUBERT THEATRE

Opened Thursday, September 5, 1946.**
Arthur Spitz presents:

YOURS IS MY HEART†

Music by Franz Lehar; Book and Lyrics by Ira Cobb and Karl Farkas; Staged by Theodore Bache; Dances by Henry Shwarze; Scenery and Costumes by H. A. Condell; Dialogue Direction by Monroe Manning; Lighting by Milton Lowe; Musical Adaptation by Felix Guenther; Musical Director, George Schick.

Cast of Characters
(in order of appearance)

Guy	Monroe Manning
Lucille	Helene Whitney
Lou	Jane Mackle
Pierre	Harold Lazaron
Fernand D'Orville	Alexander D'Arcy
Yvonne	Natalye Greene
Fifi	Dorothy Karrol
Marie	Jean Heisey
Archibald Mascotte, Impresario	Sammy White
Claudette Vernay, Prima Donna	Stella Andreva
Butler	Harvey Kier
Prince Sou Chong	Richard Tauber*
Huang Wei, Chinese Ambassador	Edward Groag
Prince Tschang, Sou Chong's Uncle	Arnold Spector
Hsi Fueng, Minister of Finance	Fred Keating
Princess Mi, Sou Chong's Sister	Lillian Held
Master of Ceremonies	Albert Shoengold
Hight Priest	Fred Briess
Li Tsi, Chinese Bride	Beatrice Eden

Solo Dancers—Trudy Goth, Henry Shwarze, Wayne Lamb, Alberto Feliciano.
Guests, Maids and Servants, Dancers, Mandarins, etc.

Musical Numbers: Music Box and Waltz, "Goodbye, Paree," "Free as the Air," "Chinese Melody," "Patiently Smiling," "A Cup of China Tea," "Upon a Moonlight Night in May," Chinese Ceremony, "Love, What Has Given You This Magic Power?," "Men of China," "Chingo-Pingo," "Yours Is My Heart Alone," Wedding Ceremony, "Paris Sings Again,"†† "Ma Petite Cherie."

An operetta in three acts. The action takes place in 1900 in the drawing room of Claudette Vernay's Paris apartment and a hall and a room in Sou Chong's Palace, Peiping.

General Manager, Jacob L. Steisel
Business Manager, Felix G. Gerstman
Company Manager, Charles Stewart
Press, Karl Bernstein, Martha Dreiblatt
Stage Manager, Monroe Manning

†Based on "Land of Smiles." This is the first production of the Lehar work on Broadway, although the Shuberts have twice tried it out on the road as "Prince Chu Chan" and "Land of Smiles."

††by French Composer, Paul Durant.

*On September 19th, Mr. Tauber was stricken with laryngitis and with the exception of three performances after that John Hendrick sang the role. It was Mr. Tauber's illness which caused show to fold.

**Closed October 5, 1946. (36 performances)

Fred Keating—Lillian Held—
Richard Tauber

Stella Andreva Richard Tauber

Stella Andreva—Alexander D'Arcy—Sammy White

ALVIN THEATRE

(Moved to ADELPHI October 5, 1946; the MUSIC BOX, October 22, 1946; the BROADWAY, November 19, 1946).

Opened Thursday, September 5, 1946.**

American League for a Free Palestine presents:

A FLAG IS BORN

By Ben Hecht; Music by Kurt Weill; Staged by Luther Adler; In Charge of Production, Jules J. Leventhal; Musical Director, Isaac Van Grove; Settings by Robert Davison; Costumes by John Boyt; Choreography by Zamira Gon.

Cast of Characters

Speaker	Quentin Reynolds *1
Tevya	Paul Muni *2
Zelda	Celia Adler
David	Marlon Brando *3
The Singer	Mario Berini *4
Saul	George David Baxter
Old One	Morris Samuylow
Middle Aged One	David Manning
Young One	John Baragrey
David The King	William Allyn *5
Solomon	Gregory Morton
American Statesman	Jonathan Harris
Russian Statesman	Yasha Rosenthal
1st English Statesman	Tom Emlyn Williams
2nd English Statesman	Jefferson Coates
French Statesman	Frederick Rudin
1st Soldier	Steve Hill
2nd Soldier	Jonathan Harris
3rd Soldier	Harold Gary

A Dramatic Spectacle without intermission. The continuous action of this plea for a Hebrew Homeland takes place in a Jewish Graveyard in ravished Europe with flashes into the Courts of Saul, David and Solomon; the Council Chamber of the Mighty; and the Road to the Holy Land.

Assistant Producer, ROSE KEANE
General Manager, MILTON WEINTRAUB
Company Manager, EDWIN A. RELKIN
Press, HENRY SENBER, NAT DORFMAN
Stage Manager, GUY EDWARD THOMAJAN

*Replacements: 1 Ruth Chatterton followed by Alexander Scourby; 2 Luther Adler, then Jacob Ben-Ami; 3 Sidney Lumet; 4 Richard Monti; 5 Allan Frank, then Rita Gam.

**Closed Dec. 15, 1946. (120 performances)

Gregory Morton as Solomon

Marlon Brando—Celia Adler—Paul Muni

Paul Muni as Tevya

CENTURY THEATRE

Opened Tuesday, September 17, 1946.**
Edwin Lester presents:

GYPSY LADY††

Music by Victor Herbert; Musical Adaptation and Direction, Orchestral and Choral Arrangements by Arthur Kay; Book by Henry Myers; Stage Direction and New Lyrics by Robert Wright and George Forrest; Vocal Numbers Staged by Lew Kesler; Dance Direction by Aida Broadbent; Scenic Designs, Boris Aronson; Costume Designs, Miles White; Lighting by Adrian Awan; Costumes executed by Walter J. Israel.

Cast of Characters

Baron Pettibois .... Clarence Derwent *1
Yvonne .... Kaye Connor
Fresco .... Jack Goode
Musetta .... Helena Bliss
Sergeant of Gendarmes .... Edmund Dorsay
The Great Alvarado .... John Tyers
Valerie .... Doreen Wilson
Imri .... Val Valentinoff *2
Rudolfo .... William Bauer
Boris .... Melville Cooper *3
Roszika .... Patricia Sims
Sandor .... George Britton
Andre .... Gilbert Russell
Stephan .... Joseph Macaulay
The Undecided Mademoiselle .... Suzette Meredith
M. Guilbert Armand .... Bert Hillner
Majordomo .... Harvey Shahan

Young Ladies of the Academy, Gypsies, Guests, Maids and Mannikins played by the Young Artist Personnel of the Los Angeles and San Francisco Civic Light Opera.

Musical Numbers: "On A Wonderful Day Like Today," "The Facts of Life Backstage," Serenade: "I Love You, I Adore You," "Life Is A Dirty Business," "My Treasure," "Romany Life†," Pantomime, "The World and I," "Piff Paff," Andalusia Bolero, "Keepsakes," "Young Lady a la Mode," "Springtide," "Reality," "Gypsy Love Song†."

An Operetta in two acts, eight scenes. The action takes place in France, about 1900, in a Room, the Garden and Cupid's Cupola at Baron Pettibois' Academy of Theatre Arts; the Gypsy Camp; a Suite and the Roof of a Paris Hotel overlooking Montmartre; Terrace of Chateau de Roncevalle; and on the Road.

General Manager, ELEANOR PINKHAM
Company Manager, GEORGE LEFFLER
Press, C. P. GRENEKER, BEN KORNZWEIG, LENNY TRAUBE
Production Manager, MICHAEL JEFFREY
Stage Manager, KAY HAMMOND

†Original Lyrics by Harry B. Smith.

††A Period Piece created to re-introduce melodies from "The Forune Teller" and "The Serenade" by arrangement with Ella Herbert Bartlett. It was tried-out by The San Francisco Civic Light Opera Association under the title "Fortune Teller" at the Curran Theatre, opening July 1, 1946. This production was brought to New York by Mr. Lester and the Shuberts. After it closed in New York it was sent to London where Jack Hylton presented it under the title "Romany Life" at His Majesty's Theatre on March 7, 1947 starring Melville Cooper and Helena Bliss. It ran 12 weeks.

*Replacements: 1 Ralph Herbert, 2 Rem Olmsted, 3 Billy Gilbert.

**Closed November 23, 1946. (79 performances)

Helena Bliss as 'Musetta'

Gilbert Russell—George Britton—Helena Bliss—John Tyers. Below: Jack Goode and the Young Ladies of the Academy.

Peter Von Zerneck   Diana Barrymore

PLYMOUTH THEATRE

Opened Thursday, September 19, 1946.*
The Messrs. Shubert in association with
Albert de Courville present:

HIDDEN HORIZON†

By Agatha Christie; Staged by Mr. de Courville; Scenery by Charles Elson; Costumes by Everett Staples.

Cast of Characters

1st Beadseller	Monty Banks Jr.
2nd Beadseller	David Andrews
Steward	Charles Alexander
Miss Ffoliot-Ffoulkes	Eva Leonard-Boyne
Christina Grant	Joy Ann Page
Smith	David Manners
Louise	Edith Kingdon
Dr. Bessner	Peter Von Zerneck
Simon Mostyn	Blair Davies
Kay Mostyn	Barbara Joyce
Archdeacon Pennyfeather	Halliwell Hobbes
Jacqueline De Severac	Diana Barrymore
McNaught, Ship's Captain	Winston Ross
Egyptian Policeman	Leland Hamilton Damian Nimer

A Murder Mystery in three acts, four scenes. The scene is laid throughout in the Observation Salon of the paddle steamer "Lotus" on the Nile between Shellal and Wadi Halfa.

Company Manager, JACK SMALL
Press, C. P. GRENEKER, BEN KORNZWEIG
Production Manager, JOHN HOLDEN

†Adapted from Miss Christie's novel "Murder on the Nile" and was originally presented in London under that title on March 19, 1946 at the Ambassadors Theatre where it ran 7 weeks.

*Closed September 28, 1946. (12 performances)

Halliwell Hobbes—Diana Barrymore—
Peter Von Zerneck

David Manners

Joy Ann Page

Joyce Van Patten—Barbara Robbins—Rosemary Rice—Sybil Stocking. Opposite: Sybil Stocking—Sylvia Lane

CORT THEATRE

(Moved to BOOTH October 8, 1946).
Opened Thursday, September 26, 1946.*
Mort H. Singer, Jr. presents:

THE BEES AND THE FLOWERS†

By Frederick Kohner and Albert Mannheimer; Staged by Mr. Mannheimer; Setting by Edward Gilbert; Costumes by Enid Gilbert.

Cast of Characters

Louise Morgan	Barbara Robbins
Nancy	Jean Frey
Alix Morgan	Sybil Stocking
Tess Morgan	Rosemary Rice
Ilka Morgan	Joyce Van Patten
Winston Atchison	Michael Dreyfuss
Tack Cooper	Russell Hardie
Dippy Marshall	Sylvia Lane
Drayman	Maurice Brenner
Tom	Leonard Bell
Jerry	Peggy Romano

A Domestic Comedy in two acts, six scenes. The entire action takes place on the terrace of the Morgan Apartment, New York City, at the present time.

Company Manager, ARTHUR SINGER
Press, C. P. GRENEKER, LEWIS HARMON
Stage Manager, JAMES H. MALONE

†Originally called "The Birds And The Bees."
*Closed October 19, 1946. (28 performances)

Russell Hardie   Barbara Robbing

Eugenie Leontovich Basil Rathbone

PLYMOUTH THEATRE

Opened Tuesday, October 1, 1946.*
Homer Curran in association with Russell Lewis and Howard Young presents:

OBSESSION†

By Louis Verneuil; Adapted by Jane Hinton; Staged by Reginald Denham; Designed and Lighted by Stewart Chaney; Gowns by Adrian.

Cast of Characters

Maurice............Basil Rathbone
Nadya............Eugenie Leontovich

A Revival of the Melodrama in three acts. The action throughout takes place in a two room combination set that represents the bedroom and sitting-room of their Paris apartment.

General Manager, Stanley Brown
Company Manager, Charles Williams
Press, Bert Stern, Helen Hoerle
Stage Manager, Glenn Jordan

†First produced on Broadway by A. H. Woods under the title, "Jealousy" and was adapted by Eugene Walter. Opened October 22, 1928 at the Maxine Elliott Theatre with John Holliday and Fay Bainter. It played 136 performances.

*Closed October 26, 1946. (31 performances)

Ray Mayer (piano)—Bobby Sherwood (trumpet)—Sidney Bechet (clarinet)—Philip Layton (trombone)—Bart Edwards (bass)—Marty Marsala (drums)

Ray Mayer Lynne Carter

Audra Lindley Bobby Sherwood

THE PLAYHOUSE

Opened Monday, October 7, 1946.*
Arthur Hopkins presents:

HEAR THAT TRUMPET

By Orin Jannings; Designed by Woodman Thompson; Staged by Mr. Hopkins.

Cast of Characters
(As they speak)

Mumford, Clarinet .... Sidney Bechet
Alonzo Armonk .... Frank Conroy
Dinger Richardson, Trumpet .... Bobby Sherwood
Floyd Amery, Piano .... Ray Mayer
Abba, Bass Viol .... Bart Edwards
Rocco, Drums .... Marty Marsala
Erica Marlowe .... Audra Lindley
Skippy, Trombone .... Philip Layton
Sally Belle .... Lynne Carter
Cleasy .... Raymond Bramley

A Comedy Drama about a Jazz-band in three acts, six scenes. The entire action takes place in Dinger's and Floyd's rooms, Chicago, in the spring of 1945.

Company Manager, TOM POWERS
Press Representative, RICHARD MANEY
Stage Manager, EDWARD A. MCHUGH

*Closed October 12, 1946. (8 performances)

Jose Ferrer as Cyrano de Bergerac

Ralph Clanton as 'Comte De Guiche' enters the Post at the Siege of Arras

Frances Reid Jose Ferrer Hiram Sherman

ALVIN THEATRE

(Moved to the BARRYMORE November 18, 1946.)
Opened Tuesday, October 8, 1946.***
Jose Ferrer presents:

CYRANO DE BERGERAC†

By Edmond Rostand, Brian Hooker's version; Staged by Melchor G. Ferrer; Settings and Costumes by Lemuel Ayers; Incidental Music composed by Paul Bowles; Production supervised by Arthur S. Friend.

Cast of Characters††
(In order of appearance)

Porter	Benedict McQuarrie
A Cavalier	Samuel N. Kirkham
A Musketeer	George Oliver
A Lackey	Stewart Long *1
Another Lackey	Ralph Meeker
A Guardsman	Charles Summers
Flower Girl	Phyllis Hill
A Citizen	Wallace Widdecombe
His Son	Walter Kelly
A Cut Purse	Nick Dennis
Orange Girl	Patricia Wheel
A Marquis	John O'Connor *2
Brissaille	Bert Whitley
Ligniere	Robert Carroll
Christian De Neuvillette	Ernest Graves
Ragueneau	Hiram Sherman
Le Bret	William Woodson
Roxane, Nee Madeleine Robin	Frances Reid
Her Duenna	Paula Lawrence
Comte De Guiche	Ralph Clanton
Vicomte De Valvert	Anthony Jordan**
Montfleury	Leopold Badia
Cyrano De Bergerac	Jose Ferrer
Bellrose	Howard Wierum
Jodelet	Robinson Stone
A Meddler	Francis Letton
A Soubrette	Mary Jane Kersey *3
A Comedienne	Jacqueline Soans
Lise	Nan McFarland
Carbon De Castel-Jaloux	Francis Compton
A Poet	Vincent Donahue
Another Poet	Leonardo Cimino
A Capuchin	Robinson Stone
A Cadet	Paul Wilson
Sister Marthe	Jacqueline Soans
Mother Marguerite	Nan McFarland
Sister Claire	Phyllis Hill
A Nun	Patricia Wheel

A Revival of the French Classic in five acts, five scenes. The action takes place in the Hall of the Hotel Bourgogne, 1640, the Bakeshop of Ragueneau; the House of Roxane in a little square in Old Marais; the Post of the Company of Carbon de Castel-Jaloux, at the Siege of Arras; and the Park of the Convent in Paris, 1655.

General Manager, JULES J. LEVENTHAL
Company Manager, VINCE McKNIGHT
Press Representative, DAVID LIPSKY
Stage Manager, JESS KIMMEL

†This play was first presented to the world on December 28, 1897 at the Theatre de la Porte Saint-Martin with Benoit Constant Coquelin in the title role. The first New York presentation was at the Garden Theatre, October 3, 1898 with Richard Mansfield. Mr. Mansfield and Walter Hampden made the Cavalier of the proboscis a familiar figure to the American theatregoers.

††As an experiment during the regular run, the cast presented two special matinees with the understudies playing the leads and the regular players doing the supporting roles (on January 16 and 22, 1947).

*Replacements: 1 Van Graves, 2 Vincent Donahue, 3 Denise Flynn.

**Alternate: Dean Cetrulo.

***Closed March 22, 1947. (195 performances)

Jose Ferrer as Cyrano de Bergerac

Frances Reid and Jose Ferrer

James Barton—Marcella Markham—John Marriott—E. G. Marshall—Paul Crabtree—Nicholas Joy—Frank Tweddell—Carl Benton Reid—Leo Chalzel

Jeanne Cagney—Tom Pedi—Ruth Gilbert

James Barton Dudley Digges

MARTIN BECK THEATRE

Opened Wednesday, October 9, 1946.**
The Theatre Guild presents:

THE ICEMAN COMETH

By Eugene O'Neill†; Directed by Eddie Dowling; Designed and Lighted by Robert Edmond Jones; Supervised by Theresa Helburn and Lawrence Langner; Associate Producer, Armina Marshall.

Cast of Characters

Harry Hope .... Dudley Digges
proprietor of a saloon and rooming house
Ed Mosher .... Morton L. Stevens
Hope's brother in law, one-time circus man
Pat McGloin .... Al McGranary
one-time Police Lieutenant
Willie Oban .... E. G. Marshall *1
a Harvard Law School alumnus
Joe Mott .... John Marriott
one-time proprietor of a Negro gambling house
Piet Wetjoen .... Frank Tweddell
"The General"—one-time leader of a Boer commando
Cecil Lewis .... Nicholas Joy
"The Captain"—one-time Captain of British infantry
James Cameron .... Russell Collins
"Jimmy Tomorrow"—one-time Boer War correspondent
Hugo Kalmar .... Leo Chalzel
one-time editor of Anarchist periodicals
Larry Slade .... Carl Benton Reid
one-time Anarchist

Joe Marr—Tom Pedi—Ruth Gilbert—Jeanne Cagney—Russell Collins—Morton L. Stevens—
Al McGranary—Dudley Digges

Jeanne Cagney—Dudley Digges—Ruth Gilbert

Rocky Pioggi .... Tom Pedi
night bartender
Don Parritt .... Paul Crabtree
Pearl } street walkers { Ruth Gilbert
Margie } street walkers { Jeanne Cagney*2
Cora } street walkers { Marcella Markham
Chuck Morello .... Joe Marr
day bartender
Theodore Hickman .... James Barton *3
"Hickey"—a hardware salesman
Moran .... Michael Wyler
Lieb .... Charles Hart

A Drama in four acts††. The action takes place in the Back Room and the Bar at Harry Hope's lower West side New York City waterfront saloon in the summer of 1912.

Company Manager, DIXIE FRENCH
Publicity Director, JOSEPH HEIDT
Press, PEGGY PHILLIPS, PHIL STEVENSON
Stage Manager, BUFORD ARMITAGE

†This is Mr. O'Neill's first new play to be produced since "Days Without End" in 1934.
††The first act runs one hour, 15 minutes; the second, 51 minutes; the third, 53 minutes; and the fourth, approximately one hour. The performance began at 5:30 with a dinner intermission. Six performances were given each week. In the middle of the run the dinner interval was omitted and the first curtain went up at 7:30.
*Replaced by: 1 Earle Larimore, 2 Anna Minot, 3 E. G. Marshall.
**Closed March 15, 1947. (136 performances)

Carl Benton Reid—James Barton—Dudley Digges—
Nicholas Joy

Howard Smith Rhys Williams Randee Sanford

Dorothy Gilchrist Thomas Coley

THE MUSIC BOX

Opened Thursday, October 10, 1946.*
Joseph M. Hyman presents:

MR. PEEBLES AND MR. HOOKER

By Edward E. Paramore, Jr.; Based on the novel by Charles G. Givens; Directed by Martin Ritt; Settings by Frederick Fox; Costumes by Eleanor Goldsmith.

Cast of Characters
(in order of appearance)

Hank, a Singer	James Robertson
Brother Alf Leland	Paul Huber
Hattie	Juanita Hall
Brother Wally Leland	Tom Coley
Bump Sorrell	Arthur Hunnicutt
Ellen Sorrell	Dorothy Gilchrist
Chauffeur	Van Prince
Mrs. Hatcher Craine	Randee Sanford
Nate Corbett	Grover Burgess
Mr. Hooker	Rhys Williams
Sheriff Todd Blakely	Ralph Stantley
Pete	Arthur Foran
Deputy	Charles Thompson
Mr. Hatcher Craine	Neil McFee Skinner
Dr. Phil Jameson	Tom Morgan
Judge Fayette	Tom Hoier
Mr. Peebles	Howard Smith
A Stranger	Jeff Morrow
Whigsey	Ken Renard
Joe Greer	Dennis Bohan

A Fantasy Folk Drama with overtones of religious allegory in a prologue, three acts, and six scenes. The prologue takes place near a fallen tree, on a hilltop overlooking a lake, several years after World War II. The rest of the action takes place in 1939 at the Leland House, and outside and within Mr. Hooker's shack—all in Tennessee.

General Manager, AL GOLDIN
Press Representative, MAX GENDEL
Production Assistant, ANN BROOKS OAKMAN
Stage Manager, EDDIE DIMOND

*Closed October 12, 1946. (4 performances)

Jack Merivale—Evan Thomas—Cecil Beaton—Rex Evans—John Buckmaster

The Drawing Room of Lord Windermere's House from "Lady Windermere's Fan."

CORT THEATRE

Opened Monday, October 14, 1946. **
Homer Curran in association with Russell Lewis and Howard Young presents:

LADY WINDERMERE'S FAN†

By Oscar Wilde; Directed by Jack Minster; Scenery, Costumes and Lighting by Cecil Beaton.††

Cast of Characters
(In order of appearance)

Lady Windermere	Penelope Ward
Parker	Thomas Louden
Lord Darlington	John Buckmaster
Duchess of Berwick	Estelle Winwood
Lady Agatha Carlisle	Sally Cooper
Lord Windermere	Henry Daniell *1
Mr. Rufford	Paul Russell *2
Miss Rufford	Jeri Sauvinet *3
Lady Paisley	Marguerite Gleason
Hon. Paulette Sonning	Tanagra Thayer
Lady Jedburgh	Elizabeth Valentine
The Bishop	Peter Keyes
Miss Graham	Pamela Wright
Sir James Royston	Jack Merivale
Lady Stutfield	Anne Curson
Mr. Dumby	Evan Thomas
Mrs. Cowper-Cowper	Leonore Elliott *4
Mr. Hopper	Stanley Bell
Lady Plymdale	Nan Hopkins *5
Lord Augustus Lorton	Rex Evans
Mr. Cecil Graham	Cecil Beaton *6
Mrs. Erlynne	Cornelia Otis Skinner
First Footman	Guy Blake
Second Footman	Richard Burns
Rosalie	Marjorie Wood *7

A Revival of the Comedy of Victorian Manners and Morals in four acts. The action takes place within twenty-four hours, beginning on a Tuesday afternoon at 5:00 o'clock and ending the next day at 1:30 P. M. — the Morning-room and Drawing-room of Lord Windermere's House in Carlton Terrace, London; and Lord Darlington's Rooms.

Company Manager, EMMETT R. CALLAHAN
Press Representative, HELEN HOERLE
Production Manager, TOM TURNER
Stage Manager, ROBERT LINDEN

†This play was produced for the first time in New York on February 5, 1894 at Palmer's Theatre. This production was produced in San Francisco, opening at the Curran Theatre on August 26, 1946.

††Mr. Beaton originally designed the John Gielgud production which ran at the Haymarket Theatre, London, from August 21, 1945 to February 8, 1947.

*Replacements: 1 David Manners, 2 Richard Burns, 3 Dorothy Kelley, 4 Jeri Sauvinet, 5 Louise Prussing, 6 Rex O'Malley, 7 Pamela Wright.

**Closed April 26, 1947. (227 performances)

Estelle Winwood

Below Left: Cornelia Otis Skinner. Below Right: Penelop Ward—Guy Blake—Thomas Louden—Estelle Winwood-Sally Cooper—John Buckmaster.

Canada Lee—Whitfield Connor—Patricia Calvert—
Elisabeth Bergner

Canada Lee John Carradine

BARRYMORE THEATRE

Opened Tuesday, October 15, 1946.**
Paul Czinner presents:

THE DUCHESS OF MALFI†

By John Webster; Adapted by W. H. Auden; Directed by George Rylands; Incidental Music by Benjamin Britten; Arranged by Ignatz Strasfogel; Scenery by Harry Bennett††; Costumes by Miles White.

Cast of Characters

Ferdinand ..... Donald Eccles
The Cardinal ..... John Carradine
Giovanno, Duchess of Malfi ..... Elisabeth Bergner
Antonio Bologna ..... Whitfield Connor
Delio ..... Richard Newton
Daniel De Bosola ..... Canada Lee*
Officers attending on the Duchess Ben Morse, Michael Bey, Lawrence Ryle, Robin Morse
Ladies attending on the Duchess Beth Holland Diana Kemble
Cariola ..... Patricia Calvert
Old Lady ..... Michelette Burani
Roderigo ..... Rupert Pole
First Guard ..... William Layton
Second Guard ..... Frederic Downs
Julia ..... Sonia Sorel
Monk ..... Michael Ellis
Pilgrim ..... Jack Cook
Antonio's Son ..... Maurice Cavell
Antonio's Daughter ..... Kathleen Moran
Priest, Lawyer, Astrologer, Doctor ..... Madmen ..... Walter Peterson, Robert Pike, Frederic Downs, Guy Spaull
Courtiers, Officers, Soldiers, Ladies and Gentlemen of the Court.

A Jacobean horror drama in three parts. The action takes place in Italy, early in the sixteenth century—in a Gallery, a Court, and a Bed-chamber of the Palace of the Duchess in Amalfi; an Apartment in the Palace of the Cardinal in Rome; near the Shrine of Our Lady of Loretto; Apartment in the Residence of Ferdinand; the Open Court of an Ancient Fortification.

Company Manager, LESTER AL SMITH
General Press Representative, JEAN DALRYMPLE
Asso. Press, PHILLIP BLOOM, MARIAN GRAHAM
Stage Manager, FORREST TAYLOR, JR.

†This play is thought to have been written in 1613, and the first public performance to have taken place at the Globe, with Richard Burbage as Ferdinand and Henry Condell as the Cardinal. This is the first presentation of this play on Broadway. It also marks Mr. Carradine's New York debut.

††A great portion of the scenery followed the designs by Roger Furse for John Gielgud's London production of last season.

*When McKay Morris withdrew during rehearsal, it was decided Mr. Lee, a Negro actor, with the aid of white make-up, would replace him.

**Closed November 16, 1946 (39 performances)

BILTMORE THEATRE

Opened Wednesday, October 16, 1946.**
Jed Harris presents:

LOCO†

By Dale Eunson and Katherine Albert; Staged by Mr. Harris; Settings by Donald Oenslager; Costumes by Emeline Roche.

Cast of Characters
(in order of appearance)

Alma Brewster	Helen Murdoch
Naomi Brewster	Beverly Bayne
McIntyre	Barry Kelley
Waldo Brewster	Jay Fassett
David Skinner	Morgan Wallace
Loco Dempsey	Jean Parker*
Ginger	Marlo Dwyer
Matron	Darin Jennings
Eben	Parker Fennelly
Pamela Brewster	Elaine Stritch
Nicky Martinez	Si Vario
Miss White	Lauretta Maxine

A Comedy in two acts, nine scenes. The action takes place within a period of ten days in February of this year in The Brewster Library, Bedroom, Hunting Lodge in Maine and Office; The Golden Bantam Club and Powder Room.

General Manager, BEN F. STEIN
Press Representative, DICK WEAVER
Stage Manager, DEL HUGHES

†This Husband and Wife collaboration is taken from a magazine story written by the former. The title—derived from the Mexican slang for the word "crazy"—is used here as a nickname, after the fad created by Harry Conover of giving an unusual one-word name to his models.

*Miss Parker's Broadway debut.

**Closed November 16, 1946. (37 performances)

Jean Parker Jay Fassett

Jay Fassett Jean Parker

BELASCO THEATRE

Opened Thursday, October 17, 1946. *
James Light and Max J. Jelin present:

LYSISTRATA

By Aristophanes, modern version by Gilbert Seldes†; Directed by James Light. Designed and Lighted by Ralph Alswang; Costumes by Rose Bogdanoff; Choreography by Felicia Sorel; Music by Henry Brant.

Cast of Characters

(In order of appearance)

Leader of Old Women's Chorus ... Pearl Gaines
Old Women's Chorus ..... Beatrice Wade, Phyllis Walker, Hilda Offley, Theresa Brooks, Olive Ball, Ethel Purnello, Wilhelmina Williams, Edyth Reid
Lysistrata ..... Etta Moten
Kalonika ..... Fredi Washington
Young Women's Chorus ... Lora Pierre, Geneva H. Fitch, Laphfawn Gumbs, Marie Cooke, Jean Stovall, Geri Bryan, Jackie Greene, Courtenay Olden, Minnie Gentry.
Myrrhina ..... Mildred Smith
Lampito ..... Mercedes Gilbert
Spartan Women: Louise E. Evans, Tica Janine
Theban Women ..... Lou Sealia Swarz, Eunice Elenora Miller
Corinthian Women ..... Margaret Tynes, Valerie Black
Leader of Old Men's Chorus ..... Leigh Whipper
Old Men's Chorus ..... Wardell Saunders, Cherokee Thornton, James H. Dunmore, Louis Sharp, Andrew Ratousheff, George Dozier, Larri E. Lauria, Service Bell
President of the Senate ..... Rex Ingram
Spartan Envoy ..... Maurice Ellis
Kinesias ..... Emmett Babe Wallace
Trygeus ..... John De Battle
Nikias ..... Larry Williams
Polydorus ..... Sidney Poitier
Senators ..... Harry Bolden, P. Jay Sidney, Bootsie Davis, Hanson Elkins, Milton J. Williams, Wilson Woodbeck
Lykon ..... Emory S. Richardson
Officers ..... Milers Winbush, George F. Carroll
Satyrs ..... Archie Savage, Jay Flashe Riley
Dancers ..... Bill O'Neil, Frank Green, H. Roderick Scott, Albert Popwell, George Thomas, Royce Wallace, Marble Hart, Erona Harris, Gwyn Hale, Hettie Stephens, Ann Henry.

A Revival of the Greek Classic with an all-negro cast in two acts. The action takes place on the Acropolis, Athens, 411 B. C. in the twenty-first year of the War between Athens and Sparta.

Company Manager, M. Eleanor Fitzgerald
Press, Marjorie Barkentin, Michael O'Shea
Stage Managers, Phil Stein, Alan Shulruff

†Mr. Seldes' modern adaptation was first presented by the Philadelphia Theatre Association, Inc. at the 44th Street Theatre on June 5, 1930 with Violet Kemble Cooper, Miriam Hopkins, Ernest Truex and Sidney Greenstreet. It ran 252 performances.

*Closed October 19, 1946. (4 performances)

Top: Emmett "Babe" Wallace and Mildred Smith. Center: Etta Moten and Rex Ingram. Bottom: Mildred Smith as 'Myrrhina,' Fredi Washington as 'Kalonika,' Etta Moten as 'Lysistrata,' and Mercedes Gilbert as 'Lampito.'

HENRY MILLER THEATRE

Opened Thursday, October 24, 1946.**
John Golden presents:

MADE IN HEAVEN†

By Hagar Wilde; Directed by Martin Manulis; Designed by Lawrence Goldwasser.

Cast of Characters

(In order of appearance)

Nancy Tennant	Katharine Bard
Marian Hunt	Sarah Burton
Laszlo Vertes	Louis Borel
Philip Dunlap	Tony Bickley
Elsa Meredith	Carmen Mathews
Zachery Meredith	Donald Cook
Harry Hunt	Lawrence Fletcher
Dorothy	Marrian Walters
Miss Crowder	Jane Middleton*
Hank	Maurice Manson
Man At Bar	Willard L. Thompson
June	Ann Thomas

A Domestic Comedy in three acts, six scenes. The action takes place at the present time in the living-room of Zachary Meredith's home—within commuting distance of New York and his office in New York; the Bar and a Room in the Hotel Revere.

Manager, MAX SIEGEL
Press, BERNARD SIMON, FRANK GOODMAN
Stage Manager, EARL McDONALD

†Formerly known as "It's A Man's World."
*Replaced by Elaine Stritch.
**Closed January 11, 1947. (91 performances and 9 previews)

Lawrence Fletcher—Ann Thomas—Donald Cook

Donald Cook—Carmen Mathews—Katharine Bard—Tony Bickley

Eithne Dunne—Barry Macollum—Burgess Meredith—J. M. Kerrigan—J. C. Nugent

Mildred Natwick—Burgess Meredith—Eithne Dunne

BOOTH THEATRE

Opened Saturday, October 26, 1946.**
Theatre Incorporated presents:

THE PLAYBOY OF THE WESTERN WORLD†

By J. M. Synge; Staged by Guthrie McClintic; Scenery and Costumes by John Boyt; Richard Aldrich, Managing Director.

Cast of Characters

Margaret Flaherty........Eithne Dunne††*
(called Pegeen Mike)
Shawn Keogh........Dennis King Jr.
Michael James Flaherty........J. M. Kerrigan
Philly Cullen........Barry Macollum
Jimmy Farrell........J. C. Nugent
Christopher Mahon........Burgess Meredith
Widow Quin........Mildred Natwick
Susan Brady........Mary Diveny
Honor Blake........Sheila Keddy
Nelly........Julie Harris
Sara Tansey........Maureen Stapleton
Old Mahon........Fred Johnson
Villagers: Robin Humphrey, Edith Shayne, Mary Lou Taylor, Mary T. Walker, Paul Anderson, Elmer Borlab, Charles Martin, James L. O'Neil, Ford Rainey.

A Revival of the Irish Folk Comedy in three acts. The scene is Flaherty's Public House near a village on the wild coast of County Mayo, Ireland.

General Manager, CHANDOS SWEET
Press, WILLIAM FIELDS, FRANCIS ROBINSON
Stage Manager, JAMES NEILSON

†First produced in January 1907 at The Abbey Theatre, Dublin, Ireland, where it caused riots, as it also did when the Abbey Theatre Players first presented it here in November, 1911 at the Maxine Elliott Theatre. It was last done here by the Abbey Company in 1937.
††First appearance in America of this actress from Dublin's Abbey and Gate Theatres.
*Alternate: Maureen Stapleton.
**Closed January 4, 1947. (81 performances)

Marta Linden—Clifton Webb—Robin Craven—Gordon Mills—Doris Dalton

Clifton Webb Evelyn Varden

Clifton Webb Marta Linden

PLYMOUTH THEATRE

Opened Tuesday, October 29, 1946.**
John C. Wilson presents:

PRESENT LAUGHTER†

By Noel Coward; Setting by Donald Oenslager; Costumes for Miss Dalton and Miss Linden by Castillo; Other Costumes supervised by Sylvia Saal; Staged by Mr. Wilson.

Cast of Characters

Daphne Stillington .... Jan Sterling††*
Miss Erikson .... Grace Mills
Fred .... Aidan Turner
Monica Reed .... Evelyn Varden
Garry Essendine .... Clifton Webb
Liz Essendine .... Doris Dalton
Roland Maule .... Cris Alexander
Morris Dixon .... Gordon Mills
Hugo Lyppiatt .... Robin Craven
Joanna Lyppiatt .... Marta Linden
Lady Saltburn .... Leonore Harris

A Light Comedy in three acts, four scenes. The action takes place at the present time in Garry Essendine's Studio in London.

General Manager, C. Edwin Knill
Company Manager, William Tisdale
Press, Willard Keefe, David Tebet
Stage Manager, Earl J. Brisgal

†The title is taken from the Clown's Song in "Twelfth Night": '*Present mirth hath present laughter.*' The original production, after touring the English provinces from September 21, 1942 as one of a bill of three, collectively known as "Play Parade," opened at the Haymarket Theatre, London, on April 29, 1943 with Mr. Coward as Garry Essendine. The following evening "This Happy Breed" opened at the same theatre and played alternately with it.

††Replaced by Diane Chadwick.
*Alternate: Diana Cheswick.
**Closed March 15, 1947. (158 performances)

Clifton Webb

Leonore Harris—Jan Sterling—Marta Linden—Clifton Webb—Doris Dalton—Evelyn Varden

Helen Hayes—Thomas Heaphy—
Louis Jean Heydt—Lorraine Miller

Helen Hayes Louis Jean Heydt

Helen Hayes Jack Diamond

BROADHURST THEATRE

Opening Thursday, October 31, 1946.
Richard Rodgers and Oscar Hammerstein 2nd. present:

HAPPY BIRTHDAY

By Anita Loos; Directed by Joshua Logan; Scenery and Lighting by Jo Mielziner; Costumes by Lucinda Ballard; Incidental Music by Robert Russell Bennett; "I Haven't Got A Worry In The World" by Rodgers and Hammerstein; Sound Consultant, Harold Burris-Meyer; Conductor, Maurice Lefton.

Cast of Characters
(In order of appearance)

Gail .... Margaret Irving
Glorious .... Musa Williams
Dad Malone .... Thomas Heaphy
Gabe .... Charles Gordon
Bella .... Florence Sundstrom
Herman .... Jack Diamond
Myrtle .... Jacqueline Paige
June .... Jean Bellows
Addie .... Helen Hayes
Maude .... Lorraine Miller
Don .... Dort Clark
The Judge .... Ralph Theadore
Paul .... Louis Jean Heydt
Policeman .... Philip Dakin
Tot .... Enid Markey
Emma .... Grace Valentine
Manuel .... Philip Gordon
Margot .... Eleanor Boleyn
Bert .... James Livingston
Mr. Bemis .... Robert Burton
Mr. Nanino .... Harry Kingston

A Sentimental Comedy about a dowdy librarian on a toot in two acts. The action takes place in the Jersey Mecca Cocktail Bar in Newark, N.J.

General Manager, MORRIS JACOBS
Company Manager, HARRY ESSEX
Press, MICHEL MOK, ABNER D. KLIPSTEIN
Stage Managers, DAVID GRAY, JR., RUTH MITCHELL

†During tryout, the parts of Ruby and the Stranger, played by Betty Lou Barto and Bethell Long respectively, were written out.

Helen Hayes—Grace Valentine—Enid Markey

Jean Bellows—Dort Clark—Helen Hayes

Dort Clark—Eleanor Boleyn—Enid Markey—Louis Jean Heydt—Philip Gordon—Margaret Irving
Charles Gordon—Helen Hayes—Jack Diamond—Jacqueline Paige

SHUBERT THEATRE

Opened Monday, November 4, 1946.**
Max Gordon presents:

PARK AVENUE

Book by Nunnally Johnson and George S. Kaufman; Lyrics by Ira Gershwin; Music by Arthur Schwartz; Book directed by Mr. Kaufman; Dances and Musical Numbers by Helen Tamiris†; Production supervised by Arnold Saint Subber; Settings and Lighting by Donald Oenslager; Costumes by Tina Leser; Miss Corbett's Gowns by Mainbocher; Orchestrations by Don Walker; Conductor, Charles Sanford.

Cast of Characters

Carlton .... Byron Russell
Ned Scott .... Ray McDonald
Madge Bennett .... Martha Stewart
Ogden Bennett .... Arthur Margetson
Mrs. Sybil Bennett .... Leonora Corbett
Charles Crowell .... Robert Chisholm
Mrs. Elsa Crowell .... Marthe Errolle
Reggie Fox .... Charles Purcell
Mrs. Myra Fox .... Ruth Matteson
Richard Nelson .... Raymond Walburn
Mrs. Betty Nelson .... Mary Wickes
Ted Woods .... Harold Mattox
Mrs. Laura Woods .... Dorothy Bird
James Meredith .... William Skipper
Mrs. Beverly Meredith .... Joan Mann
Mr. Meachem†† .... David Wayne *1
Freddie Coleman .... Wilson Smith *2
Carole Benswanger .... Virginia Gordon
Brenda Stokes .... Adelle Rasey
Brenda Follansbee .... Sherry Shadburne
Brenda Follansbee-Stokes .... Carol Chandler
Brenda Follansbee-Stokes-Follansbee .... Betty Ann Lynn
Brenda Cadwaller .... Kyle MacDonnell
Brenda Stuyvesant .... Eileen Coffman
Brenda Cathcart .... June Graham
Brenda Cathcart-Cartcath .... Betty Low
Brenda Kerr .... Virginia Morris
Brenda Ker-Ker-Ker .... Judi Blacque
Brenda Quincy Adams .... Gloria Anderson
Brenda Wright, Jr., Sr., 3rd .... Margaret Gibson

Musical Numbers: 'Tomorrow Is The Time,' 'For The Life of Me,' 'The Dew Was on the Rose,' 'Don't Be a Woman if You Can,' 'Sweet Nevada,' In The Courtroom, 'There's No Holding Me,' 'There's Nothing Like Marriage for People,' 'Hope for the Best,' 'My Son-in-Law.' 'Land of Opportunities,' 'Goodbye To All That,' Echo.

A Musical Comedy satirizing the ultra-smart set in two acts. The action passes on the terrace and in the Drawing-room of the home of Mrs. Ogden Bennett on Long Island.

General Manager, Ben A. Boyar
Company Manager, Michael Goldreyer
Press, Nat Dorfman, Martha Dreiblatt
Stage Managers, Barbara Adams, Randell Henderson

†Replaced Eugene Loring.
††Played during tryout tour by Jed Prouty.
*Replaced by: 1 George Keane, 2 Gilbert O. Herman.
**Closed January 4, 1947. (72 performances)

Top: Mary Wickes—Marthe Errolle—Robert Chisholm—Leonora Corbett—Arthur Margetson—Ruth Matteson—Charles Purcell.

Center: Martha Stewart—Leonora Corbett—Raymond Walburn.

Bottom: Byron Russell—Leonora Corbett—Ray McDonald—Mary Wickes.

AMERICAN REPERTORY THEATRE

Walter Hampden June Duprez Victor Jory

Eva Le Gallienne Margaret Webster

Richard Waring Ernest Truex Philip Bourneuf

INTERNATIONAL THEATRE

Opened Wednesday, November 6, 1946.**
American Repertory Theatre, Inc.
presents:

HENRY VIII†

By William Shakespeare††; Staged by Margaret Webster*; Scenery and Costumes by David Ffolkes; Music by Lehman Engel; Dances arranged by Felicia Sorel, Cheryl Crawford, Managing Director.

Cast of Characters
(In order of appearance)

The Prologue	Philip Bourneuf
Duke of Buckingham	Richard Waring
Duke of Norfolk	Raymond Greenleaf
Lord Abergavenny	Robert Rawlings
Cardinal Wolsey	Walter Hampden
Cromwell	Eli Wallach
Sir Thomas Lovell	Emery Battis
Sergeant of the Guard	William Windom
Henry VIII	Victor Jory
Duke of Suffolk	Efrem Zimbalist, Jr.
Katherine of Aragon	Eva Le Gallienne
Surveyor	Angus Cairns
Lord Chamberlain	Ernest Truex
Lord Sands	John Becher
Sir Harry Guildford	Arthur Keegan
Ann Bullen	June Duprez
First Chronicler	Philip Bourneuf
Second Chronicler	Eugene Stuckmann
Sir Nicholas Vaux	Donald Keyes
Cardinal Campeius	John Straub
An Old Lady	Margaret Webster
Griffith	Donald Keyes
Lady in Waiting to Katherine	Ruth Neal
Garter King of Arms	Angus Cairns
Earl of Surrey	William Windom
Archbishop of Canterbury	Theadore Tenley
Patience	Marion Evensen
A Messenger	Robert Rawlings
Capucius	Eugene Stuckmann
Duchess of Norfolk	Mary Alice Moore

Ladies of the Court, Crowd, Ladies to Katherine: Cavada Humphrey, Ann Jackson, Mary Alice Moore, Ruth Neal.

Lords, Bishops, Monks, Guards, Servants, Heralds, Pages, Executioner, Sergeant at Arms: Don Allen, John Behney, Michael Corhan, Tom Grace, Bart Henderson, Frederic Hunter, Robert Leser, Mark McCardle, Gerald McCormack, Walter Neal, James Rafferty, Theadore Tenley, Ed Woodhead.

A Revival of the Historical drama in two acts, thirteen scenes. The action takes place in London between the years 1521 and 1533—outside and within the Council Room at Whitehall Palace, a Street, Wolsey's Palace at York House, outside the Tower, the King's Apartments, the Hall at Blackfriars, the Queen's Apartments, Westminster Abbey, a Room in Kimbolton Abbey, Ante-room in the Palace, outside the Palace at Greenwich.

†This play is believed to have been the poet's last work, originally titled "All Is True," and presented for the first time at the Globe Theatre in London, on June 29, 1613. During the performance the discharge from a small cannon heralding the entrance of the king to the mask at the Cardinal's house set fire to some thatch and ultimately caused complete destruction of the Old Globe. The first New York performance was at the Park Theatre on May 13, 1799 with Lewis Hallam as Henry.

††The text of this play is thought to be only partially the work of Shakespeare—John Fletcher being a collaborator.

*In preparing this acting version Miss Webster went to 'The Chronicles of Rafael Holinshead,' which was the source for the original text, for the excerpts spoken by the two chroniclers. The song used in Act I. Scene 6 is an authentic song written by King Henry VIII to Ann Bullen.

**Closed February 21, 1947. (39 performances in Repertory)

BELASCO THEATRE

Opened Thursday, November 7, 1946.*
Nelson L. Gross and Daniel Melnick
present Katherine Dunham's Production:

BAL NEGRE

Choreography and Staging by Katherine Dunham; Costumes and Lighting by John Pratt; Orchestra directed by Gilberto Valdes.

Featuring

Katherine Dunham

Lenwood Morris	Lucille Ellis
Lawaune Ingram	Vanoye Aikens
James Alexander	Dolores Harper
Ronnie Aul	Jesse Hawkins
Wilbert Bradley	Richardena Jackson
Byron Cuttler	Eartha Kitt
Eddy Clay	Gloria Mitchell
Syvilla Fort (Guest)	Eugene Robinson
Roxie Foster	Othella Strozier

Sans-Souci Singers

Mariam Burton	Eartha Kitt
Jean Leon Destine	Mary Lewis
Rosalie King	Ricardo Morrison

Gordon Simpson

Drummers: La Rosa Estrada, Julio Mendez, Candido Vicenty

Musical and Production Numbers

Act I

Overture: 'Ylenko-Ylembe' by Gilberto Valdes; 'Congo Paillette'—Native Haitian Corn Sorting Ritual.

I. Motivos: 'Rhumba' by Gilberto Valdes; 'Son' —Cuban Slave Lament; 'Nanigo' by Valdes; 'Choro' by Gogliano—a 19th Century Brazilian quadrille; 'La Comparsa' by Ernesto Lecuona. Alone in the deserted streets in the early morning hours after carnival, a woman encounters three men. She believes that one may be her husband . . .

II. Haitian Roadside by Paquita Anderson and Gilberto Valdes. 'Soleil, O'—invocation; 'Apollon'—Carnival Meringue; 'Chocounne.' Vocal arrangements by Reginald Beane. On the dusty roads of Haiti, many things happen in the late afternoon.

III. Shango† by Baldwin Bergerson—Ritual and Dance.

Act II

I. L'Ag'Ya by Robert Sanders, from an original story by Katherine Dunham. The scene is Vauclin, a tiny 18th Century fishing village in Martinique. Front curtain by Charles Sebree.

Act III

I. Nostalgia: Ragtime—'Chong,' 'Under the Bamboo Tree,' 'Ragtime Cowboy,' 'Oh, You Beautiful Doll,' 'Alexander's Ragtime Band,' The Waltz, Fox-Trot, Ballin' the Jack, Tango, Maxixe and Turkey Trot. Vocal arrangement by Reginald Beane, Orchestration by Billy Butler, Advisor, Tom Fletcher; 'Blues' by Floyd Smith. Miss Dunham's gown by Leopold Kobrin; 'Flaming Youth, 1927' by "Brad" Gowans—Black Bottom, Mooch, Fishtail and Snake Hips.

II. Finale: Havana-1910 by Navarro; 'Para Que Tu Veas' by Bobby Capo.

A Native Music and Dance Revue in three acts, six parts.

General Manager, ROBERT MILFORD
Company Manager, RUBE BERNSTEIN
Press, CAMPBELL B. CASAD
Stage Manager, MAURY YAFFE

†From "Carib Song" with the original Jo Mielziner settings.
*Closed Dec. 22, 1946. (54 performances)

Top: 'La Comparsa' with James Alexander, Byron Cuttler, Vanoye Aikens, Miss Dunham. Second: Candido Vicenty—Julio Mendez—La Rosa Estrada—Lucille Ellis—Othella Strozier. Third: 'Blues' with Vanoye Aikens and Miss Dunham. Bottom: 'Finale' with Miss Dunham and Sans-Souci Singers.

Richard Waring June Duprez Walter Hampden Eva Le Gallienne

INTERNATIONAL THEATRE

Opened Friday, November 8, 1946.*
American Repertory Theatre, Inc.
presents:

WHAT EVERY WOMAN KNOWS†

By J. M. Barrie; Directed by Margaret Webster; Scenery by Paul Morrison; Costumes by David Ffolkes; Cheryl Crawford, Managing Director.

Cast of Characters
(In order of appearance)

Alick Wylie........Ernest Truex
James Wylie........Arthur Keegan
David Wylie........Philip Bourneuf
Maggie Wylie........June Duprez
John Shand........Richard Waring
Comtesse de la Briere........Eva Le Gallienne
Lady Sybil Tenterden........Mary Alice Moore
A Maid........Cavada Humphrey
Charles Venables........Walter Hampden
A Butler........Efrem Zimbalist Jr.

Electors of Glasgow and members of the Cowcaddens: John Becher, Angus Cairns, Cavada Humphrey, Ann Jackson, Donald Keyes, Robert Rawlings, John Straub, Eugene Stuckmann, Theodore Tenley, Eli Wallach, William Windom, Ed Woodhead, Efrem Zimbalist, Jr.

A Revival of the comedy in two acts, five scenes. The action takes place early in the nineteen hundreds, in the Wylie house in the village of the Pans, Scotland; a barber shop used as Shand's committee rooms, Glasgow; the Shand house in London; and the Comtesse's Cottage in Surrey.

†First presented in New York by Charles Frohman at the Empire Theatre, December 23, 1908 with Maude Adams as "Maggie." Revived by W. A. Brady April 13, 1926 at the Bijou with Helen Hayes.

*Closed February 15, 1947. (Played 21 performances in repertory)

Eva Le Gallienne Mary Alice Moore

Eva Le Gallienne—Mary Alice Moore—William Windom—Victor Jory—Margaret Webster

INTERNATIONAL THEATRE

Opened Tuesday, November 12, 1946.*
American Repertory Theatre, Inc.
presents:

JOHN GABRIEL BORKMAN†

By Henrik Ibsen; Direction, Translation and Production Scheme by Eva Le Gallienne; Scenery and Costumes by Paul Morrison; Musical Arrangement by Lehman Engel; Cheryl Crawford, Managing Director.

Cast of Characters
(In order of appearance)

Mrs. Borkman....Margaret Webster
Malene, her maid....Marion Evensen
Ella Rentheim, her sister....Eva Le Gallienne
Erhart Borkman, her son....William Windom
Mrs. Fanny Wilton....Mary Alice Moore
John Gabriel Borkman....Victor Jory
Frida Foldal....Ann Jackson
Vilhelm Foldal....Ernest Truex

A Revival of the Drama in five scenes, no intermission. The continuous action takes place on a winter evening in the Living-room, the upstairs Sitting-room, on the Front Porch and the Path up the Hill on the Rentheim Family Estate in the neighborhood of Christiana (Oslo), about 1896.

†Presented for the first time in New York by the Criterion Independent Theatre on November 18, 1897 at Hoyt's Theatre.
*Closed February 19, 1947. (21 performances in Repertory)

Staff For American Repertory Theatre
General Manager, John Yorke
Press, Wolfe Kaufman, Mary Ward
Stage Managers, Thelma Chandler, Emery Battis

Victor Jory Eva Le Gallienne

THE PLAYHOUSE

Opened Wednesday, November 13, 1946.*
Viola Rubber and Johnnie Walker present:

THE HAVEN†

By Dennis Hoey, based on the novel by Anthony Gilbert; Staged by Clarence Derwent; Setting by William N. Saulter; Costumes supervised by Noel Taylor.

Cast of Characters††
(In order of appearance)

Miss Martin	Viola Roache
Mrs. Hart	Queenie Leonard
Edmund Durward	Dennis Hoey
Agatha Forbes	Valerie Cossart
Arthur Cook	Melville Cooper
Grace Knowles	Eliza Sutherland
Inspector Ramsey	Charles Francis
Constable Miller	Darby Summers
Coroner	Ivan Simpson

A Murder Melodrama in two acts, six scenes. The action takes place in "The Haven," a house in the marshy Fen country of Cambridgeshire, England in 1944.

Company Manager, HAROLD HARRIS
Press, PHYLLIS PERLMAN, MARIAN BYRAM
Assistant to producer, ADRIAN LARKIN
Stage Manager, CHARLES PARSONS

†During the out of town tryout, Elmer Harris was called to assist with the re-write and direction.

††The part of a Reporter, played by Keith Palmer was written out during the tryout.

*Closed November 16, 1946. (5 performances)

Dennis Hoey Melville Cooper

Charles Francis—Ivan Simpson—Melville Cooper—Valerie Cossart

Ingrid Bergman in "Joan of Lorraine"

Sam Wanamaker **Ingrid Bergman**

ALVIN THEATRE

Opened Monday, November 18, 1946.***
The Playwrights' Company presents:

JOAN OF LORRAINE†

By Maxwell Anderson; Directed by Margo Jones*; Settings, Lighting and Costumes by Lee Simonson.

Cast of Characters

Jimmy Masters, the Director......Sam Wanamaker
(The Inquisitor)
Al, the Stage Manager......Gilmore Bush
Mary Grey......Ingrid Bergman††
(Joan)
Abbey......Lewis Martin
(Jacques D'Arc) (Cauchon, Bishop of Beauvais)
Jo Cordwell......Bruce Hall
(Jean D'Arc)
Dollner......Kenneth Tobey
(Pierre D'Arc)
Charles Elling......Charles Ellis
(Durand Laxart)
Farwell......Arthur L. Sachs
(Jean de Metz) (The Executioner)
Garder......Peter Hobbs
(Bertrand de Poulengy)
Sheppard......Berry Kroeger
(Alain Chartier)
Les Ward......Romney Brent
(The Dauphin)
Tessie......Timothy Lynn Kearse**
Ass't. Stage Manager (Aurore)
Jeffson......Roger De Koven
Kipner......Harry Irvine
(Regnault de Chartres, Archbishop of Rheims)
Long......Kevin McCarthy
(Dunois, Bastard of Orleans)
Noble......Martin Rudy
(La Hire)

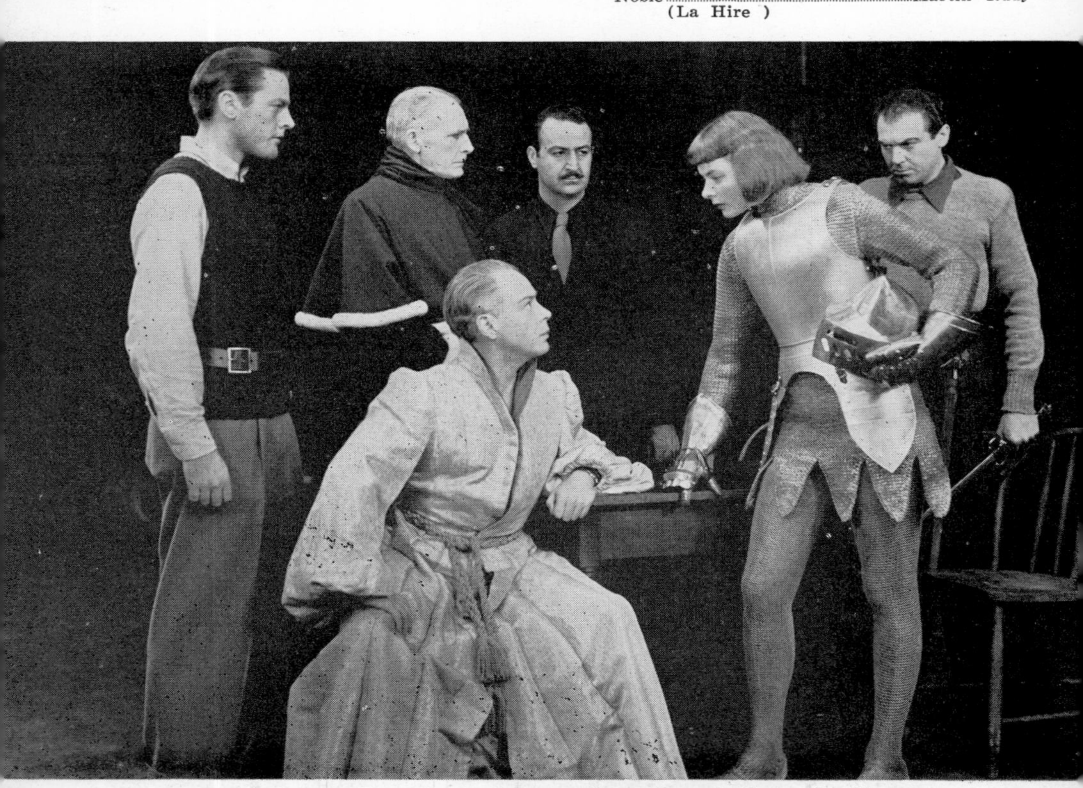

Kevin McCarthy—Harry Irvine—Romney Brent (seated)—Roger De Koven—Ingrid Bergman—Martin Rudy

Quirke .... Brooks West
(St. Michael) (D'Estivet)
Miss Reeves .... Ann Coray
(St. Catherine)
Miss Sadler .... Joanna Roos
(St. Margaret)
Champlain .... Joseph Wiseman
(Father Massieu)
Smith .... Stephen Roberts
(Thomas de Courcelles)
Marie, the Costumer .... Lotte Stavisky
Electrician .... Himself

A Drama in two acts. The play takes place within a single day on the stage of a New York Theatre during the last week of rehearsal on a play about Joan of Arc. The action begins on a bare stage with only chairs and tables as props and in modern clothes. As the scenes progress, costumes and more props are added till at the end it is like a dress rehearsal.

Company Managers, WILLIAM BLAIR, VICTOR SAMROCK
Press, WILLIAM FIELDS, WALTER ALFORD
Stage Manager, ALAN ANDERSON

†By the device of a play within a play the author puts forth some contemporary reflections while unfolding the story of the Maid of Orleans.

††This is Miss Bergman's second appearance on Broadway, her first having been in a revival of "Liliom," produced by Vinton Freedley at the 44th Street Theatre for 56 performances, opening March 25, 1940.

*During the tryout, Miss Jones was compelled to leave the play because of illness and Sam Wanamaker and Alan Anderson completed the work of direction.

**Replaced by Terese Hayden.

***Closed May 10, 1947. (198 performances)

Joseph Wiseman—Ingrid Bergman—Lewis Martin

Joseph Wiseman—Sam Wanamaker—Ingrid Bergman—Lewis Martin—Brooks West—Stephen Roberts

Patricia Neal—Mildred Dunnock—Bartlett Robinson—
Margaret Phillips—Percy Waram—Leo Genn—
Jean Hagen—Scott McKay
Opposite: Scott McKay and Jean Hagen

Scott McKay—Margaret Phillips—Leo Genn

FULTON THEATRE

Opened Wednesday, November 20, 1946.**
Kermit Bloomgarden presents:

ANOTHER PART OF THE FOREST†

By Lillian Hellman; Staged by the author; Settings and Lighting by Jo Mielziner; Costumes by Lucinda Ballard; Original Music by Marc Blitzstein; Coby Ruskin, assistant to the producer.

Cast of Characters

Regina Hubbard	Patricia Neal
John Bagtry	Bartlett Robinson
Lavinia Hubbard	Mildred Dunnock
Coralee	Beatrice Thompson
Marcus Hubbard	Percy Waram
Benjamin Hubbard	Leo Genn*
Simon Isham	Owen Coll
Oscar Hubbard	Scott McKay
Jacob	Stanley Greene
Birdie Bagtry	Margaret Phillips
Harold Penniman	Paul Ford
Gilbert Jugger	Gene O'Donnell
Laurette Sincee	Jean Hagen

A Drama in three acts, three scenes. The action takes place in the Alabama town of Bowden on the side terrace and in the living-room of the Hubbard house, June 1880.

General Manager, MAX ALLENTUCK
Press, RICHARD MANEY, ANNE WOLL
Stage Manager, RICHARD BECKHARD

†This play depicts the lives of the Hubbards twenty years before the time of "The Little Foxes," four characters are retained, Oscar, Ben and Regina Hubbard, and Birdie.

*Replaced by Wesley Addy.

**Closed April 26, 1947. (182 performances)

Mildred Dunnock—Beatrice Thompson—
Patricia Neal—Bartlett Robinson

Patricia Neal—Percy Waram—Mildred Dunnock

Leo Genn—Scott McKay—Beatrice Thompson—Mildred Dunnock—Percy Waram—Patricia Neal

Ruth Ford—Claude Dauphin—Annabella

BILTMORE THEATRE

Opened Tuesday, November 26, 1946.*
Herman Levin and Oliver Smith present:

NO EXIT†

By Jean-Paul Sartre; Adapted from the French by Paul Bowles; Directed by John Huston; Setting and Lighting by Frederick Kiesler.

Cast of Characters
(In order of appearance)

Cradeau .... Claude Dauphin††
Bellboy .... Peter Kass
Inez .... Annabella
Estelle .... Ruth Ford

A Psychological Melodrama based on Existentialist philosophy in one act, two scenes. The entire action takes place in a Room which represents a cubicle in Hell at the present time.

General Manager, PHILIP ADLER
Company Manager, SIDNEY HARRIS
Press, RICHARD MANEY, ANNE WOLL
Stage Manager, PETER KASS

†Adapted from "Huis Clos" which opened in May, 1944, at Le Theatre du Vieux Columbier in Paris. The English version had its first performance at the Arts Theatre Club in London on July 17, 1946 under the title "Vicious Circle."
††French actor making his first appearance in America.
*Closed December 21, 1946. (31 performances)

Claude Dauphin—Peter Kass—Ruth Ford

John Williams—Emily Ross—Ann Mason

THE PLAYHOUSE

Opened Wednesday, November 27, 1946.**
Jesse Long and Edward S. Hart present:

A FAMILY AFFAIR

By Henry R. Misrock; Staged by Alexander Kirkland; Setting by Sam Leve.

Cast of Characters
(In order of appearance)

Florence McConnel ..... Emily Ross
Mary ..... Amelia Barleon
Alice Jones ..... Jewel Curtis
Julia Wallace ..... Ann Mason
Walter Wallace ..... John Williams
Johnny Wallace ..... Joel Marston*
Martha ..... Lenore Thomas
Mike Cassidy ..... Allan Stevenson
George Weaver ..... Robert Smith
Peggy Wallace ..... Margaret Garland
Dr. Christopher Patterson ..... Frank Lyon
Gregorin ..... Anatole Winogradoff

A Domestic Comedy in three acts, three scenes. The action takes place in the Wallace Living-room, New York City—late summer 1946.

Press, PHYLLIS PERLMAN, MARIAN BYRAM
Stage Manager, WILLIAM JOHNSON

*Played by Peter Scott during tryout tour.
**Closed November 30, 1946. (5 performances)

John Williams Joel Marston Ann Mason

MUSIC BOX THEATRE

Opened Saturday, November 30, 1946.**
Joseph M. Hyman and Bernard Hart present:

CHRISTOPHER BLAKE†

By Moss Hart; directed by Mr. Hart; Designed by Harry Horner; Lighting by Mr. Horner and Leo Kerz; Costumes supervised by Bianca Stroock.

Cast of Characters

A Soldier	Ira Cirker *1
A Marine	Dan Frazer *2
A Radio Man	Hugh Williamson
A Photographer	Jack Garbutt
Another Photographer	Charles S. Dubin
A Radio Announcer	Kermit Kegley
A Newsreel Man	Frederic De Wilde
Another Newsreel Man	Allen Shaw
A Military Aide	Carl Judd
A General	Frank M. Thomas
An Admiral	Tom Morrison
Another General	Guy Tano
The President	Irving Fisher
Christopher Blake	Richard Tyler
Mr. Blake	Shepperd Strudwick
Mrs. Blake	Martha Sleeper
Mr. Kurlick	Francis De Sales
Mr. Caldwell	Watson White
Judge Adamson	Robert Harrison
A Courtroom Attendant	Raymond Van Sickle
The Doorman	Tom Morrison
The Stage Manager	Carl Judd
Butts	Hugh Williamson
Miss Holly	Peggy Van Vleet
An Actress	Phyllis Tyler
Johnny	Mack Twamley *3
Ray	Dickie Leone
The Headmaster	Ronald Alexander
The Janitor	Maximilian Schultz
A Beggar	Edward Pegram
An Angry Man	Allen Shaw
A Policeman	Kermit Kegley
Miss MacIntyre	Kay Loring
The Superintendent	Frank M. Thomas
The Mother	Susan Sanderson
The Father	Hugh Williamson
The Bailiff	Ronald Alexander
Photographers	Guy Tano, Bill Hoe
Three Boys	Charles Nevil, Dickie Leone, Mack Twamley
Another Bailiff	Allen Shaw
A Judge	Frank M. Thomas

Spectators and Passersby; Dorothy Beauvaire, Maylah Bradford, Eileen Burns, Lois Harmon, Johann Kley, Lillian Marr, Jennifer Moore, Diane Parker, Leslie Penha.

A Realistic and Fantastic Drama about divorce in two acts, eight scenes. The realistic action takes place in Judge Adamson's Chambers and Courtroom; and the scenes in the private world of Christopher Blake are at the White House, on the Stage of a Theatre, a street in New York City, the Poorhouse and a Courtroom.

General Manager, AL GOLDIN
Press, MICHEL MOK, ISADORA BENNETT
Production Assistant, ANN BROOKS OAKMAN
Stage Manager, DON HERSHEY

†During the run of the play the author changed the playing order of the scenes—opening with the first chambers scene; presenting the White House scene fourth instead of first; and eliminating the poorhouse scene.
*Replacements: 1 Charles S. Dubin, 2 Edgar Waldman, 3 Charles Nevil.
**Closed March 8, 1947. (114 performances)

Top: Christopher (Richard Tyler) is photographed for the Rogues' Gallery. Second: Christopher calls on the President (Irving Fisher). Third: Sheppard Strudwick—Martha Sleeper—Richard Tyler—Robert Harrison. Bottom: Christopher seeks his father in New York.

Fredric March and Florence Eldridge in "Years Ago"

Florence Eldridge—Fredric March— Patricia Kirkland

MANSFIELD THEATRE

Opened Tuesday, December 3, 1946.**
Max Gordon presents:

YEARS AGO†

By Ruth Gordon; Directed by Garson Kanin; Setting by Donald Oenslager; Costumes by John Boyt and Ruth Kanin.

Cast of Characters

Clinton Jones........Fredric March
Annie Jones........Florence Eldridge
Ruth Gordon Jones........Patricia Kirkland
Katherine Follett........Bethel Leslie
Anna Witham........Jennifer Bunker
Fred Whitmarsh........Richard Simon
Mr. Sparrow........Seth Arnold*
Mr. Bagley........Frederic Persson
Miss Glavin........Judith Cargill
Punk........A Cat

An Autobiographical Comedy in three acts, four scenes. The action takes place in the Jones' Dining-room-Sitting-room at 14 Elmwood Avenue, Wallaston, Massachusetts, in 1913.

General Manager, BEN A. BOYAR
Company Manager, CHARLES WILLIAMS
Press, NAT DORFMAN, MARTHA DREIBLATT
Stage Manager, GEORGE GREENBERG

†Tried-out last season out of town under title "Miss Jones."
*Alternate: Grover Burgess.
**Closed May 31, 1947. (199 performances)

Patricia Kirkland—Richard Simon—Fredric March—Florence Eldridge—Jennifer Bunker—Bethel Leslie

Frederic Persson—Judith Cargill—Fredric March—Florence Eldridge—Patricia Kirkland

Patricia Kirkland—Richard Simon—Bethel Leslie—Seth Arnold—Florence Eldridge

CENTURY THEATRE

Opened Thursday, December 5, 1946.*
Leonard Sillman presents:

IF THE SHOE FITS

Book by June Carroll and Robert Duke; Music by David Raksin; Lyrics by June Carroll; Book Direction by Eugene Bryden; Choreography by Charles Weidman; Settings by Edward Gilbert; Costumes by Kathryn Kuhn; Tap Routines by Don Liberto; Orchestrations by Russell Bennett; Production Manager, Archie Thomson, Musical Director, Will Irwin; Vocal Director, Joe Moon; Supervised by Leonard Sillman.

Cast of Characters

Town Crier .... Robert Penn
Singing Attendant .... Eugene Martin
Dancing Attendant .... Billy Vaux
Broderick .... Jack Williams
Acrobatic Attendants .... Jane Vinson and Paula Dee
Cinderella .... Leila Ernst
Mistress Spratt .... Jody Gilbert
Delilah } .... her daughters .... { Marilyn Day
Thais } { Sherle North
The Butcher Boy .... Richard Wentworth
First Undertaker .... Don Mayo
Second Undertaker .... Walter Kattwinkel
Loreli .... Gail Adams
Lilith .... Eileen Ayers
First Lawyer .... Harvey Braun
Second Lawyer .... Stanley Simmonds
Lady Eve .... Florence Desmond
Herman .... Joe Besser
Four Sprites ..... Vincent Carbone, Harry Rogers, Allen Knowles, Ferd Bernaski
1st Troubadour .... William Rains
2nd Troubadour .... Ray Morrissey
3rd Troubadour .... Richard Wentworth
Their Arranger .... Fin Olsen
Major Domo .... Youka Troubetzkoy
Lady Guinevere .... Eleanor Jones
Lady Persevere .... Dorothy Karroll
Dame Crackle .... Chloe Owen
The Baker .... Ray Cook
Dame Crumple .... Joyce White
Dame Crinkle .... Jean Olds
Prince Charming .... Edward Dew
Widow Willow .... Adrienne
Kate .... Barbara Perry
King Kindly .... Edward Lambert
His Magnificence, The Wizard —Frank Milton
Court Dancer .... Vincent Carbone
Sailor .... Richard D'Arcy
His Sweethearts .... { Marcia Maier
{ Maryblу Harwood

Musical Numbers: Prologue, 'Start The Ball Rollin',' 'I Wish,' 'In the Morning,' 'Come and Bring Your Instruments,' 'Night After Night,' 'Every Eve,' 'With a Wave of My Wand,' 'Am I a Man or a Mouse?,' 'I'm Not Myself Tonight,' 'Three Questions,' Entre Acte, 'If The Shoe Fits,' 'What's The Younger Generation Coming To?' 'Have You Seen The Countess Cindy?,' 'This Is The End of the Story,' 'I Took Another Look,' 'I Want To Go Back to the Bottom of the Garden,' 'My Business Man.'

A Musical Comedy based on the Cinderella Legend in a Prologue, two acts, thirteen scenes. The story takes place during the Middle Ages in one of those mythical kingdoms known only to writers of musical comedies, in this case, "The Kingdom of Nicely." The action takes place at the Town Gate, Cinderella's Kitchen, the Gate, Ballroom and Anteroom of the Palace, and in a Village Street.

General Manager, LILLIAN MILLS
Press, DOROTHY ROSS, LEWIS HARMON
Assistant to Producer, ALBERT F. CRIPPA
Stage Manager, T. C. JONES

*Closed December 21, 1946. (20 performances)

Florence Desmond Joe Besser

Edward Dew Leila Ernst

THE PLAYHOUSE

Opened Wednesday, December 11, 1946.*
Paul Feigay in association with George Somnes presents:

LAND'S END

By Thomas Job, based on the novel "Dawn in Lyonesse" by Mary Ellen Chase; Staged by Robert Lewis; Designed by Donald Oenslager†; Incidental Music by Paul Bowles.

Cast of Characters

Susan Pengilly ..... Shirley Booth
Lize ..... Amelia Romano
Ellen Pascoe ..... Helen Craig
Mr. Trevetha ..... Fred Stewart
Derek Tregonny ..... Walter Coy
Miss Penrose ..... Frieda Altman
Mrs. Bond ..... Mabel Acker
Miss Clark ..... Diane de Brett
Mr. Brooks ..... Clement Brace
Mrs. Brooks ..... Xenia Bank
Mr. Brigstocke ..... Joseph Foley
Mr. Derby ..... Sydney Boyd
Mr. Harris ..... Ross Chetwynd
The Professor ..... Theodore Newton
Dr. Gregory ..... Horace Cooper
Kitchen Boy ..... Michael Feigay
Mrs. Tregonny ..... Merle Maddern
Grandmother Tregonny ..... Minnie Dupree
The Rector ..... Jay Barney
First Fisherman ..... Joseph Foley
Second Fisherman ..... Sydney Boyd
Third Fisherman ..... Ross Chetwynd
Fourth Fisherman ..... Fred Stewart

A Folk Tragedy with an analogy to the Tristram and Iseult legend in three acts, seven scenes, set between the two world wars. The action takes place at Mr. Trevetha's fish chopping shelter at St. Ives, Cornwall, England; the Dining-lounge and Ellen's and Susan's room in the Tower Hotel, Tintagel; the Men-an-Thol Stone and the Living-room of the Tregonny's house at Land's End.

General Manager, Charles Harris
Company Manager, Joseph C. Cohne
Press, Karl Bernstein, Ben Kornzweig
Stage Managers, Robert Griffith, Daniel Sattler

†Charles Elson assisted on the settings and Rose Bogdanoff on costumes.
*Closed December 14, 1946. (5 performances)

Helen Craig Walter Coy

Joseph Foley—Sydney Boyd—Ross Chetwynd—Mabel Acker—Diane de Brett—Theodore Newton—Helen Craig

Ernest Truex John Becher

June Duprez Richard Waring

INTERNATIONAL THEATRE

Opened Thursday, December 19, 1946.**
American Repertory Theatre presents:

POUND ON DEMAND†

By Sean O'Casey; Staged by Victor Jory; Costumes and Scenery by Wolfgang Roth.

Cast of Characters

Girl .... Cavada Humphrey
Jerry .... Philip Bourneuf
Sammy .... Ernest Truex
Woman .... Margaret Webster*
Policeman .... Eugene Stuckmann

A one-act Comedy Curtain Raiser which takes place in a post office.

ANDROCLES AND THE LION†

By Bernard Shaw; Staged by Margaret Webster; Music by Marc Blitzstein; Costumes and Scenery by Wolfgang Roth; Animal heads and masks by Remo Bufano.

Cast of Characters

Lion .... John Becher
Megaera .... Marion Evensen
Androcles .... Ernest Truex
Beggar .... Arthur Keegan
Centurion .... John Straub
Captain .... Richard Waring
Lavinia .... June Duprez
Lentulus .... Eugene Stuckmann
Metullus .... Angus Cairns
Ferrovius .... Victor Jory
Spintho .... Eli Wallach
Ox-driver .... Robert Rawlings
Call-boy .... Arthur Keegan
Secutor .... Efrem Zimbalist Jr.
Retiarus .... William Windom
Editor .... Raymond Greenleaf
Menagerie Keeper .... Ed Woodhead
Caesar .... Philip Bourneuf

Christians: Emery Battis, Cavada Humphrey, Anne Jackson, Donald Keyes, Mary Alice Moore, Theodore Tenley, Gloria Valborg.

Soldiers, Slaves, Gladiators, Servants: Don Allen, John Behney, Michel Corhan, Thomas Grace, Bart Henderson, Frederic Hunter, Robert Leser, Gerald McCormack.

A Revival of the Comedy in a prologue, two acts, four scenes. The action takes place in a Jungle; on the outskirts of Rome, and the entrance to the Arena—behind the Emperor's Box and in the Arena of the Coliseum.

Managing Director, CHERYL CRAWFORD
General Manager, JOHN YORKE
Press, WOLFE KAUFMAN, MARY WARD
Stage Mgrs., THELMA CHANDLER, EMERY BATTIS

†This is the Broadway Premiere of "Pound on Demand." The Shaw play was first presented here by Granville Barker at Wallacks' Theatre on January 27, 1915 with O.P. Heggie as 'Androcles.' It was revived by the Theatre Guild in 1925.

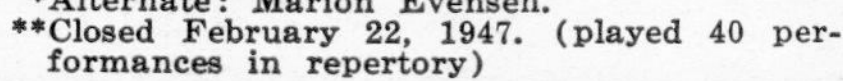

*Alternate: Marion Evensen.
**Closed February 22, 1947. (played 40 performances in repertory)

Hal Conklin—Donald Murphy—Sidney Blackmer—Philip Loeb

CORONET THEATRE

Opened Wednesday, December 25, 1946.**
Theron Bamberger in association with Richard Skinner presents:

WONDERFUL JOURNEY†

By Harry Segall; Staged by Frank Emmons Brown; Settings by Raymond Sovey; Costumes supervised by Bianca Stroock.

Cast of Characters

1st. Escort .... Phil Stein
2nd. Escort .... Michael Lewin
Joe Pendleton .... Donald Murphy
Messenger 7013 .... Wallace Acton
Mr. Jordan .... Sidney Blackmer
Ames .... Richard Temple
Tony Abbott .... Hal Conklin
Julia Farnsworth .... Fay Baker
Bette Logan .... Frances Waller *1
A Workman .... Carmen Costi
Max Levene .... Philip Loeb
Susie .... Ann Sullivan
Lieut. Williams .... Barry Kelley *2
Plain-Clothesman .... Phil Stein
Radio Announcer .... Robert Caldwell
Lefty .... Richard Taber
Trainer .... Michael Lewin
Handler .... Stephen Elliott
Doctor .... Robert Caldwell

A Whimsical Fantasy in two acts, six scenes. The action takes place somewhere in Space, the Farnsworth Drawing-room and a Dressing-room underneath the Stadium.

Company Manager, GILMAN HASKELL
Press, LEO FREEDMAN, JUNE GREENWALL
Stage Managers, ROBERT CALDWELL, PHIL STEIN

†The first Broadway production of the play which was originally entitled "Heaven Can Wait," and six years prior was filmed as "Here Comes Mr. Jordan."

*Played during tryout tour by 1 Jean Gillespie. 2 William Tubbs.

**Closed January 1, 1947. (9 performances)

Donald Murphy Sidney Blackmer

Santo Scudi and Joan Andre in "The Sheik of Araby"

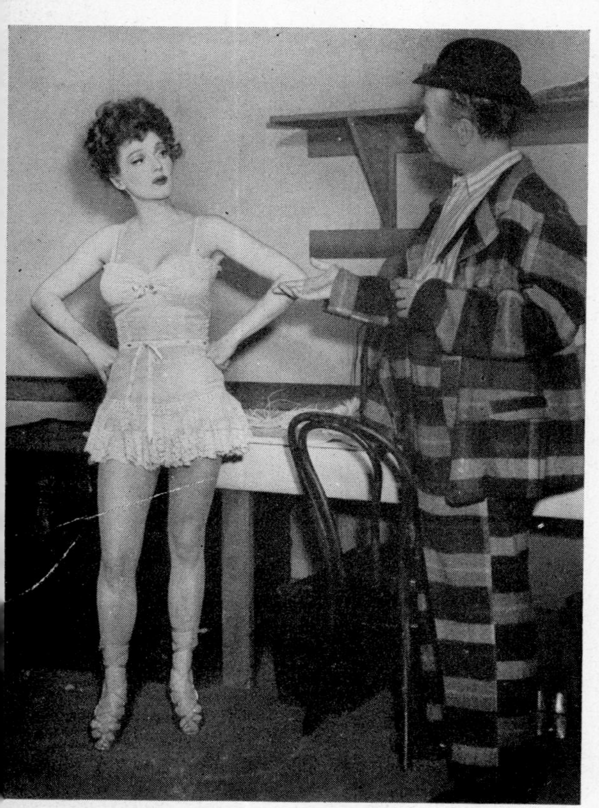

Jean Parker Bert Lahr

Bert Lahr as Skid

BELASCO THEATRE

Opening Wednesday, December 25, 1946.
Jean Dalrymple presents:

BURLESQUE†

By George Manker Watters and Arthur Hopkins; Settings by Robert Rowe Paddock; Dances by Billy Holbrook; Costumes by Grace Houston; Staged by Mr. Hopkins.

Cast of Characters

Bonny........Jean Parker
Sammy........Robert Weil
Skid........Bert Lahr
Lefty........Ross Hertz
A Fireman........Norman Morgan
Mazie........Kay Buckley **
Gussie........Jerri Blanchard
Sylvia Marco........Joyce Mathews *1
Bozo........Bobby Barry
Harvey Howell........Charles G. Martin
Jerry Evans........Harold Bostwick
A Bell Boy........Norman Morgan
Stage Carpenter........Michael Keene
Ecdysisist........Irene Allarie
Tenor........Santo Scudi
Orchestra Leader........Milton Merill
Girls of the Chorus:
Marie........Joan Andre
Kiki........Carolyn Boyce
Buster........Millicent Roy
Sugar........Ronnie Rogers
Mimi........Gene Gilmour
Mitsy........Darin Jennings
Blossom........Ruth Maitland *2
Bubbles........Jeri Archer
Cuddles........Eleanor Prentiss

Songs: 'Rhapsody,' 'The Man I Love,' 'Hallelujah.' 'Hindustan,' 'Peggy O'Neal.' 'Hold That Tiger,' 'He's Got To Get Under, Get Out and Get Under,' 'Just Around the Corner,' 'Put Your Arms Around Me,' 'Sheik of Araby,' 'There's Something About a Soldier,' 'Daughter of Rosie O'Grady.'

A Revival of the Comedy-drama in three acts, four scenes. The action occurs some years ago in a Basement Dressing-room in a Mid-West Burlesque Theatre, the Living-room of a New York Hotel Suite, the Stage of the Star Theatre, Paterson, N. J., and opening night of Lefty's Burlesque Show.

General Manager, PHILLIP BLOOM
Company Manager, ARTHUR SINGER
Press, DAVID LIPSKY, MARIAN GRAHAM
Production Assistant, SYLVIA FRIEDLANDER
Stage Managers, GUS SCHIRMER,, JR., NORMAN MORGAN

†Originally produced by Arthur Hopkins; opened at the Plymouth on September 1, 1927 with Barbara Stanwyck and Hal Shelly. It ran for 372 performances.
*Replaced by 1 Darin Jennings, 2 Patricia Leslie.
**Alternate; Patricia Leslie

Harold Bostwick—Kay Buckley—Ross Hertz—Jean Parker—Bert Lahr—Charles G. Martin

Bobby Barry—Jerri Blanchard—Jean Parker—Bert Lahr—Kay Buckley

ADELPHI THEATRE

(Moved to CORONET January 5, 1947.)
Opened Wednesday, December 25, 1946. *
David Lowe† presents:

LOVELY ME††

By Jacqueline Susann and Beatrice Cole; Directed by Jessie Royce Landis; Designed and Lighted by Donald Oenslager; Costumes supervised by Eleanor Goldsmith; Songs by Arthur Siegel and Jeff Bailey.

Cast of Characters
(In order of appearance)

Irving	Arthur Siegel
Auntie	Barbara Bulgakov
Peggy Smith	June Dayton
Matilda	Joyce Allan
Sonny	Paul Marlin
Natasha Smith	Luba Malina
Mr. Forrest	Houston Richards
Thomas van Stokes	Reynolds Evans
Stanislaus Stanislavsky	Mischa Auer
Mike Shane	Millard Mitchell

Songs; 'Life Can Be Beautiful,' 'Lovely Me.'

A Comedy in three acts, four scenes. The action takes place in the Living-room of Natasha Smith's Hotel Apartment on Central Park South, New York City, October, 1946.

Business Manager, SAMUEL FUNT
Press, KARL BERNSTEIN
Stage Director, JOSEPH OLNEY
Stage Manager, ALLEN COLLINS

†Vinton Freedley relinquished sponsorship of this production after a second tryout tour which opened at the Walnut Street Theatre in Philadelphia, November 25, 1946, and closed at the Royal Alexandra in Toronto on December 14, 1946.

††Tried out earlier this season as "The Temporary Mrs. Smith." (see page 135)

*Closed January 25, 1947. (37 performances)

Luba Malina—Paul Marlin—June Dayton

Luba Malina Millard Mitchell

June Dayton—Luba Malina—Joyce Allan

CENTURY THEATRE

Opened Thursday, December 26, 1946. **
William Cahn presents:

TOPLITZKY OF NOTRE DAME

Book and Lyrics by George Marion, Jr., Music by Sammy Fain; Additional Dialogue and Lyrics by Jack Barnett; Staged by Jose Ruben; Dances and Musical Numbers Staged by Robert Sidney; Settings by Edward Gilbert; Costumes by Kenn Barr; Musical Director, Leon Leonardi.

Cast of Characters

Army Angel .... Phyllis Lynne
Recording Angel .... Candace Montgomery
Lionel .... Harry Fleer
Angelo .... Warde Donovan
Mrs. Strutt .... Doris Patston *1
Betty .... Marion Colby *2
Dodo .... Estelle Sloan
McCormack .... Gus Van
Roger .... Walter Long
Toplitzky .... J. Edward Bromberg
A Girl .... Betty Jane Watson *3
Mailman .... Robert Bay
Leary .... Frank Marlowe
Patti .... Phyllis Lynne
Male Qurtet: Oliver Boersma, John Frederick, Eugene Kingsley, Chris Overson.

Musical Numbers; 'Let Us Gather at the Goal Line,' 'Baby, Let's Face It,' 'I Want To Go To City College,' 'Love Is a Random Thing,' 'Common Sense,' 'A Slight Case of Ecstasy,' 'Wolf Time,' 'McInerney's Farm,' 'You Are My Downfall,' 'All American Man,' 'The Notre Dame Victory March†,' 'The Notre Dame Hike Song††.'

A Musical Comedy in a Prologue and two acts, eight scenes. The action takes place in Heaven; Toplitzky's Tavern and Terrace, New York City; a Field on the Jersey Shore; Yankee Stadium.

Company Manager, HAROLD C. JACOBY
Press, IVAN BLACK, HARRY KOENIGSBERG
Production Assistant, HARRIET KAPLAN
Stage Managers, JOHN EFFRAT, STEVEN GETHERS, CHARLES CONWAY

† By Rev. Michael J. Shea and John F. Shea.
††By Joseph Casastana and Vincent F. Fagan.
*Played during tryout tour by 1 Vivienne Segal, 2 Alma Kaye, 3 Margaret Phelan.
**Closed February 15, 1947. (60 performances)

Warde Donovan   Margaret Phelan

Margaret Phelan   J. Edward Bromberg

Warde Donovan—Margaret Phelan—J. Edward Bromberg

Alfred Drake

Alfred Drake—Jet MacDonald—Zero Mostel—Rollin Smith

BROADWAY THEATRE

Opened Thursday, December 26, 1946.**
Perry Watkins and John R. Sheppard, Jr. present:

BEGGAR'S HOLIDAY†

Based on "The Beggar's Opera" by John Gay; Music by Duke Ellington; Book and Lyrics by John Latouche; Book directed by Nicholas Ray; Settings by Oliver Smith; Costumes by Walter Florell; Technical Supervision and Lighting by Peggy Clark; Choreography by Valerie Bettis; Musical Director, Max Meth; Orchestrations supervised by Billy Strayhorn.

Cast of Characters

The Beggar ..... Alfred Drake
The Pursued ..... Tommy Gomez
Cop ..... Archie Savage
Policemen ..... Herbert Ross, Lucas Hoving
Plainclothesman ..... Albert Popwell
The Lookout ..... Marjorie Belle
Macheath ..... Alfred Drake
The Cocoa Girl ..... Marie Bryant
Jenny† ..... Bernice Parks
Dolly Trull ..... Lavina Nielsen
Betty Doxy ..... Leone Hall*
Tawdry Audrey ..... Tommie Moore
Mrs. Trapes ..... Doris Goodwin
Annie Coaxer ..... Royce Wallace
Baby Mildred ..... Claire Hale
Minute Lou ..... Nini Korda
Trixy Turner ..... Malka Farber
Bessie Buns ..... Elmire Jones-Bey
Flora, the Harpy ..... Enid Williams
The Horn ..... Bill Dillard
Highbinder ..... Jack Bittner
O'Heister ..... Gordon Nelson
The Drunk ..... Perry Bruskin
Gunsel ..... Archie Savage
Fingersmith ..... Stanley Carlson
Strip ..... Lucas Hoving
Mooch ..... Perry Bruskin
The Eye ..... Pan Theodore
Wire Boy ..... Paul Godkin
The Other Eye ..... Tommy Gomez
Slam ..... Albert Popwell
The Caser ..... Douglas Henderson
Two Customers ..... Gordon Nelson, Hy Anzel
The Knife ..... Lewis Charles
Bartender ..... Herbert Ross
Careless Love ..... Avon Long
Polly Peachum ..... Jet MacDonald
Black Marketeer ..... Gordon Nelson
Mrs. Peachum ..... Dorothy Johnson
Hamilton Peachum ..... Zero Mostel
Chief Lockit ..... Rollin Smith
Lucy Lockit ..... Mildred Smith
Blenkinsop ..... Pan Theodore
The Girl ..... Marjorie Belle
The Boy ..... Paul Godkin

Musical Numbers: The Chase, 'When You Go Down by Miss Jenny's,' 'I've Got Me,' 'TNT,' 'Take Love Easy,' 'I Wanna Be Bad,' 'When I Walk With You,' Wedding Ballet, 'The Scrimmage of Life,' 'Ore From a Gold Mine,' 'Tooth and Claw,' 'Maybe I Should Change My Ways,' 'The Wrong Side of the Railroad Tracks,' 'Tomorrow Mountain,' Chorus of Citizens, 'Girls Want a Hero,' 'Lullaby for Junior,' 'Quarrel for Three,' Fol-de-rol-rol, 'Brown Penny††,' 'Women, Women, Women,' 'The Hunted.'

A Musical Comedy in two acts, thirteen scenes. The action takes place outside and inside Miss Jenny's, also in her Bedroom; at Hamilton Peachum's; on a Street; Chief Lockit's Office and Jail; under the Bridge.

General Manager, LEO ROSE
Company Manager, OTTO HARTMAN
Press, LORELLA VAL-MERY
Stage Manager, FRANK COLETTI

†Opened out of town as "Twilight Alley," with Libby Holman playing 'Jenny.'
††Lyrics based on poem by W. B. Yeats.
*Replaced by Margaret Wilson
**Closed March 29, 1947. (111 performances)

Avon Long sings "I Wanna Be Bad" at Jenny's Place

"The Wrong Side of the Railroad Track" in the Hobo Jungle

Thomas Beck—Walter Greaza—Tonio Selwart—Blanche Yurka—Reinhold Schunzel—Vilma Kurer

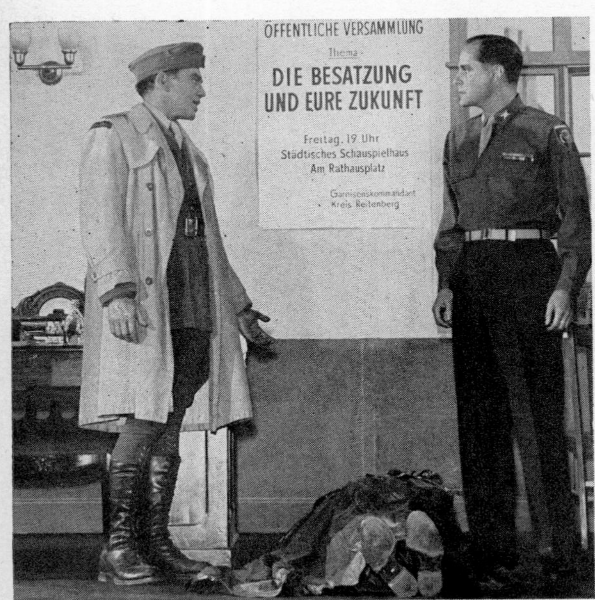

Herbert Berghof—Thomas Beck

THE PLAYHOUSE

Opened Friday, December 27, 1946.**
Barnard Straus and Roland Haas present:

TEMPER THE WIND†

By Edward Mabley and Leonard Mins; Staged by Reginald Denham; Settings by Raymond Sovey; Costumes by Anna Hill Johnstone.

Cast of Characters
(In order of appearance)

Sophie von Gutzkow	Blanche Yurka
Trudi	Charlotte London
Elisabeth Jaeger	Vilma Kurer
Hugo Benckendorff	Reinhold Schunzel
Theodore Bruce	Walter Greaza
Cpl. Tom Hutchinson	George Mathews
Erich Jaeger	Tonio Selwart
Lt. Col. Richard Woodruff	Thomas Beck
Heinrich Lindau	Martin Brandt
Capt. Karel Palivec	Herbert Berghof*
Sgt. Edward Green	Paul Tripp
Lt. James Harris	Albert Patterson
Lt. Frank Daniels	Michael Sivy

A Drama about the Military Government's occupation of Germany in three acts, five scenes. The action takes place in the small manufacturing town of Reitenberg in northeastern Bavaria at the present time in the living-room of the Benckendorff house and the American Garrison Headquarters.

General Manager, Lodewick Vroom
Press Representative, Dick Weaver
Stage Manager, Henri Caubisens

†Formerly called "Drums of Peace." It is based on an original idea of Edward Mabley and Edwin Mills, Jr.
*Replaced Robert Alvin during tryout.
**Closed January 25, 1947. (35 performances)

BILTMORE THEATRE

Opened Wednesday, January 1, 1947. **
Warren P. Munsell and Herman Bernstein present:

LOVE GOES TO PRESS†

By Martha Gellhorn and Virginia Cowles; Directed by Wallace Douglas; Settings by Raymond Sovey; Costumes by Emeline Roche.

Cast of Characters
(In order of speaking)

Leonard Lightfoot .... Gerald Andersen *
(International Information Agency)
Tex Crowder .... David Tyrrell
(Union Press)
Hank O'Reilly .... Warren Parker
(Alliance Press)
Joe Rogers .... William Post, Jr.
(San Francisco Dispatch)
Major Phillip Brooke-Jervaux .... Ralph Michael ††*
(Public Relations Officer)
Corporal Cramp .... Peter Bennett *
Daphne Rutherford (E.N.S.A.) .... Georgina Cookson *
Jane Mason .... Joyce Heron *
(New York Bulletin)
Annabelle Jones .... Jane Middleton
(San Francisco World)
Major Dick Hawkins (U.S.A.A.F.) .... Don Gibson
Captain Sir Alastair Drake .... Nigel Neilson *
(Conducting Officer)

A Comedy satirizing war correspondents in Italy in three acts, four scenes. The action takes place in the Main Press Room and a Store Room of the Allied Press Camp, Poggibonsi, Italy - February, 1944.

Company Manager, EDWARD A. HASS
Press, LEO FREEDMAN, JUNE GREENWALL
Stage Manager, FORREST TAYLOR, JR.

†This play was first presented by Anthony Hawtrey at the Embassy Theatre, London, on June 18, 1946. It had an 8 week run.
††By special permission of Ealing Studios, Ltd.
*These six performers are duplicating the roles they created in London. Also Mr. Douglas is repeating as director.
**Closed January 4, 1947. (5 performances)

Joyce Heron—Ralph Michael

Peter Bennett—Joyce Heron—Don Gibson—Jane Middleton

Claire Trevor—Philip Dorn

BOOTH THEATRE

Opened Wednesday, January 8, 1947.*
Elliott Nugent and Robert Montgomery by arrangement with David Bramson present:

THE BIG TWO

By L. Bush-Fekete and Mary Helen Fay; Staged by Mr. Montgomery; Scenery and Lighting by Jo Mielziner; Costumes supervised by Bianca Stroock.

Cast of Characters
(In order of appearance)

Karl.....Martin Berliner
Meissl.....Eduard Franz
Corp. Pat McClure.....Robert Scott
Gwendolyn.....Wauna Paul
Danielle Forbes.....Claire Trevor
Moser.....E. A. Krumschmidt
Wirth.....John Banner
Platschek.....Felix Bressart†
Captain Nicholai Mosgovoy.....Philip Dorn†
Fraulein Berger.....Olga Fabian
Sergeant Kulikoff.....Mischa Tonken
Guests: Phil Miller, Zita Rieth, Kenneth Dobbs, Fred Lorenz, Louise Svecenski.
Russian Soldiers: Marc Hamilton, Walter Palance, Charles Boaz, Jr.

A Topical Comedy in three acts, four scenes. The action takes place in the Lobby of the Waldhotel in Baden, within the Russian-occupied zone of Austria near Vienna in November, 1945.

General Manager, S. M. HANDELSMAN
Press, RICHARD MANEY, ANNE WOLL
Stage Manager, PAUL PORTER

†American stage debut.
*Closed January 25, 1947. (21 performances)

Claire Trevor—Wauna Paul—John Banner—Eduard Franz—E. A. Krumschmidt—Fred Lorenz—Zita Rieth—Kenneth Dobbs—Olga Fabian—Phil Miller—Lee Nugent—Felix Bressart

Brian Sullivan—Anne Jeffreys

Norman Cordon—Anne Jeffreys—Polyna Stoska

Irving Kaufman—Creighton Thompson—David E. Thomas—Helen Arden—Sydney Rayner—Hope Emerson—Ellen Repp—Wilson Smith

ADELPHI THEATRE

Opened Thursday, January 9, 1947.***
Dwight Deere Wiman and The Playwrights' Company present:

STREET SCENE

Book by Elmer Rice, from his Pulitzer Prize Play†; Music by Kurt Weill; Lyrics by Langston Hughes; Directed by Charles Friedman; Scenery and Lighting by Jo Mielziner; Costumes by Lucinda Ballard; Dances by Anna Sokolow; Musical Arrangements and Orchestrations by Kurt Weill; Musical Director, Maurice Abravanel.

Cast of Characters
(In order of appearance)

Abraham Kaplan .... Irving Kaufman
Greta Fiorentino .... Helen Arden
Carl Olsen .... Wilson Smith
Emma Jones .... Hope Emerson
Olga Olsen .... Ellen Repp
Shirley Kaplan .... Norma Chambers
Henry Davis .... Creighton Thompson
Willie Maurrant .... Peter Griffith
Anna Maurrant .... Polyna Stoska**
Sam Kaplan .... Brian Sullivan††1
Daniel Buchanan .... Remo Lota
Frank Maurrant .... Norman Cordon
George Jones .... David E. Thomas
Steve Sankey .... Lauren Gilbert
Lippo Fiorentino .... Sydney Rayner
Jennie Hildebrand .... Beverly Janis
Second Graduate .... Zosia Gruchala
Third Graduate .... Marion Covey
Mary Hildebrand .... Juliana Gallagher
Charlie Hildebrand .... Bennett Burrill
Laura Hildebrand .... Elen Lane
Grace Davis .... Helen Ferguson
First Policeman .... Ernest Taylor
Rose Maurrant .... Anne Jeffreys
Harry Easter .... Don Saxon
Mae Jones .... Sheila Bond
Dick McGann .... Danny Daniels
Vincent Jones .... Robert Pierson
Dr. John Wilson .... Edwin G. O'Connor*1
Officer Harry Murphy .... Norman Thomson
A Milkman .... Russell George
A Music Pupil .... Joyce Carrol
City Marshall James Henry .... Randolph Symonette*2
Fred Cullen .... Paul Lilly
An Old Clothes Man .... Edward Reichert
An Interne .... Roy Munsell
An Ambulance Driver .... John Sweet
First Nursemaid .... Peggy Turnley
Second Nursemaid .... Ellen Carleen

Hope Emerson—Helen Arden—Ellen Repp

Danny Daniels and Sheila Bond

A Married Couple .... { Bette Van, Joseph E. Scandur*3 }
Passersby, Neighbors, Children, etc.: Aza Bard, Diana Donne, Juanita Hall, Marie Leidal, Biruta Ramoska, Marcella Uhl, Larry Baker, Tom Barragan, Mel Bartell, Victor Clarke, Bobby Horn, Wilson Woodbeck.

Musical Numbers††2: 'Ain't It Awful, the Heat?', 'I Got a Marble and a Star,' 'Get a Load of That,' 'When a Woman Has a Baby,' 'Somehow I Never Could Believe,' 'Ice Cream,' 'Let Things Be Like They Always Was,' 'Wrapped in a Ribbon and Tied in a Bow,' 'Lonely House,' 'Wouldn't You Like To Be On Broadway?,' 'What Good Would the Moon Be?,' 'Moon-Faced, Starry-Eyed,' 'Remember That I Care††*,' 'Catch Me If You Can,' 'There'll Be Trouble,' 'A Boy Like You,' 'We'll Go Away Together,' 'The Woman Who Lived Up There,' 'Lullaby,' 'I Loved Her, Too,' 'Don't Forget the Lilac Bush††*.'

A Dramatic Musical in two acts, three scenes. The action takes place on the Sidewalk in front of a Sandstone Tenement House in New York City.

Business Managers, FORREST C. HARING, J. H. DEL BONDIO
Press, WILLIAM FIELDS, JOHN L. TOOHEY, ARTHUR CANTOR
General Stage Manager, JOHN E. SOLA
Stage Managers, AMBROSE COSTELLO, GEORGE NICHOLS

†Presented in New York by William A. Brady at the Playhouse, on January 10, 1929. It ran 601 performances.
††During tryout tour: 1 played by Richard Manning, 2 'Italy in Technicolor' was dropped from the score.
††*The poem "When Lilacs Last in the Dooryard Bloomed" referred to in these numbers, was written by Walt Whitman.
*Replaced by: 1 John Sweet, 2 Joseph E. Scandur, 3 Russell George.
**Alternate: Bette Van.
***Closed May 17, 1947. (148 performances)

Albert Sharpe and Ella Logan arrive in Rainbow Valley, Missitucky

46TH STREET THEATRE

Opening Friday, January 10, 1947.
Lee Sabinson and William R. Katzell present:

FINIAN'S RAINBOW

Book by E. Y. Harburg and Fred Saidy; Lyrics by E. Y. Harburg; Music by Burton Lane; Directed by Bretaigne Windust; Scenery and Lighting by Jo Mielziner; Choreography and Musical Numbers by Michael Kidd; Costumes by Eleanor Goldsmith; Orchestrations by Robert Russell Bennett and Don Walker; Vocal Arrangements by Lyn Murray; Musical Director, Milton Rosenstock.

Cast of Characters

(In order of appearance)

Sunny (Harmonica Player)........Sonny Terry
Buzz Collins........Eddie Bruce
Sheriff........Tom McElhany
1st Sharecropper........Alan Gilbert
2nd Sharecropper........Robert Eric Carlson*1
Susan Mahoney........Anita Alvarez
Henry........Augustus Smith, Jr.
Finian McLonergan........Albert Sharpe*2†
Sharon McLonergan........Ella Logan*3
Woody Mahoney........Donald Richards
3rd Sharecropper........Ralph Waldo Cummings*4
Og (A Leprechaun)........David Wayne
Howard........William Greaves
Senator Billboard Rawkins........Robert Pitkin
1st Geologist........Lucas Aco
2nd Geologist........Nathaniel Dickerson*5
Singer........Dolores Martin
Diane........Diane Woods*6
Jane........Jane Earle
John (The Preacher)........Roland Skinner
4th Sharecropper........Maude Simmons*7
Mr. Robust........Arthur Tell
Mr. Shears........Royal Dano
1st Passion Pilgrim Gospeler........Jerry Laws
2nd Passion Pilgrim Gospeler........Lorenzo Fuller
3rd Passion Pilgrim Gospeler........Louis Sharp
1st Deputy........Michael Ellis*8
2nd Deputy........Robert Eric Carlson*1
3rd Deputy........Harry Day
Other Children, Norma Jane Marlowe, Elayne Richards

Musical Numbers: 'This Time of the Year,' 'How Are Things in Glocca Morra?,' 'Look to the Rainbow,' 'Old Devil Moon,' 'Something Sort of Grandish,' 'If This Isn't Love,' 'Necessity,' 'Great Come-and-Get-It-Day,' 'When the Idle Poor Become the Idle Rich,' Dance o' the Golden Crock, 'The Begat,' 'When I'm Not Near the Girl I Love.'

A Humorous Musical Fantasy with satire and social significance about an Irishman who borrows a crock of gold from the Leprechauns of Ireland and brings it to America, in two acts, ten scenes. The action passes at The Meetin' Place, The Colonial Estate of Senator Rawkins, a Path in the Woods, and a Wooded Section of the Hills in Rainbow Valley, Missitucky.

General Manager, CHARLES HARRIS
Company Manager, MICHAEL GOLDREYER
Press, SAMUEL J. FRIEDMAN
Production Stage Manager, JAMES GELB
Stage Managers, JAMES RUSSO, MICHAEL ELLIS

†Mr. Sharpe's American debut.

*Replaced by: 1 Brayton Lewis, 2 James N. O'Neill, then Patrick J. Kelly followed by Ian Martin, 3 Dorothy Claire, 4 Maude Simmons, 5 William McDaniel, 6 Mary Dawson, 7 William Scully, 8 George Charles.

Anita Alvarez and David Wayne

Donald Richards—Ella Logan—Albert Sharpe

'Great Come and Get It Day,' First Act Finale of "Finian's Rainbow."

'When The Idle Poor Become The Idle Rich,' Second Act Opening of "Finian's Rainbow."

Wallis Clark—Otto Kruger—Robert Willey

Otto Kruger—Ottilie Kruger—Jessie Royce Landis

Jessie Royce Landis—Otto Kruger
Below: Frances Bavier—Jessie Royce Landis—Ottilie Kruger—Wallis Clark—Otto Kruger

HENRY MILLER THEATRE

Opened Wednesday, January 15, 1947.*
Sam Nasser presents:

LITTLE A

By Hugh White; Staged by Melville Burke; Setting by Watson Barratt; Lighting by Leo Kerz; Harry Lambert, associate producer.

Cast of Characters

Aaron Storm	Otto Kruger
Lucinda Storm	Jessie Royce Landis
Mary Howard	Ottilie Kruger
Phoebe Painter	Frances Bavier
Clyde Painter	Harry Mehaffey
Dr. Duncan Brown	Wallis Clark
Donald Storm	Robert Willey

A Psychological Tragedy in three acts, three scenes. The action takes place in the Living-room of the Storm home in Rockbridge, a small town in Northern California, at the present time.

General Manager, JOHN TUERK
Company Manager, JOSEPH ROTH
Press, NAT DORFMAN, MARTHA DREIBLATT
Stage Manager, GORDON DUFF

*Closed February 1, 1947. (21 performances)

Bobby Clark in "Sweethearts"

Robert Shackleton—Gloria Story—Mark Dawson

Marjorie Gateson—Bobby Clark

SHUBERT THEATRE

Opening Tuesday, January 21, 1947.
Paula Stone and Michael Sloane present:

SWEETHEARTS†

Music by Victor Herbert, Arrangements by Russell Bennett; Original Book by Harry B. Smith and Fred De Gresac, Revisions by John Cecil Holm; Lyrics by Robert B. Smith; Staged by John Kennedy; Ensembles by Catherine Littlefield; Choreography by Theodore Adolphus; Scenery by Peter Wolf; Costumes by Michael Lucyk; Vocal Direction by Pembroke Davenport; Musical Director, Edwin McArthur.

Cast of Characters

Daughters:
- Doreen .... Marcia James
- Corinne .... Nony Franklin
- Eileen .... Janet Medlin
- Pauline .... Betty Ann Busch
- Kathleen .... Martha Emma Watson
- Nadine .... Gloria Lind*1

Gretchen .... Eva Soltesz
Hilda .... Muriel Bruenig
Lt. Karl .... Robert Shackleton
Dame Lucy .... Marjorie Gateson
Peasants .... Robert Reeves, Raynor Howell
Liane**1 .... June Knight
Mikel Mikeloviz .... Bobby Clark
Sylvia**2 .... Gloria Story*2
Prince Franz .... Mark Dawson
Peter .... Richard Benson
Hans .... Ken Arnold*3
Baron Petrus Von Tromp .... Paul Best
Hon. Butterfield Slingsby .... Anthony Kemble Cooper
Prima Ballerina .... Janice Cioffi
Adolphus, Homberg .... Footmen .... John Anania, Cornell MacNeil
Ambassadors .... Robert Feyti, Louis De Mangus
Captain Laurent .... Tom Perkins
Karl (dance suitor) .... James Russell
Von Tromp (dance suitor) .... Bruce Cartwright
Slingsby (dance suitor) .... Peter Holmes
Fourth Dancer .... John Ward

Musical Numbers: 'Iron, Iron,' 'On Parade,' 'Sweethearts,' 'For Every Lover Must Meet His Fate,' 'Lorelei,' 'The Angelus,' 'Jeanette and Her Little Wooden Shoes,' 'Pretty as a Picture,' 'Land of My Own Romance,' 'I Might Be Your Once-in-a-While,' 'Pilgrims of Love.'

A Revival of the Operetta in two acts. The action takes place in the Village Square and the Palace, in the mythical town of Zilania.

General Manager, Ben F. Stein
Company Manager, Samuel C. Brin
Press, Zac Freedman
Associate Executive, Dixie Love Dean
Stage Mgrs. Mortimer O'Brien, Fred Hebert

†First presented in New York by Werba and Luescher at the New Amsterdam Theatre on September 8, 1913 with Christie MacDonald. It ran 136 performances.

*Replaced by: 1 Rosemary O'Shea, 2 Gloria Lind, 3 Phil Crosbie.

**Played during tryout tour by: 1 Gloria Story, 2 Margaret Spencer.

Arthur Kennedy—Ed Begley—Eugene Steiner

Beth Merrill and Ed Begley in "All My Sons"

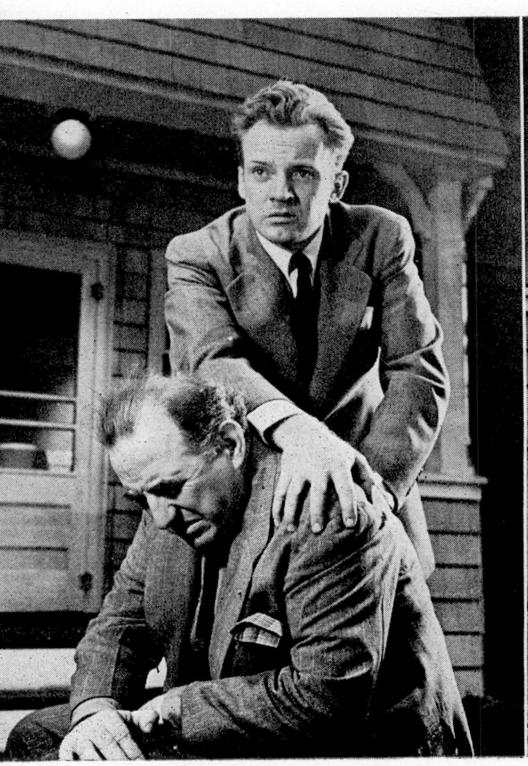

Ed Begley—Arthur Kennedy

Arthur Kennedy—Lois Wheeler

CORONET THEATRE

Opening Wednesday, January 29, 1947.
Harold Clurman, Elia Kazan and Walter Fried in association with Herbert H. Harris present:

ALL MY SONS†

By Arthur Miller; Staged by Elia Kazan; Designed and Lighted by Mordecai Gorelik; Costumes by Paul Morrison.

Cast of Characters
(In order of appearance)

Joe Keller	Ed Begley
Dr. Jim Bayliss	John McGovern
Frank Lubey	Dudley Sadler
Sue Bayliss	Peggy Meredith
Lydia Lubey	Hope Cameron
Chris Keller	Arthur Kennedy *1
Bert	Eugene Steiner *2††
Kate Keller	Beth Merrill
Ann Deever	Lois Wheeler *3
George Deever	Karl Malden

A Postwar Drama in three acts, three scenes. The action takes place on a Sunday in the backyard of the Keller House, on the outskirts of an American town.

Company Manager, OTTO HARMON
Press, JAMES D. PROCTOR, LEWIS HARMON
Stage Manager, ROBERT F. SIMON

†Formerly known as "The Sign of the Archer."
††Alternate: Donald Harris.
*Replacements: 1 John Forsythe, 2 Maurice Cavell, 3 Ann Shepherd.

Arthur Kennedy—Beth Merrill

Ed Begley—Dudley Sadler—Beth Merrill—Arthur Kennedy—Karl Malden—Lois Wheeler

Vivian Vance   Martha Scott

BILTMORE THEATRE

Opened Monday, February 3, 1947.*
George Abbott and Richard Aldrich
present:

IT TAKES TWO†

By Virginia Faulkner and Dana Suesse; Directed by George Abbott; Setting by John Root.

Cast of Characters
(As They Speak)

Connie Frazier	Martha Scott
Mr. Fine	Julius Bing
Mrs. Loosbrock	Reta Shaw
Bee Clark	Vivian Vance
Elevator Boy	Robert Edwin
Todd Frazier	Hugh Marlowe
Monk Rathburn	Anthony Ross
Comfort Gibson	Temple Texas
Bill Renault	John Forsythe

A Comedy about the housing shortage and marital troubles in three acts, five scenes. The entire action takes place in the Living-room of the Frazier's Apartment, in the Murray Hill section of New York, in the late fall of 1946.

General Manager, Charles Harris
Press, Richard Maney, Ned Armstrong
Stage Managers, Robert Griffith, George Smith

†Formerly called "Apartment 17-B." During the out of town tryout the part of 'Walter Clark,' played by George Smith was written out.

*Closed February 8, 1947. (8 performances)

Hugh Marlowe   Martha Scott   Anthony Ross

Tom Ewell—Lyle Bettger—William Prince

Nina Foch—Ralph Chambers

Wililam Prince—Nina Foch—Tom Ewell

BOOTH THEATRE

(Moved to MUSIC BOX, March 17, 1947).
Opening Tuesday, February 4, 1947.
Richard Rodgers and Oscar Hammerstein 2nd. in association with Joshua Logan present:

JOHN LOVES MARY

By Norman Krasna; Directed by Joshua Logan; Scenery and Lighting by Frederick Fox; Costumes by Lucinda Ballard.

Cast of Characters
(In order of appearance)

Mary McKinley........Nina Foch†
Oscar Dugan........Ralph Chambers
Fred Taylor........Tom Ewell
John Lawrence........William Prince
Senator James McKinley........Loring Smith
Mrs. Phyllis McKinley........Ann Mason
Lt. Victor O'Leary........Lyle Bettger
George Beechwood........Max Showalter
Lily Herbish........Pamela Gordon
Harwood Biddle........Harry Bannister

A Comedy in three acts, four scenes. The action of the play takes place in the Living-room of the Apartment of Senator James McKinley in the St. Regis Hotel, New York.

General Manager, MORRIS JACOBS
Company Manager, MANNING GURIAN
Press, MICHEL MOK, ABNER D. KLIPSTEIN
Stage Manager, SHELLY HULL
†Courtesy of Columbia Pictures.

Nina Foch **Wiliam Prince**

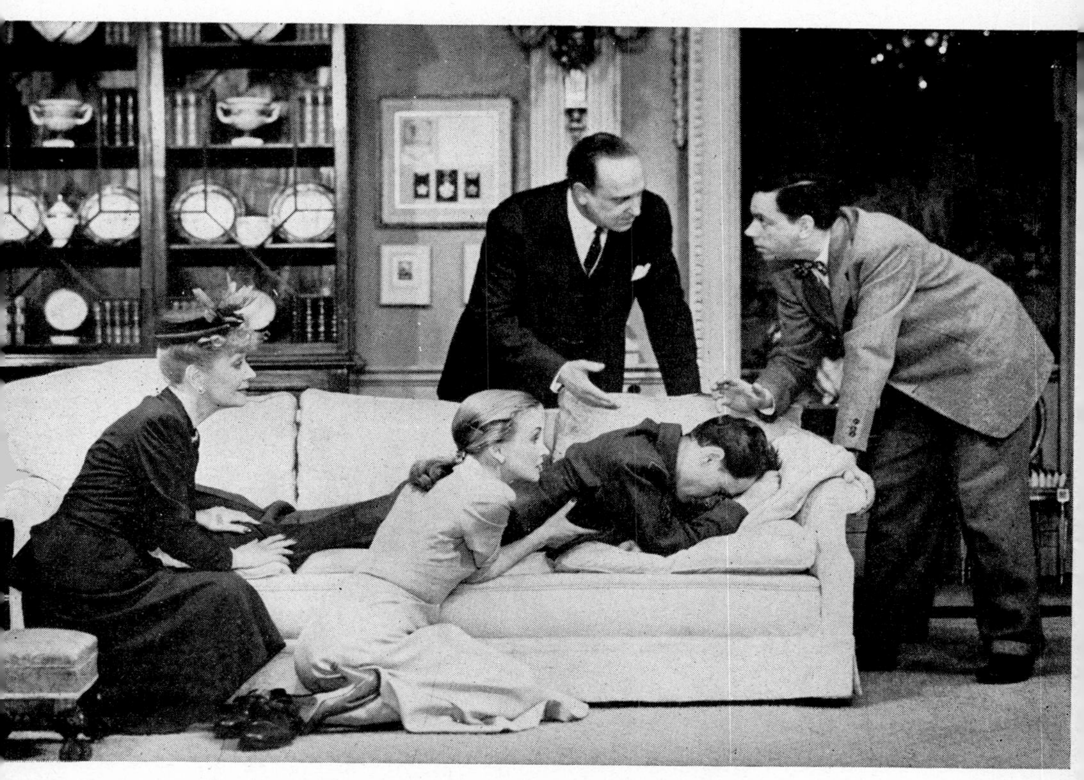

Ann Mason—Nina Foch—Loring Smith—William Prince—Tom Ewell

Elizabeth Ross—Dorothy Gish—Graham Denton

Elizabeth Ross—Kent Smith—Dorothy Gish

Kent Smith—Dorothy Gish—Richard Sanders

HENRY MILLER THEATRE

Opened Saturday, February 8, 1947.*
Russell Lewis and Howard Young present:

THE STORY OF MARY SURRATT†

By John Patrick; Directed by the author; Settings by Samuel Leve; Lighting by Girvan Higginson.

Cast of Characters

Anna Surratt	Elizabeth Ross
Mary Surratt	Dorothy Gish
Louis Weichman	Bernard Thomas
Louis Payne	Don Shelton
George Atzerodt	Zachary Berger
David Herold	Michael Fox
John Surratt	John Conway
John Wilkes Booth	James Monks
Captain William Smith	Graham Denton
Sgt. Day	Larry Johns
Colonel Burnett	Douglas McEachin
General Joshua Holden	Richard Sanders
Brigadier General Ekin	Wallis Roberts
Reverdy Johnson	Kent Smith
Major General Hunter	Edward Harvey
Brigadier General Harris	Frank McFarland
Major General Wallace	Robert Neff
Major General Kautz	Thomas Glynn
Brigadier General Howe	Robert Morgan
Brigadier General Foster	Dallas Boyd
Colonel Tompkins	Lee Malbourne
Colonel Clendenin	Arthur Stenning
Special Provost Marshal	Tom Daly
Major Henry Rathbone	Gordon Barnes
Lt. Henry Von Steinacker	Bill Hitch
General Jubal Bentley	John Pimley
Father Wiget	Harlan Briggs
W. E. Doster	Hugh Mosher
Dr. Samuel Mudd	Tom J. McGivern
Edward Spangler	Lytton Robinson
Michael O'Laughlin	Bill Reynolds
Samuel Arnold	Larry Johns
Guard	Earl Dawson
Soldier	Michael Roane
Soldier	Clyde Cook

Guards, Soldiers

A Historical Tragedy based on the trial of Mary Surratt who was hanged for alleged complicity in the assassination of Abraham Lincoln, in three acts, six scenes. The action takes place in the Living-room of Mary Surratt's Boarding House and an improvised Courtroom and a Cell in the old penitentiary building on the U.S. Arsenal grounds at Washington, D.C., 1865.

General Manager, EMMETT CALLAHAN
Company Manager, LOUIS LISSNER
Press, BERT STERN, HELEN HOERLE
Stage Manager, GLEN JORDAN

†Formerly known as "This Gentle Ghost."
*Closed February 15, 1947. (9 performances)

THE PLAYHOUSE

Opened Wednesday, February 12, 1947.*
Gant Gaither presents:

CRAIG'S WIFE†

By George Kelly; Staged by Mr. Kelly; Designed by Stewart Chaney; Decor by Jensen's.

Cast of Characters
(In order of appearance)

Miss Austin..........Kathleen Comegys
Mrs. Harold..........Viola Roache
Mazie..........Dortha Duckworth
Mrs. Craig..........Judith Evelyn
Ethel Landreth..........Virginia Dwyer
Walter Craig..........Philip Ober
Mrs. Frazier..........Virginia Hammond
Billy Birkmire..........Herschel Bentley
Joseph Catelle..........Hugh Rennie
Harry..........Allan Nourse
Eugene Fredericks..........John Hudson

A Revival of the Drama in three acts. The action takes place in the Reception Room at the home of the Walter Craigs.

General Manager, PAUL VROOM
Production Assistant, MARGARET PERRY
Press, DAVID LIPSKY, PHILLIP BLOOM
Stage Manager, HUGH RENNIE

†First produced on Broadway by Rosalie Stewart on October 14, 1925 at the Morosco Theatre with Chrystal Herne. It ran for 360 performances.

*Closed April 12, 1947. (69 performances)

Judith Evelyn as Mrs. Craig

Above: Virginia Dwyer—John Hudson
Below: Philip Ober—Judith Evelyn

Philip Ober—Kathleen Comegys—Virginia Hammond

CENTURY THEATRE

Opened Tuesday, February 18, 1947.*
Hall Shelton by arrangement with Advance Players Association, Ltd.†
presents:

KING LEAR††

By William Shakespeare; Settings and Costumes by Ernest Stern; Music arranged by Rosabel Watson.

Cast of Characters

Lear, King of Britain .... Donald Wolfit
King of France .... David Dodimead
Duke of Burgundy .... George Bradford
Duke of Cornwall .... Josef Shear
Duke of Albany .... Robert Algar
Earl of Kent .... Alexander Gauge
Earl of Gloucester .... Eric Maxon
Edgar, son to Gloucester .... Kempster Barnes
Edmund, bastard son to Gloucester .... Frederick Horrey
Curan, a courtier .... Malcolm Watson
Oswald, steward to Goneril .... John Wynyard
Tenant to Gloucester .... George Bradford
Doctor .... Malcolm Watson
Fool .... Geoffrey Wilkinson
Officer .... David Dodimead
Herald .... Richard Blythe
Goneril, Regan, Cordelia } Daughters to King Lear .... { Violet Farebrother, Ann Chalkley, Rosalind Iden
Knights of Lear's train, Officers, Messengers, Soldiers and Attendants.

A Revival of the Tragedy of the King of Britain in two acts.

†This is the first appearance in the United States of Mr. Wolfit and his London Company of thirty-five. He and his troupe have given some 2500 performances of the Bard during their ten years of operation in London, in the British Provinces, before troops in North Africa, France and Belgium, and recently in Canada.

††The first presentation of this play in New York took place on January 14, 1754 at the Nassau Street Theatre.

*Closed March 8, 1947. (8 performances in Repertory)

Donald Wolfit as King Lear

Geoffrey Wilkinson—Eric Maxon—Alexander Gauge

Donald Wolfit—Rosalind Iden

CENTURY THEATRE

Opened Thursday Matinee, February 20, 1947.*
Hall Shelton by arrangement with Advance Players Association, Ltd. presents:

AS YOU LIKE IT†

By William Shakespeare; Settings and Costumes by Ernest Stern; Music arranged by Rosabel Watson.

Cast of Characters

Duke, living in exile		Alexander Gauge
Frederick, his brother		David Dodimead
Jacques	Lords attendant	John Wynyard
Lord	upon the banished	George Bradford
Amiens	duke	Robert Algar
Le Beau		Geoffrey Wilkinson
Charles, a wrestler		Josef Shear
Oliver	Sons of Sir Roland	Frederick Horrey
Jacques	de Bois	David Dodimead
Orlando		Kempster Barnes
Adam	Servants to Oliver	Eric Adeney
Dennis		Charles Ollington
Touchstone, a clown		Donald Wolfit
Sir Oliver Martext		David Dodimead
Corin	Shepherds	Malcolm Watson
Silvius		Richard Blythe
William		Josef Shear
Hymen		Robert Algar
Rosalind		Rosalind Iden
Celia		Penelope Chandler
Phoebe		Ann Chalkley
Audrey		Marion Marshall

Lords, Pages, Foresters and Attendants

A Revival of the Comedy in two acts. The action takes place in Oliver's Orchard, the Usurper's Court, and the Forest of Arden.

†First performance in New York was at the John Street Theatre with Mrs. Kenna as 'Rosalind' on July 14, 1786.
*Closed March 8, 1947. (4 performances in Repertory)

Donald Wolfit

Rosalind Iden

Rosalind Iden—Marion Marshall—Kempster Barnes

Donald Wolfit and Rosalind Iden in "The Merchant of Venice"

CENTURY THEATRE

Opened Saturday Matinee, February 22, 1947.*

Hall Shelton by arrangement with Advance Players Association, Ltd. presents:

THE MERCHANT OF VENICE†

By William Shakespeare; Costumes by Shelia Jackson; Music arranged by Rosabel Watson.

Cast of Characters

Duke of Venice	Eric Adeney
Prince of Morocco	Robert Algar
Prince of Aragon	David Dodimead
Antonio	Alexander Gauge
Bassanio	John Wynyard
Solanio	Frederick Horrey
Salarino	Richard Blythe
Gratiano	Josef Shear
Lorenzo	Kempster Barnes
Shylock	Donald Wolfi
Tubal	Eric Maxo
Launcelot Gobbo	Geoffrey Wilkinso
Old Gobbo	Malcolm Watso
Balthasar	George Bradfor
Stephano	Margaret Stallar
Clerk to the Court	David Dodimea
Portia	Rosalind Ide
Nerissa	Marion Marsha
Jessica	Zilla Tomli

Magnificoes of Venice, Officers of the Cour of Justice, Gaolers, Servants and other At tendants.

A Revival of the drama in three acts. Th action passes in a Street, before Shylock' House and the Courtroom in Venice, and a Portia's House at Belmont.

†This play was first presented in New Yor at the John Street Theatre on January 28 1768 with Lewis Hallam as 'Shylock.'

*Closed March 6, 1947. (6 performances i Repertory)

CENTURY THEATRE

Opened Monday, February 24, 1947.*
Hall Shelton by arrangement with Advance Players Association, Ltd.
presents:

VOLPONE†

By Ben Jonson; Settings devised by Donald Wolfit; Music arranged by Rosabel Watson.

Cast of Characters

Volpone	Donald Wolfit
Mosca	John Wynward
Voltore	Frederick Horrey
Corbaccio	Eric Maxon
Corvino	Alexander Gauge
Bonario	Kempster Barnes
Sir Politick Would-Be	Robert Algar
Peregrine	Malcolm Watson
Nano	Richard Blythe
Ca Strone	Geoffrey Wilkinson
Androgyno	David Dodimead
Three Magistrates	Malcolm Watson George Bradford Josef Shear
Celia	Rosalind Iden

A Satiric Comedy of greed and dishonesty brought to justice with heavy punishments in two acts. The action passes in Venice during the 17th. Century at Volpone's House, in a Street, Corvino's House and the Senate House.

†This is the first production of the original Jonson text to be presented on Broadway. On April 9, 1928 the Theatre Guild presented a German adaptation by Stefan Zweig which was translated back into English by Ruth Langner with Dudley Digges as "The Fox." The same production was revived on March 10, 1930 at the Liberty Theatre for one week with Sidney Greenstreet.

*Closed March 6, 1947. (3 performances in Repertory)

Donald Wolfit Rosalind Iden

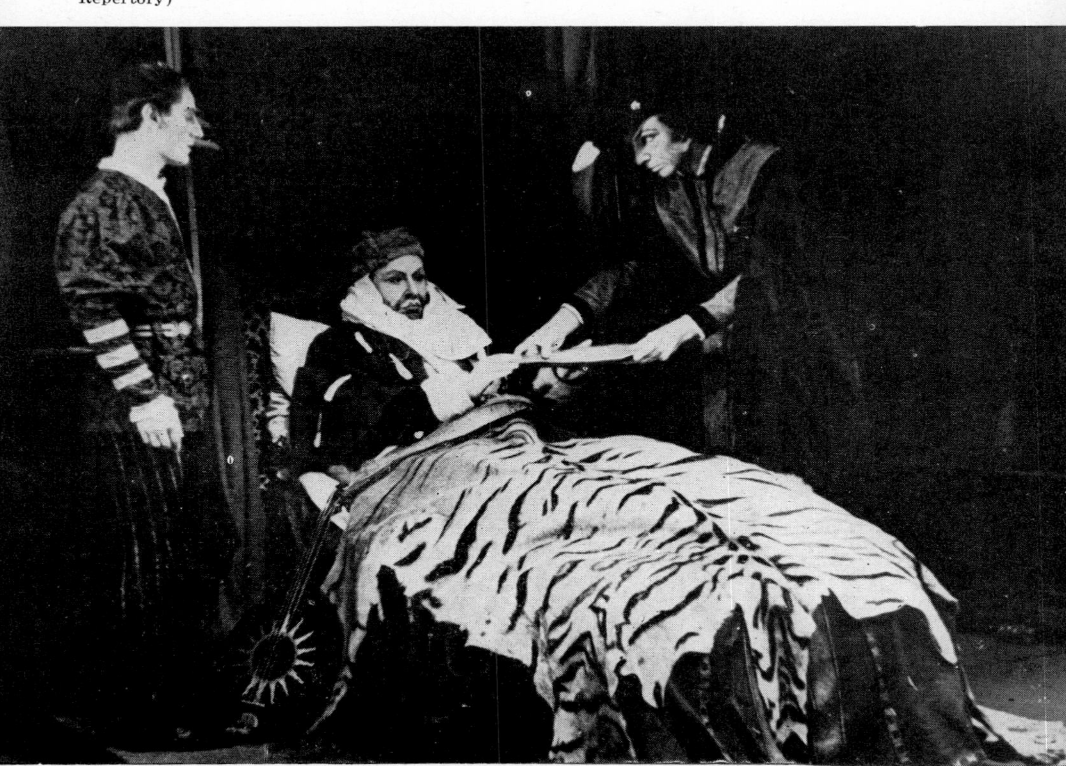

John Wynyard Donald Wolfit Frederick Horrey

Rosalind Iden

and

Donald Wolfit

in

"Hamlet"

CENTURY THEATRE

Opened Wednesday, February 26, 1947.*
Hall Shelton by arrangement with Advance Players Association, Ltd. presents:

HAMLET†

By William Shakespeare; Designed by Donald Wolfit and Eric Adeney; Music arranged by Rosabel Watson.

Cast of Characters

Hamlet, Prince of Denmark..........Donald Wolfit
Claudius, King of Denmark.....Alexander Gauge
Horatio..........John Wynyard
Ghost..........Eric Adeney
Polonius..........Eric Maxon
Rosencrantz / Guildenstern / Osric — Courtiers: Robert Algar / David Dodimead / Richard Blythe
Marcellus / Bernardo / Francisco — Soldiers: George Bradford / David Dodimead / Richard Blythe
Laertes..........Kempster Barnes
Sailor..........Hugh Cross
First Player..........Josef Shear
Second Player..........Frederick Horrey
Player Queen..........Marion Marshall
First Gravedigger..........Malcolm Watson
Second Gravedigger..........Geoffrey Wilkinson
Priest..........Robert Algar
Reynaldo..........Geoffrey Wilkinson
Fortinbras..........Frederick Horrey
Gertrude, Queen of Denmark
Violet Farebrother
Ophelia..........Rosalind Iden

Ladies in Waiting, Pages and Courtiers

A Revival of the Tragedy of the Prince of Elsinore in two acts.

General Manager, GRAHAM POCKETT
Company Manager, CHARLES G. STEWART
Press, WILLIAM FIELDS, WALTER ALFORD
Artistic Director, CHRISTOPHER EDE
Stage Manager, ROY HAWKINS

†On November 26, 1761 Lewis Hallam played 'Hamlet' at the Chapel Street Theatre; this is thought to be the first performance of the play in New York.

*Closed March 7, 1947. (2 performances in Repertory)

INTERNATIONAL THEATRE

Opened Thursday, February 27, 1947.*
American Repertory Theatre, Inc.†
presents:

YELLOW JACK††

By Sidney Howard, in collaboration with Paul de Kruif; Staged by Martin Ritt; Designed by Wolfgang Roth; Music arranged by Lehman Engel.

Cast of Characters

O'Hara	Arthur Keegan
McClelland	William Windom
Busch	Eli Wallach
Brinkerhof	John Becher
Miss Blake	Ann Jackson
Walter Reed	Raymond Greenleaf
Aristides Agramonte	Efrem Zimbalist, Jr.
James Carroll	Victor Jory
Colonel Tory	John Straub
Wm. Crawford Gorgas	Eugene Stuckmann
Jesse W. Lazear	Alfred Ryder
Roger P. Ames	Emery Battis
Major Cartwright	Angus Cairns
Dr. Carlos Finlay	Philip Bourneuf
William H. Dean	Robert Rawlings
An Army Chaplain	Donald Keyes
A Commissary Sergeant	Ed Woodhead

Soldiers, orderlies, etc.: Don Allen, John Behney, Michel Corhan, Will Davis, Thomas Grace, Bart Henderson, Fred Hunter, Robert Leser, Gerald McCormack, Walter Neal, James Rafferty.

A Revival of the Dramatization of the events which led to man's conquest of Yellow Fever in two acts. The action takes place in and around the Laboratory of the Army Medical Commission in Cuba during the summer and fall of 1900.

General Manager, JOHN YORKE
Press, WOLFE KAUFMAN, MARY WARD
Stage Managers, THELMA CHANDLER, EMERY BATTIS

†With this production ART changed its policy from repertory to the straight run of a single play.

††Based upon a chapter in Dr. de Kruif's "Microbe Hunters." It was first produced by Guthrie McClintic on March 6, 1934 at the Martin Beck Theatre where it ran for 79 performances with James Stewart playing O'Hara.

*Closed March 15, 1947 (20 performances)

Alfred Ryder as Dr. Lazear

Robert Rawlings—Raymond Greenleaf

William Windom—Eli Wallach—Arthur Keegan—Ann Jackson

Robert Flemyng—Jean Cadell—John Kidd—Jane Baxter—John Gielgud

Margaret Rutherford—Jean Cadell

Robert Flemyng—Richard Wordsworth—
Margaret Rutherford

ROYALE THEATRE

Opened Monday, March 3, 1947.*
The Theatre Guild and John C. Wilson in association with H. M. Tennent Ltd. of London present John Gielgud's Company in:

THE IMPORTANCE OF BEING EARNEST†

By Oscar Wilde; Directed by John Gielgud; Decor by Motley††; Lighting by William Conway; Music Arranged by Leslie Bridgewater.

Cast of Characters

Lane .... Richard Wordsworth
Algernon Moncrieff .... Robert Flemyng
John Worthing, J.P. .... John Gielgud
Lady Bracknell .... Margaret Rutherford
Hon. Gwendolen Fairfax .... Pamela Brown
Cecily Cardew .... Jane Baxter
Miss Prism .... Jean Cadell
Rev. Canon Chasuble, D.D. .... John Kidd
Merriman .... Stringer Davis
Footman .... Donald Bain

A Revival of the Satire on late 19th. Century English Society in three acts. The action takes place in Algernon Moncrieff's Rooms in Piccadilly and the Garden and Morning-room at the Manor House, Woolton, Hertfordshire.

General Manager, PETER DAVIS
Company Manager, CHANDOS SWEET
Press, WILLARD KEEFE, DAVID TEBET
General Stage Director, WILLIAM CONWAY
Stage Manager, DONALD BAIN

†This play was first presented in New York on April 22, 1895 at the Empire Theatre. This production was first produced by Mr. Gielgud at the Globe Theatre in London on January 31, 1939.

††The physical production, its furniture and other properties have been brought here from Mr. Gielgud's Repertory Theatre in London.

*Closed May 10, 1947. (80 performances)

Pamela Brown John Gielgud

John Gielgud

Joan Vohs—Carol Wheeler—Walter Abel

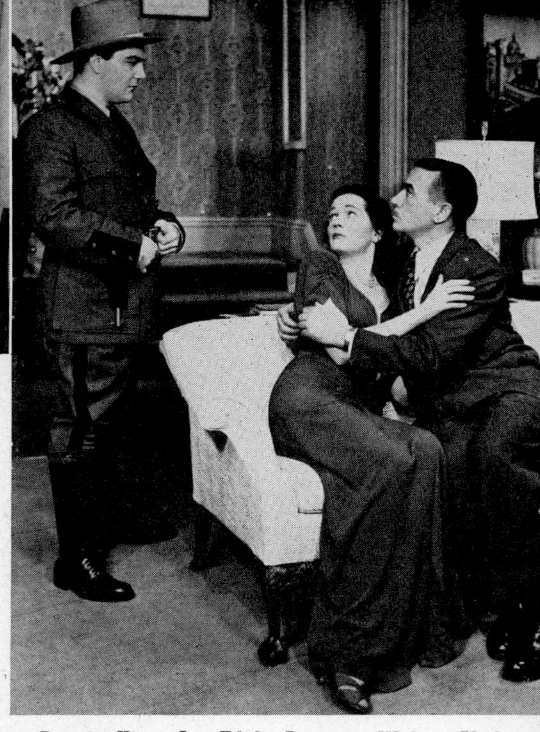

Dennis King, Jr.—Edith Atwater—Walter Abel

BILTMORE THEATRE

Opened Tuesday, March 4, 1947.*
Paul Streger presents:

PARLOR STORY

By William McCleery; Setting by Raymond Sovey; Costumes by Bianca Stroock; Staged by Bretaigne Windust.

Cast of Characters
(In order of appearance)

Marian Burnett .... Edith Atwater
Katy .... Joan Vohs
Charles Burnett .... Walter Abel
Christine .... Carol Wheeler
Eddie West .... Richard Noyes
Mike } State Troopers { Frank Wilcox
Lainson } { Dennis King Jr.
Mrs. Bright .... Dorothy Eaton
Governor Sam Bright .... Paul Huber
Mel Granite .... Royal Beal

A Comedy of corrupt politics within a State University in three acts, three scenes. The action all happens on a Friday evening in October, in the Living-room of a professor's house in a University Town somewhere West of the Missouri River.

Company Manager, EDGAR RUNKLE
Press, WILLARD KEEFE, JAMES P. DAVIS
Stage Manager, MAURY TUCKERMAN
*Closed March 22, 1947. (23 performances)

Walter Abel—Richard Noyes—Carol Wheeler

Paul Huber—Royal Beal—Walter Abel

CENTURY THEATRE

Opened Wednesday, March 12, 1947.*
J. H. Del Bondio and Hans Bartsch for the Delvan Company present:

THE CHOCOLATE SOLDIER†

Music by Oscar Straus; Book by Rudolph Bernauer and Leopold Jacobson; American Version by Stanislaus Stange; Revised Book by Guy Bolton; Revised and Additional Lyrics by Bernard Hanighen; Directed by Felix Brentano; Settings and Lighting by Jo Mielziner; Costumes by Lucinda Ballard; Choreography by George Balanchine; Orchestrations and Musical Direction by Jay Blackton.

Cast of Characters
(In order of appearance)

Nadina........Frances McCann
Mascha........Gloria Hamilton
Aurelia........Muriel O'Malley
Bumerli........Keith Andes
Massakroff........Henry Calvin
Popoff........Billy Gilbert
Alexius........Ernest McChesney
Stefan........Michael Mann
Katrina........Anna Wiman
Premiere Danseuse........Mary Ellen Moylan
Premier Dancer........Francisco Moncion

Musical Numbers: 'We Are Marching Through the Night,' 'Lonely Women,' 'My Hero,' 'The Chocolate Soldier,' 'Sympathy,' 'Seek the Spy,' 'Bulgaria Victorious,' 'Thank the Lord the War Is Over,' 'Slavic Dance††,' 'After Today††,' 'Forgive,' 'Tale of the Coat,' 'Falling in Love,' 'Waltz Ballet,' 'Just a Connoisseur††,' 'The Letter Song,' 'That Would Be Lovely,' 'After Today Gala Polkan††.'

A Revival of the Operetta in three acts. The action takes place in Nadina's Bedroom and the Courtyard of the Popoff House, situated in a small town in Bulgaria—during the 19th Century.

Company Manager, EDWARD HAAS
Press, TOM WEATHERLY
General Stage Manager, EDWARD BRINKMAN
Stage Managers, RUDY BROOKS, KARL SITTLER

†First produced in New York by F. C. Whitman at the Lyric Theatre on September 13, 1909. It ran for 296 performances. The original Bernauer-Jacobson Libretto was based on G. B. Shaw's "Arms and the Man."
††Arranged and adapted by Jay Blackton from Straus melodies.
*Closed May 10, 1947. (69 performances)

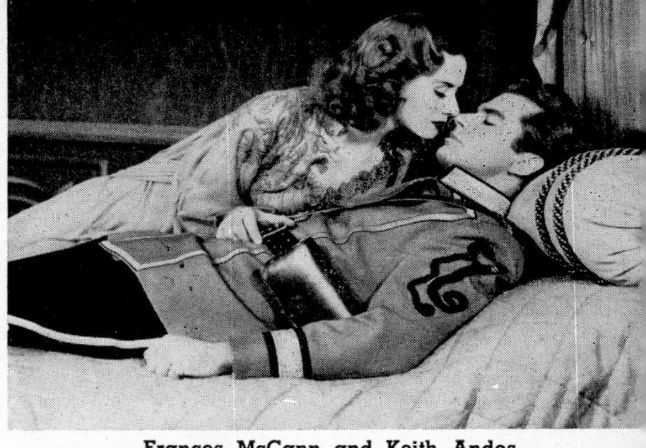

Frances McCann and Keith Andes

Ernest McChesney—Billy Gilbert—Muriel O'Malley—Gloria Hamilton—Frances McCann

David Brooks—Marion Bell

Virginia Bosler—William Hansen—Lee Sulliva

George Keane—David Brooks—William Hansen

ZIEGFELD THEATRE

Opening Thursday, March 13, 1947.
Cheryl Crawford presents:

BRIGADOON

Book and Lyrics by Alan Jay Lerner; Music by Frederick Loewe; Dance and Musical Numbers by Agnes de Mille†; Staged by Robert Lewis; Scenery†† by Oliver Smith; Costumes by David Ffolkes; Vocal Arrangements by Mr. Loewe; Orchestrations by Ted Royal; Lighting by Peggy Clarke; Musical Director, Franz Allers.

Cast of Characters

Tommy Albright .... David Brooks
Jeff Douglas .... George Keane
Archie Beaton .... Elliott Sullivan
Harry Beaton .... James Mitchell
Fishmonger .... Bunty Kelley
Angus MacGuffie .... Walter Scheff**1
Sandy Dean .... Hayes Gordon*1
Andrew MacLaren .... Edward Cullen
Fiona MacLaren .... Marion Bell
Jean MacLaren .... Virginia Bosler
Meg Brockie .... Pamela Britton
Charlie Dalrymple .... Lee Sullivan
Maggie Anderson .... Lidija Franklin
Mr. Lundie .... William Hansen
Sword Dancers ...... Roland Guerard, George Drake
Frank .... John Paul*2
Jane Ashton .... Frances Charles
Bagpipers ...... James MacFadden, Arthur Horn
Stuart Dalrymple .... Paul Anderson**2
MacGregor .... Earl Redding
Townsfolk of Brigadoon

Musical Numbers: 'Once in the Highlands,' 'Brigadoon,' 'Down on MacConnachy Square,' 'Waitin' for My Dearie,' 'I'll Go Home with Bonnie Jean,' 'The Heather on the Hill,' 'The Love of My Life,' 'Jeannie's Packin' Up,' 'Come to Me, Bend to Me,' 'Almost Like Being in Love,' 'The Wedding Dance,' 'Sword Dance,' 'The Chase,' 'There But for You Go I,' 'My Mother's Weddin' Day,' Funeral Dance, 'From This Day On.'

A Musical Fantasy about a mythical Scottish Village that comes to life for one day each century, in two acts, eleven scenes. The action takes place in a Forest in the Scottish Highlands; a Road, MacConnachy Square, an open Shed, The MacLaren House, outside the House of Mr. Lundie, The Churchyard, a Forest and the Glen, all in the village of Brigadoon; and a Bar in New York City.

General Manager, JOHN YORKE
Press, WOLFE KAUFMAN, MARY WARD
Production Stage Manager, WARD BISHOP
Stage Managers, JULES RACINE, JOHN HERMAN

†Assisted in research on Scotch dances by James Jamison.
††Settings painted under the supervision of Victor Graziano.
*Played during tryout tour by: 1 Jeff Warren, 2 Wendell Phillips. The part of Kate Mac Queen, played by Margaret Hunter was written out.
**Replaced by: 1 Jules Racine, 2 Delbert Anderson.

Top: "Jeannie's Packin' Up" at MacLaren's House. Center: "The Sword Dance" in the Churchyard at dusk. Bottom: A Forest in the Scottish Highlands.

Above: Helmut Dantine and Tallulah Bankhead. Below: Clarence Derwent and Helmut Dantine.

Helmut Dantine—Tallulah Bankhead

PLYMOUTH THEATRE

Opened Wednesday, March 19, 1947. **
John C. Wilson presents:

THE EAGLE HAS TWO HEADS†

By Jean Cocteau, adapted from the French by Ronald Duncan; Settings by Donald Oenslager; Costumes by Aline Bernstein; Staged by Mr. Wilson.

Cast of Characters
(In order of appearance)

Countess Edith De Berg.....Eleanor Wilson
Maxim, Duke of Willenstein.....Kendall Clark*1
The Queen.....Tallulah Bankhead
Stanislas.....Helmut Dantine *2
Tony.....Cherokee Thorton
Baron Foehn.....Clarence Derwent

A Romatic Melodrama with tragic consequences in three acts. The action takes place in the Queen's Bedroom and the Library, in a Mythical Kingdom.

General Manager, C. EDWIN KNILL
Company Manager, CHARLES MULLIGAN
Press, RICHARD MANEY, WILLARD KEEFE
Stage Manager, STEPHEN EUGENE COLE

†Originally known in English as "Azrael" and in French as "La Mort Ecoute aux Porte." It was first presented in London on September 6, 1946 at the Lyric Theatre, Hammersmith with Eileen Herlie. It was later presented in Paris at the Theatre Herbertot under the title "L'Aigle a Deux Tetes." This production was first called "Angel of Death" and opened its pre-Broadway tour as "Eagle Rampant."

*Played during tryout tour by: 1 Colin Keith-Johnston followed by Jeff Morrow, 2 Marlon Brando.

**Closed April 12, 1947. (29 performances)

BARRYMORE THEATRE

Opened Wednesday, March 26, 1947.*
Maximilian Becker and Lee K. Holland in association with Sylvia Friedlander present:

BATHSHEBA

By Jacques Deval; Staged by Coby Ruskin†; Settings, Costumes and Lighting by Stewart Chaney; Lyrical research and arrangements by Elma Stern; production supervised by Sylvia Friedlander.

Cast of Characters
(In order of appearance)

Gershoum .... Martin Ashe
Hiram .... Carleton Scott Young
Joab .... Rusty Lane
Manasseh .... Paul Donah
Shari .... Hildy Parks
Uriah .... Phil Arthur
Niziah .... Leonore Rae
Aroussia .... Blanche Zohar
David .... James Mason††
Ghazil .... Horace Braham
Obram .... Michael Sivy
Nathan .... Thomas Chalmers
Hanoufati .... Maud Scheerer
Agreb .... Joseph Tomes
Bathsheba .... Pamela Kellino††
Sourab .... Patricia Robbins
Micale .... Jane Middleton
Bahila .... Barbara Brooks
Orphie .... Lenka Peterson
Lady-in-waiting .... Vega Keane

A Comedy-Drama based on the Old Testament Story of King David's affair with Bathsheba in three acts, nine scenes. The action takes place during the summer of the year 1030 B.C. in a Tent before Rabah and the Top Terrace of King David's Palace in Jerusalem.

General Manager, LEE K. HOLLAND
Press, JAMES D. PROCTOR, LEWIS HARMON
Stage Manager, WALTER DAVIS

†After opening night of the tryout in Princeton Robert H. Gordon resigned and Mr. Ruskin succeeded him, accenting the comedy and subduing the biblical overtones.
††Mr. and Mrs. Mason's American debut.
*Closed April 19, 1947. (29 performances)

James Mason as King David

Phil Arthur—James Mason

Pamela Kellino—James Mason

BILTMORE THEATRE

Opened Thursday, March 27, 1947.**
Walter Fried and Paul F. Moss present:

THE WHOLE WORLD OVER†

By Konstantine Simonov, adaptation by Thelma Schnee; Directed by Harold Clurman; Settings and Costumes by Ralph Alswang; Song, "To The Future": Music by I. Dunaevski, Lyrics by Harold Rome.

Cast of Characters
(In order of appearance)

Feodor Vorontsov .... Joseph Buloff
Nadya .... Beatrice De Neergaard
Olya Vorontsov .... Uta Hagen
Sergei Sinitsin .... Sanford Meisner*1
Sasha .... Elisabeth Neumann
Stepan Cheezov .... Fred Stewart
Dmitri Savelev .... Stephen Bekassy*2
Nicolai Nekin .... Michael Strong
Vanya Shpolyanski .... George Bartenieff
Colonel Ivanov .... Lou Polan
Major Anna Orlov .... Jo Van Fleet

A Comedy about reconversion and housing shortage in two acts, five scenes. The action takes place in the Apartment of Professor Feodor Vorontsov in Moscow shortly after the end of the war.

Company Manager, WALTER FRIED
Press, RICHARD MANEY, NED ARMSTRONG
Stage Manager, MORTIMER HALPERN

†Presented in Moscow last season under the name of "So It Will Be."
*Replacements: 1 Paul Mann, 2 Herbert Berghof.
**Closed June 21, 1947. (100 performances)

Uta Hagen Stephen Bekassy

Michael Strong—George Bartenieff—Stephen Bekassy—Joseph Buloff—Fred Stewart—Uta Hagen—Beatrice de Neergaard—Elizabeth Neumann—Jo Van Fleet

Standing: Ralph Brooke—Jean Muir—William David. Kneeling: Edward De Valde—Henry Lascoe—James Fallon—Joshua Shelley—Forrest Taylor, Jr.—Dean Harens.

Betty Caulfield and Jackie Kelk

BOOTH THEATRE

Opened Wednesday, April 2, 1947.**
Saul Fischbein† presents:

TENTING TONIGHT††

By Frank Gould; Directed by Hudson Faussett; Setting by John Root; Costumes supervised by Robert Moore.

Cast of Characters

Peter Roberts	Richard Clark
Edna Roberts	June Dayton
Lester Pringle	Michael Road
Leonie Roberts	Jean Muir
Phil Alexander	Dean Harens
Stanley Fowler	Ralph Brooke*
Sue Fowler	Betty Caulfield
Theda Henderson	Ethel Remey
Marvin Henderson	William David
Elliot Smollens	Jackie Kelk
Joe Wollinski	Joshua Shelley
Yock Janowski	Henry Lascoe
Sherman	Michael Lewin
Harry Nash	Forrest Taylor Jr.
Billy Heffernan	Edward De Valde
Sammy Foley	James Fallon

A Comedy about Veteran Housing Shortage at a college in three acts, four scenes. The action of the play takes place in the combination Living-room Study of the home of Peter Roberts, a teacher of chemistry in a small college town—September, the present time.

Company Manager, SAM NIXON
Press, JAMES PROCTOR, LEWIS HARMON
Stage Mgrs FORREST TAYLOR JR. LIONEL WILSON

†Originally produced by Judith Abbott and Mary Mason—relinquished during tryout.
††Formerly known as "Snow Job."
*During tryout, played by Robert White, 'Nancy' played by Jean Hogan was deleted.
**Closed May 10, 1947. (46 performances)

Billy Redfield Nancy Walker
Below: Sociology Classroom Scene with Philip Coolidge as Professor Schultz

MARTIN BECK THEATRE

Opened Thursday, April 3, 1947.**
George Abbott presents:

BAREFOOT BOY WITH CHEEK

Book by Max Shulman, from his novel of the same name; Music by Sidney Lippman; Lyrics by Sylvia Dee; Scenery and Lighting by Jo Mielziner; Choreography by Richard Barstow; Vocal Arrangements by Hugh Martin; Costumes by Alvin Colt; Orchestrations by Philip Lang; Musical Director, Milton Rosenstock; Production staged by George Abbott.

Cast of Characters

Roger Hailfellow....Jack Williams
Shyster Fiscal....Red Buttons*
Van Varsity....Ben Murphy
Charlie Convertible....Loren Welch
Freshman....Patrick Kingdon
Asa Hearthrug....Billy Redfield
Eino Fflliikkiinnenn....Benjamin Miller
Noblesse Oblige....Billie Lou Watt
Clothilde Pfefferkorn....Ellen Hanley
Yetta Samovar....Nancy Walker
Professor Schultz....Philip Coolidge
Peggy Hepp....Shirley Van
Kermit McDermott....Jerry Austen
Boris Fiveyearplan....Solen Burry
Playwright....Marten Sameth
Bartender....James Lane
Muskie Pike....Tommy Farrell
First Band Member....Harris Gondell
Second Band Member....Nathaniel Frey

Musical Numbers: 'A Toast to Alpha Cholera,' 'We Feel Our Man Is Definitely You,' 'The Legendary Eino Fflliikkiinnenn,' 'Too Nice a Day to Go to School,' 'I Knew I'd Know,' 'I'll Turn a Little Cog,' 'Who Do You Think You Are?, 'Everything Leads Right Back to Love,' 'Little Yetta's Gonna Get a Man,' 'Alice in Boogieland,' 'After Graduation Day,' 'There's a Lot of Things You Can Do With Two (But Not With Three),' 'The Story of Carrot,' 'When You Are Eighteen,' 'Star of the North Star State,' 'It Couldn't Be Done (But We Did It).'

A Musical Comedy Caricature of non-academic phases of campus-life in two acts, fifteen scenes. The action takes place on the Campus of the University of Minnesota, the Alpha Cholera Fraternity House, College Class Room, Corridor, and Publication Office, The Sty, a Street, The Knoll and the Polling Place.

General Manager, CHARLES HARRIS
Press, RICHARD MANEY, NED ARMSTRONG
General Stage Manager, ROBERT GRIFFITH
Stage Managers, DANIEL SATTLER, FRED HEARN

*Replaced by Joshua Shelley.
**Closed July 5, 1947. (108 performances)

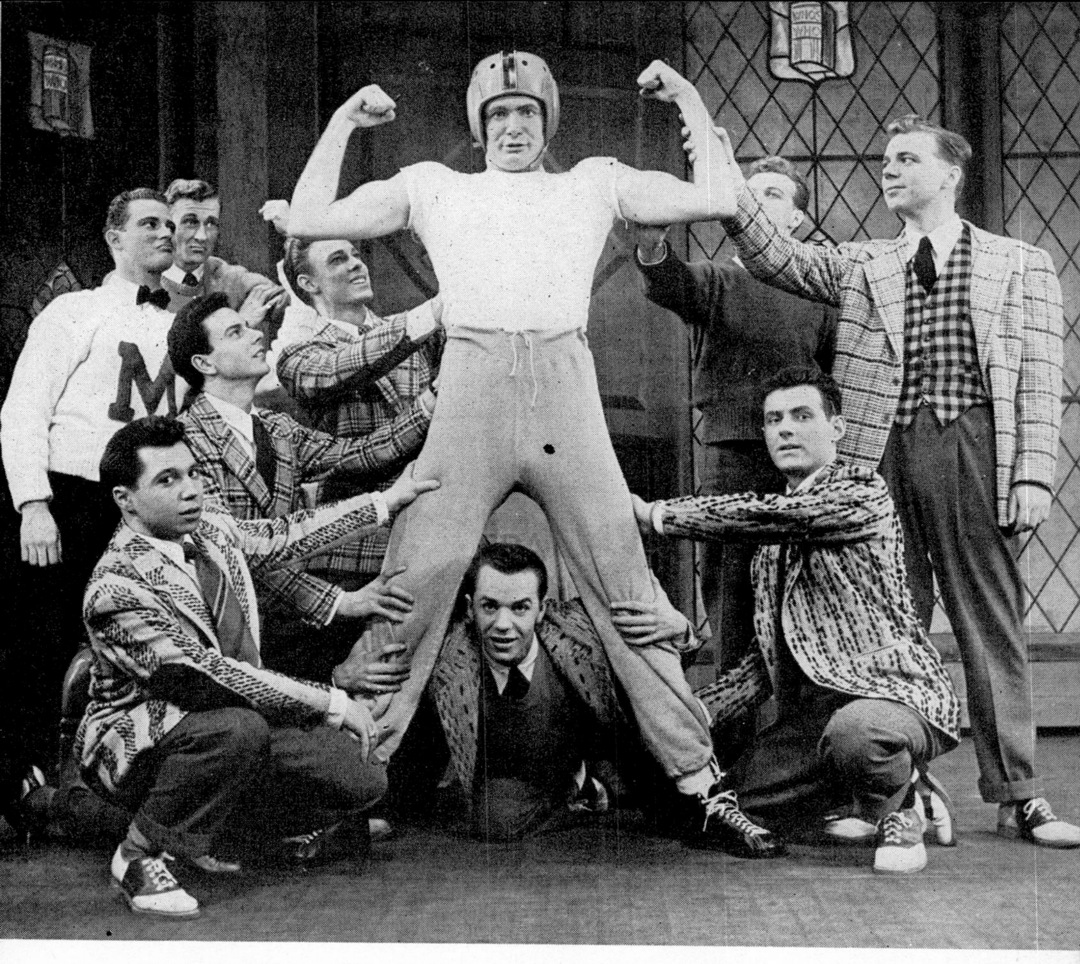

Above: Benjamin Miller as "The Legendary Eino Fflliikkiinnenn." Below left: Billie Lou Watt, Billy Redfield, Nancy Walker, Ellen Hanley. Below right: Billy Redfield and Billie Lou Watt.

INTERNATIONAL THEATRE

(Moved to MAJESTIC May 28, 1947)
Opened Saturday, April 5, 1947. **
Rita Hassan and The American Repertory Theatre present:

ALICE IN WONDERLAND† and Through the Looking Glass

By Lewis Carroll, adapted for the stage by Eva Le Gallienne and Florida Friebus, based on the Tenniel Drawings; Music by Richard Addinsell; Scenery by Robert Rowe Paddock; Costumes by Noel Taylor; Masks and Marionettes by Remo Bufano; Choreography by Ruth Wilton; Conductor, Tibor Kozma; Production devised and directed by Eva Le Gallienne.

Characters in Part One

Alice	Bambi Linn††
White Rabbit	Julie Harris, William Windom
Mouse	Henry Jones
Dodo	John Straub
Lory	Angus Cairns
Eaglet	Arthur Keegan
Crab	Don Allen
Duck	Eli Wallach
Caterpilllar	Theodore Tenley
Fish Footman	Ed Woodhead
Frog Footman	Robert Rawlings
Duchess	Raymond Greenleaf
Cook	Don Allen
Cheshire Cat	Donald Keyes *1
March Hare	Arthur Keegan
Mad Hatter	Richard Waring
Dormouse	Don Allen *2
2 of Spades	Eli Wallach
5 of Spades	Robert Rawlings
7 of Spades	Donald Keyes
Queen of Hearts	John Becher
King of Hearts	Eugene Stuckmann
Knave of Hearts	Frederick Hunter
Gryphon	Jack Manning
Mock Turtle	Angus Cairns
3 of Clubs	John Behney
5 of Clubs	Bart Henderson
7 of Clubs	John Straub
9 of Clubs	Thomas Grace

Bambi Linn as Alice

Top: The Caucus Race. Second: The Duchess Receives an Invitation. Frog Footman (Robert Rawlings), Fish Footman (Ed Woodhead). Third: The Queen's Croquet Party. Duchess (Raymond Greenleaf), Queen of Hearts (John Becher). Bottom: By The Sea. Gryphon (Jack Manning), Mock Turtle (Angus Cairns).

Hearts: Don Allen, Robert Carlson, Michel Corhan, Will Davis, Robert Leser, Gerald McCormack, Walter Neal, James Rafferty, Dan Scott, Carles Townley.

Characters in Part Two

Red Chess Queen .... Margaret Webster
Train Guard .... John Straub
Gentleman Dressed in White Paper
William Windom
Goat .... Don Allen
Beetle Voice .... Donald Keyes
Gnat Voice .... Cavada Humphrey
Gentle Voice .... Angus Cairns
Other Voices ..... Mary Alice Moore, Eli Wallach
Tweedledum .... Robert Rawlings
Tweedledee .... Jack Manning
White Chess Queen .... Eva Le Gallienne
Sheep .... Theodore Tenley
Humpty Dumpty .... Henry Jones
White Knight .... Philip Bourneuf *3
Horse .... Charles Townley and Will Davis
Old Frog .... Donald Keyes
Shrill Voice .... Angus Cairns
Singers .... Eloise Roehm, Mara Lunden
Marionettes worked under the direction of A. Spolidoro.

A Revival of the Fantasy in two parts. Part One: Alice at home. The looking glass house. White Rabbit. Pool of Tears. Caucus Race. Caterpillar. Duchess. Cheshire Cat. Mad Tea Party. Queen's Croquet Ground. By the Sea. The Trial.
Part Two: Red Chess Queen. Railway Carriage. Tweedledum and Tweedledee, White Chess Queen. Wool and Water. Humpty Dumpty. White Knight. Alice Crowned. Alice with the Two Queens. The Banquet. Alice at Home Again.

General Manager, JOHN YORKE
Press, WOLFE KAUFMAN, MARY WARD
Stage Mgrs. THELMA CHANDLER, EMERY BATTIS

†First produced by Miss Le Gallienne at her Civic Repertory Theatre on West Fourteenth Street on December 12, 1932. It ran for 127 performances.
††By arrangement with David O. Selznick.
*Replaced by: 1 Margaret Webster, 2 Theodore Tenley, 3 Hugh Franklin.
**Closed June 28, 1947. (97 performances, 3 previews)

Richard Waring as Mad Hatter

Top: The Trial. King of Hearts (Eugene Stuckmann), Queen of Hearts (John Becher). Second: Tweedledee (Jack Manning) and Tweedledum (Robert Rawlings). Third: The White Knight (Philip Bourneuf). Bottom: Alice with the White Queen (Eva Le Gallienne) and The Red Queen (Margaret Webster).

Miriam Hopkins　　Mady Christians

Mady Christians—Roger Pryor—Peter Cookson

Roger Pryor　　Mady Christians

PLYMOUTH THEATRE

Opened Wednesday, April 16, 1947.*
Stanley Gilkey and Barbara Payne in association with Henry Sherek, Ltd. present:

By James Parish; Directed by Elliott Nugent; Setting by Donald Oenslager; Miss

MESSAGE FOR MARGARET†

Christians' clothes by Bergdorf Goodman; Miss Hopkins' by Valentina.

Cast of Characters
(In order of appearance)

Margaret Hayden .... Mady Christians
Stephen Austin .... Roger Pryor
Adeline Chalcot .... Miriam Hopkins
Robert Chalcot .... Peter Cookson
Maid .... Janice Mars

A Drama in three acts, six scenes. The action takes place in Margaret Hayden's apartment in Gramercy Park, New York City.

Company Manager, THOMAS BODKIN
Press Representative, SOL JACOBSON
General Stage Manager, JAMES NEILSON
Stage Manager, WINDSOR LEWIS

†This play was presented earlier this season in London by Sherek Players Ltd. at the Westminster Theatre on August 28, 1946 with Flora Robson as Margaret. It ran for 26 weeks. In London there were only four characters; when the locale was changed from London to New York the part of the maid was added.

*Closed April 19, 1947. (5 performances)

Frederic Tozere—Julie Haydon—Victor Kilian

Julie Haydon—Victor Kilian—E. A. Krumschmidt

Julie Haydon

THE PLAYHOUSE

Opened Friday, April 25, 1947.**
Archer King and Harrison Woodhull present:

MIRACLE IN THE MOUNTAINS†

By Ferenc Molnar; Settings and Costumes by Robert Davison; Staged by the author.*

Cast of Characters

Clement........Kermit Kegley
Dominic........Norman Wallace
Ambrose........Salem Ludwig
The Prior........John McKee
The Attorney........Victor Kilian
Cicely........Julie Haydon
Simon........E. A. Krumschmidt
Sergeant........John Frederick
Gendarme........Mace Gwyer
Veronica........Consuelo O'Connor
Cornelia........Gloria O'Connor
The Squire........Lawrence Tibbett, Jr.
The Judge........Manart Kippen
The Mayor's Wife........Katherine Anderson
The Doctor........Bernard Randall
The Mayor........Frederic Tozere
The Baron........Len Patrick
Butler........Carl Wallace
Young Woman........Vivi Janiss
Court Attendant........Louis Cruger
Girl........Vivian King
Old Woman........Marjorie Dalton
The Prosecutor........Dayton Lummis
The Schoolmaster........Pitt Herbert
Members of the Elders' Council—Jack Hallen, Harry Miller, Jack O'Brien, Charles Russel, C. E. Smith, Augustus Vaccaro.
Little Boy........Maurice Cavell
Townswomen........Elaine Flippen, Janice Cavell, Jane DuFrayne

A Folk Legend in two acts, four scenes. The action takes place in a Monastery, The Mayor's House, The Judgment Hall, and at the foot of the "Hill" in a small town, somewhere in the dark Carpathian Mountains about a hundred years ago.

General Manager, Max Siegel
Press, Richard Maney, Reuben Rabinovitch
Production Assistant, Leon King
Stage Managers, William McFadden, Louis Cruger

†Written for a religious festival and first produced in Budapest at the Vig Szinhaz in 1933.
*When Elizabeth Miele resigned, the author took over.
**Closed April 26, 1947. (3 performances)

Bart Roe—Bill Talman—Donald Hastings—Ronnie Jacoby—Richard Leone—Roy Sterling—Lenore Lonergan

PLYMOUTH THEATRE

Opening Tuesday, April 29, 1947
Henry Adrian presents:

A YOUNG MAN'S FANCY†

By Harry Thurschwell and Alfred Golden; Staged by Robert E. Perry; Scenery and Lighting by Ralph Alswang; Costumes supervised by Lou Eisele.

Cast of Characters

Harold Greenley†1.......Bill Talman
Sylvia Wilson†2.......Lynne Carter*
Girl Camper†3.......Colette MacMahon
Dr. Spee†4.......Hugh Reilly
Dorothy Bennett.......Joan Lawrence
Duvie†5.......Richard Leone
Grilly.......Donald Hastings
Jokey Stephen.......Roy Sterling
Buddy.......Bart Roe
Helen Greenley†6.......Lenore Lonergan
Dickie Crandell.......Ronnie Jacoby
Oliver Crandell†7.......Raymond Bramley
Mrs. Mary Crandell.......Lee Carney
Faith.......Joan Shepard
Miss Weatherhead.......Myrtle Ferguson
Boy Camper.......Ronnie Smith
Camp Trilby Boy.......Mickey Carroll

A Farce Comedy about progressive education in a summer camp in three acts, six scenes. The action takes place in a boys' bunkhouse at Camp Freedom, in Connecticut.

Producer's Associate and General Manager, EMANUEL EPSTEIN
Company Manager, ROY JONES
Press, BERNARD SIMON
Stage Mgrs. HAL PERSONS, RICHARD BALDWIN

†Tried out from January 3, 1947 at Playhouse, Wilmington, to January 18, 1947, Copley, Boston, with: 1 David Durston, 2 Ann Sorg, 3 Naoma Yuenger, 4 George Eden, 5 Paul White, 6 Sheila Bromley, 7 Albert Bergh. Taken off for repairs; resumed tour at Locust Street, Philadelphia, April 15, 1947. Former title: "S'Wonderful."

*Miss Carter was hospitalized a week before opening; her understudy, Margaret Langley opened and played the first few weeks.

Lenore Lonergan—Lynne Carter—Bill Talman

BARRYMORE THEATRE

Opening Thursday, May 1, 1947.
Chandler Cowles and Efrem Zimbalist, Jr. in association with Edith Lutyens present the Ballet Society's production† of:

THE TELEPHONE
("L'Amour A Trois")

Music, Book and Lyrics by Gian-Carlo Menotti; Directed by the composer; Settings and Costumes by Horace Armistead; Lighting by Jean Rosenthal; Musical Director, Emanuel Balaban.

Cast of Characters

Lucy.......Marilyn Cotlow
Ben.......Frank Rogier

A Comic Opera curtain raiser in one act. The action takes place in Lucy's apartment and a telephone booth around the corner.

THE MEDIUM

Cast of Characters

Monica.......Evelyn Keller
Toby, A Mute.......Leo Coleman
Madame Flora (Baba).......Marie Powers
Mrs. Gobineau.......Beverly Dame
Mr. Gobineau.......Frank Rogier
Mrs. Nolan.......Virginia Beeler

A Tragic Opera in two acts. The action takes place in Madame Flora's Parlor at the present time.

General Manager, PHIL ADLER
Company Manager, EDWARD O'KEEFE
Press, DOROTHY ROSS, FRANK GOODMAN
Executive Secretary, DONALD NEVILLE-WILLING
Stage Manager, NANNANNE PORCHER

†Originally presented at the Heckscher Theatre on February 18, 1947, under the musical direction of Leon Barzin.

Marie Powers

Marilyn Cotlow Frank Rogier

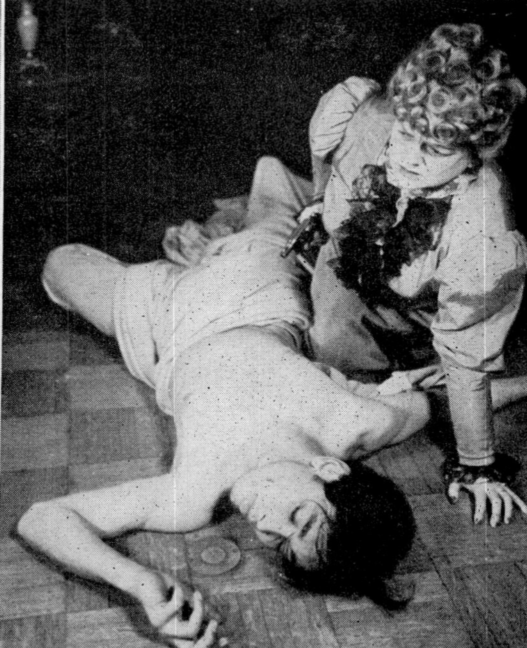

Leo Coleman Marie Powers

CORT THEATRE

Opened Friday, May 2, 1947.*
Your Theatre, Inc.† in association with the theatre going public presents:

HEADS OR TAILS

By H. J. Lengsfelder and Ervin Drake; Directed by Edward F. Cline; Settings by Watson Barratt; Lighting by Leo Kerz; Costumes by Alice Gibson.

Cast of Characters
(In order of appearance)

Cornelius T. Sheldon........Les Tremayne
Amy........Lulu Belle Clarke
Helen Sheldon........Audra Lindley
Burton Snead........Joseph Silver
Frank Jones........Gregory Robbins
Marion Gilmore........Lucie Lancaster
Alice Milford........Jean Cobb
Philip McGill........Jed Prouty
Barney McGill........Ralph Simone
Eric Petersen........Werner Klemperer
Mrs. Warren........Lelah Tyler
Ernest Milford........Joseph Graham
Mr. Green........Anthony Gray
Senor Costamara........Frank de Kova
Humperdinck........Richard Barron
McNulty........Paul Lipson

A Farce in three acts, five scenes. The action takes place on the Terrace of the Country Home of Cornelius Sheldon, in Barney McGill's Office and the Milford Living-room.

Company Manager, JOSEPH MOSS
Press, STANLEY SEIDEN, JOSEPH I. RICHMAN
Stage Manager, JOHN HOLDEN

†Two years ago, Mr. Lengsfelder formed this organization to permit advance ticket purchasers to become shareholders in the venture. The play was financed to the extent of $150,000; half of the capitalization came from 3,146 ticket "angels" and the other half from regular backers.

*Closed May 31, 1947. (35 performances)

Lucie Lancaster Jed Prouty

Ralph Simone Werner Klemperer

Les Tremayne—Joseph Silver—Audra Lindley

Donald Cook Claire Luce

Thomas Coley Dorothea Jackson

Mary Michael Barry Kelley

BOOTH THEATRE

Opened Wednesday, May 14, 1947. *
David Lowe and Edgar F. Luckenbach present:

PORTRAIT IN BLACK†

By Ivan Goff and Ben Roberts; Staged by Reginald Denham; Setting and Lighting by Donald Oenslager; Costumes supervised by Helene Pons.

Cast of Characters
(In order of appearance)

Tanis Talbot	Claire Luce
Gracie McPhee	Mary Michael
Peter Talbot	David Anderson
Winifred Talbot	Dorothea Jackson
Cob O'Brien	Barry Kelley
Rupert Marlowe	Sidney Blackmer
Dr. Philip Graham	Donald Cook
Blake Ritchie	Thomas Coley

A Murder Thriller in two acts, five scenes. The action takes place in the Drawing-room of the Talbot Home in San Francisco.

Company Manager, EDGAR RUNKLE
Press, KARL BERNSTEIN
Stage Manager, HARRY ALTNER

†This play was tried out last season on the road by Leland Hayward. Also produced in London on May 30, 1946 at the Piccadilly Theatre with Diana Wynyard as Tanis Talbot. It ran 14 weeks.
*Closed July 5, 1947. (61 performances)

Cyril Ritchard—Adrianne Allen—George Hayes—John Gielgud

John Gielgud Pamela Brown

ROYALE THEATRE

Opened Monday, May 26, 1947.*
The Theatre Guild and John C. Wilson in association with H. M. Tennent Ltd. of London present John Gielgud's Company in:

LOVE FOR LOVE†

By William Congreve; Directed by Mr. Gielgud; Settings by Rex Whistler††; Costumes by Jeannetta Cochrane; Lighting by William Conway; Incidental Music arranged and the songs 'A Nymph and a Swain,' 'Cynthia,' and 'Charmion,' composed to Congreve's own words by Leslie Bridgewater.

Cast of Characters

Valentine	John Gielgud
Jeremy	Richard Wordsworth
Scandal	George Hayes
Tattle	Cyril Ritchard
Mrs. Frail	Adrianne Allen
Foresight	John Kidd
Robin	Donald Bain
Nurse	Philippa Gill
Angelica	Pamela Brown
Sir Sampson Legend	Malcolm Keen
Mrs. Foresight	Marian Spencer
Miss Prue	Jessie Evans
Ben	Robert Flemyng
Buckram	Sebastian Cabot
Jenny	Mary Lynn

Singer: Eric Goldie

A Revival of the Restoration Comedy in two acts, five scenes. The action takes place in London, 1695 at Valentine's Lodgings and at Foresight's House.

General Manager, Peter Davis
Company Manager, Chandos Sweet
Press, Willard Keefe, David Tebet
Stage Managers, Mary Lynn, Donald Bain

†This production was first presented by Mr. Gielgud at the Phoenix Theatre in London on April 8, 1943.

††The physical production, its furniture and other properties have been brought here from Mr. Gielgud's Repertory Theatre in London.

*Closed July 5, 1947. (48 performances)

Jessie Evans—Robert Flemyng—Marian Spencer—Adrianne Allen

Kenneth Leslie—Charles Cavanaugh—
Berenice Odell—Kay Corcoran—Beth Stevens

Joe Jackson, Jr.

CENTER THEATRE

Opening Wednesday, May 28, 1947.
Sonja Henie and Arthur M. Wirtz present:

ICETIME OF 1948†

Production by Sonart Productions; Executive Director, Arthur M. Wirtz; Production Director, William H. Burke; Lyrics and Music by James Littlefield and John Fortis; Staging and Choreography by Catherine Littlefield; Settings by Bruno Maine and Edward Gilbert; Costumes by Lou Eisele, Billy Livingston and Kathryn Kuhn; Assistant Choreographer Dorothie Littlefield; Lighting by Eugene Braun; Skating Direction by May Judels; Musical arrangements by Paul Van Loan; Conductor, David Mendoza.

Featuring

Skippy Baxter — Joan Hyldoft
Freddie Trenkler — Joe Jackson Jr.

The Bruises:
Monty Stott, Geoffe Stevens, Sid Spalding
Helga and Inge Brandt

Edward Berry — John Kasper
Grace Bleckman — Kenneth Leslie
Ray Blow — Berenice Odell
Edward Brandstetter — Buck Pennington
James Caesar — Ragna Ray
James Carter — Jerry Rehfield
Paul Castle — Lucille Risch
Charles Caminiti — Jean Sakovich
Charles Cavanaugh — Joe Shillen
Kay Corcoran — James Sisk
Claire Dalton — Charles Slagle
Fritz Dietl — Beth Stevens
Lou Folds — Cissy Trenholm
Buster Grace — James Trenholm
Fred Griffith — Janet Van Sickle
Garry Keran — Wally Van Sickle

John Walsh

Vocals: Nola Fairbanks, Richard Craig, Melba Welch.

Songs: 'Breaking The Ice'††, 'Mandy,' 'Cuddle Up,' 'Dream Waltz,' 'Garden of Versailles,' 'Lovable You.'

Production Numbers: Overture, Breaking The Ice, Precision Plus, Goldilocks and the Three Bears, Mountain Echoes, Cossack Lore, Design in Rhythm, Bit of Old Erin, Light and Shadow, Toss-up, The Nutcracker, Bouncing Ball of the Ice, When The Minstrels Come To Town, Entr'acte, The Dream Waltz, Zouaves, Double Vision, Garden of Versailles, Over The Top, Man of Distinction, Setting The Pace, Lovable You, Style on Steel, The Bruises, Finale.

Fifth Edition of the musical Ice-travaganza in two acts, twenty-five scenes.

Company Manager, JOHN BERGER
Press, S. J. BRODY
Stage Director, BURTON MCEVILLY

†The first edition, "It Happens on Ice," featuring Joe Cook, opened October 10, 1940.
††By Al Stillman and Paul McGrane.

Claire Dalton and Fred Griffith

Donald Randolph—Ruth Hammond—Mary Loane

Donald Randolph Mary Loane

David Garden—Mary Loane—David Anderson (on floor)—Donald Randolph—(behind sofa) Robert Donnelly—Harvey Collins

EMPIRE THEATRE

(Moved to BIJOU September 9, 1945; ALVIN June 16, 1947.)
Opened Wednesday, November 8, 1939.***
Oscar Serlin presents:

LIFE WITH FATHER†

By Clarence Day, made into a play by Howard Lindsay and Russel Crouse; Staged by Bretaigne Windust; Setting and Costumes by Stewart Chaney.

Cast of Characters

Annie	Mary McNamee
Vinnie††	Mary Loane
Clarence	Harvey Collins*1
John	Robert Donnelly*2
Whitney**	David Garden*3
Harlan	Preston Zucker*4
Father††	Donald Randolph*5
Margaret	Dorothy Bernard††*
Cousin Cora	Ruth Hammond††*
Mary Skinner	Pamela Gillespie*6
The Rev. Dr. Lloyd	Richard Sterling††*
Delia	Ellen Humphrey*7
Nora	Elaine Ivans
Dr. Humphreys	A. H. Van Buren††*
Dr. Sommers	Charles Collier
Maggie	Ruth McArthur*8

A Comedy in three acts, six scenes. The entire action takes place in the morning room of the Day House on Madison Avenue. The time is late in the 1880's.

General Manager, HARRY D. KLINE
Press, HARRY FORWOOD
Production Director, A. H. VAN BUREN
Stage Manager, CHARLES COLLIER

†On June 5, 1947 Firth Shephard opened a London duplication at the Savoy Theatre with Leslie Banks and Sophie Stewart. In America the New York Company and the nine road duplicates have grossed more than $10,000,000 and have been witnessed by six and a half million playgoers.

††On June 14, 1947 when the production played its 3,183rd performance and passed the long run record formerly held by "Tobacco Road," the original Vinnie and Father, Dorothy Stickney and Howard Lindsay re-entered the company for two weeks.

††*These four members of the original company remained with the play throughout its run.

*Replaced by: 1 Gene Fuller, 2 Dean Kenny followed by James Christie, 3 David Frank, 4 Tommy Dineen, 5 Brandon Peters, 6 Ellen Humphrey, 7 Kathleen McLean, 8 Barbara Barton.

**Alternate: David Anderson.

***Closed July 12, 1947. (A World's record of 3,213 consecutive performances)

Harold Keel

Mary Hatcher

David Burns

Harold Keel and Mary Hatcher

ST. JAMES THEATRE

Opening Wednesday, March 31, 1943.
The Theatre Guild presents:

OKLAHOMA!†

Based on the play, "Green Grow the Lilacs," by Lynn Riggs; Music by Richard Rodgers; Book and Lyrics by Oscar Hammerstein 2nd; Directed by Rouben Mamoulian; Dances by Agnes de Mille; Settings by Lemuel Ayers; Costumes by Miles White; Supervised by Lawrence Langner and Theresa Helburn.

Cast of Characters

Aunt Eller .... Ruth Weston
Curly .... Harold Keel*1
Laurey**1 .... Betty Jane Watson*2
Ike Skidmore .... John Alda
Fred .... Allen Sharp
Slim .... Herbert Rissman
Will Parker .... James Parnell
Jud Fry .... Bruce Hamilton
Ado Annie Carnes .... Bonita Primrose*3
Ali Hakim .... David Burns
Gertie Cummings .... Vivienne Allen*4
Ellen .... Gemze De Lappe*5
Kate .... Mae Muth
Sylvie .... Beatrice Lynn*6
Armina .... Nancy Hachenberg*7
Aggie**2 .... Ruth Harte
Andrew Carnes .... Florenz Ames
Cord Elam .... Owen Martin
Jess .... Vladimir Kostenko
Chalmers .... Erik Kristen*8
Joe .... Stokely Gray
Sam .... Remi Martel

Musical Numbers: Oh, What a Beautiful Mornin'; The Surrey With the Fringe on Top; Kansas City; I Can't Say No; Many a New Day; It's a Scandal! It's an Outrage!; People Will Say; Pore Jud; Lonely Room; Out of My Dreams; The Farmer and the Cowman; All er Nothin'; Oklahoma.

A Musical Play in two acts, six scenes. The action takes place in Indian Territory (now Oklahoma) just after the turn of the Century: The front yard, The Smoke House, A Grove, and the Back Porch on Laurey's Farm; The Skidmore Ranch and Kitchen Porch.

Company Manager, MAX A. MEYER
Press, JOSEPH HEIDT, PEGGY PHILLIPS
Stage Manager, TED HAMMERSTEIN

†On April 30, 1947 the Theatre Guild opened a London Company at the Drury Lane Theatre with Harold Keel and Betty Jane Watson heading an American Company.

*Replaced by: 1 Jack Kitty, 2 Mary Hatcher, 3 Dorothea MacFarland followed by Vivienne Allen, 4 Patricia Allen, 5 Alicia Krug, 6 Jane Fischer, 7 Ginger Vetrand followed by Jacqueline Dodge, 8 Boris Runanin.

**Alternate: 1 Ann Crowley, 2 Margaret Nelson.

Alan Baxter Beatrice Pearson

Beatrice Pearson Alan Baxter

MOROSCO THEATRE

Opening Wednesday, December 5, 1943.
Alfred De Liagre, Jr., presents:

THE VOICE OF THE TURTLE†

By John van Druten; Staged by Mr. van Druten; Setting by Stewart Chaney.

Cast of Characters

(In order of appearance)

Sally Middleton .... Beatrice Pearson*
Olive Lashbrooke .... Vicki Cummings
Bill Page .... Alan Baxter

A Comedy in three acts. The action takes place over a weekend in the early spring of 1945 in an apartment in the East Sixties, near Third Avenue, New York City.

Company Manager, SAMUEL SCHWARTZ
Press, JEAN DALRYMPLE, PHILLIP BLOOM
Assistant Press, MARIAN GRAHAM
Stage Manager, EDWIN GORDON

†A London duplication with Margaret Sullivan and Wendell Corey was opened by Gilbert Miller at the Piccadilly Theatre on July 9, 1946.

*Replaced by Phyllis Ryder.

Vicki Cummings Beatrice Pearson

Alan Baxter Beatrice Pearson

John Morley Romola Robb

Frank Fay Romola Robb

48TH STREET THEATRE

Opening Wednesday, November 1, 1944.
Brock Pemberton presents:

HARVEY

By Mary Chase; Directed by Antoinette Perry; Settings by John Root.

Cast of Characters

Myrtle Mae Simmons	Jane Van Duser
Veta Louise Simmons	Josephine Hull*1
Elwood P. Dowd	Frank Fay*2†
Miss Johnson	Lee Truhill*3
Mrs. Ethel Chauvenet	Frederica Going
Ruth Kelly, R.N.	Romola Robb*4
Marvin Wilson	Jesse White
Lyman Sanderson, M.D.	John Morley
William R. Chumley, M.D.	Fred Irving Lewis
Betty Chumley	Dora Clement
Judge Omar Gaffney	John Kirk
E. J. Lofgren	Robert Gist

The Play is in three acts, five scenes. The action takes place in a city in the Far West in the library of the Old Dowd Family Mansion and the reception room of Chumley's Rest.

General Manager and Press Representative THOMAS KILPATRICK
Company Manager, CLARENCE TAYLOR
Stage Manager, BRADFORD HATTON

†On July 14, 1947 James Stewart assumed the role of Elwood P. Dowd during Mr. Fay's vacation.

*Alternates: 1 Ruth McDevitt, 2 Bert Wheeler, 3 Anita Webb, 4 Toni Favor.

esse White—Frank Fay—Romola Robb—John Morley

Josephine Hull Jane Van Duser

Kay Francis Ralph Bellamy

Kay Francis—Margalo Gillmore—Ralph Bellam

Ralph Bellamy—Myron McCormick—
Kay Francis—Minor Watson

Kay Francis—Minor Watson—Ralph Bellamy

HUDSON THEATRE

Opening Wednesday, November 14, 1945.
Leland Hayward presents:

STATE OF THE UNION

By Howard Lindsay and Russel Crouse; Staged by Bretaigne Windust; Settings by Raymond Sovey; Costumes by Emeline Roche; Gowns by Hattie Carnegie.

Cast of Characters†
(In order of speaking)

James Conover .... Minor Watson
Spike McManus .... Myron McCormick
Kay Thorndyke .... Margalo Gillmore
Grant Matthews .... Ralph Bellamy
Norah .... Helen Ray
Mary Matthews .... Kay Francis**
Stevens .... John Rowe
Bellboy .... Howard Graham
Waiter .... Robert Toms
Sam Parrish .... Herbert Heyes*1
Swenson .... Fred Ayers Cotton
Judge Jefferson Davis Alexander
G. Albert Smith
Mrs. Alexander .... Maidel Turner
Jennie .... Madeline King
Mrs. Draper .... Aline McDermott
William Hardy .... Victor Sutherland*2
Senator Lauterback .... George Lessey

A Political Comedy about the present presidential race, in three acts. Scenes: Study and Bedroom in James Conover's Home, Washington, D.C., Living-room of a Suite in the Book-Cadillac Hotel, Detroit, and the Living-room of the Matthews' Apartment in New York.

General Manager, HERMAN BERNSTEIN
Press, LEO FREEDMAN
General Stage Director, WALTER WAGNER
Stage Manager, VICTOR SUTHERLAND

†To allow the players a four-week holiday without interrupting the engagement, on May 19, 1947, the Third Company, headed by Conrad Nagel, Irene Hervey and Henry O'Neill was brought in from the road for two weeks, followed on June 2, 1947 by the Second Company starring Neil Hamilton, Erin O'Brien-Moore and James Rennie for another two weeks.

*Replaced by: 1 Victor Sutherland, 2 Donald McClelland.

**Replaced Ruth Hussey.

MPIRE THEATRE

Opened Wednesday, January 23, 1946.*
The Theatre Guild and John C. Wilson present:

O MISTRESS MINE

By Terence Ratigan; Settings by Robert avison; Miss Fontanne's dresses by Molyeaux; Directed by Mr. Lunt.

Cast of Characters
(In order of appearance)

livia Brown .... Lynn Fontanne
olton .... Margery Maude
iss Dell .... Esther Mitchell
ir John Fletcher .... Alfred Lunt
ichael Brown .... Dick Van Patten
iana Fletcher .... Ann Lee
iss Wentworth .... Marie Paxton

A Comedy in three acts. Time: London, 1944.
cenes: A House in Westminster and a Flat Baron's Court.

General Manager, C. Edwin Knill
Company Manager, Lawrence Farrell
Press, Joseph Heidt, Howard Newman
Stage Managers, Charva Chester, Charles Bowden

*Vacationed from June 30, 1946 to August 26, 1946. Run interrupted from January 12, 1947 to February 24, 1947 due to illness of Mr. Lunt.
Closed May 31, 1947. (482 performances)

Lynn Fontanne   Alfred Lunt

Alfred Lunt—Ann Lee—Lynn Fontanne

Alfred Lunt—Lynn Fontanne—Dick Van Patten

Larry Oliver—Paul Douglas—Gary Merrill—Judy Holliday—Frank Otto—Otto Hulett

Paul Douglas Judy Holliday

LYCEUM THEATRE

Opening Monday, February 4, 1946.
Max Gordon presents:

BORN YESTERDAY†

By Garson Kanin; Staged by the author; Setting by Donald Oenslager; Costumes supervised by Ruth Kanin Aronson.

Cast of Characters
(In order of appearance)

Helen	Ellen Hall
Paul Verrall	Gary Merrill
Eddie Brock	Frank Otto
Bellhop	William Harmon
Bellhop	James Daly
Harry Brock	Paul Douglas
The Assistant Manager	John S. Clubley*1
Billie Dawn	Judy Holliday**
Ed Devery	Otto Hulett
Barber	Ted Mayer
Manicurist	Mary Laslo
Bootblack	Parris Morgan*2
Senator Norval Hedges	Larry Oliver
Mrs. Hedges	Mona Bruns
Waiter	C. L. Burke

A Comedy in three acts. The scene: Grand Suite of exclusive Washington, D.C., Hotel, 1945.

General Manager, BEN A. BOYAR
Press, NAT N. DORFMAN
Stage Manager, DAVID M. PARDOLL

†On January 23, 1947, Laurence Olivier presented a London duplication at the Garrick Theatre with Yolanda Donlan and Hartley Power.

*Replaced by: 1 Gerald Cornell, 2 Lawrence Hall, followed by Johnny Long.

**Alternate: Eleanor Lynn.

Betty Lou Holland and Bill Callahan

David Nillo Maria Karnilova

Jane Kean

NATIONAL THEATRE

Opening Thursday, April 18, 1946.
Melvyn Douglas and Herman Levin present:

CALL ME MISTER

Music and Lyrics by Harold Rome; Sketches by Arnold Auerbach, The Sketches, "Once Over Lightly" and "Off We Go," written in collaboration with Arnold B. Horwitt; Directed by Robert H. Gordon; Dances by John Wray; Musical Direction by Lehman Engel; Scenery by Lester Polakov; Costumes by Grace Houston.

Featuring

Jane Kean** Jules Munshin*1
Betty Lou Holland Bill Callahan
Paula Bane Danny Scholl
Maria Karnilova David Nillo
Lawrence Winters

Robert Baird Joan Bartels
Harry Clark Joe Calvan
Chandler Cowles Fred Danieli
Virginia Davis Alex Dunaeff
Bettye Durrence Ruth Feist
Shellie Filkins Kate Friedlich
Ward Garner Darcy Gardener
Betty Gilpatrick George Hall
Bruce Howard George Irving
Tommy Knox Henry Lawrence
Sid Lawson Betty Lorraine
Rae MacGregor Howard Malone
Alan Manson William Mende
Marjorie Oldroyd Doris Parker
Patricia Penso Paula Purnell
Roy Ross Evelyn Shaw
Edward Silkman Kevin Smith*2
Alvis Tinnin Eugene Tobin
Glen Turnbull

Musical Numbers:† "The Jodie Chant," "Goin' Home Train," "Along With Me," "Surplus Blues," "The Drug Store Song," "The Red Ball Express," "Military Life," "Call Me Mister," "Yuletide, Park Avenue," "When We Meet Again," "The Face on the Dime," "A Home of Our Own," "His Old Man," "South America, Take It Away," "The Senators' Song."

Sketches: Welcome Home, The Army Way, Off We Go, Yuletide, Park Avenue, Once Over Lightly, A Home of Our Own, South Wind.

A Musical Revue in two acts, twenty-three scenes.

General Manager, PHIL ADLER
Press, DOROTHY ROSS
Production Stage Manager, B. D. KRANZ
Stage Managers, STEVE ALLISON, DAVID KANTER

†When Mr. Munshin left the show, the sketch, America's Square Table of the Air, was added to replace his special material.
*Replaced by: 1 Jack C. Carter, 2 Jay Lloyd.
**Replaced Betty Garrett.

IMPERIAL THEATRE

Opening May 16, 1946.
Richard Rodgers and Oscar Hammerstein II present:

ANNIE GET YOUR GUN†

Music and Lyrics by Irving Berlin; Book by Herbert and Dorothy Fields; Directed by Joshua Logan; Sets and Lighting by Jo Mielziner; Dances by Helen Tamiris; Costumes by Lucinda Ballard; Orchestra directed by Jay S. Blackton.

Cast of Characters
(In order of appearance)

Little Boy .... Warren Berlinger
Little Girl .... Mary Ellen Glass
Charlie Davenport .... Marty May
Iron Tail .... Daniel Nagrin*1
Yellow Foot .... Earl Sauvain*2
Mac (Property Man) .... Cliff Dunstan
Cowboys .... Rob Taylor, Bernard Griffin, Jack Pierce
Cowgirls .... Mary Grey*3, Evelyn Giles
Foster Wilson .... Art Barnett
Coolie .... Beau Tilden*4
Dolly Tate .... Lea Penman
Winnie Tate .... Betty Anne Nyman
Tommy Keeler .... Kenny Bowers
Frank Butler .... Ray Middleton
Girl with Bouquet .... Katrina Van Oss
Annie Oakley .... Ethel Merman
Minnie (Annie's Sister) .... Nancy Jean Rabb*5
Jessie (Another Sister) .... Camilla De Witt*6
Nellie (Another Sister) .... Marlene Cameron
Little Jake (Her Brother) .... Clifford Sales*7
Harry .... Don Liberto
Mary .... Ellen Hanley*8
Col. Wm. F. Cody (Buffalo Bill) William O'Neal
Mrs. Little Horse .... Alma Ross
Mrs. Black Tooth .... Elizabeth Malone
Mrs. Yellow Foot .... Nellie Ranson
Trainman .... John Garth III
Waiter .... Leon Bibb
Porter .... Clyde Turner
Riding Mistress .... Lubov Roudenko
Major Gordon Lillie (Pawnee Bill) George Lipton
Chief Sitting Bull .... Harry Bellaver
Mabel .... Mary Woodley
Louise .... Ostrid Lind
Nancy .... Dorothy Richards
Timothy Gardner .... Jack Byron*9
Andy Turner .... Earl Sauvain*10
Clyde Smith .... Noel Gordon
John .... Rob Taylor
Freddie .... Robert Dixon

Ray Middleton Ethel Merman

Ethel Merman Harry Bellaver

The Wild Horse (Ceremonial Dancer) Daniel Nagrin*11
Pawnee's Messenger .... Milton Watson
Major Domo .... John Garth III
1st Waiter .... Clyde Turner
2nd Waiter .... Leon Bibb
Mr. Schuyler Adams .... Don Liberto
Mrs. Schuyler Adams .... Dorothy Richards
Dr. Percy Ferguson .... Bernard Griffin
Mrs. Percy Ferguson .... Marietta Vore
Debutante .... Ruth Vrana
Mr. Ernest Henderson .... Art Barnett
Mrs. Ernest Henderson .... Truly Barbara*12
Sylvia Potter-Porter .... Marjorie Crossland
Mr. Clay .... Rob Taylor
Mr. Lockwood .... Fred Rivett
Girl in Pink .... Jet MacDonald*13
Girl in White .... Mary Grey*3

Musical Numbers: "Buffalo Bill," "I'm a Bad Bad Man," "Doin' What Comes Naturally," "The Girl That I Marry," "You Can't Get a Man With a Gun," "Show Business," "They Say It's Wonderful," "Moonshine Lullaby," "I'll Share It All with You," "Ballyhoo," "My Defenses Are Down," Wild Horse Ceremonial Dance, "I'm an Indian, Too," Adoption Dance, "Lost in His Arms," "Who Do You Love, I Hope?" "Sun in the Morning," "Anything You Can Do."

A Musical Comedy in two acts, nine scenes: Wilson House, a summer hotel on the outskirts of Cincinnati, Ohio; Pullman Parlor in an Overland Steam Train; Fair Grounds at Minneapolis, Minn.; Arena and a Dressing-room of the Big Tent; Deck of a Cattle Boat; Ballroom of the Hotel Brevoort; Aboard the Governor's Island Ferry; Governor's Island, near the Fort.

General Manager, MORRIS JACOBS
Company Manager, MAURICE WINTERS
Press, MICHEL MOK, ABNER D. KLIPSTEIN
General Stage Manager, CHARLES ATKIN
Stage Manager, JOHN SOLA

†On June 7, 1947 the London Company produced by Emile Litter opened at the Coliseum Theatre with Dolores Gray and Bill Johnson heading an otherwise all-British cast.

*Replacements: 1 Jack Beaber, 2 Fred Rivett, 3 Andrea Downing, 4 Phil McEneny, 5 Camilla De Witt, 6 Beverly Sales, 7 Clifford Tatum, Jr., 8 Helene Whitney, 9 Pete Civello, 10 Joseph Cunneff, 11 Jack Beaber, 12 Rose Marie Elliott, 13 Claire Saunders followed by Christina Lind.

Peter Gibbons

David Wayne as 'Og' in "Finian's Rainbow," Ingrid Bergman as "Joan of Lorraine," Estelle Winwood as 'the Duchess of Berwick' in "Lady Windermere's Fan," John Gielgud as 'Valentine' in "Love for Love," and Katherine Dunham.

CHARACTUETTES of 1947

By Mary Green, New York Artist, from the Daniel Blum Collection

PLAYS OPENING IN PAST SEASONS THAT CLOSED DURING THE SEASON OF 1946-47

The Play	*Performances*	*Opened*	*Closed*
Song of Norway	(859)	Aug. 21, 1944	Sept. 7, 1946
Anna Lucasta	(956)	Aug. 30, 1944	Nov. 30, 1946
I Remember Mama	(713)	Oct. 19, 1944	June 29, 1946
Dear Ruth	(680)	Dec. 13, 1944	July 27, 1946
Glass Menagerie, The	(563)	Mar. 31, 1945	Aug. 3, 1946
Carousel	(881)	Apr. 19, 1945	May 24, 1947
Deep Are The Roots	(477)	Sept. 26, 1945	Nov. 16, 1946
Red Mill, The	(531)	Oct. 16, 1945	Jan. 18, 1947
Are You With It?	(264)	Nov. 10, 1945	June 29, 1946
Dream Girl	(348)	Dec. 14, 1945	Dec. 14, 1946
Billion Dollar Baby	(219)	Dec. 21, 1945	June 29, 1946
Pygmalion	(181)	Dec. 26, 1945	June 1, 1946
Show Boat	(417)	Jan. 5, 1946	Jan. 4, 1947
Magnificent Yankee, The	(159)	Jan. 22, 1946	June 8, 1946
O Mistress Mine	(482)	Jan 23, 1946	May 31, 1947
Lute Song	(142)	Feb. 6, 1946	June 8, 1946
Three To Make Ready	(323)	Mar. 7, 1946	Dec. 14, 1946
St. Louis Woman	(113)	Mar. 30, 1946	July 6, 1946
This Too Shall Pass	(63)	Apr. 30, 1946	June 22, 1946
Old Vic Theatre Company	(50)	May 6, 1946	June 15, 1946
On Whitman Avenue	(148)	May 8, 1946	Sept. 14, 1946
Swan Song	(155)	May 15, 1946	Sept. 28, 1946
Around The World	(74)	May 31, 1946	Aug. 3, 1946

PLAYS AT THE NEW YORK CITY CENTER

Michael Todd presents:

HAMLET

By William Shakespeare; Staged by George Schaefer; Scenery by Frederick Stover; Costumes by Irene Sharaff; Music by Roger Adams, conducted by William Brooks. Played at City Center from June 4, 1946 to June 16, 1946. (16 performances)

Cast of Characters

(In order of appearance)

Bernardo	William Weber
Francisco	Robert Berger
Marcellus	Alexander Lockwood
Horatio	Whit Connor
Ghost of Hamlet's Father	Victor Thorley
Claudius, King of Denmark	Thomas Gomez
Hamlet, Prince of Denmark	Maurice Evans
Gertrude, Queen of Denmark	Lili Darvas
Polonius, Secretary of State	Harry Sheppard
Laertes, son of Polonius	Emmett Rogers
Ophelia, daughter of Polonius	Frances Reid
Reynaldo	Victor Rendina
Rosencrantz	Howard Morris
Guildenstern	Booth Colman
Player King	William Le Massena
Player Queen	Blanche Collins
Player Villain	Alan Dreeben
Player Prologue	Howard Otway
Fortinbras, Prince of Norway	Leon Shaw
Norwegian Captain	William Le Massena
Osric	Richard Newton

Frances Reid and Maurice Evans

A return engagement of the Tragedy in two acts, sixteen scenes. The action takes place in Denmark—the Battlements, the Main Hall, the Apartment of Polonius, the Chapel, the Open Court, the Queen's Apartment, a Cellar Room and a Hall at the Castle at Elsinore, also a Street leading to the Port.

General Manager, JAMES COLLIGAN
Company Manager, ROBERT RAPPORT
Press Representative, BILL DOLL
Company Press, MORTON NATHANSON, DICK WILLIAMS
Stage Manager, WALTER WILLIAMS

John C. Wilson in Association with Nat Goldstone presents:

BLOOMER GIRL

Music by Harold Arlen; Lyrics by E. Y. Harburg; Book by Sig Herzig and Fred Saidy; Based on the Play by Lilith and Dan James; Dances by Agnes De Mille; Orchestrations by Russell Bennett; Book Directed by William Schorr; Settings and Lighting by Lemuel Ayers; Costumes by Miles White; Production Staged by E. Y. Harburg; Musical Director, Jerry Arlen. Played at City Center from January 6, 1947 to February 15, 1947. (48 performances)

Cast of Characters
(In order of appearance)

Serena		Mabel Taliaferro
Octavia	The Applegate Daughters	Holly Harris
Lydia		Ellen Leslie
Julia		Dorothy Cothran
Phoebe		Claire Stevens
Delia		Claire Minter
Daisy		Peggy Campbell
Horatio		Matt Briggs
Gus		John Call
Evelina		Nanette Fabray
Wilfred Thrush	The Sons-in-Law	Walter Russell
Joshua Dingle		Carlos Sherman
Ebenezer Mimms		Lester Towne
Herman Brasher		Victor Bender
Hiram Crump		Byron Milligan
Dolly		Olive Reeves-Smith
Jeff Calhoun		Dick Smart
Paula		Lily Paget
Prudence		Noella Pelloquin
Hetty		Alice Ward
Pompey		Hubert Dilworth
Sheriff Quimby		Joe E. Marks
1st Deputy		Edward Chapel
2nd Deputy		Ralph Sassano
3rd Deputy		Donald Green
Hamilton Calhoun		John Byrd
State Official		John Byrd
Governor Newton		Sidney Bassler
Augustus		Arthur Lawson

Musical Numbers: 'When The Boys Come Home', 'Evelina,' 'Welcome Hinges,' 'Farmer's Daughter,' 'It Was Good Enough For Grandma,' Dance Specialty, 'The Eagle and Me,' 'Right as the Rain,' 'T'morra', T'morra',' 'Rakish Young Man With The Whiskers,' 'Pretty as a Picture,' Waltz, 'Sunday in Cicero Falls,' 'I Got a Song,' 'Lullaby,' 'Simon Legree,' 'Liza Crossing the Ice,' 'I Never Was Borned,' 'Man for Sale,' Civil War Ballet.

A return engagement of the Musical Comedy in two acts and ten scenes. The action takes place in Cicero Falls; the conservatory of the Applegate mansion; Applegate bathroom; The Lily; the hedge outside the Applegate estate; the Yellow Pavilion; The Garden; The Village Green; The Town Jail; The Opera House. Time: In the spring of 1861.

General Manager, C. EDWIN KNILL
Company Manager, JAMES TROUP
Press, WILLARD KEEFE, CARLTON MILES
General Stage Manager, WARD BISHOP
Stage Managers, ROBERT CALLEY, ARTHUR GRAHL

Dick Smart and Nanette Fabray

The Applegate Family.
Seated, Matt Briggs and Mabel Taliaferro.

Michael Todd presents:

UP IN CENTRAL PARK

Book by Herbert and Dorothy Fields; Lyrics by Dorothy Fields; Music by Sigmund Romberg; Staged by John Kennedy; Dances by Helen Tamiris; Singing ensemble numbers by Lew Kesler; Settings and Lighting by Howard Bay; Costumes by Grace Houston and Ernest Schraps; Orchestra conducted by William Parson; Orchestrations by Don Walker; Stage supervised by Sammy Lambert. Played at the City Center from May 19, 1947 to May 31, 1947. (16 performances)

Cast of Characters
(In order in which they speak)

A Laborer .... Oren Dabbs
Danny O'Cahane .... Walter Burke
Timothy Moore .... Russ Brown
Bessie O'Cahane .... Betty Bruce
Rosie Moore .... Maureen Cannon
John Matthews, of the New York Times
Earle MacVeigh
Thomas Nast, of Harper's Weekly
Guy Standing, Jr.
Andrew Munroe .... James Judson
William Dutton .... John Quigg
Vincent Peters .... Paul Reed
Mayor A. Oakey Hall .... Rowan Tudor
Richard Connolly, Comptroller of the City of New York .... George Lane
Peter Sweeney, Park Commissioner
Harry Meehan
William Marcey Tweed, Grand Sachem of Tammany Hall .... Malcolm Lee Beggs
Butler .... Dick Hughes
Maid .... Louise Holden
2nd Maid .... Eve Harvey
Mildred Wincor .... Lillian Withington
Joe Stewart .... Jack Stanton
Porter .... John Thorne
Lotta Stevens .... June MacLaren
Fanny Morris .... Janet Roland
Clara Manning .... Lilias MacLellan
James Fisk, Jr. .... Jack Howard
George .... George Bockman
The Gnome .... Kenneth Owen
Governess .... Louise Holden
1st Child .... Joanne Lally
2nd Child .... Janet Lally
Head Waiter .... John Quigg
Arthur Finch .... Wally Coyle
George Jones, Owner of the New York Times
Rowan Tudor
Newsboy .... Hobart Streiford
Organ Grinders .... { Edward Pate / Kenneth Owen

Musical Numbers: 'Up From the Gutter,' 'Carrousel in the Park,' 'It Doesn't Cost You Anything to Dream,' 'Boss Tweed,' 'When She Walks in a Room,' 'Currier and Ives,' 'Close as Pages in a Book,' 'Rip Van Winkle,' 'The Fireman's Bride,' 'When the Party Gives a Party,' 'Maypole Dance,' 'The Big Backyard,' 'April Snow,' 'The Birds & The Bees.'

A Return Engagement of the Musical in two acts and eleven scenes. The action takes place at a site, the Park Commissioner's Temporary Office, the Bird House in the Zoo, the Gardens, the Picnic Grounds, the Mall and the Bandstand in Central Park; the Lounge of the Stetson Hotel (formerly McGowan's Pass Tavern); the office of George Jones (owner of the New York Times); and Central Park West. Time: 1870-1872.

General Manager, JAMES COLLIGAN
Company Manager, WILLIAM G. NORTON
Press Representative, BILL DOLL
Stage Managers, TONY JOCHIM, DAVE EDISON

Betty Bruce   Maureen Cannon

Maureen Cannon   Earle MacVeigh

"THE TROJAN WOMEN"—Abbie Webster, Leslie Hill, Sala Staw, holding Jonathan Marlowe, Elaine Stacey and Kay Parker.

THE EQUITY-LIBRARY THEATRE

By George Freedley

The first of June halted Equity-Library Theatre activities after its fourth and most prolific season in the little theatres located in branches of the New York Public Library. Fifty-six productions set a new record, particularly after a late start since the curtain didn't go up on the first production "Rosmersholm" until November 20th. Only the unfailing purse and willing cooperation of John Golden, the indefatigable patience and skill of Sam Jaffe, the enthusiasm of Benne Franklin as executive secretary, the untiring consideration of branch library staffs and the custodians who went without sleep made all this possible.

Other November openings included "The Milky Way," dreamed up by a group in the South Pacific during the war and realized through ELT, "The Shining Hour" (also staged two seasons ago with a different cast), "The Long Goodbye" and "Hello Out There" in double bill, and finally Carl Shain's excellent direction of "Kiss Them For Me," which won the approbation of Herman Shumlin and Luther Davis, director and adapter, respectively, of the original production.

December saw an ambitious production of "L'Aiglon," "The Second Man," W. S. Gilbert's "Engaged," Day Tuttle's fine handling of "Our Town," Edward Ludlom's imaginative staging of "Abe Lincoln in Illinois," "Angel Street," "Elizabeth The Queen" with a cast of young players from Jose Ferrer's "Cyrano de Bergerac" production, "The Constant Nymph" and O'Neill's "Ah Wilderness!"

1947 was begun with James Joyce's only play, "Exiles," expertly handled by Roland von Weber, "Rocket to the Moon," "The Good Fairy," "The Petrified Forest," "The Green Goddess," "The Church Mouse," and Webster's rarely produced "The White Devil," a great Elizabethan classic for its New York premiere.

Beth Shea and David Bell in "Our Town."

The February shows consisted of "The Dybbuk," "Tomorrow and Tomorrow," "Beyond The Horizon," "Fata Morgana," "Six Characters in Search of an Author," "Uncle Harry," "The Inspector General," "The Great God Brown," three Chekhov comedies directed by Jose Ferrer, "The Mistress of the Inn," and the extraordinarily successful playing of Sidney Howard's "Paths of Glory."

A group of Thornton Wilder one-acters began the month of March and were followed by "Awake and Sing," "Hotel Universe," "Milestones," "A Sound of Hunting," "Home of the Brave," "The Detour," "Peer Gynt," "Justice," and "The Sabine Women." April brought "Success Story," in David Yellen's production. Then came "Arms and the Man," "The Trojan Women," "The Cenci," "There's Always Juliet," "John Ferguson," "The First Year," "Karl and Anna" and "The Lower Depths."

The final month brought several of the most exciting productions of the season, notably Pirandello's obscure but fascinating "Henry IV," adapted and staged by John Reich. The others were "The Circle," "The Three Sisters," "Much Ado About Nothing" in Henry Jones' skillful cutting, and finally "Hedda Gabler," the 56th production of this season and the 144th since ELT began.

Five library theatres were employed: Hudson Park, George Bruce, 115th Street, Hamilton Grange and Fort Washington. In January through the friendly cooperation of C. V. Ericksons, the Greenwich Mews Playhouse at 141 West 13th Street was added.

Ibsen and O'Neill were the most popular dramatists with three plays each. Pirandello, Chekhov, Wilder, Barry, Sherwood and Odets were tied with two productions each. This is a high average of excellence in choice of dramatists for production.

Strictly for the record, George Freedley was again co-chairman of the Equity-Library Theatre.

ONE-MAN SHOWS

EMPIRE THEATRE

Opened Sunday, January 12, 1947.*
John C. Wilson presents:

RUTH DRAPER

in her old and new
Character Sketches
First Program

1. Opening a Bazaar
   Scene: Terrace of a country house in England.
2. Doctors and Diets
   Scene: In a restaurant.
3. Three Women and Mr. Clifford
   Miss Nichols in the office.
   Mrs. Clifford in the Motor Car.
   Mrs. Mallory in her apartment.
4. The Return†
   Scene: Living-room of English Cottage, June, 1945.
   Mrs. Drew
   Mrs. Hancock, postmistress.
5. Vive La France†
   Scene: a beach in Brittany, a night in Autumn, 1940.
   Wife of young Frenchman who is about to sail across the Channel to join the forces of the Fighting French in England.

Second Program

1. The Italian Lesson
2. Three Generations
   Scene: Court of Domestic Relations.
3. A Class in Greek Poise
4. On the Porch
   In a Maine Coast Village.
5. In a Church in Italy—Before the War
   An English Artist—a Beggar—an American Tourist—a Young Girl—a German Tourist—a Peasant.

General Manager, C. EDWIN KNILL
Company Manager, LAWRENCE FARRELL
Press, WILLARD KEEFE
Stage Manager, CHARLES BOWDEN
†New to American Audiences.
*Closed February 23, 1947. (42 performances)

Ruth Draper

Maurice Chevalier

HENRY MILLER THEATRE

Opened Monday, March 10, 1947.*
Arthur Lesser presents:

MAURICE CHEVALIER

in an evening of
songs and impressions
Accompanied by Irving Actman

Act I

1. La Marche de Menilmontant
   Music: B. Clerc. Lyrics: M. Vandair.
2. La Lecon de Piano
   Music: H. Betti. Lyrics: M. Vandair.
3. American Medley
   'You Brought a New Kind of Love to Me,' 'My Love Parade,' 'Hello, Beautiful,' 'Baby,' 'Mimi.'
4. Vingt ans
   Music: M. Fontenoy. Lyrics: M. Chevalier.
5. A Barcelone
   Music: H. Betti. Lyrics: M. Chevalier.

Act II

1. Weeping Willie
   Music: Revil. Lyrics: R. Pirosch.
2. Quai de Bercy
   Music: Alstone. Lyrics: M. Chevalier.
3. Mandarinade
   Music: H. Betti. Lyrics: Pierre Gilbert and M. Chevalier.
4. Place Pigalle
   Music: Alstone. French Lyrics: M. Chevalier. English Lyrics: R. Pirosch.
5. La Symphonie des Smelles de Bois
   Music: V. Scotto. Lyrics: M. Chevalier.

Encore
'Louise,' 'Just a Bum,' 'Valentine.'

Business Manager, JESSE LONG
Press, LEONARD TRAUBE
*Closed April 19, 1947. (46 performances)

NAUGHTY NAUGHT '00

A Revival of the Musical Melodrama in three acts, ten scenes, and a handy adjacent bar. Produced by Paul Killiam in association with Oliver Rea; Lyrics by Ted Fetter; Music by Richard Lewine; Book by John Van Antwerp; Directed by Mr. Fetter; Musical Direction by Mr. Lewine; Dances by Ray Harrison; Physical Production conceived and lighted by Kermit Love, executed by Herbert Brodkin; Costumes by Robert Moore; Orchestra Direction and Arrangements by Leroy Anderson. Played at the Old Knickerbocker Music Hall from October 19, 1946 to Nov. 9, 1946. (21 performances)

Cast of Characters

P. De Quincy Devereux .... John Cromwell
Spunky .... Teddy Hart
Frank Plover .... Leonard Hicks
Jack Granville .... Kenneth Forbes
Stub .... Shepard Curelop
Fred .... King Taylor
Claire Granville .... Ottilie Kruger
Jim Pawling .... Marshall Jamison
Joe .... Roy Wolvin
Tom .... Len Smith, Jr.
Bartender .... George Spelvin
Cathleen .... Virginia Barbour
Pugsy .... L. A. Nicoletti

Naughty Naught Girls

Aza Bard — Rhoda Johannson
Helen Franklin — Diane Renay
Dorothy Hill — Mildred Roane

Entr'Acte Olios

Myrtle Dunedin .... Unicyclist Extraordinary
Maxine and Bobby .... A Man and His Dog
Ullaine Malloy .... Aerialist Supreme

Musical Numbers: 'Goodbye Girls, Hello Yale,' 'Naughty-Naught,' 'Mother Isn't Getting Any Younger,' 'When We're in Love,' 'Zim Zam Zee,' 'Coney-by-the-Sea,' 'What's Good About Good Morning?,' 'Pull the Boat for Eli,' 'Just Like a Woman.'

The action passes at Yale Campus, Frank and Jack's Dormitory Room, Moriarity's Saloon, New Haven Railroad Station, Boathouse near Thames, the River Bank, at the Race.

General Manager, HENRY D. ROMANOW
Company Manager, EDGAR RUNKLE
Press, RICHARD MANEY
Stage Manager, DAVID CAMPBELL

THE PEACEMAKER

A Farce-Fantasy in three acts, four scenes by Kurt Unkelbach. Produced by the American Negro Theatre; Directed by Marjorie Hildreth; Setting by Frank Neal; Costumes by Geneva Fitch. Opened at the ANT Playhouse, Harlem, November 25, 1946. (16 performances)

Cast of Characters

The Widow Mary .... Cecil Scott
Nellie .... Willie Lee Johnson
Lena .... Chickie Evans
Arthur .... Elwood Smith
Deacon Spooner .... Charles Henderson
Sheriff Swift .... Kenneth Manigault
Basil McGee .... Fred Carter
827 .... Howard Augusta
General Swanson .... Hilda Haynes
Sister Maloney .... Clarice Taylor
P. D. Morgwalk .... Frederick O'Neal
The President .... John S. Brown
Secretary .... Letitia Toole
Professor Volga .... Maurice Lisby

The action takes place in the Widow Mary's Farmhouse and the President's Office in Washington, D.C.

Business Manager, JEFFERSON DAVIS, JR.
Press, EVELIO GRILLO
Technical Director, CHARLES SEBREE
Stage Managers, LETITIA TOOLE, ERNEST TRUESDALE

Walter Craig—Dorothy Patterson—Octavia Kenmore—John Jordan—Edmond Le Comte

The Experimental Theatre, Inc. under the sponsorship of American National Theatre and Academy presents Theatre Incorporated's production of:

THE WANHOPE BUILDING

A Fantasy Drama in three acts by John Finch; Staged by Bett Warren; Scenery and Lighting by Wolfgang Roth; Musical Score composed by Arthur Kreutz. Opened at Princess Theatre, February 9, 1947. (5 performances)

Cast of Characters

4-F .... Haskell Coffin
Flashy Page .... John Jordan
Maggie .... Dorothy Patterson
George .... Walter Craig
Eddie .... Martin Balsam
Mrs. Mead .... Octavia Kenmore
Michael .... Edmond Le Comte
Sleeping Drunk .... Courtney Burr, Jr.
Housewife .... Winifred Cushing
Guard .... Frank Richards
Professor Thornstein .... Frederic Cornell
Interviewer .... Clark Howat
Medical Examiner .... Don Peters
Secretary .... Penelope Sack
Brown Hat .... Will Kuluva
Announcer .... Robert Wark
Quiz Master .... Blair Cutting
Baritone .... Billy Rollo
Mr. 10 .... Walter Craig
Mr. 11 .... Anthony Grey
Mr. 12 .... Courtney Burr, Jr.
1st Customer .... Ford Rainey
2nd Customer .... Frederic Cornell
Attendant .... Frank Richards
Felina .... Beatrice Straight
Arnold .... Lex Richards
Young Lovers .... { Penelope Sack / Robert Wark }
Miss Queen .... Margaret Barker
Pomeroy .... Anthony Grey
Madam Endor .... Frieda Altman
Jo Light .... Don Peters
Max .... Robert Wark
John B. Sherman .... Ford Rainey
Policy Committee .... { Blair Cutting / Frank Richards }
Pilot .... Clark Howat

The play begins and ends in Michael's Bar; the rest of the action takes place in the reception room, an Elevator car, a broadcasting studio, the Wanhope baths, a suicide chamber, the salon of Madam Endor, a committee room, a laboratory and John B. Sherman's Office in the Wanhope Building.

Executive Assistant, ROBERT C. SCHNITZER
Company Manager, ZELDA DORFMAN
Production Manager, DOROTHY DAVIES
Stage Managers, CHARLES DURAND, COURTNEY BURR, JR.

Walter Coy as "O'Daniel"

The Experimental Theatre, Inc. under the sponsorship of American National Theatre and Academy presents the Theatre Guild's production of:

O'DANIEL

A Play in three acts, eleven scenes, a prologue, and an epilogue by Glendon Swarthout and John Savacool; Staged by Paul Crabtree; Scenery and Lighting by Herbert Brodkin; Music composed and Directed by Alex North. Opened at Princess Theatre, February 23, 1947. (5 performances)

Cast of Characters

Dan.......Walter Coy
Alex.......Anne Burr
Lee.......Jack Manning
Photographers.......Philip McEneny, Norman Budd
Reporter.......William Munroe
Bellhop.......James Holden
Rudy Bond, Keen Crockett — Politicians.......Billy M. Greene, Robert P. Lieb
Pvt. Sumian.......James Holden
Company Clerk.......William Munroe
Bartender.......Rudy Bond
Ethel.......Isabel Bishop
Potty.......Billy M. Greene
Colonel Basil.......Robert P. Lieb
Technician 4th Grade.......Norman Budd
Corporal.......James Holden
Italian Girl.......Isabel Bishop
Workman.......Billy M. Greene
Cleaning Woman.......Georgia Simmons
Vignati.......Royal Raymond
J. P. Collins.......Keene Crockett

The play opens and closes in a Chicago Hotel Room 1952. The action flashes back to Barracks, 1943, a Bar, 1943, a Dugout, 1944, Apartment Living-room, 1945, Lee's Office, 1947, Dan's Office, 1947, a Telephone Booth, 1948, Dan's Office, 1950, Philadelphia, 1951, Campaign Headquarters, 1951, and an Airport, 1952.

Executive Assistant, ROBERT C. SCHNITZER
Company Manager, ZELDA DORFMAN
Production Manager, STEPHEN ALEXANDER
Stage Managers, PHILIP MCENENY, SUE ANN YOUNG

WINNERS AND LOSERS

A Drama in three acts, four scenes by Nicholas Biel; Produced by the Associated Playwrights, Inc.; Directed and Designed by Edward R. Mitchell. Opened at The Henry Street Playhouse on February 26, 1947. (6 performances

Cast of Characters

Burgermeister.......Sy Travers
Frau Froebel.......Ruth Lilienthal
Young Froebel.......Sam Dortch
Rathner.......Arthur Seelen
Krasnewski.......Charles Dorrey
Dietrich.......William Gershick
Princess Bathildis.......Hanna Gunther
Security Guard.......Louis Filett
Corporal Gilbert Wanstead.......Gaylord Mason
Miss Nebelschein.......Regina Sands
Schwannbaum.......Howard Levine
Lieutenant Tucker.......Robert Fierman
Captain Teveren.......Charles Lilienthal
Scharf.......George Higgins
Lieutenant Albergh.......West Hooker
Heidi.......Ingrid Fleming
Ursula.......Kit Barton
Lieutenant Landley.......Ellis Charles
The Landrat.......Louis Freilich
Private Newman.......Gustav Breuer
Miss Eisenach.......Annette Erlanger
Staff Sergeant Garden.......Pete Rodgers
Lieutenant Colonel Poole.......Marvin Horne
Soldier.......Allen Joseph
Prince Georg Ferdinand of Thalbach and Himmelberg.......Anton Diffring
Lieutenant Ives.......Stuart Hoover
Technical Sergeant O'Grady.......Robert Weston
Luftwaffe Captain VonDobeneck.......Lawrence Ryle
Second Lieutenant Peabody.......Gordon Ayres
Sergeant.......James Trierweiler
Soldiers.......Jack Shaw, Howard Levine
Major Cushing, C.I.C.......John Harwood

The scene is Headquarters of Detachment I 27, Co. F, of the 5th European Civil Affairs Regiment, in the Courthouse at Hellestadt, Germany: Summer, 1945.

Press, SOL JACOBSON
Assistant Director, PATRICIA IRONSIDE
Technical Director, RICHARD BROWN
Stage Manager, LEE LAWRENCE

TIN TOP VALLEY

A Drama in three acts, nine scenes by Walter Carroll; Produced by the American Negro Theatre; Staged by Abram Hill; Settings by Roger Furman; Incidental Music by Hattie King-Reaves; Choral Direction by Elfreeda S. Wright. Opened at the ANT Playhouse, Harlem, February 27, 1947. (45 performances)

Cast of Characters

Ruth Talbot.......Lillian Adams
Mildred Price.......Betty Haynes*1
Greg Talbot.......Charles Nolte
Buck Price.......Frederick O'Neal†*2
Soldier.......Michael Lloyd
Willie Turner.......James Jackson*3
First Man.......Joe Nathan
Second Man.......Kenneth Porter
Third Man.......Michael Lloyd
Wilks.......Walter Carroll*4
First Neighbor.......Vivian Hogan*5
Second Neighbor.......Lulu Hairston
A Photographer.......William Malkin*6
Preacher Wilson.......Frederick Carter*7

†Mr. O'Neal performed in white-face.
*Alternates: 1 Rae Abruzzo, 2 Owen Tolbert-Hewitt, 3 Ernest Truesdale, 4 Allen Joseph, 5 Doris Luper, 6 Willie Lee Johnson, 7 Charles Griffin.

A Mourner ..... Maggi Coates
A Crippled Woman ..... Sadie Stockton
Organist ..... Bessie Powers
Members of the Congregation and Choir—
Josephine Cooper, Garfield Love
Lucille Harris, Lulu Peterson
Urylee Leonardos, Mildred Pollard
Hilda Levine, Bertha Reubel

The action takes place at the present time outside the Price and Talbot shacks in Tin Top, at a clearing in the woods, and in a Church.

Business Manager, JEFFERSON DAVIS, JR.
Press, EVELIO GRILLO
Technical Director, RICHARD BERNSTEIN
Stage Manager, HOWARD AUGUSTA

Joel Ashley—Dorothea MacFarland—Sylvia Stone—William Lee—Somer Alberg

The Experimental Theatre, Inc. under the sponsorship of American National Theatre and Academy presents Jose Ferrer's production of:

AS WE FORGIVE OUR DEBTORS

A Comedy in two acts, four scenes by Tillman Breiseth; Scenery and Costumes by Carl Kent; Lighting by Herbert Brodkin. Opened at the Princess Theatre, March 9, 1947. (5 performances)

Cast of Characters

Mrs. Torvik ..... Mary Fletcher
Mrs. Ness ..... Sara Floyd
Gullick Sturkelson ..... Somer Alberg
Molla Sturkelson ..... Jeannette Dowling
Mr. Svensrud ..... Cyrus Staehle
Oscar Svensrud ..... Kenneth Tobey
Agnet Benstad Foss ..... Sylvia Stone
Chistina Benstad ..... Joyce Ross
Odin Sturkelson ..... William Lee
Lars Foss ..... Joel Ashley
Gonda Sturkelson ..... Dorothea MacFarland
Pastor Flaten ..... Paul Ford
Mr. Torvik ..... Graham Velsey

The action takes place on a Friday of early Spring, in the Kitchen, Parlor and large Bedroom of the Farmhouse of the deceased Miss Etta Sturkelson in Southern Minnesota.

Executive Assistant, ROBERT C. SCHNITZER
Company Manager, ZELDA DORFMAN
Production Manager, JESS KIMMEL
Stage Manager, KENNETH TOBEY

THE DEPUTY OF PARIS

A Drama in three acts by Edmund B. Hennefeld; Produced by the Associated Playwrights, Inc.; Directed by Day Tuttle; Setting by Edward R. Mitchell. Opened at the Henry Street Playhouse on March 21, 1947. (8 performances)

Cast of Characters

Jacques Dubois ..... Alexander Scourby
Pierre ..... Ellis Charles
Henriette Dubois ..... Melva Doney
Sebastien Dubois ..... Arthur Seelen
Adolphe Thiers ..... George Higgins
Casimir Perier ..... John Harwood
Philippe, Duke of Orleans ..... Sam Cohen
Amelie, Duchess de Regnac ..... Annette Erlanger
Auguste, Duke de Regnac ..... Anton Diffring
Marie-Joseph, Marquis de Lafayette ..... Lawrence Ryle
Robert Cabet ..... Marvin Horne
Captain Coignet ..... James Trierweiler

The action takes place in the Salon of Jacques Dubois, Liberal Deputy of Paris, the week of July 26, 1830—"The Glorious Days."

Press, SOL JACOBSON
Assistant Director, BUD IRVING
Technical Director, RICHARD BROWN

Thomas Coley—Howard Brockway—Robert P. Lieb—Frances Waller

The Experimental Theatre, Inc. under the sponsorship of American National Theatre and Academy presents T. Edward Hambleton's production of:

THE GREAT CAMPAIGN

A Folk Play with music in two acts, fourteen scenes by Arnold Sundgaard; Staged by Joseph Losey; associate, Helen Tamiris; Choreography by Anna Sokolow; Settings by Robert Davison; Costumes by Rose Bogdanoff; Music composed and directed by Alex North. Opened at Princess Theatre, March 30, 1947. (5 performances)

Cast of Characters

Emily Trellis ..... Kay Loring
Sam Trellis ..... Millard Mitchell
Jeff Trellis ..... Thomas Coley
Trivett ..... John Eaton
Jane ..... Clara Cordery
Paula ..... Ruth Rowen
Wilderness ..... Philip Robinson
Trumpeter ..... Howard Brockway
Mr. Cook ..... John O'Shaughnessy
Kenneth ..... Ray Boyle
Kenneth's Girl ..... Mary Lou Taylor
Laneth ..... Frances Waller
Barber ..... Glen Tetley
Henry ..... Alan Manson
John ..... William Roerick
Wallie P. Hale ..... Robert P. Lieb
Sidney Gat ..... Erik Rhodes
Roscoe Dray ..... Robert Alvin
Hamp ..... Paul Bain
Laura ..... Marsh McLeod
Eddie ..... Gayne Sullivan
Anna ..... Ann d'Autremont
Avery ..... Howard Wendell
Dancers ..... Clara Cordery, Margaret McCallion, Ruth Rowen, Solvei Wiberg, Richard Astor, John Eaton, Glen Tetley.

The action takes place in the U.S.A.: a field in Minnesota; a farm and road in Illinois; a barber shop and campaign headquarters in Columbus, Ohio; the Trellis home in Zanesville, Ohio; and a highway across the U.S.A.

Executive Assistant, ROBERT C. SCHNITZER
Company Manager, ZELDA DORFMAN
Stage Manager, ALFRED BOYLEN

Alan MacAteer—Don McLaughlin—
Jimsey Somers—Jetti Preminger

The Experimental Theatre, Inc. under the sponsorship of American National Theatre and Academy presents Leonard Field's production of:

VIRGINIA REEL

A Play in three acts by John and Harriett Weaver; Staged by Gerald Savory; Scenery by Richard Bernstein; Lighting by Herbert Brodkin. Opened at Princess Theatre, April 3, 1947. (5 performances)

Cast of Characters

Old Man Henry Haskins ... Alan MacAteer
Ruth Joy Pomfritt ... Jimsey Somers
Creed Haskins ... Barbara Leeds
John Larkin ... Don McLaughlin
Hobe Kelvin ... James Daly
Keen Sowers ... Philip Youmans Remer
The Widow Curtis ... Reta Shaw
Ernie Brunk ... Robert Emhardt
May Belle Haskins ... Jetti Preminger
Tuck Henry ... Richard Shankland
Two Movers ... { C. J. Parsons / William Tregoe

The scene is the country store of Old Man Henry Haskins, in the Blue Ridge Hill Country, a few miles from Royalton, Virginia.

Executive Assistant, ROBERT C. SCHNITZER
Company Manager, ZELDA DORFMAN
Stage Manager, CHARLES J. PARSONS

THE FLIES†

A Drama based on the Orestes and Electra myth in three acts, four scenes and a newsfilm prologue by Jean-Paul Sartre, translated by Stuart Gilbert. Producted by the Dramatic Workshop of the New School; Directed by Paul Ransom; Settings by Willis Knighton; Choreography by Trudl Dubsky-Zipper; Costumes by Mathilda Ziegler; Lighting by Doris S. Einstein; Murals and Projections by John McGrew; Music composed and conducted by Harold Holden; Supervised by Erwin Piscator. Opened at the President Theatre, April 17, 1947. (21 demonstrations)

Cast of Characters

Women of Argos ... Maia Abilea, Helen Bernstein, Naomi Feigenbaum, Mary Key, Dianthe Pattison, Lillian Pintar
Orestes ... Dan Matthews
Tutor ... Nehemiah Persoff
Idiot Boy ... Fred Halpern
Zeus ... Jack Burkhart
Old Woman ... Leola Harlow
Electra ... Carol Gustafson
Clytemnestra ... Frances Adler
Mother ... Naomi Feigenbaum
Child ... Richard Rosenfeld
Nervous ... Robert Schwartz
Sentimental Man ... Bert Neil
Average Man ... Harry Adler
Cynical Man ... Joseph Sargent
Segestes ... Thom Carney
Nicias ... Bernie Schwartz
Other Men ... Syd Parfrey, Harry Heyman, John Lehne, Steve Gottleib
Young Woman ... Maia Abilea
Another Woman ... Helen Bernstein
1st Officer ... John Miller
2nd Officer ... David Miller
Soldiers ... Paul Browne, Harry Bergman, Paul Pfenley
High Priest ... Gerry Cobert
Aegistheus ... Alfred Linder
Children ... Denise Duross, Richard Rosenfeld, Caroline Stolper, Davey Miller, Ellen Shaff, Morton Lang, Fred Halpern
1st Soldier ... Walter Matthau
2nd Soldier ... Jean Saks
Servants ... Robert Schwartz, Syd Parfrey
1st Fury ... Judith Malina, Diane Mayne
2nd Fury ... Mary Key
3rd Fury ... Leola Harlow
4th Fury ... Joan Andrews
5th Fury ... Lillian Pintar

The action takes place in a Public Square in Agras, a Mountain Temple, the Throne room of the Palace, and the Temple of Apollo.

Executive Secretary, HENRY WENDRINER
Publicity, M. ELEANOR FITZGERALD
Technical Director, BERNARD SACHS
Stage Manager, GEORGE QUICK

†"Les Mouches."

OUR LAN'†

A Drama with music in two acts, ten scenes, by Theodore Ward; Produced by the Associated Playwrights, Inc.; Staged and Designed by Edward R. Mitchell; Costumes by Jerry Stone and Sylvia Spiegel; Music arranged and directed by Joshua Lee. Opened at the Henry Street Playhouse on April 18, 1947. (12 performances)

Cast of Characters

Edgar Price ... Edmund J. Cambridge
Gabe Peltier ... John W. Smith
Emanuel Price ... Charles Sebree
Patsy Ross ... Theresa Hines*1
Joe Ross ... Jay Brooks
Charlie Setlow ... Service Bell
Ellen, his daughter ... Valerie Black*2
James ... Harold Conklin
Daddy Sykes ... Luther Henderson
Roxanna, Delphine's Sister ... Margo Washington
Delphine ... Muriel Smith
Beulah ... Dolores Woodard
Ruth ... Martha Evans
Tom Taggert ... Clarence Williams
Sarah, his wife ... Estelle B. Evans
Joshuah Tain ... William Veasey
Georgana, his daughter ... Hileary Glover
Dosia ... Edith-Atuka Reid
Ollie Webster ... Louis Peterson
Lem ... Chauncey Reynolds
Chester ... Lars Murphy
Hank Saunders, overseer ... Charles Lilienthal
Captain Bryant ... Frank McArdle
Libeth Arbarbanel ... Jennie Breines
Oliver Webster ... John Harwood
Yank Sergeant ... William Gershick
Yankee Soldiers ... Howard Levine, Charles Rosen, Bob Mayo, Alan Fiesler
Captain Stewart ... Bob Fierman
John Burkhardt, a planter ... Jack Becker
A Cotton Broker ... Paul Hoffman
1st Rebel Soldier ... Nathan Adler
2nd Rebel Soldier ... Stuart Hoover

The action takes place on the Road to Savannah, January, 1865, and on an Island off the Coast of Georgia.

Press, SOL JACOBSON
Assistant Director, PAUL L. BEAUDRY
Technical Director, RICHARD BROWN
Stage Manager, COURTNEY BURR, JR.

†Won the Theatre Guild Award in 1945.
*Alternates: 1 Blanche Christopher, 2 Ursala Plinton.

CHICAGO SEASON

By William Leonard

Subjected for the last four or five years to derogatory remarks from the East about the lack of discrimination on the part of midwestern theatre-goers, Chicago found cause for self-satisfaction in at least one of the 31 attractions which played the Loop in the season of 1946-47.

Ever since "Good Night Ladies!," a hoked-up revival of "Ladies' Night," ran two years in Chicago, the town has had an unjustified reputation as one in which rough, bawdy, preferably sleazy, theatrical fare was almost sure to succeed, while subtlety, grace and theatrical artistry were equally sure to fail.

When his support kept "The Glass Menagerie" alive, a few years ago, until the Tennessee Williams play could summon the courage to essay a try at Broadway, the Chicago theatre-goer felt a little better about it all. And when "Follow the Girls," after two years in New York, starved to a deserved death in six fast weeks in Chicago, his pride in his judgment was saved again.

But a more satisfying tonic for midwestern morale was yet to eventuate. "Lute Song," the Sidney Howard-Will Irwin adaptation of an ancient Chinese classic, which had been only moderately successful in its seventeen and one-half weeks in New York, caught on slowly in a four-week Autumn engagement at the Studebaker Theatre, then came back to Chicago in January and lingered until mid-May. Its stay of twenty weeks not only bettered its run on Broadway, and made Producer Michael Myerberg think kind thoughts about the Windy City, but reaffirmed the fact that worthwhile shows are not always a poor risk in Illinois.

The statistics of the 1946-47 season indicate that the wartime boom which enabled "Good Night Ladies!," "Kiss and Tell," "The Voice of the Turtle" and "Maid in the Ozarks" to prosper all the way 'round the calendar has ended. The 31 shows which opened in Chicago between June 1, 1946 and June 1, 1947, compared with a total of 37 in the preceding year, and with 39 the year before that. The number of playgoing weeks also decreased, the town's eight theatres being lit a total of 281 weeks in 1946-47, compared with 326 weeks for nine theatres in 1945-46 and 302 weeks for eight theatres in 1944-45.

The season's content was little changed from that of recent years. Thirteen of the 31 arrivals were musicals, the same number as in the preceding season. Eleven of them were revivals or return engagements, compared with ten in 1945-46, and a marked decrease from the 17 revivals and returns of the 1944-45 year.

There were far fewer "pre-Broadway" presentations than a year earlier. Only five shows with New York as their goal were seen at Loop theatres on their way East. Only two of them, "Sweethearts" and "Obsession" reached Manhattan, and "Obsession" might just as well have saved itself the trip.

Of the three other "pre-Broadway" shows, "Laura" decided Miriam Hopkins wasn't the actress for the title role and started all over again under new management and with a new cast, "Come On Up" decided discretion was the better part of valor and headed back to the West Coast without having seen the bright lights of New York, and Max Wylie's "The Greatest of These," a melodramatic harangue about British policy in India, was a failure at the Selwyn despite Eddie Dowling's sincere direction and a cast headed by Gene Raymond, Mary Boland, Bramwell Fletcher and Sam Jaffe.

"Harvey" was the long-run champion of the season, a second company with Joe E. Brown in the Frank Fay role playing 43 weeks at the Harris. Next longest run in the 1946-47 year went to "State of the Union," the last 32 of whose 42 Chicago weeks were subsequent to June 1, 1946. "Lute Song's" twenty weeks constituted the third longest run.

"Song of Norway" was at the Shubert for 16 weeks, of which only the first ten or twelve really were prosperous. "Born Yesterday," in a second company with Richard Rober, Jan Sterling and Laurence Hugo playing the roles originated on Broadway by Paul Douglas, Judy Holliday and Gary Merrill, had been at the Erlanger 14 weeks when the end of the 1946-47 season rolled around.

Other fairly lengthy engagements included "Three to Make Ready," 13 weeks at the Blackstone; "Up In Central Park" (a holdover from 1945-46), twelve weeks at the Shubert; "Dream Girl," twelve weeks at the Selwyn, and "Oklahoma!," in a return engagement, ten sell-out weeks at the Erlanger.

Outlook for 1947-48 is uncertain, but one thing it will share with the season sketched above. Both began with "Laura." The dramatization of Vera Caspary's mystery novel started things off on June 10, 1946, at the Harris Theatre, and it was back, with a new cast, at the same house, June 1, 1947.

PLAYS THAT OPENED OUT OF TOWN BUT DID NOT ARRIVE ON BROADWAY

MERRY WIVES OF WINDSOR

A Comedy in two acts, sixteen scenes, by William Shakespeare. Produced by the Theatre Guild; Directed by Romney Brent; Settings by Stewart Chaney; Supervised by Lawrence Langner and Theresa Helburn. Opened at the Playhouse, Wilmington, Friday, March 15, 1946.**

Cast of Characters†

Shallow, a country justice....Baldwin McCaw
Sir Hugh Evans, a Welsh parson....Charles Francis
Slender, nephew to Shallow....Frank Leslie
Master Page....Robin Craven
Sir John Falstaff....Charles Coburn*
Bardolph (Followers of Falstaff)....George Rees
Pistol (Followers of Falstaff)....Lionel Ince
Nym (Followers of Falstaff)....Allen Collins
Mistress Page....Gina Malo
Anne Page, her daughter....Jennifer Howard
Simple....Jules Racine
Mistress Quickly....Wauna Paul
Rugby, servant to Dr. Caius....Howard Whitfield
Dr. Caius, a French physician....Romney Brent
Fenton, a young gentleman....Douglas Watson
Host of the Carter Inn....Whitford Kane
Mistress Ford....Jessie Royce Landis
Master Ford....David Powell
Robin, page to Falstaff....Judson Rees
Servants to Ford....Dennis Dengate, Robert Stinson
Servants to Mistress Ford....Lucille Patton, Emma Knox

The action takes place in Windsor, England: a public square, a street, a room in Dr. Caius' house, a field near Windsor, a field near Frogmore, a room in Ford's House, and at Herne's Oak.

Company Manager, JOHN H. POTTER
Press, DOROTHY JOHNSON
Stage Manager, MORTIMER HALPERN

†Cast as of June 2, 1946, Erlanger Theatre, Chicago.
*Replaced by Alan Reed.
**Closed at His Majesty's Theatre, Montreal, September 14, 1946.

COME ON UP

A Comedy in two acts, four scenes, and a prologue by Miles Mander, Fred Schiller and Thomas Dunphy; Produced by Select Operating Corporation; Directed by Russell Fillmore; Setting by Ernest Glover; Miss West's gowns by Peter Johnson. Opened at Oakland Auditorium, Oakland, Monday, May 20, 1946.**

Cast of Characters
(In order of appearance)

General Quantillo....Charles La Torre
Ramon Rodriguez....Robert Tafur
Krafft....John Doucette
Carliss Dale....Miss Mae West
Jeff Bentley....Michael Ames*1
Lottie....Cleo Desmond
J. W. Bentley....Roy Gordon
Doug Wade....Charles G. Martin*2
Annette....Francesca Rotoli
Mike Hannegan....Joe McTurk
Twilby....Harold Bostwick*3
Buddy, Sailor....Allan Nixon
Lou Baker, Sailor....Harry (The Hipster) Gibson*4
Nick....Don Harvey
Senator Carlton....Willis Claire
Larkin....Jon Anton
Bell Captain....John Hampton
Ed....Peter Dunne*5
Frank....George Spelvin
General Housenborough....Robert Long

The Prologue takes place in a private room in a penthouse above the "El Flamingo" night club in Mexico City and the four scenes in Carliss Dale's apartment, Washington, D.C., at the present time.

Company Manager, HARRY MIRSKY*6
Press, JOHN J. HILL
Stage Manager, CHARLES LA TORRE

*Replaced by: 1 Richard Davies, 2 Tom De Graffenried, 3 Phillip Russell, 4 Leonard Marvin, 5 Scott Davis, 6 Eddie Lewis.
**Closed at Biltmore Theatre, Los Angeles, February 22, 1947.
(see picture on page 134)

Mae West—Cleo Desmond

MARY HAD A LITTLE

A Farce Comedy in two acts, five scenes, by Muriel Herman, Arthur Herzog, Jr. and Al Rosen. Produced by Al Rosen; Directed by Leon Errol; Designed by Richard Jackson; Gowns by Jacks of Hollywood. Opened at Geary Theatre, San Francisco, July 15, 1946.*

Cast of Characters

Dolores McQuade .... Claire Carleton
Mary White .... Mary Brian
Thomas Cranton III .... Edmund Lowe
Dr. James Hamilton (Jimmie) .... Fred Sherman
Esther Stuart, R.N. .... Lynne Lyons
Betty .... Kathleen Maguire
Mrs. Daisy Jones .... Virginia Belmont
Princess Olga Romanoff .... Lori Irving
Mrs. Lucy Bell .... Jean Dean
Basil Chumley .... Gerald Oliver Smith
A Minister .... Jack Hayes
Max (a waiter) .... Frank E. Bristow

The action takes place in Dolores' Hotel room, Dr. Hamilton's office and Tommie's Apartment.

Company Manager, GEO. B. HUNT
Press, WILLIAM RODDY
Stage Manager, MUNI DIAMOND

*Closed at Copley Theatre, Boston, December 14, 1946.

CORDELIA

A Comedy in three acts, four scenes by George Batson. Produced by Jules J. Leventhal; Directed by Russell Fillmore; Setting by Charles Elson; Costumes by Edith Head. Opened at Shubert Theatre, New Haven, August 23, 1946.*

Cast of Characters

Glory .... Phyllis De Bus
Amity .... Susan Steel
Captain Winkle .... Curtis Cooksey
Candy .... Patty Pope
Professor Harriman .... William Van Sleet
Cordelia Tuttle .... Zazu Pitts
Lon .... Gordon McDonald
Ellie .... Lotus Robb
Millicent .... Nancy Davis
Mr. Todd .... Robert Lyon
Maudie .... Kitty Kelly
Mrs. Dodge .... Valerie Valaire

The scene is Cordelia's home along the waterfront somewhere on the North Shore of Massachusetts, Summertime in the early Nineteen Hundreds.

Business Manager and Press, GEORGE "LEFTY" MILLER
Company Manager, MAURICE COSTELLO
Stage Manager, CHARLES OBERMEYER

*Closed at Auditorium, Trenton, September 28, 1946.

Zazu Pitts

THE LEGEND OF LOU

A Comedy in two acts, three scenes by Stephen Gross. Produced by Arthur Grossman; Directed by Ralph Murphy; Setting by Tony Reveles; Costumes by Judd Johnson; Lighting by Malcom Megley. Opened at Cass Theatre, Detroit, September 2, 1946.*

Cast of Characters

Ezra .... J. Lewis Johnson
Lou Kennedy .... Jane Darwell
Reverend Flowerton .... Peter Keys
Jim Farr .... Frederick Burton
Dawson Kennedy .... Lyle Talbot
Clara Kennedy .... Dian Fauntelle
Grace Kennedy .... Keven McClure
Nome Kennedy .... Lynn Whitney
Louise Kennedy .... Elena Verdugo
Frank Farr .... Ray Barons
Klondike Kennedy .... Tom Tully
The 'Ragtime' Kid .... Lake Reynolds
The Sheriff .... Roger Gray

The scene is the living-room of Mrs. Louise Kennedy in the exclusive residential section of San Francisco—Nob Hill.

Associate Producer, DR. H. A. CONWAY
Treasurer, ARLENE CONWAY
Press, ROGER ROGERS
Stage Manager, ROGER GRAY

*Closed at Cass Theatre, Detroit, September 14, 1946.

THE MAGNIFICENT HEEL

A Comedy in three acts by Constance O'Hara. Produced and Directed by Brock Pemberton; Setting and Costumes by John Root. Opened at the Erlanger Theatre, Buffalo, September 4, 1946.*

Cast of Characters

Kearny Scott	Alan Ross
Susan Woodward	Peggy Wood
Jesse Coxe	Oscar Polk
Earl Bond, Jr.	Paul C. Fielding
Leslie Paul	Nina Sittler
Denis Reardon	Frank Merlin
Melissa Morgan	Edith Meiser
Trask Morgan	Melville Ruick
J. Murray Woodward	Richard Verney
"Slugs" Devine	William Sharon
James Huston	Bert Lytell
Charles Edwards	Booth Colman
Frank Adamson	Richard Aiken

The scene is the living-room of J. Murray Woodward's Calvert County, Maryland, Farmhouse at the present time.

General Manager, THOMAS KILPATRICK
Company Manager, LODEWICK VROOM
Press, THOMAS KILPATRICK, HORACE G. MCNAB
Stage Manager, ELAINE PERRY

*Closed at the National Theatre, Washington, D.C., September 14, 1946.

Alan Ross—Bert Lytell—Booth Colman—Richard Verney—Peggy Wood

BARNABY AND MR. O'MALLEY

A Comedy in two acts by Jerome Chodorov, based on Crockett Johnson's comic strip. Produced by Barney Josephson and James D. Proctor; Staged by Charles Friedman; Settings by Ralph Alswang; Costumes by Ruth Kanin. Opened at the Playhouse, Wilmington, Delaware, September 6, 1946.*

Cast of Characters

Sally Baxter	Louise Campbell
John Baxter	Clark Howat
Barnaby Baxter	Thomas Hamilton Damien George Drew
Jane Shultz	Iris Mann
Mr. O'Malley	J. M. Kerrigan
Launcelot McSnoyd	Solen Burry
Dr. Blackman	Sam Bonnell
Fred Shultz	K. Elmo Lowe
Alice Shultz	Muriel Campbell
Lion	Add Bates
State Trooper	Charles Durand
Lion Trainer	Robert Pierson
Assistant	Perry Bruskin
Reporter	Jamie Schmitt
Photographer	Charles Mendick
Gus	Royal Dano
Gorgon	Jack Bittner

The action takes place in a cross-section set of the suburban house of the Baxters, showing the living-room and kitchen on the first floor and Barnaby's bedroom on the second, and the woods adjoining it. The time is early summer through late fall in the immediate future.

Business Manager, VICTOR SAMROCK
Company Manager, MAX SIEGEL
Press, FRANK GOODMAN
Stage Managers, BEN ROSS BERENBERG, PERRY BRUSKIN

*Closed at Ford's Theatre, Baltimore, September 14, 1946.

Jack Bittner (dog)—J. M. Kerrigan—Thomas Hamilton

THE TEMPORARY MRS. SMITH

A Comedy in two acts, five scenes by Jacqueline Susann and Beatrice Cole. Produced by Vinton Freedley; Directed by Billy Gilbert; Setting and Lighting by Donald Oenslager; Costumes by Eleanor Goldsmith; Richard Krakeur, Associate Producer. Opened at the Playhouse, Wilmington, Delaware, September 13, 1946.*

Cast of Characters

Irving	Arthur Siegel
Joe Vinelli	Silvio Minciotti
Auntie	Fania Marinoff
Peggy Smith	Joy Geffen
Matilda	Joyce Allan
Sonny	Paul Marlin
Natasha Smith	Francine Larrimore
Thomas van Stokes	Howard St. John
Stanislaus Stanislavsky	Mischa Auer
Stu	Ben Laughlin
Mrs. Townsend	Nella Webb
Miss de Haven	Millicent McKean
Miss Frick Tilford	Sonya Yarr
Mr. Penniman	George Pine
Mr. Pritchard	Arthur Schrieber
Mrs. Hemingway	Lois Bolton
Mike Shane	Millard Mitchell
Chatana	By Herself

The scene is the living-room of Natasha Smith's Hotel Apartment on Central Park South, New York City.

Business Manager, EDGAR RUNKLE
Press, KARL BERNSTEIN, MARTHA DREIBLATT
Stage Director, HARRY HOWELL
Stage Manager, JAMES C. WICKER

*Closed Ford's Theatre, Baltimore, September 28, 1946.

SWEET BYE AND BYE

A Musical Comedy in two acts, thirteen scenes, by S. J. Perelman and Al Hirschfeld, Lyrics by Ogden Nash, Music by Vernon Duke. Produced and Staged by Nat Karson; Directed by Curt Conway; Settings by Boris Aronson; Dances by Fred Kelly; Charles Blackman, Musical Director. Opened at Shubert Theatre, New Haven, October 10, 1946.**

Cast of Characters

Grover Slump........Robert Strauss
Don Fox........Le Roi Operti
Cameraman........Jack Blair
Workman........Billy Parsons
Diver........Fred Hearn
Dr. Moon........Leonard Stocker
Miss Parker........Kay Rich
Secretary in Television........Sandra Grubell
Lovers........Doris York, Joey Thomas
Solomon Bundy........Gene Sheldon*
Policewomen........Jennie Lewis, Nevada Smith
Pedestrians......Leonard Claret, Rosemary Schaefer, George O'Leary, Gretchen Houser, Jay Lloyd, Charlotte Bergmeier
Dancer........Billy Parsons
Egon Pope........Walter O'Keefe
Executives........Stella Anderson, Kay Borron, Arthur Carroll, Kenneth Bonjukian, Eddy Di Genova, Walter Holland
Brimmer........Percy Helton
Diana Janeway........Dolores Gray†
Mr. Twenty-Four........Robert Strauss
Dr. Cody........Le Roi Operti
Borvis........Fred Hearn
Mr. Fugazy........Nat Dana
Joan........Joanne Jaap
Bubbles........Betty Bartley
Stoat........Jack Blair
Miss Pittman........Eleanor French
Mr. Flack........Leonard Stocker
Neon Flack........Jerry Boyar
Mrs. Flack........Kay Borron
Nora........Miriam Lavelle
Dr. Knife........A. Winfield Hoeny
Department Store Executive......Sandra Grubell
Magazine Editor........Arthur Carroll
Executive........Lee Ketcham
Bundy's Double........Gene Wilson
Tramp........Tom Glazer
Stevedores........Jennie Lewis, Nevada Smith
J. Walter Noodnik........Robert Strauss
Kimona (His daughter)........Kay Rich
Eskimoes........Fred Hearn, Jack Blair

Musical Numbers: 'Sweet Bye and Bye,' 'Old Fashioned Tune,' 'Yes, Yes,' 'Diana,' 'Good Deed for Today,' Factory Ballet, 'Low and Lazy,' 'Breakfast in Bed,' 'Crisp and Crunchy,' 'Let's Be Young,' 'Roundabout,' 'Hymn,' 'My Broker Told Me So,' 'Just Like a Man,' 'It's Good,' 'Where is Bundy?', 'We Love Us,' 'Eskimo Bacchante.'

The action takes place July 4, 2076 at Flushing Meadows, Curator's Workroom, Museum of the City of New York, Prospect Park, Office of the General Manager and the Factory of the Futurosy Candy Corporation; Janeway Personality Builders Salon, Solomon's Bedroom, Futurosy Park, Assembly Hall of Executives Anonymous, Diana's Bedroom, the Baggage Compartment of a Spaceliner, an Eskimo Village on the rim of the North Pole.

General Manager, ROBERT MILFORD
Company Manager, HUGO SCHAAF
Press, IVAN BLACK, HENRY SENBER
Production Associate, E. W. NASH
Stage Managers, DAVID JONES, GEORGE HUNTER

†Replaced Pat Kirkwood during rehearsals.
*Replaced by Erik Rhodes.
**Closed at Erlanger Theatre, Philadelphia, November 5, 1946.

SET 'EM UP TONY

A Comedy in two acts, three scenes by George Lynn. Produced by Mack Hilliard; Directed by Edgar Macgregor; Setting by Cirker & Robbins; Animal Heads by Frank Koetzner. Opened at the Erlanger Theatre, Buffalo, November 27, 1946.*

Cast of Characters

Goldie........Virginia Smith
Mrs. Rose........Lulu Bates
Detective........Alonzo Price
Policeman........Fred Walton
Tony........Tito Vuolo
Winnie........Robert Watson
Homer Hyde........Charles Gerrard
Lewis Hannegan........Paul Hammond
Jim Morrelli........Richard Allen
Francesca........Lucille Marsh
Gloria........Susan Vall
Major McCracken........Fred Hillebrand
Taxi Driver........William Monroe
Brother Judson........Bernard Randall
Joe........Bruce Adams
Maria........Grazia Narcisco
Comfort McCracken........Georgia Harvey

The scene is Tony's spaghetti joint and saloon.

Business Manager and Press, GEORGE "LEFTY" MILLER
Company Manager, GEORGE ZORN
Stage Manager, ZAC CAULLY

*Closed at Newark Opera House, December 7, 1946.

IN GAY NEW ORLEANS

A Musical Comedy in two acts, seventeen scenes with Book and Lyrics by Forbes Randolph, Music by Carl Fredrickson. Produced by Mr. Randolph; Settings by Watson Barratt; Costumes by Mary Grant; Dances by Felicia Sorel; Lighting by Leo Kerz; Orchestrations by Robert Russell Bennett; Ray Kavanaugh, Conductor. Opened at Colonial Theatre, Boston, December 25, 1946.*

Cast of Characters

Peppi........Pat Meaney
Suzanne........Maria Gambarelli
Stage Door Johnnies........Glenn Martin, Keny McCord, Bernard Sloane, Al Stewart
Agatha........Bertha Powell
Lucinda Bonnet........Monica Coryeo
George Monteux (Conductor)........John Cherry
Annette........Jeanne Grant
Queenie (Wardrobe Mistress)........Betty O'Rear
Dora........Katherine Barlow
Clara........Ruth Shor
Page Boy........Charles Julian
Maurice........Richard Oneto
Phillip (his valet)........Tom Fletcher
Marie (Conductor's Maid)........Betty Voorhees
Maestro........Marek Windheim
La Duchesse........Helen Raymond
Robert Randall........Gilbert Russell
Blackamoors........{ R. Davis Williams, Richard Williams
Spanish Singer........Clifford Jackson
Waiter........Charles Julian
Proprietor........Keny McCord
Colored Women........Rhoda Boggs, Jean Johnson, Delphine Roach
Charles Blauvelt........Glenn Martin
George........Charles Colman
Mary Lou........Louvinia White
Merrymaker........Nat Dano
Michelle........Janie Janvier
Julie Le Blanc........Penny Carroll

Belles of Basin Street .... Katherine Barlow, Penny Carroll, Teresa Castagna, Jeanne Grant, Patricia Hall, Janie Janvier, Ruth Shor, Leona Vanni
Stephen (Robert's Man) .... Charles Welch
Seconds .... Berton Davis, Clifford Jackson, Glenn Martin, Bernard Sloane
Director .... Al Stewart
Conjure Woman .... Catherine Ayers
Colored Man .... John Diggs
Colored Woman .... Rhoda Boggs
Theatre Manager .... Berton Davis
Charwomen .... Janie Janvier, Betty O'Rear, Leona Vanni
Stage Door Man .... Al Stewart
Siren .... Maria Gambarelli

Musical Numbers: 'New Orleans Saga,' 'Don't Pull the Wool Over My Eyes,' 'Just to Say That I Love You,' 'Concert Waltz,' 'Madame, La Duchesse,' 'Music at Night,' 'What Would You Do,' 'Now and Forevermore,' 'Heavens Declare,' 'House on a Cloud,' 'Wind from the Bayou,' 'Forever Spring,' 'In a Hundred Years from Now,' 'Lonely Straggler,' 'Love Came By,' 'Belles of Basin Street,' 'If He Hollers,' Carnaval, 'When the Weddin' March is Ended,' 'Barcarolle' from "Anthony and Cleopatra," 'What Kind of Noise Annoys an Oyster,' 'Sky of Stars,' 'Is Fou Happy-Go-Lucky,' 'Charwomen's Song,' 'Don't Break the Spell.'

The action takes place on the street outside the Stage Door, inside the Stage Door and the Reception and Dressing Rooms of the Lyric Theatre, New Orleans, 1829; Studio in the house of the Conductor; Cafe de L'Opera; the Levee, Garden of Lucinda's home; the Lawn and Library of the home of La Duchesse; Duelling Oaks; Lobby, Stage and Grand Foyer of New Orleans French Opera House, 1835.

General Manager, CHARLES STEWART
Press, LEO FREEDMAN
General Stage Manager, FRANK HALL
Stage Managers, DAVID JONES, GEORGE HUNTER

*Closed at Colonial, Boston, January 31, 1947.

ROPE

A Revival of the Melodrama in three acts by Patrick Hamilton. Produced by Leonard Altobell and Alfred E. Cohan; Staged by Mr. Altobell; Setting by Harry Gordon Bennett. Opened at Town Hall, Toledo, December 30, 1946.*

Cast of Characters

Wyndham Brandon .... Lawrence Slade
Charles Granillo .... Kurt Richards
Sabot .... John O. Hewitt
Kenneth Raglan .... Gene Lyons
Leila Arden .... Margaret Parmentier
Sir Johnstone Kentley .... J. Roland Hogue
Mrs. Debenham .... Elise Bernard
Rupert Cadell .... John Carradine

The scene is a room on the first floor of a house in Mayfair, London, shared by Brandon and Granillo. The continuous action takes place in one evening at the present time.

Company Manager, GEORGE D. SUTTON
Press, ROD WAGGONER
Stage Manager, VERN ARMSTRONG

*Closed at Shubert Lafayette Theatre, Detroit, January 11, 1947.

A LADY PASSING FAIR

A Comedy in three acts by Harry Wagstaff Gribble. Produced by Henri Leiser in association with Gribble Productions, Inc.; Staged by Mr. Gribble; Settings by Frederick Fox; Costumes supervised by Harrietta Harra; "Sensemaya" by Nicolas Guillen, adapted into English by Ben Frederic Carruthers, set to music by Heitor Villa Lobos; Dances by Claude Marchand, Fencing by Ernest Sarracino; Music supervised by Paquita Anderson. Opened at Lyric Theatre, Bridgeport, January 3, 1947.*

Cast of Characters

Claude Harper .... Ernest Sarracino
Miss James .... Judith Allen
Patrick Manico .... Richard Angarola
Paul Freeman .... Frederick O'Neal
Joan Freeman .... Hilda Simms
Dominick Meriwether .... George Fisher
Everett Du Shane (Babe) .... Earle Hyman
Diane Giles .... Basile Spears

The action takes place in the private office of the president of Manico Aeronautics, Inc., and the living-room in the home of Paul and Joan Freeman, uptown somewhere above 125th Street, New York City, the summer of 1946.

General Manager, IRVING COOPER
Company Manager, CLARENCE GRAY
Press Representative, RICHARD MANEY
Production Assistant, LENORE FORSTAD
Stage Manager, JAMES EDWARDS

*Closed at Newark Opera House, January 11, 1947.

BEST OF SPIRITS†

A Comedy in three acts, six scenes by Martyn Coleman. Produced by Marjorie and Sherman Ewing; Staged by Jerome Coray; Setting by Raymond Sovey; Costumes supervised by Emeline Roche. Opened at Bushnell Memorial, Hartford, January 3, 1947.**

Cast of Characters

Mr. Ladd .... Ralph Cullinan
Sarah Thacker .... Janet Tyler
Kitty Thacker .... Dorothy Stickney
Aunt Cora .... Linda Carlon Reid*
Granny .... Daisy Belmore
Mrs. Harris .... Lucille Benson
Captain Wattle .... Roland Culver
Dwight Roland .... Thomas Coley

The scene is the living-room behind Kitty Thacker's Antique Shop.

General Manager, J. H. DEL BONDIO
Company Manager, WARREN MUNSELL, JR.
Press, FRANK GOODMAN, BERNARD SIMON
Stage Manager, ARTHUR MARLOWE

†Originally called "A Little for the Bottle."
*Replaced by Kathryn Givney.
**Closed at Walnut Street Theatre, Philadelphia, January 25, 1947.

Dorothy Stickney—Roland Culver

MISS JULIE†

A One-act Drama by August Strindberg, American acting version by John LaTouche. Produced by Paul Czinner; Staged and adapted by Theodore Komisarjevski; Settings by Harry Bennett; Costumes by Rose Bogdanoff. Opened at Forrest Theatre, Philadelphia, January 21, 1947.*

Cast of Characters

Christine .... Joan Field
Jean .... Raymond Burr
Miss Julie .... Elisabeth Bergner

The action takes place on the country estate in Sweden around the turn of the last century.

A MARRIAGE PROPOSAL

A One-act Comedy by Anton Chekhov.

Cast of Characters

Stepan Stepanitch Tchouboukov
a landowner .... Harrison Dowd
Natalya Stepanna
his daughter .... Elisabeth Bergner
Ivan Vassilitch Lomov
their neighbor .... Jerome Thor
Pasha, a servant .... Jeanne North

The scene is Russian countryside of Czarist Russia before the first World War.

General Manager, LESTER AL SMITH
Press, BYRON BENTLEY
Stage Manager, JOAN NORLANDER

†"Countess Julie."
*Closed at Shubert Theatre, New Haven, February 15, 1947.

WASHINGTON SQUARE

A Drama in three acts, six scenes by Ruth Goodman and Augustus Goetz, suggested by the Henry James novel. Produced by Oscar Serlin; Directed by Jack Minster; Settings and Costumes by Donald Oenslager; The Song "Comme tu es different" by Dorothie Bigelow. Opened at Shubert Theatre, New Haven, January 23, 1947.**

Cast of Characters

Maria .... Fiona O'Shiel
Lavinia Penniman .... Louise Prussing
Dr. Austin Sloper .... John Halliday*
Catherine Sloper .... Barbara Leeds
Elizabeth Almond .... Ivy Troutman
Marian Almond .... Joy Page
Arthur Townsend .... William Corrigan
Morris Townsend .... Peter Cookson
Mrs. Montgomery .... Betty Linley

The entire action of the play takes place in the front parlor of Dr. Sloper's House in Washington Square, New York City—1847.

General Manager, HARRY D. KLINE
Company Manager, JESSE LONG
Press, HARRY FORWOOD, SOL JACOBSON
Production Assistant, BARNA OSTERTAG
Stage Manager, WILLIAM MENDREK

*Replaced by Richard Barbee.
**Closed at Colonial Theatre, Boston, February 1, 1947.

A DANGEROUS WOMAN†

A Comedy in three acts by George Batson and Jack Kirkland. Produced by David Lowe and John Huntington; Staged by Mr. Kirkland; Setting by Charles Elson. Opened at Erie Theatre, Schenectady, January 24, 1947.*

Cast of Characters

Smiley .... John Gerard
Joey .... Lee Sanford
Professor Harriman .... Bruce Adams
Captain Winkle .... Paul Lipson
Glory .... Phyllis DeBus
Candy .... Nancy Hoadley
Cordelia Tuttle .... Zazu Pitts
Todd .... Frank Lyon
Amity Haines .... Margaret Callahan
Priscilla Haines .... Jean Carson
Lon Dagett .... Gordon McDonald
Mrs. Hodge .... Valerie Valaire
"Boston" Bennie .... Anthony Rivers
The Deacon .... Allan Tower

The scene is Cordelia Tuttle's Boarding House along the waterfront on the North Shore of Massachusetts in the early 1900's.

Business Manager, GEORGE "LEFTY" MILLER
Company Manager, MAURICE COSTELLO
Stage Manager, CHARLES BUTLER

†A Rewriting and restaging of "Cordelia."
*Closed at Ford's Theatre, Baltimore, February 15, 1947.

CARROT AND CLUB

A Drama in two acts, four scenes, by John Wexley. Produced by William Herz, Jr.; Directed by Mr. Wexley; Setting by Frederick Fox. Opened at Shubert Theatre, New Haven, January 30, 1947.*

Cast of Characters

Ronnie James .... Polly Rowles
Florist Boy .... Joe Burns
Patricia Gibbs .... Diane Chadwick
Kit Trevor .... John Beal
Telegraph Messenger .... Thomas Hume
Bram Carter .... Kendall Clark
Stanley Moore .... Bert Lytell
Radio Voice of E. T. Pritchard Manart Kippen
Radio Commentator .... Earl Hammond

The action takes place in two adjoining apartments, 1407¼ and 1407½, in the Casa Paloma Courts, Los Angeles.

General Manager, MILTON BARON
Press, JAMES D. PROCTOR, LEWIS HARMON
Production Stage Manager, BEN ROSS
Stage Manager, THOMAS HUME

*Closed at Walnut Street Theatre, Philadelphia, February 8, 1947.

Bert Lytell—Diane Chadwick—John Beal

DARLING, DARLING, DARLING†

A Comedy in three acts, four scenes by Patricia Coleman. Produced by William Cahn; Directed by George Schaefer and Elliott Nugent; Setting by Ralph Alswang; Costumes by Pat Havens. Opened at McCarter Theatre, Princeton, January 31, 1947.*

Cast of Characters

Martin Fife .... Edmon Ryan
Lillian .... Gee Gee James
Linda Burgess .... Lenore Lonergan

Jennifer Mason .... Adele Longmire
Miss Brown .... Ruth McDevitt
Gaby Brown .... Richard Stapley
Becky Philips .... Buff Cobb
Andy Fielding .... Arthur Franz

The entire action takes place in the studio living-room of a house on the East River in New York.

General Manager, GEORGE GOODRICH
Company Manager, JAMES MCKECHNIE
Press, IVAN BLACK, HARRY KOENIGSBERG
Production Assistant, HARRIET KAPLAN
Stage Managers, JOHN EFFRAT, ALFRED BOYLEN

†Originally called "The First Hundred Years."

*Closed at Wilbur Theatre, Boston, February 8, 1947.

THE GREATEST OF THESE

A Drama in three acts, seven scenes by Max Wylie. Produced by Frank Satenstein, in association with Edgar F. Luckenbach, Jr. and Richard Krakeur; Staged by Eddie Dowling; Settings by Donald Oenslager; Costumes by Mary Schenck. Opened at Shubert-Lafayette, Detroit, February 18, 1947.*

Cast of Characters

Mangat .... Frank de Silva
Terrence Philipson .... Bramwell Fletcher
Hackley Chard .... Gene Raymond
Aziz .... Al Singh
Mahmud .... Andrew Kumar Singha
Lady Elizabeth Bates .... Mary Boland
Piyar Siraj-Uddin .... Barbara Young
Sir Harry Chadbourne .... Edwin Jerome
Maha Maya .... Kumara Singha
Rashid Siraj-Uddin .... Peter Coe
Spencer .... A. J. Herbert
Batchie Ram .... George Beshara
Khan Mirza Siraj-Uddin .... Sam Jaffe
Indian Policeman .... Rajah Rama
Garnesh Chatterji .... Dari Singh
Umar Qitab .... Frank de Kova
English Police Captain .... Charles Gerrard

The action takes place in Hackley Chard's Living-room—Punjab, India; Outside and in the living-room of the Siraj-Uddin home, during the month of April.

General Manager, LEO ROSE
Press, CHARLOTTE BAYLIE
Stage Manager, HERBERT HIRSCHMAN

*Closed at Selwyn Theatre, Chicago, March 15, 1947.

Eddie Dowling—Gene Raymond—Sam Jaffe—Bramwell Fletcher—Mary Boland

A MOON FOR THE MISBEGGOTEN

A Drama in four acts by Eugene O'Neill. Produced by the Theatre Guild; Directed by Arthur Shields; Designed and Lighted by Robert Edmond Jones; Supervised by Theresa Helburn and Lawrence Langner. Opened at Hartman Theatre, Columbus, February 20, 1947.**

Cast of Characters

Josie Hogan .... Mary Welch
Phil Hogan, her father .... J. M. Kerrigan*
Mike Hogan, her brother .... J. Joseph Donnelly
James Tyrone, Jr. .... James Dunn
T. Stedman Harder .... Lex Lindsey

The action takes place outside the Hogan Farmhouse with the interior of the sitting room revealed, early September, 1923.

Company Manager, HUGO SCHAAF
Press, JOSEPH HEIDT
Stage Managers, EDWARD P. DIMOND, RICHARD CARLYLE

*Replaced by Rhys Williams.

**Closed American Theatre, St. Louis, March 29, 1947.

James Dunn—Mary Welch—Arthur Shields (the director)

TEN O'CLOCK SCHOLAR†

A Comedy in three acts by Joseph Schrank. Produced by Lewis J. Deak in association with Lee Shubert; Staged by Thomas Mitchell; Setting by Richard Jackson. Opened at Geary Theatre, San Francisco, February 24, 1947.*

Cast of Characters

Emily Wilkins .... Fay Bainter
Herbert Wilkins .... Thomas Mitchell
Jimmy .... Buddy Swan
Eleanor Wilkins .... Jean Ruth
Bill Wilkins .... Paul Langton
Arthur Wilkins .... Skip Homeier
Sam Tucker .... Edward Ryan
Mary .... Helene Stanley
Mr. Muller .... Paul Maxey

The scene is the living-room of the Wilkins' Home.

Company Manager, LEWIS J. DEAK
Press, GEORGE B. HUNT
Stage Manager, RALPH SIMONE

†Formerly titled "The World and Mrs. Wilkins."

*Closed at Geary Theatre, San Francisco, March 15, 1947.

HEARTSONG

A Comedy Drama in three acts by Arthur Laurents. Produced by Irene M. Selznick; Directed by Phyllis Loughton†; Designed and Lighted by Stewart Chaney; Associate Producer, Irving Schneider. Opened at Shubert Theatre, New Haven, February 27, 1947.**

Cast of Characters

Joe Bannion .... Lloyd Bridges*1
Ivy .... Susan Douglas
Uncle Ted .... Jay Fassett
Malloy .... Shirley Booth
Kate Bannion .... Kay Stewart*2
Arnold Everett .... Vinton Hayworth
Lt. Adams .... Mark Wayne

The action takes place in the Bannion's Apartment in New York City.

Company Manager, MAX SIEGEL
Press, WILLARD KEEFE
Stage Manager, ROBERT DOWNING

†Melchor G. Ferrer took over after opening.
*Replaced by 1 Barry Nelson, 2 Phyllis Thaxter.
**Closed at Walnut Street Theatre, Philadelphia, March 29, 1947.

Phyllis Thaxter—Barry Nelson—Shirley Booth

HEY DAY

A Comedy Fantasy in two acts, ten scenes by Donald Richardson. Produced by Howard Lang; Staged by the author; Designed by Stewart Chaney. Opened at Shubert Theatre, New Haven, March 13, 1947.*

Cast of Characters

Mr. Pepper .... Roscoe Karns
Doctor .... Hugh Franklin
Molly Pepper .... Mary Wickes
Brutus Lovelace .... John Craven
Patrolman .... Andrew Duggan
Steve O'Flaherty .... Robert Keith, Jr.
Kipper .... John Marsh
Pinky .... Iggie Wolfington
Marjorie .... Margot Stevenson
Eunice .... Elizabeth Dewing
Agatha .... Pauline Drake
Doona Rafferty .... Timothy Kearse
1st Bodyguard .... John Hix
2nd Bodyguard .... Sid Sawyer
Mr. Lenehan .... Bert Wilcox
Electioneer .... Jus Addiss
Mrs. O'Flaherty .... Kathleen Bolton

The action takes place in Mr. Pepper's Bedroom, the street, the store, the park, and the side door of Mr. Lenehan's Residence.

General Manager, HAROLD KUSELL
Company Manager, IRVING BECKER
Press, LEO FREEDMAN, JUNE GREENWALL
Stage Managers, JUS ADDISS, SID SAWYER

*Closed at Shubert Theatre, New Haven, March 15, 1947.

John Craven—Timothy Kearse—Roscoe Karns

ACCIDENTALLY YOURS

A Comedy in three acts, five scenes by Pauline Williams. Produced by James S. Elliott and Herbert J. Freezer; Staged by Harry Ellerbe and Mr. Elliott; Setting by Ben Edwards. Opened at Junior College Auditorium, Sacramento, March 15, 1947.*

Cast of Characters

Gladys Mosby .... Billie Burke
Marietta .... Leora Thatcher
Olive .... Betty de Cormier
Vivienne .... Barbara Billingsley
Lawrence Conwell .... Phil Warren
Jean Erwin .... Eve McVeagh
Spencer Mosby .... Grant Mitchell
Miss Featherby .... Kathryn Sheldon
Llewellyn Johnson .... Don Grusso
Mrs. Esterhazy .... Paula Trueman
Martin .... Liam Dunn
Photographer .... Jack Whitmore
Dr. Field .... David Bond
Mr. Cavendish .... Edwin Cooper

The action takes place in the living-room of the Mosby's home in a small Mid-Western College Town, at the present time.

General Manager, ALBERT H. ROSEN
Press, GEORGE H. ATKINSON
Stage Manager, JOSEPH OLNEY

*Closed at Selwyn Theatre, Chicago, June 14, 1947.

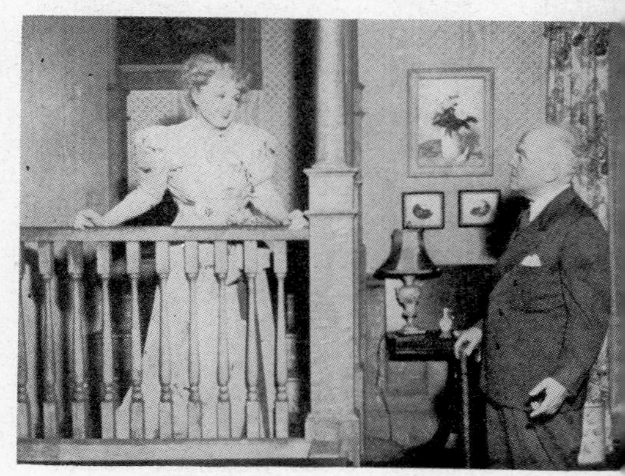

Billie Burke—Grant Mitchell

TROUBLE FOR RENT

A Comedy Mystery in three acts by Monroe Manning. Produced by Frank P. Atha, Inc.; Directed by the author. Opened at the English Theatre, Indianapolis, April 3, 1947.*

Cast of Characters

John Anderson........John Shay
Marion Woodcock........Carol Hughes
Officer Delahanty........Dave Ward
Pete Durkin........Raymond Bond
Helen Durkin........Estelle Taylor
Al........Lyle Talbot
Otto Morris........Charles Jordan
J. H. Tasker........George J. Spelvin

The continuous action takes place in the living-room of an old deserted mansion on the high and dangerous cliffs of Marin County in Northern California.

Company Manager, ROGER ROGERS
Press, ZACK HARRIS
Stage Manager, DAVE WARD

*Closed at American Theatre, St. Louis, April 26, 1947.

THREE INDELICATE LADIES

A Mystery Farce in three acts, four scenes, by Hugh Evans. Produced by Hunt Stromberg, Jr. and Thomas Spengler in association with Irving Cooper; Directed by Jessie Royce Landis; Setting and Lighting by Stewart Chaney; Gowns by Robert Lanza; Production Associate, Thomas Elwell. Opened at Shubert Theatre, New Haven, April 10, 1947.*

Cast of Characters

Kelly........Jayn Fortner
Roberts........Elaine Stritch
Mr. Max........Joey Faye
Morgan........Ann Thomas
Alfred Brook........Alexander Clark
Sam Phelps........Ray Walston
Joe The Heart........Jack Arnold
Francis X. O'Rourke........Bela Lugosi
Mrs. Henrietta Brook........Frances Brandt
Bernice Desos........Katherine Squire
Gus........Charles Mendick
Sergeant........Robert Schulee
Paul Austin........Stratton Walling

The scene is the private office of the late Michael Bludgeon in New York City.

Company Manager, RALPH KRAVETTE
Press, FRANK GOODMAN
Stage Managers, PHIL JOHNSON, JACK CASSIDY

*Closed at Wilbur Theatre, Boston, April 19, 1947.

SUMMER THEATRE CIRCUIT

By Torben Prestholdt

The warm weather months of 1946 saw remarkable activity and revived interest in the "Straw Hat" theatre. When we consider that in both the previous summers there had been less than 30 theatres in operation, and that during the current season there were more than 100, we get a good idea of the increase in business. It was, in fact, one of the most successful seasons in summer theatre history.

Most of this activity was centered in rural areas of the eastern coast from Maine to Virginia, but there were other playhouses scattered throughout the country. In Dallas, St. Louis, Louisville, Los Angeles and San Francisco there was a thriving season of musical stock, and in Denver, the Elitch Gardens continued the high quality of their summer resident company. But it was the small eastern "Barn Theatres" that were the heart of the movement. Many of them were poorly equipped as to stage facilities, and had small seating capacities, but vacationists and natives alike eagerly turned out to see the shows.

Some of these companies used the resident stock system, and several groups of this type did outstanding work. More popular, however, was the visiting star system, and many well known names from the legitimate stage as well as from Hollywood helped keep business teeming.

Among these troupers we found such top stage favorites as Helen Hayes, Gertrude Lawrence, Tallulah Bankhead, Bert Lahr and Jane Cowl. And among the people from the film capital answering the call of the footlights were Olivia de Haviland, Gregory Peck, Gene Raymond, Jean Pierre Aumont, Roddy MacDowell and Charles Korwin.

The longest run was achieved by Edward Everett Horton, who played "Springtime for Henry" for a period of 11 weeks, in as many different theatres. "Night Must Fall" with Dame May Whitty and "Angel Street" with Francis Lederer were the runners-up, each of these having been performed for a period of 8 weeks. The play which was given the most performances was Noel Coward's "Blithe Spirit."

The scale of admission prices was not low. In many theatres it was about the same as that of Broadway, but despite the discomfort of hard seats and warm weather, the audience response was heartening. An all time record for summer stock in Connecticut was established by Tallulah Bankhead in "Private Lives." In the 600 seat Greenwich Playhouse, the take was $11,000 for eight performances. The Cape Playhouse in Dennis, Mass. also broke its record with a week's gross of $9,600 for "The Man in Possession." Gene Raymond was the star of the show, and the leading lady was one Alexandra Dagmar, "A Danish personality of wide experience in the Theatre," who turned out to be none other than Gertrude Lawrence.

The straw hat circuit offered an opportunity for the roving theatregoer to see again many favorite plays. Among them were "The Playboy of the Western World" with Gregory Peck, "Candida" with Jane Cowl, "Alice-Sit-By-The-Fire" with Helen Hayes, "The Circle" with Grace George, and "Pygmalion" with Gertrude Lawrence.

Mary Boland revived "Meet the Wife," Elissa Landi played in "Theatre," Fred Stone did "Lightin'," and Gloria Swanson trouped in "A Goose for the Gander." Florence Reed played "Rebecca," Ruth Chatterton did "Caprice," Estelle Winwood was seen in "The Royal Family" and Olivia de Haviland revived "What Every Woman Knows."

Other plays which were frequently done were "Autumn Crocus," "Anna Christie," "Skylark," "Rope," "Arsenic and Old Lace," and "Brother Rat." There were also productions of "Young Woodley," "The Show Off," "Papa Is All," "Personal Appearance," "The Man Who Came To Dinner," "The Petrified Forest," "Candlelight," "The Vinegar Tree," and "They Knew What They Wanted."

There was a total of 43 new plays tried out during the season. Of these, only five finally reached Broadway. "Drums of Peace" arrived as "Temper The Wind;" "S'wonderful" as "A Young Man's Fancy;" "Made In Heaven" had been tried out as "It's A Man's World;" "Little A" came in under its original title; and "Heaven Can Wait" arrived as "Wonderful Journey." In addition to these plays, Bert Lahr's revival of "Burlesque" had been successfully tested on the summer circuit before it was brought to Broadway.

From the 1945 season of the 24 tryouts, not a single one arrived on Broadway, and only 2 of the new plays tried out in 1944 made the grade. On the other hand, back in 1938, 12 of the Broadway hits of that season had been tried out in summer stock. One of the difficulties connected with a tryout is the fact that the average rehearsal period is only one week, and generally this is an insufficient time for a production of high standards. Nevertheless, tryouts of new plays seem an established part of the summer theatre pattern.

The "Barn Theatres" offer a unique and highly rewarding training ground for new talent. Practical experience in the theatre is given young actors, directors and scenic artists, as well as new playwrights. In this way the legitimate theatre is greatly helped.

The popularity and financial success of the summer theatre during the 1946 season is ample proof of a thriving future. The summer theatre is here to stay, and more and more it should prove to be a potent and exciting factor in American life.

David Wayne in "Finian's Rainbow"
(See page 195)

GALLERY OF PORTRAITS OF PROMISING PERSONALITIES

Dorothea MacFarland in "Oklahoma!"
(See page 180)

Peter Cookson in "Message for Margaret"
(See page 164)

Patricia Neal in "Another Part of The Forest"

(See page 185)

John Jordan in "The Wanhope Building"

(See page 176)

Ann Crowley in "Carousel"
(See page 165)

James Mitchell in "Brigadoon"
(See page 184)

Marion Bell in "Brigadoon"
(See page 156)

George Keane in "Brigadoon"
(See page 176)

Keith Andes in "The Chocolate Soldier"
(See page 153)

Ellen Hanley in "Barefoot Boy With Cheek"
(See page 172)

Sara Allgood

Charles Alexander

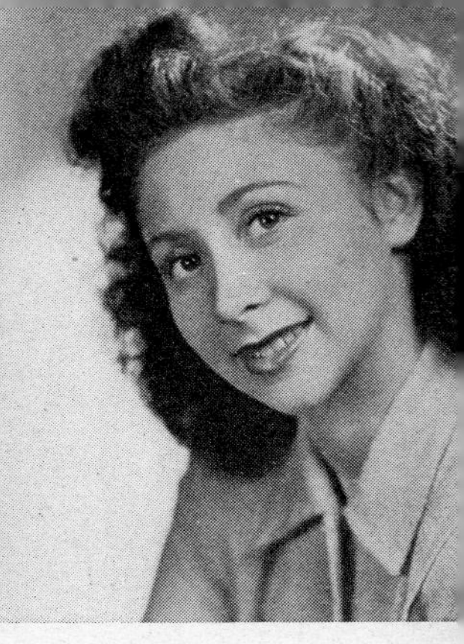

Joyce Allen

BIOGRAPHIES OF POPULAR BROADWAY PLAYERS

ABEL, WALTER. Born in St. Paul, Minn., June 6, 1898. Received his stage training at the American Academy of Dramatic Arts. First N.Y. appearance at Manhattan Opera House, 1919, in "Forbidden." Made more recent N.Y. appearances in "When Ladies Meet," "Wife Insurance," "Invitation to a Murder," "Merrily We Roll Along," and "The Wingless Victory." After a long session in films, he returned to the Broadway stage in "The Mermaids Singing," and played this season in "Parlor Story."

ACKER, MABEL. Early Broadway appearances included "Twin Beds," "Nearly Married," "Mlle. Modiste," "Mother Carey's Chickens," and "Cousin Lucy." After many years of retirement, returned to the N.Y. stage in "The Late George Apley," and played this season in "Land's End."

ADDY, WESLEY. Born in 1912 in Omaha, Neb. His N.Y. appearances include Maurice Evans' productions of "Henry IV," "Hamlet," and "Twelfth Night," Leslie Howard's "Hamlet," Laurence Olivier's "Romeo and Juliet," and more recently "Antigone" and Katharine Cornell's 1946 revival of "Candida." This season he replaced Leo Genn in "Another Part of the Forest."

ADLER, LUTHER. Born in N.Y.C., May 4, 1903. Educated at Lewis Institute, Chicago. Made his first stage appearance in 1908 at the Thalia Theatre, Bowery, N.Y. as a child in a Yiddish play "Schmendrick." His Broadway plays include "Night Over Taos," "Success Story," "Alien Corn," "Men in White," "Gold Eagle Guy," "Awake and Sing," "Paradise Lost," "Johnny Johnson," "Golden Boy," "Rocket to the Moon," "The Russian People," "Two on an Island," "Common Ground," "Beggars are Coming To Town," "Dunnigan's Daughter," and "A Flag is Born."

ADLER, STELLA. Born in N.Y.C., Feb. 10, 1902. Educated N.Y.U. Received her stage training with her father, Jacob Adler, and with Maria Ouspenskaya. First stage appearance with her father in 1906 at the Garden Theatre, N.Y. in "Broken Hearts." Recent stage roles include "House of Connelly," "Success Story," "Night Over Taos," "Gentlewoman," "Gold Eagle Guy," "Awake and Sing," "Paradise Lost," and more recently "Sons and Soldiers," "Pretty Little Parlor," and the revival of "He Who Gets Slapped."

AHERNE, BRIAN. Born in King's Norton, Worcestershire, England, May 2, 1902. Educated at Malvern College. On Feb. 9, 1931, made his Broadway debut in "The Barretts of Wimpole Street." Also appeared with Katharine Cornell in "Lucrece," "Romeo and Juliet," and "Saint Joan." In 1937 he played Iago in "Othello." Between 1937 and 1945 he spent most of his time in Hollywood. Returned to Broadway for a revival of "The Barretts of Wimpole Street," and "The French Touch."

ALEXANDER, CHARLES K. Born in Cairo, Egypt, May 4, 1919. Education at Egyptian Univ., Cairo. Toured Middle East with repertory company. Made Broadway debut in "Hidden Horizon."

ALEXANDER, CRIS. Born in Tulsa, Okla., 1920. Made Broadway debut in revival of "Liliom." More recently was seen in "On The Town" and "Present Laughter."

ALEXANDER, KATHARINE. Born in Ft. Smith, Arkansas, 1901. Made Broadway bow in 1917 in "A Successful Calamity." Other appearances include "Little Accident," "Hotel Universe," "The Left Bank," "Letters to Lucerne," and "Little Brown Jug."

ALLEN, ADRIANNE. Born Feb. 7, 1907 in Manchester, England. Educated in London, and on the continent. Studied for the stage in London at the Royal Academy of Dramatic Art. Made Broadway debut in 1931 in "Cynara." Since then has been seen in "The Shining Hour," "Pride and Prejudice" and "Love for Love."

ALLEN, JOYCE. Born in N.Y.C., Jan. 28, 1926. Educated at Julia Richman High School, Faegan's School of Dramatic Arts and Mme. Daykahonova Speech and Diction School. Made her Broadway debut in "Lovely Me."

ALLEN, ROBERT. Born Mt. Vernon, N.Y., March 28, 1906. Educated N.Y. Military Academy and Dartmouth College. Spent fifteen years in movies, radio, and stock companies. Appeared on Broadway in "Blessed Event," "A Few Wild Oats," "I Killed the Count," "Kiss Them for Me," and "Show Boat."

ALLEN, VERA. Born N.Y.C. Made her debut on N.Y. stage in 1925 in "The Grand Street Follies." Recent appearances include "At Home Abroad," "The Show is On," "Susan and God," "A Woman's a Fool To Be Clever," "Glorious Morning," "The Philadelphia Story," and "Strange Fruit."

ALLGOOD, SARA. Born Dublin, Ireland, Oct. 31, 1883. Recent N.Y. stage appearances include "Storm Over Patsy," "Shadow and Substance," and a revival of "Juno and the Paycock."

Judith Anderson

Cris Alexander

Joan Andre

ALLYN, WILLIAM. Born Jan. 22, 1927 in N.Y.C. Educated at Horace Mann School, N.Y., and Texas Univ. where he studied drama. Made his Broadway debut in "A Flag Is Born."

ALTMAN, FRIEDA. Born Boston, Mass., Aug. 18, 1904. Educated at Wellesley College. Received her stage training at American Laboratory Theatre. Made her Broadway debut in "Carrie Nation," and since then has appeared in "We, the People," "Another Language," "Spring Song," "Paradise Lost," "Guest in the House," "Ah, Wilderness," Hickory Stick," "Days to Come," "Counsellor-at-Law," "The Naked Genius," "A Joy Forever," "Little Brown Jug," and "Land's End."

ALVAREZ, ANITA. Born Oct. 13, 1920 in Tyrone, Pa. Educated at Washington Irving High School, N.Y.C. Was with Martha Graham group for three years. Appeared on Broadway in "All in Fun," "Something for the Boys," "Allah Be Praised," the revival of "A Connecticut Yankee," "One Touch of Venus," and "Finian's Rainbow."

ANDERS, GLENN. Born Los Angeles, Calif., Sept. 1, 1890. Educated at Columbia University. Made first appearance on the stage with Los Angeles stock company in 1910 as Lennox in "Macbeth." Since then he appeared in "Just Around the Corner," "Civilian Clothes," "Scrambled Wives," "The Ghost Between," "The Demi-Virgin," "Hell-Bent for Heaven," "Bewitched," "They Knew What They Wanted," "The Constant Nymph," "Murray Hill," "Strange Interlude," "Dynamo," "Farewell to Arms," "Hotel Universe," "Tomorrow and Tomorrow," "Another Language," "Love and Babies," "I Was Waiting for You," "False Dreams, Farewell," "Moor Born," "A Sleeping Clergyman," "On to Fortune," "If This Be Treason," "There's Wisdom in Women," "The Masque of Kings," "Three Waltzes," "Call It a Day," and more recently "Skylark," "Get Away, Old Man," "Career Angel," and "Soldier's Wife."

ANDERSEN, GERALD. Born April 28, 1910 in London, Eng. Educated at Houghton School, England. Made Broadway debut in "Love Goes To Press."

ANDERSON, JUDITH. Born in Adelaide, Australia, Feb. 10, 1898. Made her American debut in 1918 with a stock company on Fourteenth Street, N.Y.C. Made her Broadway bow in 1923 in "Peter Weston." Since then has appeared in "Cobra," "The Dove," "Behold the Bridegroom," "Anna," "Strange Interlude," "As You Desire Me," "Mourning Becomes Electra" (on tour), "Firebird," "Conquest," "The Mask and the Face," "The Drums Begin," "Come of Age," "Divided by Three," "The Old Maid," the Queen to John Gielgud's Hamlet, "Family Portrait," and more recently Lady Macbeth to Maurice Evans' Macbeth.

ANDES, KEITH. Born Ocean City, N.J., July 12, 1920. Educated at Upper Darby High School, Upper Darby, Pa., St. Edward's School, Oxford, England, and received B.S. degree at Temple Univ. Made Broadway debut in "Winged Victory." Appeared in the films: "Winged Victory," and "The Farmer's Daughter." Played the title role in "The Chocolate Soldier" during the current season.

ANDRE, JOAN. Born in N.Y.C. April 5, 1929. Educated at Washington Irving High School and the New School for Social Research. Made Broadway debut in revival of "Burlesque."

ANDREWS, ANN. Born in Los Angeles, 1895. Appeared on Broadway in "The Hottentot," "The Champion," "The Dark," "The Captive," "The Royal Family," "Dinner at Eight," "De Luxe," and "Reflected Glory."

ANDREWS, TOD. (Formerly Michael Ames). Born in N.Y.C., Nov. 10, 1914. Educated at Washington State College. Stage training at Pasadena Playhouse. Brroadway plays: "Quiet, Please," "My Sister Eileen," "Storm Operation," "Mrs. Kimball Presents," and "That Old Devil."

ANGLIN, MARGARET. Born Ottawa, Canada, April 3, 1876. Educated Loretto Abbey, Toronto, and Convent of the Sacred Heart, Montreal. Made N.Y. debut 1894 in "Shenandoah." Since then her brilliant career included roles in "Mrs. Dane's Defense," "Diplomacy," "The Importance of Being Earnest," "Camille," "The Marriage of Kitty," "Frou-Frou," "The Second Mrs. Tanqueray," "The Great Divide," "The Awakening of Helena Richie," "Antigone," "Green Stockings," such Shakespearian roles as Viola, Katherine, Rosalind and Cleopatra, "Beverly's Balance," "Iphigenia in Tauris," "Electra," "The Woman in Bronze," "Foot-Loose," "A Woman of No Importance," and more recently "Fresh Fields."

ANNABELLA. Born in Paris, France, 1913. Made numerous French films, and appeared on the London and Vienna stages before her debut in Hollywood pictures in 1937. Has appeared on Broadway in "Jacobowsky and the Colonel," and "No Exit."

ARCHER, JOHN. Born in Osceola, Neb., May 8, 1915. Educated at Hollywood High School and Univ. of Southern Calif. Played in many motion pictures before coming to N.Y. for his stage debut in "The Odds on Mrs. Oakley." "One Man Show," "A Place of Our Own," and "The Day Before Spring" followed.

ARCHIBALD, WILLIAM. Born March 7, 1915, in Trinidad, he came to the United States in 1937 and joined the Weidman Dance Group. His first Broadway show was "One for the Money." Since then he has appeared in "Two for the Show," "All in Fun," "Dancing in the Streets," Youman's "Ballet Revue," "Laughing Room Only," and "Concert Varieties." He also wrote the book and lyrics of "Carib Song."

Edith Atwater

Mischa Auer

Ellis Baker

ARTHUR, PHIL. Educated at William and Mary College. Appeared on the road in "The Doughgirls" and "Dream Girl," and played on Broadway in "A Bell for Adano" and "Bathsheba."

ATWATER, EDITH. Born in Chicago, Ill., April 22, 1909. Received theatre apprenticeship at the American Academy. Made Broadway debut in "Brittle Heaven," and has since appeared in "The Masque of Kings," "The Country Wife," "Susan and God," "The Man Who Came to Dinner," "Tomorrow the World," "Deep are the Roots," and "Parlor Story." Also appeared in "State of the Union" on the road.

AUER, MISCHA. Born in St. Petersburg, Russia, Nov. 17, 1905. Educated at Ethical Culture School. Made his Broadway debut 1925 in "The Wild Duck." Other Broadway plays include "Call of Life," "Cyrano de Bergerac," "Magda," and "The Riddle Woman." Went to Hollywood where he appeared in many films. Returned to Broadway for "The Lady Comes Across," and this season appeared in "Lovely Me."

BACLANOVA, OLGA. Born in Moscow, Russia, August 19, 1899. Educated Cherniavsky Institute, Moscow. A product of the Moscow Art Theatre, she made her Broadway debut in 1925 in "Lysistrata." Subsequently appeared in "Carmencita and the Soldier," "Love and Death," and "The Fountain." In 1926 played the Nun in "The Miracle" on tour. Recent appearances include "Grand Hotel," "Twentieth Century," and "Idiot's Delight" on tour, and in N.Y. "$25 an Hour," "Murder at the Vanities," "Mahogany Hall," and "Claudia."

BADIA, LEOPOLD. Born Jan. 2, 1905 in Seville, Spain. Graduated from American Academy of Dramatic Arts. Made Broadway debut in Sept. 1927 in "Speakeasy." Among the many plays in which he has appeared are "Machinal," "Siege," "One Third of a Nation," "The Cradle Will Rock" and "The Big Story." More recently he was seen in "A Bell For Adano," and the revival of "Cyrano de Bergerac."

BAIN, DONALD. Born August 5, 1922 in Liverpool, England. Educated at Winchester and King's College, Cambridge. Since 1944 has played in many London productions and made Broadway debut in "The Importance of Being Earnest." Also seen in "Love For Love."

BAINTER, FAY. Born in Los Angeles, Dec. 7, 1892. Made her Broadway bow in 1912 in "The Rose of Panama." After several seasons of stock at Albany, Des Moines and Toledo, she made her first N.Y. hit in "Arms and the Girl." This was followed by "The Willow Tree," "The Kiss Burglar," "East is West," "The Lady Cristilinda," "The Other Rose," "The Dream Girl," "The Enemy," a revival of "The Two Orphans," "First Love," "Fallen Angels," revivals of "She Stoops to Conquer," "The Beaux Stratagem," "The Admirable Crichton," and "Lysistrata." More recently she appeared in "Jealousy," "For Services Rendered," as Topsy in Players' Club revival of "Uncle Tom's Cabin," "Move On, Sister," "Dodsworth" and "The Next Half Hour." This season played "Ten O'Clock Scholar" on the West Coast.

BAKER, ELLIS. Born Muskegan, Mich., Oct. 26, 1898. Educated at St. Agatha. Made stage debut at age of five in "The Point of View." Supported such stars as Grace George and Otis Skinner. Recent N.Y. appearance in "I Like It Here."

BAKER, FAY. Born in N.Y.C. and educated at Smith College. Had dramatic training with Ouspenskaya and Lee Strasberg. Made Broadway bow in "Danton's Death," and has since appeared in "Dear Octopus," with the Lunts in "The Taming of the Shrew," "Journey to Jerusalem," "Harriet," "Another Love Story," "Violet" and "Wonderful Journey."

BANE, PAULA. Born in Seattle, Wash. Educated at Cornish School of Arts. Received stage training at Seattle Repertory Playhouse. Made her Broadway bow in "Seven Lively Arts." "Call Me Mister" followed.

BANKHEAD, TALLULAH. Born in Huntsville, Ala., Jan. 31, 1902. Received education in Montgomery, Ala., in N.Y.C. and in Washington, D.C. Made N.Y. stage debut in 1918 in "Squab Farm." This was followed by "39 East," "Footloose," "Nice People," "Everyday," "Danger," "Her Temporary Husband," and "The Exciters." In 1923 went to London, where she became the toast of the town. Her London appearances included "The Dancers," "This Marriage," "The Creaking Chair," "Fallen Angels," "The Green Hat," "Scotch Mist," "The Lady of the Camellias," "They Knew What They Wanted," "The Gold Diggers," "The Garden of Eden," "Let Us Be Gay," "Blackmail," "Mud and Treacle," and "Her Cardboard Lover." Returning to the United States in 1930 she made a number of films in Hollywood before re-appearing on Broadway in 1933 in "Forsaking All Others." This was followed by "Dark Victory," "Something Gay," "Reflected Glory," and revivals of "Rain," "The Circle," and "Antony and Cleopatra." Next came "The Little Foxes," "Clash By Night," "The Skin of Our Teeth," and "Foolish Notion." Her recent screen appearances include "Lifeboat" and "A Royal Scandal," and she was seen on the stage this season in "The Eagle Has Two Heads."

BANNERMAN, MARGARET. Born in Toronto, Canada, Dec. 15, 1896. Educated at Mt. St. Vincent, Halifax, N.S. Made her stage debut in London in 1915 in "Tina." Starred in many London productions. then toured New Zealand and Australia, heading her own company. Her first Broadway appearance was in "By Jupiter," followed by "Rebecca," and "The Deep Mrs. Sykes."

Leopold Badia

Fay Baker

James Barton

BARNARD, HENRY. Born in Birmingham, Ala., March 1, 1921. Has appeared on Broadway in "The First Million," "Theatre," "Othello," "Mrs. January and Mr. X," "The Searching Wind," "The Wind is 90," and "Home of the Brave."

BARNES, KEMPSTER. Born July 10, 1923 in Johannesburg, South Africa. Attended college in South Africa, and studied for the stage there under Sheila Munroe. He played with several English stock companies before his first London engagements, and has been with the Donald Wolfit company for the past two years. Made his Broadway debut with this company on Feb. 18, 1947.

BARRY, BOBBY. Born October, 1887 in Brooklyn. Has been in the theatre since childhood. For three years he played George M. Cohan roles on the road, and also toured Australia. More recently he has been seen in "Hellzapoppin," "Sons of Fun," the revival of "He Who Gets Slapped," and this season's revival of "Burlesque."

BARRY, GENE. Born in N.Y.C., June 14, 1919. Educated at New Utrecht High School. Appeared on Broadway in revival of "New Moon," "Rosalinda," "The Merry Widow," "Catherine was Great," and "The Would-Be Gentleman."

BARRY, JOHN. Born in Amsterdam, N.Y., June 13, 1915. Educated at Univ. of Pa., where he sang with the Mask and Wig. Spent two years with the Philadelphia Opera Company. Made Broadway debut in 1945 in "Follow the Girls."

BARRYMORE, DIANA. Born March 3, 1921 in N.Y.C. Daughter of the late John Barrymore and Michael Strange. Educated at the American Academy, and made Broadway debut in 1939 in "The Romantic Mr. Dickens." This was followed by "The Happy Days," and "The Land is Bright." After a two year stay in Hollywood she returned to Broadway in "Rebecca," and was seen this season in "Hidden Horizon."

BARRYMORE, ETHEL. Born in Philadelphia, August 15, 1879. Made N.Y. debut at the Empire Theatre, Jan. 25, 1894, in "The Rivals." Among the many plays she has appeared in are "Captain Jinks of the Horse Marines," "Cousin Kate," "Alice-Sit-By-The-Fire," "Mid-Channel," "The Twelve Pound Look," "A Slice of Life," "Tante," "The Shadow," "Our Mrs. McChesney," "The Lady of the Camellias." "The Off-Chance," "Belinda," "Declassee," "Claire de Lune," "The Constant Wife," "Scarlet Sister Mary," "The Kingdom of God," "The Love Duel," and revivals of "The Second Mrs. Tanqueray," "The School for Scandal," and "Trelawney of the Wells." Her recent Broadway engagements include "An International Incident," "Ghost of Yankee Doodle," "Whiteoaks," "Farm of Three Echoes," "The Corn is Green," "Embezzled Heaven," and she toured in "The Joyous Season." Made several early silent pictures, also "Rasputin and the Empress," "None but the Lonely Heart," "The Circular Staircase," and "The Farmer's Daughter."

BARTENIEFF, GEORGE. Born in Berlin, Germany on Jan. 24, 1933. Made Broadway debut in "The Whole World Over."

BARTON, JAMES. Born Gloucester, N.J., Nov. 1, 1890. Spent his early years in stock companies in Middle West and South. Made his first Broadway appearance in "The Passing Show of 1919." Since then appeared in "The Last Waltz," "The Rose of Stamboul," "Dew Drop Inn," "The Passing Show of 1924," "Artists and Models," "No Foolin'," "Sweet and Low," and on tour in "Burlesque." More recently, "Tobacco Road," and this season "The Iceman Cometh."

BAVIER, FRANCES. Born in N.Y.C., Jan. 14, 1905. Upon leaving American Academy of Dramatic Arts, made her Broadway debut in 1925 in "The Poor Nut." Other Broadway appearances in "Marching Song," "Bitter Stream," "On Borrowed Time," "Native Son," "The Strings, My Lord, Are False," "Kiss and Tell," and "Little A."

BAXTER, ALAN. Born East Cleveland, Ohio, Nov. 19, 1908. Educated Cleveland Heights public schools, Williams College, and Yale Univ. (Dept. of Drama, 1930-32). Appeared on Broadway in "Lone Valley," "Men in White," "Gold Eagle Guy," "Black Pit," "Winged Victory," "Home of the Brave," and "The Voice of the Turtle." Has also played in many motion pictures.

BAXTER, FRANK. Born Bola Cynwyd, Pa., March 25, 1922. Received his stage training at Barter Theatre, Abingdon, Va., and the Neighborhood Playhouse. Has appeared on Broadway in "Janie," revival of "R. U. R.," and "Catherine Was Great."

BAXTER, JANE. Born Sept. 9, 1909 in Brake, Germany. Educated in England, where she studied for the theatre under Italia Conti. After considerable success on the London stage, she made her Broadway debut on March 3, 1947 in "The Importance of Being Earnest."

BAYNE, BEVERLY. Born in Minneapolis, Minn., Nov. 22, 1896. Educated at Hyde Park High School, Chicago. Was famous star in silent pictures with the old Essanay and Metro film companies. Has appeared on Broadway in "Gala Night," "Piper Paid," "Claudia," "I Like It Here," and "Loco."

BEAL, JOHN. Born in Joplin, Mo., Aug. 13, 1909. Educated Joplin High School and Univ. of Pa. Studied for stage with Jasper Deeter at the Hedgerow Theatre. Made his first appearance on the N.Y. stage as a page in "Give Me Yesterday" in 1931. Subsequently appeared in "Wild Waves," "Another Language," "She Loves Me Not," "Russet Mantle," "Soliloquy," "Miss Swan Expects," and "Liberty Jones." Returned to Broadway after a session in Hollywood and the U.S. Army in "The Voice of the Turtle."

Rolly Beck

Marion Bell

Thomas Beck

BEAL, ROYAL. Born in Brookline, Mass., and educated at Harvard. He has appeared in "Take A Chance," "Elizabeth the Queen," "All That Glitters," "Page Miss Glory," "Noah," "Boy Meets Girl," "The Lady Has a Heart," "Susannah and the Elders," "Without Love," "Kiss and Tell," and "Woman Bites Dog." His most recent appearance was in "Parlor Story."

BEATON, CECIL. Born in London, England, on Jan. 14, 1904. Educated at Harrow and Cambridge. He is best known as an artist and photographer, but this season made his Broadway debut as an actor in "Lady Windemere's Fan," for which production he also designed the costumes and scenery.

BECK, ROLLY. Born Feb. 21, 1918 in Waterbury, Conn. Played in vaudeville, burlesque and television before making Broadway debut in this season's revival of "The Front Page."

BECK, THOMAS. Born Dec. 28, 1909 in N.Y.C. Educated at Johns Hopkins Univ. Made Broadway debut in 1932 in "Mademoiselle," and was also seen in "Her Majesty, The Widow," as well as in numerous films. Returned to Broadway in "Temper The Wind."

BEECHER, JANET. Born in Jefferson City, Mo., Oct. 21, 1884. Made her N.Y. debut as a walk-on in 1904 in "The Two Orphans." Among her many successes were "The Concert," "The Lottery Man," "The Purple Road," "The Great Adventure," "Fair and Warmer," "Call a Doctor," "A Bill of Divorcement," "Courage," and "Men Must Fight." In 1932 she deserted Broadway for Hollywood, where she remained for twelve years, appearing in many films. Since her return, played in "Slightly Scandalous" and "The Late George Apley."

BEGLEY, ED. Born March 25, 1901 in Hartford, Conn. Played in fairs, carnivals, vaudeville before making his Broadway debut in 1943 in "Land of Fame," followed by "Pretty Little Parlor" and "Get Away, Old Man." This season he was seen in "All My Sons."

BEL GEDDES, BARBARA. Born in N.Y.C., Oct. 31, 1923. Her first stage role was as a walk-on in "School for Scandal" with Ethel Barrymore at the Clinton (Conn.) Playhouse. Made her Broadway bow in "Out of the Frying Pan." Since then has appeared in "Little Darling," "Nine Girls," "Mrs. January and Mr. X" and "Deep are the Roots."

BELL, MARION. Studied singing in Rome, and made first stage appearance in her native Calif. with the San Francisco Opera Co. "Brigadoon" marked her Broadway bow.

BELLAMY, RALPH. Born in Chicago, Ill., June 17, 1904. Made his Broadway debut in 1929 in "Town Boy." This was followed by "Roadside" which led him to Hollywood where he remained, making pictures from 1930 until 1943 when he returned to Broadway to act in "Tomorrow the World." Since then he played in "State of the Union."

BELLMORE, BERTHA. Born in Manchester, England, Dec. 20, 1882. Made her debut in America in 1910 with the Ben Greet Players. Played Portia in William Faversham's production of "The Merchant of Venice." Was in "Ziegfeld Follies" of '27 and '28, and in Ziegfeld's "Show Boat." Recent appearances include "Heart of a City," "By Jupiter," "Rhapsody," and "Antigone."

BELLOWS, JEAN. Born in N.Y.C., where she attended Friends' Seminary and The Lenox School. Made Broadway debut in 1934 in "Small Miracle." Since then has been seen in "New Faces of 1936," "I Am My Youth," "Three's a Family," "Hand in Glove" and "Happy Birthday."

BEN-AMI, JACOB. Born in 1890 in Minsk, Russia. Is well known on both the Yiddish and English speaking stage. Has appeared on Broadway in "Samson and Delilah," "Johannes Kreisler," "The Failures," "Welded," "Man and the Masses," the revival of "Diplomacy," and with Eva Le Gallienne in "The Sea Gull," "The Cherry Orchard," "The Living Corpse," "Romeo and Juliet," and "Camille." More recently appeared in "A Ship Comes In" and "A Flag is Born."

BENNETT, PETER. Born Sept. 17, 1917 in London, and educated at Malvern College. Studied for the theatre at the Royal Academy of Dramatic Art, and played many roles on the London stage. Made Broadway bow in "Love Goes to Press."

BERGHOF, HERBERT. Born Sept. 13, 1909 in Vienna, where he received his education. Was a leading actor for many years in Vienna, Berlin, and in the Salzburg Festivals for Max Reinhardt. Made Broadway debut in 1942 in "Nathan the Wise." Since then appeared in "The Russian People," "Innocent Voyage," "Jacobowsky and the Colonel," "The Man Who Had All the Luck," "Beggars are Coming to Town," "Temper the Wind" and "The Whole World Over."

BERGMAN, INGRID. Born August 29, 1917 in Stockholm, Sweden, where she studied at the Royal Dramatic Theatre. She appeared both on stage and screen in her native land before coming to Hollywood in 1939. Made her Broadway debut in April 1940 in a revival of "Liliom" with Burgess Meredith. After a conspicuous success in the films she returned to the New York stage in "Joan of Lorraine."

BERGNER, ELISABETH. Born in Vienna, August 22, 1900. Began stage career at fourteen. Toured with a Shakespearian company in Germany and Austria, and later became one of Max Reinhardt's greatest stars. In 1934 went to England, where she starred in such films as "Catherine the Great," "Escape Me Never," "As You Like It,"

Jean Bellows

George Blackwood

Sheila Bond

and "Dreaming Lips." Her Broadway appearances were in "Escape Me Never," "The Two Mrs. Carrolls," and "The Duchess of Malfi."

BEST, PAUL. Born in Berlin, Germany, Aug. 30, 1908. His Broadway appearances include "La Vie Parisienne," "Rosalinda," "The Merry Widow," "Firebrand of Florence," "The Day Before Spring," and "Sweethearts."

BETTGER, LYLE. Born Feb. 13, 1915. Studied at the American Academy, and made Broadway debut in 1937 in "Brother Rat." Since then has been seen in "Dance Night," "The Flying Gerardos," "The Moon Is Down," "All for All," "The Eve of St. Mark," "Oh, Brother," and "John Loves Mary."

BICKLEY, TONY. Born in Philadelphia, and educated at Wesleyan Univ. For three years did repertory work at the Hedgerow Theatre before making Broadway debut in 1936 in "Ten Million Ghosts." Since then has appeared in "My Sister Eileen," "Without Love," and "Made in Heaven."

BIRCH, PETER. Born in N.Y.C., Dec. 11, 1922. Made his debut as a dancer with the Fokine Ballet. "One Touch of Venus," "Dream With Music," and "Carousel" are his Broadway engagements.

BISHOP, RICHARD. Born in Hartford, Conn., April 27, 1898. Educated at Hartford Public School. Broadway plays include "Missouri Legend," "An International Incident," "Sweet Mystery of Life," "One Good Year," "Where Do We Go From Here?," "Key Largo," and "I Remember Mama."

BLACKMER, SIDNEY. Born in Salisbury, N.C., July 13, 1894. Educated at Warrenton High School, and Univ. of N. C. Appeared in stock and on the road before making Broadway debut in 1917 in "The Morris Dance." Other Plays include "Not So Long Ago," "The Mountain Man," "The Thirteenth Chair," "The Love Child," "The Moon-Flower," "Quarantine," "The Carolinian," "Scaramouche," "Love In A Mist," "Trimmed in Scarlet," "39 East," "The Springboard," "Mima," "The Sandy Hooker," "Chicken Every Sunday" and "Round Trip." He also appeared extensively in the films, both silent and talking. Most recent Broadway engagements were in "Wonderful Journey" and "Portrait in Black."

BLACKWOOD, GEORGE. Born July 17, 1904 in Dalton, Ohio. Made Broadway debut in 1920 in "Aphrodite." Among the many plays in which he has appeared are "Claire de Lune," "The Yellow Jacket," "Sweet Nell of Old Drury," "Rose Briar," "Elizabeth the Queen," "So Many Paths," and "Over 21."

BLAKELY, GENE. Born Osceola, Iowa, June 8, 1922. Educated at Univ. of Wis. Toured in "The Eve of St. Mark," and "Janie." Made Broadway debut in "Brighten the Corner."

BLISS, HELENA. Born in St. Louis, Mo., Dec. 31, 1919. Educated at Hosmer Hall and Washington Univ. Plays on Broadway: "Very Warm for May," "Du Barry Was a Lady," "Song of Norway," and "Gypsy Lady."

BOLAND, MARY. Born in Philadelphia, Jan. 28, 1885. Educated at Sacred Convent in Detroit. Received her stage training in stock. Was John Drew's leading lady in "Inconstant George," "Smith," "The Single Man," "The Perplexed Husband," "The Will," "The Tyranny of Tears," and "Much Ado About Nothing." Her important appearances on Broadway include "My Lady's Dress," "Clarence," "The Torch-Bearers," "Meet the Wife," "Cradle Snatchers," "Women Go On Forever," "Ada Beats the Drum," "The Vinegar Tree," and more recently "Jubilee," and the Theatre Guild revival of "The Rivals." This season she toured in "The Greatest of These."

BOLGER, RAY. Born in Dorchester, Mass., Jan. 10, 1906. Made Broadway bow in 1926 in "The Merry World." Followed by "A Night in Paris," "The Passing Show of 1926" (on tour), "Heads Up," "George White's Scandals of 1931," "Life Begins at 8:40," "On Your Toes," "Keep Off the Grass," and "Three to Make Ready."

BOLSTER, ANITA. Born in Glenlohane, Ireland, Aug. 28, 1900. Received her stage training at the Abbey Theatre, Dublin. Made her Broadway bow in 1939 in "Where There's A Will." "Lady in Waiting" followed, and a session in Hollywood. Returned to Broadway for "Pygmalion."

BOND, SHEILA. Born in N.Y.C., March 16, 1928. Studied for the theatre since age of four, and made Broadway debut in 1942 in "Let Freedom Sing." Since then appeared in "Allah Be Praised," "Artists and Models," and "Street Scene."

BOOTH, SHIRLEY. Born in N.Y.C. Broadway plays include "Bye, Bye, Baby," "Laff That Off," "The War Song," "Too Many Heroes," "Three Men on a Horse," "Excursion," "The Philadelphia Story," "My Sister Eileen," "Hollywood Pinafore," and "Land's End."

BORDONI, IRENE. Born in Paris, France, Jan. 16, 1895. First N.Y. stage appearance in 1912 in "The First Affair." This was followed by "Broadway to Paris," "Miss Information," "Hitchy-Koo, 1918," "Sleeping Partners," "As You Were," "The French Doll," "Little Miss Bluebeard," "Naughty Cinderella," "Paris," and more recently "Great Lady," and "Louisiana Purchase."

BOREL, LOUIS. Born Oct. 6, 1906 in Amsterdam, Holland. Appeared on the stage in Holland, Germany, and England before his first appearance in N.Y.C. with Helen Hayes in "Candle in the Wind." He has both acted and written in Hollywood, and returned to Broadway this season in "Made in Heaven."

Kenny Bowers

Billie Burke

J. Edward Bromberg

BOSTWICK, HAROLD. Born in Brooklyn, N.Y. Before the war was a featured pianist with Leo Reisman's orchestra. Toured with Mae West in "Come on Up," and made Broadway debut in revival of "Burlesque."

BOURNEUF, PHILIP. Has appeared on Broadway in "Dead End," "Two Bouquets," "On The Rocks," "One for the Money," "Native Son," "The Rivals," "Moon Vine," "Winged Victory" and "Flamingo Road." This season he appeared with A.R.T. and was seen in "Henry VIII," "What Every Woman Knows," "Androcles and the Lion," "Yellow Jack," and "Alice in Wonderland."

BOWERS, KENNY. Born in Jersey City, N.J., March 10, 1923. Educated at Jersey City Grammar and Junior High. Has appeared on Broadway in "Best Foot Forward," and "Annie Get Your Gun."

BOYD, SYDNEY. Born in Glasgow, Scotland, Feb. 25, 1901. Educated at Battle Creek High School. Has appeared in vaudeville, minstrel, night clubs, and on the radio. "Are You With It?" marked his Broadway debut.

BOYLAN, MARY. Born in Plattsburg, N.Y. Educated at Mount Holyoke College. Received stage training at Barter Theatre. Made Broadway bow 1938 in "Dance Night." This was followed by "Susanna and the Elders," "The Walrus and the Carpenter," the revival of "Our Town," and "Live Life Again."

BRAHAM, HORACE. Born London, July 29, 1896. Educated City of London School. Made N.Y. debut 1914 as Lentulus in "Androcles and the Lion." His N.Y. appearances include "The Shatter'd Lamp," "Too Many Boats," the Le Gallienne revival of "L'Aiglon," "Journey to Jerusalem," "Antigone," and "Bathsheba."

BRAMLEY, RAYMOND. Born in Cleveland, Ohio. Educated at Shenandoah College. Studied for the theatre at American Academy and made Broadway debut in 1926 in "Not Herbert." Since then has been seen in "East Wind," "Dangerous Corner," "Whatever Goes Up," "Sleep No More," and "Hear That Trumpet."

BRANDO, MARLON. Born April 3, 1924. Served his apprenticeship at the New School of Social Research. Made Broadway debut Oct. 19, 1944 in "I Remember Mama." Since then has appeared in "Truckline Cafe," the Cornell revival of "Candida," and "A Flag Is Born."

BRANDT, MARTIN. Born May 7, 1908 in Germany, and educated on the continent. Made Broadway debut in "Men in Shadow," and this season was seen in "Temper the Wind."

BRENT, ROMNEY. Born in Saltillo, Mexico, Jan. 26, 1902. Educated in Mexico, Paris, London and Brussels. Made N.Y. debut in Sept. 1921 in "He Who Gets Slapped." Among the many plays in which he has appeared on the N.Y. stage are "The Garrick Gaieties," "The Simpleton of the Unexpected Isles," "The Warrior's Husband," "The Deep Mrs. Sykes," "The Winter's Tale," and "Joan of Lorraine."

BRIAN, DONALD. Born St. John's, Newfoundland, Feb. 17, 1877. Made first N.Y. appearance 1899 in "On The Wabash." His important appearances on Broadway include "Little Johnny Jones," "Forty-Five Minutes from Broadway," "The Merry Widow," "The Dollar Princess," "The Siren," "The Marriage Market," "The Girl from Utah," "Sybil," "Her Regiment," "The Girl Behind the Gun," "Buddies," and more recently "Fly Away Home," and "Very Warm for May."

BRISSON, CARL. Born Copenhagen, Denmark, Dec. 24, 1895. Only N.Y. legitimate appearance in 1936 in "Forbidden Melody." Recently has had great success as a night club entertainer.

BROMBERG, J. EDWARD. Born Temesvar, Hungary, Dec. 25, 1904. Studied under Leo Bulgakov, and made N.Y. debut at Provincetown Theatre in 1926 in "Princess Turandot." From 1927 to 1930 supported Eva Le Gallienne in Civic Repertory Theatre, appearing in many roles. Later was seen in "The Inspector-General," "The House of Connelly," "Night Over Taos," "Men in White," "Both Your Houses," "Gold Eagle Guy," and "Awake and Sing." After a session in Hollywood he returned to the Broadway stage in "Toplitsky of Notre Dame."

BROOKE, RALPH. Born N.Y.C. May 22, 1920. Educated at Columbia. Studied acting with Max Reinhardt. Appeared on Broadway in the Olivier-Leigh production of "Romeo and Juliet," "All in Favor," and "A Sound of Hunting."

BROOKS, DAVID. Born Sept. 24, 1917 in Portland, Ore. Educated at Univ. of Washington, and Curtis Institute of Music. Made Broadway debut in Oct. 1944 in "Bloomer Girl," and was seen this season in "Brigadoon."

BROOKS, GERALDINE (Stroock). Born N.Y.C., Oct. 29, 1925. Studied for the theatre at the Neighborhood Playhouse and American Academy. Made debut on Broadway in "Follow the Girls" and more recently was seen in "The Winter's Tale."

BROOKS, LAWRENCE. Born in Westbrook, Maine, Aug. 7, 1915. Educated at Westbrook High School. Received his stage training with the Portland, Maine, Players. Made first appearance on Broadway in "Song of Norway."

BROTHERSON, ERIC. Born in Chicago, Ill., May 10, 1911. Educated Univ. of Wisconsin. Made his Broadway debut 1937 in "Between the Devil." Other appearances include "Set to Music," "Lady in the Dark," and "My Dear Public."

BROWN, JOE E. Born Holgate, Ohio, July 28, 1892. Started theatrical career as a child actor,

Donald Buka

Sarah Burton

John Buckmaster

and for a time was a professional baseball player. Later appeared in road companies of "Listen Lester," and made first N.Y. appearance in 1920 in "Jim Jam Jems." Also appeared in "The Greenwich Village Follies," "Betty Lee," "Captain Jinks," "Twinkle, Twinkle," "Elmer the Great," "Square Crooks," and "Shore Leave." Since 1928 appeared frequently in the films. Returned to stage to play on road in "Harvey."

BROWN, PAMELA. In recent years has appeared with great success on the London stage, in roles varying from "Claudia" to Goneril in "King Lear." Made her Broadway debut this season in "The Importance of Being Earnest" and "Love for Love."

BRUCE, BETTY. Born in N.Y.C., May 2, 1921. Educated at the Professional Children's School. As a child, danced in the Metropolitan Opera Ballet. Appeared on Broadway in "The Boys from Syracuse," "Keep Off the Grass," "High Kickers," "Something for the Boys," and "Up in Central Park."

BRUNING, FRANCESCA. Born Miles City, Mont., March 13, 1907. Studied for the stage in Paris and New York. First Broadway appearance in 1928 with Mrs. Fiske in "The Merry Wives of Windsor." Since then has been seen in "A Month in the Country," "One Sunday Afternoon," "Amourette," "Remember the Day," "Men in White," "Escape This Night," "Bright Rebel," and "Junior Miss."

BRUNS, MONA. Born in St. Louis, Mo., and educated at St. Mary's Convent, Belleville, Ill. Made her debut on Broadway 1918 in "Chin Chin." More recently has appeared in "Wednesday's Child," "Chicken Every Sunday," and "Born Yesterday."

BRYANT, NANA. Born in Cincinnati, Ohio. Appeared in N.Y. in "The Firebrand," "The Wild Rose," "The Circus Princess," "A Connecticut Yankee," "The First Apple," and more recently "Marriage is for Single People."

BUCKMASTER, JOHN. Born Frinton-on-sea, Essex, England, July 18, 1915. Educated at Eton College. First appeared on the stage in London, and made N.Y.C. debut in 1936 in "Call It a Day," followed by "Oscar Wilde," in which he played the role of Lord Alfred Douglas. Scored considerable success as a night club entertainer, and returned to Broadway this season in "Lady Windermere's Fan."

BUKA, DONALD. Born in Cleveland, Ohio, 1921. Discovered by the Lunts when he was a drama student at Carnegie Tech. Toured a full season with the Lunts, then played a minor role in the Maurice Evans-Helen Hayes production of "Twelfth Night." Replaced Richard Waring opposite Ethel Barrymore in "The Corn is Green." Since then has been seen in "Bright Boy," "Helen Goes to Troy," "Sophie," and "Live Life Again."

BULOFF, JOSEPH. Born in Russia in 1901. Made N.Y. debut in "Don't Look Now." Other Broadway appearances: "Call Me Ziggy," "To Quito and Back," "The Man from Cairo," "Morning Star," "Spring Again," "My Sister Eileen," "Oklahoma," and "The Whole World Over."

BURKE, BILLIE. Born Washington, D.C., Aug. 7, 1885. First stage appearance was in England in 1903 in "The School Girl." Made N.Y. debut opposite John Drew in "My Wife" in 1907. First starred in "Love Watches," and later appeared in "Mrs. Dot," "The Runaway," "The 'Mind-the-Paint' Girl," "The Amazons," "The Land of Promise," "Jerry," "The Intimate Strangers," "Rose Briar," "The Marquise," "The Happy Husband," "Family Affairs," and "The Truth Game." First appeared in silent films in 1916, and since 1936 has been seen in many pictures. More recently was seen on Broadway in "This Rock," and "Mrs. January and Mr. X," and toured this season in "Accidentally Yours."

BURKE, GEORGIA. Born in Atlanta, Ga., Feb. 27, 1908. Educated at Claflin University of Orangeburg, S.C. Began her stage career in Lew Leslie's first edition of "Blackbirds." Appearances followed in "Five-Star Final," "Savage Rhythm," "In Abraham's Bosom," "Old Man Satan," "They Shall Not Die," "Mamba's Daughter," "Cabin in the Sky," "No Time for Comedy," "Sun Field," "Decision," and "Anna Lucasta."

BURKE, MAURICE. Born in Hartford, Conn., April 13, 1902. Made Broadway appearances in "Ladies of Creation," "Helena's Boys," "The Marquise," "Kiss the Boys Goodbye," "In Time to Come," "The Doughgirls," and "Up in Central Park."

BURKE, WALTER. Appeared on N.Y. stage in "The Eve of St. Mark," "The World's Full of Girls," "Sadie Thompson," and "Up in Central Park."

BURR, ANNE. Born in Boston, Mass., June 10, 1920. First N.Y. appearance was in "Plan M." This was followed by "Native Son," "Dark Eyes," "Lovers and Friends," "While the Sun Shines," and "The Hasty Heart." This season she was seen in the Experimental Theatre production of "O'Daniel."

BURTON, SARAH. Born March 20, 1912 in London, where she first appeared on the stage. Made her N.Y. debut in 1936 in "Horse Eats Hat," and since then has been seen in "Set to Music," "What a Life," "A Kiss for Cinderella," and this season in "Made in Heaven."

BUSLEY, JESSIE. Born Albany, N.Y., March 10, 1869. First appeared with R. B. Mantell's Co. and made first N.Y. success in "The Bells of Haslemere," in 1894. Later she played in "Charley's

Red Buttons

Jeanne Cagney

Bill Callahan

Aunt," "The New Boy," "The Sporting Duchess," "Hearts are Trumps," "The Girl With the Green Eyes," "Little Mary," "Mice and Men," "The Admirable Crichton," "Mrs. Leffingwell's Boots," "The Painful Predicament of Sherlock Holmes." For a time she was seen in vaudeville, and later appeared in "In The Bishop's Carriage," "Beverly of Graustark," "Old Heidelberg," "Half a Husband," "Pollyanna," "Daisy Mayme," "The Bride the Sun Shines on" and "Alien Corn." More recently she appeared in "The Great Waltz," "First Lady," "The Women," "The Birds Stop Singing," "Over 21," and "The Rich Full Life."

BUTLER, JOHN. Born in Greenwood, Miss., Sept. 29, 1920. Educated at Univ. of Miss. Studied dancing with Martha Graham and Eugene Loring. Appeared on Broadway in "On the Town," "Hollywood Pinafore," and "Oklahoma."

BUTTONS, RED. Born Feb. 5, 1919 in N.Y.C. Went into vaudeville at age of 11, and appeared as a cafe entertainer and in burlesque before making his debut in "The Admiral Takes a Wife." Since then has been seen in "Vickie," "Wine, Women and Song" and "Winged Victory." This season he appeared in "Barefoot Boy With Cheek."

BYRD, SAM. Born Jan. 18, 1908 in Mt. Olive, N. C. Studied for the stage at the Goodman Memorial Theatre in Chicago. Made Broadway bow in 1929 in "The House of Mander." Since then has been seen in "The Novice and the Duke," "Street Scene," "Cafe," "Tobacco Road," "White Man," and "Of Mice and Men."

CADELL, JEAN. Born in Edinburgh, Scotland, Sept. 13, 1884. Educated in Paris and Edinburgh. First played in repertory companies in England where she achieved great success. Made N.Y. bow in 1911 in "Bunty Pulls the Strings." She returned to this country in 1926 and played in "At Mrs. Beam's." More recently New Yorkers have seen her in "Spring Meeting" and "The Importance of Being Earnest."

CAGNEY, JEANNE. Born in New York City, March 25, 1919. Educated at Hunter College, and received stage training at Pasadena Playhouse. Made N.Y. debut in 1943 in "I'll Take the High Road." Since then she has been seen in "The Streets are Guarded," "A Place of Our Own," and "The Iceman Cometh."

CAHILL, LILY. Born in Texas, 1891. She made first stage appearance in 1909 in support of Mrs. Leslie Carter in "Vasta Hearne." Later appeared in "Two Women," "The Concert," "Joseph and his Brethern," "Under Cover," "The Melody of Youth," "Rosamund," "Over Here," "The Purple Mask," "Opportunity," "So This is London," "Lovely Lady," "Caprice," "The Tyrant," "As Husbands Go," "Chrysalis," "Alien Corn," "Women Kind," "And Be My Love," "Reunion in Vienna," "Rain from Heaven," "First Lady," and "Life With Father."

CALHERN, LOUIS. Born N.Y.C., Feb. 19, 1895. Appeared first as a child actor, and in 1914 went into stock. Played with Margaret Anglin, and served in first world war. Reappeared in N.Y.C. in 1922 in "The White Peacock," and later appeared in "The Czarina," "Roger Bloomer," "The Song and Dance Man," "Cobra," "In a Garden," "Hedda Gabler," "The Woman Disputed," "Up the Line," "A Distant Drum," "The Love Duel," "The Tyrant," "Give Me Yesterday," "Brief Moment," "Dinner at Eight," "Birthday," "Agatha Calling," "Hell Freezes Over," and "Robin Landing." More recently he has appeared in "Life With Father," "The Great Big Doorstep," "Jacobowsky and the Colonel," and "The Magnificent Yankee."

CALL, JOHN. Born in Philadelphia, Nov. 3, 1915. Educated at Univ. of Penn. Theatre apprenticeship in Toy Theatre of Atlantic City. N.Y. appearances in "Father Malachy's Miracle," "Merchant of Yonkers," "As You Like It," "Be So Kindly," "But for the Grace of God," "The Flying Gerardos," "So Proudly We Hail," "Bet Your Life," and "Bloomer Girl."

CALLAHAN, BILL. Born in N.Y.C., Aug. 23, 1926. Educated at Barnard School for Boys, Fordham Prep School, and Fordham Univ. Made his Broadway debut Jan. 7, 1943 in "Something for the Boys." Appearances in "Mexican Hayride" and "Call Me Mister" followed.

CALVIN, HENRY. Born May 25, 1918 in Dallas, Texas. Was bass soloist at the Radio City Music Hall, and appeared on concert and operetta stages throughout the country. Appeared on Broadway this season in "The Chocolate Soldier."

CAMP, RICHARD. Born in Perry, Iowa, April 11, 1923. Edcated at Univ. of Iowa and Drake Univ. Appeared on Broadway in "Junior Miss," "Three's a Family," "Men to the Sea," "Little Women," and "This, Too, Shall Pass."

CANNON, MAUREEN. Born in Chicago, Ill., Dec. 3, 1926. Only Broadway appearances in "Best Foot Forward," and "Up in Central Park." Sang the leading roles of "Irene," "No, No, Nanette," and "Hit the Deck," with the St. Louis Municipal Opera Co.

CANTOR, EDDIE. Born in N.Y.C., Jan. 31, 1892. Made first stage appearance in vaudeville in 1907, and later appeared in "Not Likely," "Canary Cottage," "The Midnight Revue," "The Ziegfeld Follies" 1917-1919, "Broadway Brevities of 1920," "Make it Snappy," "Follies of 1927," "Kid Boots," "Whoopee," and more recently in "Banjo Eyes." In recent years has devoted most of his time to radio.

CARGILL, JUDITH. Born in Milwaukee, Wisc. Educated at Milwaukee Downer College, and studied for the stage at American Academy. After apprenticeship in summer stock, she made Broad-

Henry Calvin

Judith Cargill

Richard Camp

way debut in 1943 in "Pillar to Post." She toured with the USO circuit during the war, and was seen this season in "Years Ago."

CARR, ANTHONY. Born in Reading, Pa., Feb. 6, 1924. Educated at Albright College. Received his stage training in summer stock. Made his Broadway debut in "Dear Ruth."

CARROLL, ALBERT. Born in Chicago in 1898. First professional appearance was with Ben Greet Players in Shakespearian repertoire. First role on Broadway was in "39 East." Then followed ten years with the Neighborhood Playhouse in plays, ballets, and several editions of "The Grand Street Follies." Also appeared with Theatre Guild in "Peer Gynt," "Morn to Midnight," "Taming of the Shrew," and "Garrick Gaieties." Other N.Y. appearances include "Ziegfeld Follies," "Americana," "As Thousands Cheer," Leslie Howard's "Hamlet," and "Seven Lively Arts."

CARROLL, LEO G. Born in Weedon, England, 1892. Made stage debut 1911 as a walk-on in "The Prisoner of Zenda." Came to America twenty years ago and made N.Y. debut with Noel Coward in "The Vortex." Since then appeared in "The Constant Nymph," "The Perfect Alibi," "The Green Bay Tree," "Petticoat Fever," "The Mask of Kings," "The Two Bouquets," "Angel Street," and "The Late George Apley."

CARSON, FRANCES. Born in Philadelphia, April 1, 1895. Received her stage training in stock in Ottawa. Made N.Y. debut in 1914 in "Poor Little Thing." Then played leads in "The Bad Man," "The White Feather," and "The Hottentot." Went to London where she had great success for the past twenty years. Returned to Broadway in 1944 in "Slightly Scandalous," and "The Visitor."

CASTO, JEAN. Born in Boston, Mass. Studied at American Academy of Dramatic Arts. N.Y. appearances in "Three Men on a Horse," "All That Glitters," "Pal Joey," "By Jupiter," "Decision," and "Carousel."

CHALKLEY, ANN. Born April 26, 1922 in London. Went to finishing schools in Oslo and Paris, and studied for the theatre in London. Made debut on N.Y. stage on Feb. 18, 1947 with the Donald Wolfit Co.

CHALMERS, THOMAS. Sang leading roles at the Metropolitan Opera Company for several seasons before making his first appearance on Broadway as a legitimate actor. Has appeared on the N.Y. stage in "The Wild Duck," "Beyond the Horizon," "Mourning Becomes Electra," the Players Club revival of "Uncle Tom's Cabin," "Outward Bound," and "Antony and Cleopatra." More recently was seen in the G.I. "Hamlet," and in "Bathsheba."

CHASE, ILKA. Born in N.Y.C., 1900. First N.Y. stage role in "The Red Falcon." Among the other plays in which she has appeared are "Shall We Join the Ladies?," "Antonia," "Embers," "The Happy Husband," "The Animal Kingdom," "Forsaking All Others," "Days Without End," "While Parents Sleep," "Wife Insurance," "Small Miracle," "Revenge With Music," "Keep Off the Grass," "Beverly Hills," "The Women," and "In Bed We Cry."

CHASE, STEPHEN. Born in Huntington, L.I., N.Y., April 11, 1902. Educated at Loomis School, Windsor, Conn. Until 1941 appeared on the stage as Alden Chase. Among his many appearances are "Wooden Kimono," "The Silver Cord," "Zeppelin," "People on the Hill," "Reflected Glory," "Uncle Harry," and "Strange Fruit."

CHATTERTON, RUTH. Born in N.Y.C., Dec. 24, 1893. Made first appearance on stage in stock in Washington in 1909. N.Y. debut in 1911 in "The Great Name," and since then has appeared in "Standing Pat," "The Rainbow," "Daddy Long Legs," "Frederic Le Maitre," "Come Out of the Kitchen," "A Bit o' Love," "Perkins," "A Marriage of Convenience," "Moonlight and Honeysuckle," "Mary Rose," "La Tendresse," "The Changlings," "The Magnolia Lady," "The Little Minister," "The Man With the Load of Mischief" and "The Devil's Plum Tree." After a long session in Hollywood returned to stage in "West of Broadway," on the road. This was followed by a long tour of "Private Lives." "Second Best Bed" was her most recent N.Y. appearance.

CHEVALIER, MAURICE. Born Sept. 12, 1893 in Paris, France. After great success in Paris, he was first seen in 1928 in N.Y.C. at the New Amsterdam Roof. This was followed by a highly successful venture in American films. In 1934 he made his first N.Y. appearance in a one man show. He returned to Broadway this season and scored a great hit in his one man show at the Henry Miller Theatre.

CHISHOLM, ROBERT. Born Melbourne, Australia, April 18, 1898. Received his stage training at Royal Academy of Music, London. Made his Broadway debut in "Golden Dawn." Since then, New Yorkers have seen him in "Sweet Adeline," "Luana," "Nina Rosa," "The Two Bouquets," "Higher and Higher," "Knights of Song," "Without Love," the revivals of "A Connecticut Yankee" and "The Merry Widow." His more recent appearances were in "On The Town," "Billion Dollar Baby," and "Park Avenue."

CHRISTI, VITO. Born in Philadelphia, Dec. 28, 1924. Educated at Central School for Boys, Philadelphia. Received his stage training with Neighborhood Players and in stock at Plymouth, Mass. Made first Broadway appearance in "Hickory Stick," followed by "Pick-Up-Girl," "The Tempest," and "The Rugged Path."

Ina Claire

Leo Coleman

Marion Colby

CHRISTIANS, MADY. Born Vienna, Austria, Jan. 19, 1900. Before coming to this country achieved fame in many of Max Reinhardt's productions. Made her N.Y. stage debut in "The Divine Drudge." Since then has appeared in Orson Welles' production of "Heartbreak House," Maurice Evans' productions of "Hamlet" and "Henry IV," "The Lady Who Came to Stay," "Watch on the Rhine," "I Remember Mama," and "Message for Margaret."

CHRISTIE, AUDREY. Born in Chicago, Ill., June 27, 1911. Educated at Yates Grammar School and Lake View High School in that city. Her Broadway plays number "Follow Thru," "Sweet and Low," "Sailor, Beware," "Sons of Guns," "The Women," "I Married an Angel," "Banjo Eyes," "Without Love," "The Voice of the Turtle," and "The Duchess Misbehaves."

CLAIRE, INA. Born Washington, D.C., Oct. 15, 1895. Educated Holy Cross Academy. First stage appearance was in vaudeville in 1907. Later appeared in "Jumping Jupiter," "The Quaker Girl," "The Honeymoon Express," "Lady Luxury," "The Follies" of 1915 and 1916, "Polly With a Past," "The Gold Diggers," "Bluebeard's Eighth Wife," "The Awful Truth," "Grounds for Divorce," "The Last of Mrs. Cheyney," "Our Betters," "Biography," "Ode to Liberty," "Love is not so Simple," "Barchester Towers," "Once is Enough," and "The Talley Method." She returned to Broadway this season in "The Fatal Weakness."

CLANTON, RALPH. Born in Fresno, Calif., Sept. 11, 1914. Received his stage training at Pasadena Community Playhouse. Made Broadway appearances in "Victory Belles," Evans' production of "Macbeth," George Colouris' production of "Richard III," "A Strange Play," "Othello," with Paul Robeson, "Lute Song," and "Cyrano de Bergerac."

CLARISSA. Born in Colorado, 1924. Appeared on Broadway in "Three Waltzes," "Something for the Boys," and a revival of "The Desert Song."

CLARK, BOBBY. Born in Springfield, Ohio, June 16, 1888. With his partner, Paul Mc Cullough, appeared for years in vaudeville. Made his first N.Y. appearance at Madison Square Garden with Ringling Bros. Circus in 1905. New Yorkers have seen him in "The Music Box Revue" (1922), "The Ramblers," "Strike Up the Band," "Here Goes the Bride," "Walk a Little Faster," "Thumbs Up" and "Ziegfeld Follies." More recently he has appeared in "Streets of Paris," the Players Club revival of "Love for Love," "All Men are Alike," the Theatre Guild's revival of "The Rivals," "Star and Garter," "Mexican Hayride," "The Would-Be Gentleman," and "Sweethearts."

CLARK, DORT. Born Oct. 1, 1917 in Wellington, Kan. Graduated from Kansas State Teacher's College, and first appeared on stage in stock in Erie, Pa. Made Broadway bow in 1942 in "Sweet Charity," and since then has been seen in "The First Million," "Lower North," "Snafu," and "Happy Birthday."

CLARK, KENDALL. First appeared on stage in support of Eva Le Gallienne in "L'Aiglon" and "Camille." Since then has been seen in "End of Summer," "Ghost of Yankee Doodle," "The Fifth Column," "George Washington Slept Here," "Home of the Brave," and "Eagle Has Two Heads."

CLARK, ROGER. Born in Hartford, Conn., and educated at Dartmouth. Made Broadway bow as walk-on in "The Man From Cairo." Since then has been seen in "Kiss the Boys Goodbye," "The Man Who Killed Lincoln," "Alice in Arms," and the revival of "The Front Page."

CLARK, WALLIS. Born in England March 2, 1888. First appeared on stage in that country as a member of the Sarah Thorne stock co. His N.Y. appearances include "Justice," "Jane Clegg," "Peter Ibbetson," "The Betrothal," "The Light of the World," "Dulcy," "The Exile," "Tweedles," "The Laughing Lady," "White Cargo," "Zeppelin," the last Gillette revival of "Sherlock Holmes," and more recently "Suspect," "Life With Father," and "Little A."

CLIFF, OLIVER. Born in Sebring, Ohio, June 4, 1918. Educated at Los Angeles City College. Appeared on Broadway in the Olivier-Leigh production of "Romeo and Juliet," "Othello," "Jacobowsky and the Colonel," "Ten Little Indians," "Antigone," and the Cornell revival of "Candida."

CLIFT, MONTGOMERY. Born in Omaha, Neb., Oct. 17, 1920. Made his N.Y. stage bow in "Fly Away Home." Since then has appeared in "Jubilee," "Your Obedient Husband," "Dame Nature," "The Mother," "There Shall be No Night," "Mexican Mural," "Skin of Our Teeth," revival of "Our Town," "The Searching Wind," "Foxhole in the Parlor," and "You Touched Me."

COBURN, CHARLES. Born Macon, Ga., June 19, 1877. First played in stock in Chicago and made N.Y. debut in 1901 in "Up York State." Later he toured in "The Christian," after which he organized the Coburn Shakespearian Players, which he maintained for many years, and with which he played many roles. He also played in "The Coming of Mrs. Patrick," "The Yellow Jacket," "The Imaginary Invalid," "The Better 'Ole," "French Leave," "The Bronx Express," "So This is London," "The Farmer's Wife," "Trelawney of the Wells," "The Right Age to Marry," "Old Bill," "M.P.," "The Tavern," "Falstaff," "The Plutocrat," "The First Legion," "The County Chairman," and "Sun Kissed." Recently toured with "Merry Wives of Windsor."

COCA, IMOGENE. Born in Philadelphia, Nov. 18, 1908. Began her N.Y. career in chorus of "When

Thomas Coley

Blanche Collins

John Conway

You Smile." Other appearances include "Garrick Gaieties," "Flying Colors," "New Faces," "Fools Rush In," "Who's Who," "Folies Bergere," "Straw Hat Revue," "All in Fun," and "Concert Varieties."

COLBY, MARION. Born Aug. 27, 1923 in Los Angeles. First appeared on Broadway in "Meet the People," in 1940. Since then has appeared in many night club engagements, and has also been seen in "Are You With It?" and "Toplitsky of Notre Dame."

COLEMAN, LEO. Born March 9, 1919 in Antioch, La., and educated in Detroit, Mich. Made Broadway bow this season as the mute in "The Medium."

COLEY, THOMAS. Born July 29, 1917 in Bethayres, Penna., and educated at Washington and Lee Univ. Played at the Barter Theatre before making his Broadway bow in 1935 with the Lunts in "Taming of the Shrew." Since then has been seen in "Our Town," "Swingin' the Dream," "Return Engagement," "Cue For Passion," "Mr. Peebles and Mr. Hooker" and "Portrait in Black."

COLL, OWEN. Born Oct. 30, 1887 in St. John, NB. Canada, and had first stage experience in stock. Made Broadway debut in 1930 in "The New Yorkers." Since then has been seen in "Man on Stilts," "Walk a Little Faster," "Double Dummy," "The Philadelphia Story," "Public Relations," "Catherine Was Great," "Ten Little Indians," "Swan Song," and "Another Part of the Forest."

COLLINGE, PATRICIA. Born in Dublin, Ireland, Sept. 20, 1894. Made her debut in England, and her first N.Y. appearance was in 1908 in "The Queen of the Moulin Rouge." Later she played in "The Girl and the Wizard," "The Bluebird," "The Thunderbolt," "Everywoman," "The New Henrietta," "Billy," "He Comes Up Smiling," "The Show Shop," "A Regular Business Man," "Pollyanna," "Tillie," "Golden Days," "Just Suppose," "Tarnish," "The Dark Angel," "Venus," "The Lady With the Lamp," "Another Language," "Autumn Crocus," "To See Ourselves," and "The Little Foxes."

COLLINS, BLANCHE. Born N.Y.C. May 12, 1918. Educated at Columbia Univ. Appearances on Broadway include "Scarlet Sister Mary," "Strike Me Pink," "The Cradle Will Rock," and Maurice Evans' G.I. version of "Hamlet."

COLLINS, RUSSELL. Born in Indianapolis, Ind., Oct. 6, 1897. Educated at Indiana State Univ. and Carnegie Tech Drama School. The Cleveland Playhouse was the scene of his stage training. On Broadway has had important roles in "Men in White," "Gold Eagle Guy," "Waiting for Lefty," "Johnny Johnson," "Star Wagon," "Here Come the Clowns," "Mornings at Seven," "The Heavenly Express," "The Moon is Down," revival of "Juno and the Paycock," "In Time to Come," "Carousel," revival of "He Who Gets Slapped," and "The Iceman Cometh."

COLMAN, BOOTH. Born in Portland, Ore., March 8, 1923. Educated Univ. of Washington. Received stage training at Showboat and Penthouse theatres, Seattle. Made Broadway bow in "The Assassin." Maurice Evans' G.I. "Hamlet" followed.

COMDEN, BETTY. Born in Brooklyn, and educated at Brooklyn Ethical Culture School, Erasmus Hall, and N.Y.U. Spent five years with The Revuers, a night club act. "On the Town" marked her N.Y. stage debut.

COMEGYS, KATHLEEN. Born in Shreveport, La. Appeared on Broadway in "If This Be Treason," "The Ghost of Yankee Doodle," "Call it a Day," and the revival of "Craig's Wife."

CONKLIN, PEGGY. Born Dobbs Ferry, N.Y., 1912. First N.Y. stage appearance in 1929 in "The Little Show." Later she was seen in "His Majesty's Car," "Purity," "Old Man Murphy," "Hot Money," "Mademoiselle," "The Party's Over," "The Ghost Writer," "The Pursuit of Happiness," "The Petrified Forest," "Co-respondent Unknown," "Yes, My Darling Daughter," "Miss Swan Expects," "Casey Jones," "Mr. and Mrs. North," "Alice in Arms," and "Feathers in a Gale."

CONNOR, KAYE. Born Dec. 20, 1925 in Vancouver, B.C., Canada. Made Broadway debut in "Song of Norway" in 1944, and was seen this season in "Gypsy Lady."

CONROY, FRANK. Born in Derby, Eng., Oct. 14, 1890. Made his first professional appearance at the Spa Theatre, Scarborough, 1908 as the second murderer in "Macbeth." Made his N.Y. debut at the Bandbox Theatre in 1915 in "Helena's Husband." Other plays include "The Bad Man," "The Constant Wife," and more recently "On Borrowed Time," "The Little Foxes," "For Keeps," "One Man Show," and "Hear That Trumpet."

CONWAY, JOHN. Born in Elgin, Ill., and educated at Univ. of Wisc. Had stage training on the West Coast, and first appeared on Broadway in 1942 in "The World's Full of Girls." Since then has been seen in "But Not Goodbye," "Love on Leave," "Lower North," "The Late George Apley," "You Touched Me," and "The Story of Mary Suratt."

COOK, DONALD. Born in Portland, Ore., Sept. 26, 1901. Dramatic training with Kansas City Community Playhouse. Plays on Broadway include "N.Y. Exchange," "Paris Bound," "Rebound," "Wine of Choice," "American Landscape," "Skylark," "Claudia," "Foolish Notion," "Made in Heaven" and "Portrait in Black."

COOKSEY, CURTIS. Born Dec. 9, 1892 in Kentucky. Started acting at age of fourteen with travelling stock companies. Made Broadway debut in 1916 in "The Heart of Wetona." Among the many plays in which he has appeared are "Man and Woman," "Welded," "The Fountain," "House of Women," "The Beautiful People," the revival of "Vagabond King," and "Ryan Girl."

Gladys Cooper

Robin Craven

Jane Cowl

COOKSON, GEORGINA. Born Dec. 19, 1918 in Cornwall, England, and studied for the theatre at Royal Academy of Dramatic Art. Appeared in numerous plays in London, before making Broadway debut this season in "Love Goes to Press."

COOKSON, PETER. Born May 8, 1915 in Portland, Ore. First stage experience was with the Pasadena Community Playhouse. Made Broadway debut this season in "Message for Margaret."

COOLIDGE, PHILIP. Born in Concord, Mass. Made Broadway debut in "Our Town" in 1938. Since then has been seen in "Merchant of Yonkers," "Family Portrait," "Margin for Error," "In Time to Come," "Jacobowsky and the Colonel," "Sing Out, Sweet Land," and "Barefoot Boy With Cheek."

COOPER, ANTHONY KEMBLE. Born London, Eng., Feb. 6, 1908. Is a descendant of the Kembles, one of England's oldest acting families. Made his first N.Y. appearance in 1925 in "Lass O' Laughter." Since then has played in "The School for Scandal," "His Majesty's Car," "The Command to Love," "Quiet Please," "Anne of England," "Hay Fever," "Mary of Scotland," "Age 26," "Sheppey," "Ten Little Indians" and "Sweethearts."

COOPER, DULCIE. Born in San Francisco, Nov. 3, 1907. Educated Hollywood High School and Columbia Univ. Appeared in N.Y. in "Happily Ever After," "Peter Flies High," "Courage," "The Little Spitfire," "Married and How," "Three's a Family," "Brighten the Corner" and "Open House."

COOPER, GLADYS. Born Lewisham, Eng., Dec. 18, 1888. After a distinguished career on the British stage, made her N.Y.C. debut in 1934 in "The Shining Hour." Since then she has been seen in "Othello," "Macbeth," "Call it a Day," "White Christmas," and "Close Quarters."

COOPER, MELVILLE. Born in Birmingham, Eng., Oct. 15, 1896. Made his Broadway bow in "Laburnum Grove." Since then had leading roles in "Jubilee," "The Merry Widow," "While the Sun Shines," "Firebrand of Florence," the revival of "Pygmalion," and "The Haven."

CORBETT, LEONORA. Born in London, June 28, 1908. She studied scenic and costume design before acting on the London stage. Made her N.Y.C. debut in Oct. 1941 in "Blithe Spirit," and was seen again on Broadway this season in "Park Avenue."

CORDNER, BLAINE. Born in Jacksonville, Florida, Aug. 21, 1901. Played on Broadway in "We, the People," "Bridal Quilt," "Blow, Ye Winds," "The World Waits," "First Flight," "A New Life," "Arsenic and Old Lace," and "Bloomer Girl."

COREY, WENDELL. Born Dracut, Mass., March 20, 1914. Made his Broadway debut May 26, 1942 in "Comes the Revelation." Since then New Yorkers have seen him in "The Life of Reilly," "Strip for Action," "The First Million," "It's Up to You," "Jackpot," "Manhattan Nocturne," "But Not Goodbye," "The Wind is Ninety," and "Dream Girl."

CORNELL, KATHARINE. Born Berlin, Germany, Feb. 16, 1898. Made N.Y. debut Nov. 13, 1916 with the Washington Square Players in "Bushido." Plays since then include "Nice People," "A Bill of Divorcement," "Will Shakespeare," "The Enchanted Cottage," "Casanova," "The Way Things Happen," "The Outsider," "Tiger Cats," "Candida," "The Green Hat," "The Letter," "The Age of Innocence," "Dishonored Lady," "The Barretts of Wimpole Street," "Lucrece," "Alien Corn," "Romeo and Juliet," "Flowers of the Forest," "St. Joan," "The Wingless Victory," "Herod and Marianne," "No Time for Comedy," "The Doctor's Dilemma," "The Three Sisters," "Lovers and Friends," and "Antigone."

COSSART, ERNEST. Born Cheltenham, Eng., Sept. 24, 1876. First appeared on the English stage in 1896, and made his N.Y. debut in 1910 in "The Girls from Gottenburg." Has played in "Mrs. Dot," "Love Among the Lions," "Marrying Money," "Androcles and the Lion," and many other plays. Recent appearances include "Reunion in Vienna," "The Mask and the Face," "Accent on Youth," "Madame Bovary," and "Devils Galore."

COTTON, FRED AYRES. Born in Central City, Neb. Educated Hastings College and Columbia Univ. Stage training in stock at Elitch's Gardens Theatre, Denver, Colo. Played on Broadway in "Swing Your Lady," "Tide Rising," "The Brown Danube," "Winged Victory," and "State of the Union."

COULOURIS, GEORGE. Born Manchester, Eng., Oct. 1, 1903. Appeared first in N.Y.C. in "The Novice and the Duke" in 1929. Later he played in "The Apple Cart," "The Late Christopher Bean," "Best Sellers," "Mary of Scotland," "Valley Forge," "Blind Alley," "St. Joan," "Ten Million Ghosts," "Julius Caesar," "The Shoemaker's Holiday," "Madame Capet," "The White Steed," and "Richard III."

COWL, JANE. Born Boston, Mass., Dec. 14, 1890. Made her debut in 1903 in "Sweet Kitty Bellairs." Among her most successful roles were "Within the Law," "Common Clay," "Lilac Time," "Smilin' Through," "Romeo and Juliet," and "The Road to Rome." More recently she appeared in "Rain from Heaven," "First Lady," "The Merchant of Yonkers," and "Old Acquaintance."

COWLES, CHANDLER. Born in New Haven, Conn., Sept. 29, 1917. Educated at Yale. Received stage training at Bennington Theatre School and Dramatic Workshop of the New School. Made his Broadway debut April 18, 1946 in "Call Me Mister."

CRABTREE, PAUL. Born in Virginia; educated at Syracuse University. Trained for the stage at

Helmut Dantine   Constance Cummings   Richard Davis

The Barter Theatre. Made first Broadway appearance in "Men To The Sea." "Skydrift" and "The Iceman Cometh" followed.

CRAIG, HELEN. Born in San Antonio, Tex., May 13, 1914. Educated at Scarborough School, N.Y. Received her stage training at Hedgerow Theatre. Made her Broadway debut Jan. 16, 1936 in "Russet Mantle." Other plays on Broadway include "New Faces," "Julius Caesar," "Soliloquy," "Family Portrait," "The Unconquered," "Johnny Belinda," "As You Like It," "Lute Song" and "Land's End."

CRANDALL, EDWARD. Born in Brooklyn, March 2, 1904. Educated at Hackley School, Tarrytown, and Oxford Univ., Eng. Plays on Broadway: "Young Woodley," "The Play's the Thing," "Heavy Traffic," "Our Betters," "Lady of the Orchids," "Give Me Yesterday," "Absent Father," "A Party," "Small Miracle," and "Kiss Them for Me."

CRAVEN, ROBIN. Born in London, Sept. 20, 1910. Educated at Oxford Univ., and studied for the stage at the Royal Academy of Dramatic Art. Made Broadway debut in 1938 in "Dear Octopus." Since then he has been seen in "Foreigners," "Glamour Preferred," "Claudia," "Hand in Glove" and "Present Laughter."

CROWLEY, ANN. Born in Scranton, Pa., October 17, 1929. Graduated from Julia Richman High School, N.Y.C. Played the lead in the Theatre Guild's productions "Oklahoma" and "Carousel."

CUMMINGS, CONSTANCE. Born in Seattle, Wash., May 15, 1910. Was a chorus girl in "The Little Show." Other N.Y. engagements include "Treasure Girl," "This Man's Money," "June Moon," "Accent on Youth," "Young Madame Conti," "Madame Bovary," "If I Were You," and "One Man Show."

CUMMINGS, VICKI. Born in Northampton, Mass. Has appeared on Broadway in "The Time, the Place, and the Girl," "Sunny River," "Mrs. Kimball Presents," "Lady in Danger," and "The Voice of the Turtle."

CUNNINGHAM, RONNIE. Born in Washington, D.C., Nov. 3, 1923. Educated at Academy-of-the-Immaculate Conception. Plays on Broadway include "Banjo Eyes," "Lady Says Yes," and "Marinka."

DALE, MARGARET. Born in Philadelphia, March 6, 1880. Made stage debut at Girard Ave. Theatre of that city in 1897. Was leading lady to such famous stars as John Drew, E. H. Sothern, Henry Miller, William H. Crane and George Arliss. More recently has appeared in "Dinner At Eight," "Tovarich," "Lady in the Dark," and "The Late George Apley."

DALTON, DORIS. Born March 18, 1912 in Sharon, Mass. Educated at Wellesley College. Appeared in several stock companies before her Broadway debut in 1935 as leading lady in "Petticoat Fever." Since then has been seen in "Sweet Aloes," "Blow, Ye Winds," "The Fabulous Invalid," and "Another Love Story." More recently she played on Broadway in "The Ryan Girl" and "Present Laughter."

DANIELL, HENRY. Born in London, March 5, 1894. First appeared on the stage in England in 1913, and made N.Y.C. debut in "Claire de Lune" in 1921. After that he alternated acting in both countries and his most outstanding work here has been in "Serena Blandish" and "Kind Lady." He has appeared in many films, and most recently has been seen on the Broadway stage in "Murder Without Crime," "Lovers and Friends," "The Winter's Tale," and "Lady Windermere's Fan."

DANIELS, DANNY. Born in Albany, N.Y., Oct. 25, 1924. Appeared on Broadway in "Best Foot Forward," "Count Me In," "Billion Dollar Baby," and "Street Scene."

DANTINE, HELMUT. Born in Vienna, Oct. 7, 1918. Educated in Vienna, and received theatre apprenticeship at Pasadena Community Playhouse. Appeared in a number of Hollywood films before making his Broadway debut in March 1947 opposite Tallulah Bankhead in "The Eagle Has Two Heads."

DARLING, JEAN. Born in Santa Monica, Calif., Aug. 23, 1925. Was the little girl with the golden curls in "Our Gang" comedies some years ago. Made her Broadway debut in "Count Me In." Since then has played in "Marianna," and "Carousel."

DARVAS, LILI. Born in Budapest, Hungary, and is the wife of Ferenc Molnar. Discovered by Max Reinhardt, she played in many of his famous productions. Made her first English-speaking appearance in America in "Criminals" at the New School. "Soldier's Wife" marked her Broadway debut. She was last seen in Evans' G.I. "Hamlet."

DAUPHIN, CLAUDE. Born in France, where his first connection with the theatre was as a designer of costumes and scenery. From 1933 he was actively engaged as an actor in French productions and also appeared in French films. Made his Broadway debut in "No Exit."

DAVIS, EVELYN. Born in N.Y.C., Oct. 31, 1906. Began her stage career in "Run, Lil' Children." Since then New Yorkers have seen her in "Two on an Island," "Vickie," "The Perfect Marriage," and "Flamingo Road."

DAVIS, RICHARD. Born in Boston, Mass. Made his first stage appearance in "Siege." After a session in Hollywood and the Army, returned to Broadway in "Kiss Them For Me."

DAWSON, JON. Born in Bay Port, Mich., Jan. 1, 1910. Educated at Carnegie Tech, where he graduated from the drama dept. Had further training with the Bonstelle Theatre in Detroit before mak-

Philip Dorn Beatrice de Neegaard Warde Donovan

ing Broadway debut in 1942 in "The Russian People." More recently appeared in "Maid in the Ozarks."

DAWSON, MARK. Born in Philadelphia where he studied at the Philadelphia Conservatory of Music, and was a soloist with the Philadelphia Orchestra. He appeared on Broadway in "Dancing in the Streets," "By Jupiter," and more recently in "Sweethearts."

DAYTON, JUNE. Born in Dayton, Ohio. Educated in Chicago and Mundelein College, and served stage apprenticeship with Dayton Civic Theatre and Port Players, Milwaukee. Made her Broadway debut in "Lovely Me," and was also seen in "Tenting Tonight."

DEERING, OLIVE. Made her N.Y. debut in "Girls in Uniform." Since then has appeared in "Growing Pains," "Picnic," "Daughters of Atreus," "The Eternal Road," "Winged Victory," "Skydrift," and revival of "The Front Page."

DE KOVEN, ROGER. Born Oct. 22, 1907 in Chicago. Educated at Univ. of Chicago, Northwestern, and Columbia. Stage apprenticeship with Theatre Guild School and Stuart Walker Stock Company. Made Broadway debut in 1926 in "Juarez and Maxmilian," and appeared in "Once in a Lifetime," "Murder in the Cathedral," "The Eternal Road," and "Brooklyn, U.S.A." More recently was seen in "The Assassin" and "Joan of Lorraine."

de NEERGAARD, BEATRICE. Appeared for seven years with Eva Le Gallienne's Civic Repertory Company, where she made her first N.Y. stage appearance. Later she played with Nazimova in "Ghosts," and "Doctor Monica." More recently she was seen in "Squaring the Circle," "Live Life Again," "Land of Fame," "Letters to Lucerne," and "The Whole World Over."

DERWENT, CLARENCE. Born in London, March 23, 1884. Appeared on the English stage for fifteen years before making his Broadway debut. New Yorkers have seen him in "The Three Musketeers," "Serena Blandish," "Topaze," "Mary of Scotland," "The Doctor's Dilemma," "The Pirate," "Lady in Danger," "Lute Song," and "The Eagle Has Two Heads." Recently elected President of Actors' Equity Association.

DEW, EDWARD. Born in Sumner, Wash., Jan. 29, 1909. Educated at Pomona College. Appeared in many motion pictures. Made his Broadway debut in revival of "The Red Mill," and has since appeared in "If The Shoe Fits."

DIGGES, DUDLEY. Born in Dublin, Ireland, 1880. Has appeared in many plays among which are "Bonds of Interest," "John Ferguson," "Jane Clegg," "The Guardsman," "Ned McCobb's Daughter," "Marco Millions," "Pygmalion," "Liliom," "The Doctor's Dilemma," "Major Barbara," "The Brothers Karamazov," "Juarez and Maxmilian," "A Month in the Country," "The Masque of Kings," "On Borrowed Time," Cornell's revival of "Candida," "Listen, Professor," "The Searching Wind," and "The Iceman Cometh."

DIXON, JEAN. Born in Waterbury, Conn., July 14, 1905 and attended St. Margaret's School. Her many Broadway engagements include "Golden Days," "To The Ladies," "The Wooden Kimono," "Behold the Bridegroom," "Heavy Traffic," "June Moon," "Once in a Lifetime," "Dangerous Corner," "Heat Lightning," "George Washington Slept Here," and "The Deep Mrs. Sykes."

DOLIN, ANTON. Born in Sussex, England on July 27, 1904. He studied for the theatre with Italia Conti, Seymour Hicks, and Dion Boucicault. Scored tremendous success as a dancer, and made his debut with the Diaghilev Russian Ballet in 1924. He also played on the English stage before making his Broadway debut in 1930 in "The International Revue." Since then he is better known in this country as a dancer, but has also acted in "The Seven Lively Arts," and "The Dancer."

DONOVAN, WARDE. Born Feb. 25, 1919 in Los Angeles. Educated at Oxford, England, and received stage apprenticeship at the Pasadena Playhouse. Before the war he was seen with the Los Angeles and San Francisco Light Opera Companies, and made his Broadway debut this season in "Toplitzky of Notre Dame."

DORN, PHILIP. Born in Holland where he first appeared on the stage. He also toured the Dutch possessions as an actor, and in 1940 first appeared in Hollywood pictures. Made Broadway debut this season in "The Big Two."

DOUCET, CATHARINE. Born Richmond, Va. Broadway appearances include "The Devil in the Cheese," "The Royal Family," "The Perfect Alibi," "Dynamo," "Camel Through the Needle's Eye," "Topaze," "As Husband Go," "When Ladies Meet," "Last Stop," and "Oh, Brother!"

DOUGLAS, KIRK. Made his initial Broadway appearance as a singing Western Union boy in "Spring Again." Since then has had roles in "Kiss and Tell," Cornell's revival of "Three Sisters," "Alice in Arms," "The Wind is Ninety," and "Woman Bites Dog."

DOUGLAS, MILTON. Born in N.Y.C., Dec. 7, 1901. Received his stage training in vaudeville, burlesque and night clubs. Appeared on Broadway in "Texas Guinan's Padlocks," "Summer Wines," and "Follow the Girls."

DOUGLAS, PAUL. Was better known as a sports announcer on the radio until his outstanding success in "Born Yesterday." Only other N.Y. stage appearance made in "Double Dummy" in 1935.

Joe Downing

Johnny Downs

Buddy Ebsen

DOUGLAS, SUSAN. Born in Czechoslovakia in 1926. Educated in her native country and England. Appeared extensively on radio until her Broadway debut March 20, 1946 in "He Who Gets Slapped."

DOUGLASS, MARGARET. Born in Dallas, Tex. Broadway roles: "Russet Mantle," "The Women," "Out from Under," "Yesterday's Magic," "Eight O'Clock Tuesday," "The Damask Cheek," "Bloomer Girl," and "The Fatal Weakness."

DOWLING, EDDIE. Born Woonsocket, R.I., Dec. 9, 1895. Broadway audiences have seen him in "She Took a Chance," "Ziegfeld Follies of 1919," "The Magic Melody," "The Girl in the Spotlight," "Hello America," "The Fall Guy," "Sally, Irene and Mary," "Honeymoon Lane," "Sidewalks of New York," "The Rainbow Man," "Thumbs Up," "Here Come the Clowns," "The Time of Your Life," "Hello Out There," "Magic," and "The Glass Menagerie."

DOWNING, JOE. Born N.Y.C., June 26, 1904. Appeared on Broadway in "Garrick Gaieties," "Farewell to Arms," "Shooting Star," "Heat Lightning," "Page Miss Glory," "Ceiling Zero," "Dead End," and "Ramshackle Inn."

DOWNS, JOHNNY. Born in Brooklyn, N.Y. Was one of the original kids in "Our Gang" comedies. Appeared on Broadway in "Strike Me Pink," "Growing Pains," and "Are You With It?"

DRAKE, ALFRED. Born Oct. 7, 1914 in N.Y.C. Graduated from Brooklyn College and studied voice with Clytie Hine Mundy. Has appeared on Broadway in "The White Horse Inn," "Babes in Arms," "Two Bouquets," "One for the Money," "Straw Hat Revue," "Two for the Show," "Out of the Frying Pan," "As You Like It," "Admiral Had a Wife," "Yesterday's Magic," "Oklahoma," "Sing Out, Sweet Land," and "Beggar's Holiday."

DUNCAN, AUGUSTIN. Born San Francisco, Calif., April 17, 1873. Made his first N.Y.C. appearance with Richard Mansfield in "Henry V" in 1900. He has had a long career both here and in England, and has produced and staged plays as well as acted in them. Most recent Broadway appearance was in "Lute Song."

DUNHAM, KATHERINE. Born in Chicago, June 22, 1912. Graduate of Univ. of Chicago. Appeared on Broadway in "Cabin in the Sky," "Tropical Revue," "Carib Song," and "Bal Negre."

DUNNE, EITHNE. Studied acting at the Abbey Theatre School in Dublin, and later played leading roles at both the Abbey and the Gate Theatres. She made her Broadway bow this season in the role of Pegeen Mike in the revival of "Playboy of the Western World."

DUNNOCK, MILDRED. Born in Baltimore, and holds A.B. from Goucher, and M.A. from Columbia. Before going on the stage she taught school, and acted with various amateur groups. In 1933 she made her Broadway debut in "Birth." Since then she has been seen in "The Eternal Road," "The Corn is Green," "The Cat Screams," "Only the Heart," "Richard III," "Foolish Notion," "Lute Song," and "Another Part of the Forest."

DUPREZ, JUNE. Born May 14, 1918 in London. Educated in London and in France, and had first stage experience with the Coventry Repertory Company. She became well known to the American public through her work in such films as "Four Feathers," "The Thief of Bagdad," and "None but the Lonely Heart." She made her debut on Broadway on Nov. 6, 1946 as one of the leading players in the American Repertory Theatre.

EATON, DOROTHY. Studied for the theatre at Yale Drama School, and made Broadway debut in 1941 in "The Trojan Women." Since then has appeared in "The Sun Field" and "Parlor Story."

EBSEN, BUDDY. Educated at Rollins College, Fla. First N.Y. job in chorus of "Whoopee." Since then has appeared in "Flying Colors," "Ziegfeld Follies of 1936," "Yokel Boy," the Chicago company of "Goodnight Ladies," and the revival of "Show Boat."

EDEN, TONY. Born in N.Y.C., March 31, 1927. Educated at Fairfax Hall, Va., and Ethical Culture, N.Y.C. Plays on Broadway: "Up in Central Park," "Dark of the Moon," and "Devils Galore."

EDNEY, FLORENCE. Born in London, Eng., June 2, 1879. First N.Y. stage appearance in 1906 in "The Price of Money," and since then has appeared in many plays, both here and in England. Recently she appeared in "Waterloo Bridge," "Topaze," "Twentieth Century," "Barchester Towers," and "Angel Street."

ELDRIDGE, FLORENCE. Born Sept. 5, 1901 in Brooklyn, N.Y. Made N.Y. debut as a chorus girl in "Rock-a-Bye Baby." Since then has appeared in many plays, among which are "Ambush," "The Cat and the Canary," "Six Characters in Search of an Author," "The Dancers," "Young Blood," and "The Great Gatsby." More recently she has been seen in "The Skin of Our Teeth," and "Years Ago."

ELLERBE, HARRY. Born in Columbia, S.C., Jan. 13, 1905. Made his initial Broadway appearance in "Philip Goes Forth." Other roles followed in "Thoroughbred," "Strange Orchestra," "The Man on Stilts," "The Mad Hopes," the Nazimova revivals of "Ghosts," and "Hedda Gabler," "Outward Bound," "Whiteoaks," and "Sleep, My Pretty One."

ELLIOTT, JAMES. Born N.Y.C., Jan. 15, 1924. Plays on Broadway as an actor: "Junior Miss," "Men to the Sea," and "Love's Old Sweet Song." Has the title of the youngest producer on Broadway, where he has presented "Arlene," "The First Million," and "Too Hot for Maneuvers."

Judith Evelyn Hope Emerson Nanette Fabray

EMERSON, HOPE. Born in Iowa, and had first stage experience in stock and vaudeville. Made Broadway debut in 1930 in "Lysistrata." Since then has been seen in "Smiling Faces," "Swing Your Lady," "Chicken Every Sunday," and "Street Scene." Has also been active on radio, and has appeared frequently in night clubs.

ERNST, LEILA. Born July 28, 1922 in Jaffrey, N.H. Had stage training in Ogunquit, Maine, Playhouse. Made Broadway debut in 1939 in "Too Many Girls," and since then has been seen in "Pal Joey," "Best Foot Forward," "The Doughgirls," "Truckline Cafe," and "If the Shoe Fits."

EVANS, MAURICE. Born Dorchester, Dorset, Eng., June 3, 1901. Made first professional appearance in England in 1926 in "The Orestia," of Aeschylus. First N.Y. appearance was as Romeo in Katharine Cornell's "Romeo and Juliet" in 1935. Since then has appeared in "Saint Joan," "St. Helena," "Richard II," "Henry IV, Part I," "Hamlet," "Twelfth Night," "Macbeth" and his G.I. version of "Hamlet."

EVANS, REX. Born April 13, 1903 in Southport, England. Educated at Marlborough College in England. First appeared on stage in his native country in musical revues, and made Broadway bow in 1933 in "Three Penny Opera." Well known, both here and abroad, as a night club entertainer. After a session in Hollywood films, he returned to Broadway this season in "Lady Windermere's Fan."

EVANS, WILBUR. Born in Philadelphia, 1905. Educated at Curtis Institute of Music. Made his stage debut at the Curran Theatre, San Francisco in 1930 in "Bambina." Was in the Carnegie Hall productions of "The Merry Widow," and "The New Moon." Also sang in the New Opera Company production of "La Vie Parisienne." His most recent roles were in "Mexican Hayride" and "Up in Central Park."

EVELYN, JUDITH. Born in Seneca, S.D., March 20, 1913. Educated at University of Manitoba. Went to England where she appeared in a number of roles, both modern and classic, and in 1941 made her Broadway bow with outstanding success in "Angel Street." Since then she has been seen in "The Overtons," and "The Rich Full Life," after which she toured in the National company of "State of the Union." Returned to Broadway this season in revival of "Craig's Wife."

EVEREST, BARBARA. Born in London, June 9, 1890. First appeared in England in 1912 in "The Voysey Inheritance," and had a long and successful career in that country. Made her American debut in "Anne of England," and since then has been seen in "Sheppie."

EWELL, TOM. Born April 29, 1909 in Owensboro, Ky., and educated at Univ. of Wis. Played in mid-western stock before making Broadway debut in 1934 in "They Shall Not Die." Since then he has been seen in "Sunny River," "Ethan Frome," "Family Portrait," "Merchant of Yonkers," "Liberty Jones," "Tobacco Road" and "Brother Rat." After his service in the Navy he returned to Broadway in "Apple of His Eye," and was seen this season in "John Loves Mary."

FABIAN, OLGA. Born in Vienna, Austria. Played on stage in her native country for twenty-five years. Appeared on road in "Play With Fire," and "Judy O'Connor." Made Broadway debut in "The Big Two."

FABRAY, NANETTE. Born in San Diego, Calif., Oct. 27, 1922. Educated at Hollywood High School, and had stage training at Max Reinhardt Workshop. As a child she danced in a Fanchon and Marco vaudeville unit, and appeared in "Our Gang" comedies. Made Broadway debut in 1940 in "Meet the People." Since then she has been seen in "Let's Face It," "By Jupiter," "Jackpot," "My Dear Public," and "Bloomer Girl."

FAREBROTHER, VIOLET. Born in Grimsby, England, Aug. 22, 1888. Received her dramatic training at Royal Academy of Dramatic Art. Played with Sir Frank Benson in Shakespearian repertory. Made Broadway debut with Donald Wolfit's Repertory Company.

FASSETT, JAY. Educated at Harvard. Played with Jane Cowl in "Malvaloca" and Walter Hampden in "Cyrano de Bergerac." Other Broadway appearances include "As Husbands Go," "Biography," "Tovarich," "Our Town," "Dark Eyes" and "Loco."

FAY, FRANK. Born in San Francisco, Nov. 17, 1897. Made his stage debut at seven in "Babes in Toyland." Was a child actor with Rose Stahl in "The Chorus Lady." Later he appeared with Sir Henry Irving and E. H. Sothern in Shakespearian roles. In the golden days of vaudeville he was one of the headliners at the Palace. Starred in "Jim Jam Jems," "Frank Fay's Fables," and the recent vaudeville show "Laugh Time." "Harvey" marks his first straight play since his child actor days.

FELLOWS, EDITH. Born May 20, 1923 in Boston, Mass. Educated in private school and with a studio tutor when she was a child actress in the movies. Appeared in over 500 movies before making her Broadway debut in Oct. 1946 in "Marinka." Since then was seen as the lead in "Louisiana Lady."

FERGUSON, ELSIE. Born N.Y.C., Aug. 19, 1883. First appearance was in the chorus of "The Belle of New York" in 1900. Among her outstanding successes are "Such a Little Queen," "The Strange Woman," "Outcast" and "Sacred and Profane Love." More recently she has appeared in "The House of Women," "Scarlet Pages" and "Outrageous Fortune."

Edith Fellows | Lawrence Fletcher | Nina Foch

FERRER, JOSE. Born in San Turce, Puerto Rico, Jan. 8, 1909. Educated at Princeton, where he first acted in the Princeton Triangle Shows. He played in summer stock and with a show boat company before making his Broadway debut in 1935 in "A Slight Case of Murder." Since then he has been seen in "Spring Dance," "Brother Rat," "How to Get Tough About It," "Missouri Legend," "Mamba's Daughters," "Key Largo" and "Charlie's Aunt." For a time he took over the Danny Kaye role in "Let's Face It." More recently has appeared in "Othello" and "Cyrano de Bergerac."

FIELD, BETTY. Born Boston, Mass., Feb. 8, 1918. Studied at the American Academy of Dramatic Art, but her first role was in London in 1934 in "She Loves Me Not." In N.Y. she has appeared in "Page Miss Glory," "Three Men on a Horse," "Room Service," "Angel Island," "If I Were You," "What a Life," "The Primrose Path," "Two on an Island" and "Flight to the West." More recently she has been seen in "A New Life," "The Voice of the Turtle" and "Dream Girl."

FIELD, ROBERT. Born in Attleboro, Mass., March 25, 1916. Educated at Deerfield Academy and Tufts College. Made his Broadway bow in 1937 in "Babes in Arms." Other N.Y. engagements include "Knickerbocker Holiday," "Higher and Higher," "The Merry Widow," the title role in revival of "Robin Hood," and "The Day Before Spring."

FLEMYNG, ROBERT. Born in Liverpool, England, Jan. 3, 1912. Educated at London Univ. Made Broadway debut Dec. 6, 1938 in "Spring Meeting." New Yorkers have also seen him in "No Time for Comedy," "The Importance of Being Earnest" and "Love for Love."

FLETCHER, BRAMWELL. Born Feb. 20, 1904 in Bradford, Yorkshire, Eng. Made his American debut in 1926 and since then has appeared in "Ten Minute Alibi," "Lady Precious Stream," "Within the Gates," the revivals of "Outward Bound" and "The Doctor's Dilemma," "Storm Operation" and "Rebecca."

FLETCHER, LAWRENCE. Born March 5, 1904 in Canton, Ohio. Educated at Howe Military School and Wabash College. Played for two years with the Stuart Walker Company before making Broadway debut in 1926 in "The Poor Nut." Other N.Y. appearances have been in "Marriage on Approval," "The King Can Do No Wrong," "The Game of Love and Death," "Karl and Anna," "Subway Express," "Another Language," "Sailor Beware," "Boy Meets Girl," "Antony and Cleopatra," "Julius Caesar," "No Time for Comedy," "Romantic Mr. Dickens," "Spring Again," "Hickory Stick," "The Man Who Had All the Luck," "Signature" and "Too Hot for Maneuvers." Most recent appearances were in "The Rugged Path" and "Made in Heaven."

FOCH, NINA. Born in Leyden, the Netherlands, April 20, 1924. Educated at Columbia Univ. and Parsons Art School. Received stage training at American Academy of Dramatic Arts. Appeared in several motion pictures before making her Broadway bow in "John Loves Mary."

FONTANNE, LYNN. Born in London, 1887. She made her first stage apparance in "Alice-Sit-By-The-Fire" with Ellen Terry in 1905. First seen in N.Y. in 1910 in "Mr. Preedy and the Countess." Among her more important plays are "Dulcy," "The Guardsman," "Goat Song," "At Mrs. Beam's," "The Second Man," "Strange Interlude," "Caprice," "Elizabeth the Queen," "Reunion in Vienna," "Design for Living," "Idiot's Delight," "Amphitryon 38," a revival of "The Sea Gull." More recently she appeared in "There Shall Be No Night," "The Pirate," and "O Mistress Mine."

FORBES, BRENDA. Born in London, England. Made her American debut with Katharine Cornell in "The Barretts of Wimpole Street." Since then she has appeared in "Candida," "Lucrece," "Flowers of the Forest," "Pride and Prejudice," "Storm Over Patsy," "Heartbreak House," "One for the Money," "Two for the Show," "Yesterday's Magic," "The Morning Star," "Suds in Your Eye" and "Three to Make Ready."

FORBES, RALPH. Born in London, England, Sept. 30, 1902. Made his Broadway debut in 1924 in "Havoc." Since then has had leading roles in "The Man With the Load of Mischief," "Stronger than Love," the revivals of "The Doctor's Dilemma" and "A Kiss for Cinderella," "A Highland Fling," "The Visitor" and "Second Best Bed." He has also played in over fifty films.

FORD, PAUL. Born in Baltimore, Md., Nov. 2, 1901. Educated at Dartmouth. Made Broadway debut in "Decision" on Feb. 4, 1944. Since then appeared in "Lower North," "Kiss Them for Me," "Flamingo Road," "On Whitman Avenue" and "Another Part of the Forest."

FOY, EDDIE, JR. Born in New Rochelle, N.Y., Feb. 4, 1905. Educated at St. Gabriel's School. Appeared on Broadway in "Smiles," "Show Girl," "Ripples," "Cat and the Fiddle," "At Home Abroad," "Orchids Preferred" and the revival of "The Red Mill."

FRANCIS, ARLENE. Born in Boston, Mass., and made her N.Y. bow in Orson Welles' production of "Horse Eats Hat," and again was a member of his Mercury Co. in "Danton's Death." Made other Broadway appearances in "All That Glitters," "Journey to Jerusalem," "The Doughgirls," "The Overtons" and "The French Touch."

Lidija Franklin

Eduard Franz

Marjorie Gateson

FRANCIS, KAY. Born in Oklahoma City, Okla., Jan. 13, 1899. Made her N.Y. debut at the Booth Theatre, Nov. 9, 1925 as Player Queen in modern dress version of "Hamlet." Since then appeared in "Crime," "Venus," and "Elmer the Great" before commencing her film career in 1930. Returned to the stage in 1945 when she toured in "Windy Hill," and was seen on Broadway this season in "State of the Union."

FRANKLIN, LIDIJA. Born May 17, 1922 in Russia. Appeared in England with the Joos Ballet before making her Broadway debut in "Bloomer Girl." Seen more recently in "Brigadoon."

FRANZ, EDUARD. Born Oct. 31, 1902 in Milwaukee, Wis. His first N.Y. appearance was with the Provincetown Players in "The Saint." Broadway audiences have seen him in "Miss Swan Expects," "Farm of Three Echoes," "The Russian People," "Cafe Crown," "Outrageous Fortune," "The Cherry Orchard," "Embezzled Heaven," "The Stranger," "Home of the Brave" and "The Big Two."

GALLAGHER, SKEETS. Born in Terre Haute, Ind., July 28, 1896. Educated at Terre Haute High School and Univ. of Indiana. Received his stage training in vaudeville and has appeared in many musical comedies; among them "Up in the Clouds," "The City Chap," "Lucky," "The Magnolia Lady," "No, No, Nanette," "Rose Marie," and "Up She Goes." Went to Hollywood where he played in over one hundred films. Returned to the N.Y. stage in "Good Night Ladies."

GANON, JAMES. Born in Jersey City, N.J. A graduate of the Feagin School of Dramatic Arts, he served his apprenticeship in stock in Clinton, Conn. Had his first Broadway opportunity in "Richard III" and since then was in "Dark Hammock" and "Lady in Danger."

GARRETT, BETTY. Born in St. Joseph, Mo., May 23, 1919. Received her education at the Annie Wright Seminary, Tacoma, Wash., and her stage training at the Neighborhood Playhouse, N.Y. Made appearance on Broadway in "Of Thee I Sing," "Let Freedom Ring," "Something for the Boys," "Jackpot," "Laffing Room Only," and "Call Me Mister."

GARY, HAROLD. Born in N.Y.C., May 7, 1910. Acted with the Neighborhood Playhouse before making Broadway debut in 1928 in "Diamond Lil." More recently has been seen in "Fiesta," "The World We Make," "Arsenic and Old Lace," "Billion Dollar Baby," and "A Flag is Born."

GATESON, MARJORIE. Born in Brooklyn, N.Y. Educated at Pacific Collegiate Institute and Brooklyn Conservatory of Music. Made Broadway debut in "Little Cafe," and among the many plays in which she appeared are "Little Simplicity," "Love Letter," "For Goodness Sake" and "As Good As New." After appearing in many Hollywood films she returned to Broadway in "Sweethearts."

GAUGE, ALEXANDER. Born July 29, 1914 in China. Educated in England where he appeared in many plays. Made Broadway bow in 1935 in "Eden End," and returned to the N.Y. stage this season with the Wolfit Co.

GAXTON, WILLIAM. Born in San Francisco, Dec. 2, 1893. Educated at the Univ. of Calif. Made his first Broadway appearance in the second "Music Box Revue." Since then has played leading roles in "Betty Lee," "Miss Happiness," "All for You," and the original version of "A Connecticut Yankee." Teamed up with Victor Moore and starred with him in "Of Thee I Sing," "Let 'Em Eat Cake," "Anything Goes," "Leave it to Me," "Louisiana Purchase," "Hollywood Pinafore," and "Nellie Bly."

GEAR, LUELLA. Born in N.Y.C., Sept. 5, 1897. Made her Broadway debut in 1917 in "Love O' Mike." Since then has acted in "The Gold Diggers," "Elsie," "Poppy," "Queen High," "The Optimist," "Ups-a-Daisy," "The Gay Divorcee," "Life Begins at 8:40," "On Your Toes," "Crazy With the Heat," "The Streets of Paris," "Count Me In," and "That Old Devil."

GEER, WILL. Born March 9, 1902 in Frankfort, Ind. Educated at Univ. of Chicago and Columbia Univ. His most recent appearances on Broadway include "Tobacco Road," "Abe Lincoln in Illinois," "The Cradle Will Rock," "Of Mice and Men," "Sophie," "Flamingo Road," and "On Whitman Avenue."

GENN, LEO. Born Aug. 9, 1905 in London. Educated at Cambridge Univ., and had early stage training at the Old Vic. Made Broadway debut in 1939 in "The Flashing Stream," and was seen this season in "Another Part of the Forest."

GEORGE, GRACE. Born N.Y.C. Dec. 25, 1879. Training at American Academy of Dramatic Arts. N.Y. debut, Standard Theatre, June 23, 1894, as a schoolgirl in "The New Boy." Among her famous roles are "Under Southern Skies," "Clothes," "Divorcons." "Sauce for the Goose," "The Truth," "The New York Idea," "Major Barbara," "Captain Brassbound's Conversion," "The 'Ruined' Lady," "The First Mrs. Fraser," "Mademoiselle," and more recently "Kind Lady," "Matrimony Pfd.," "Spring Again," and a revival of "The Circle."

GIBSON, DON. Born Waynesburg, Pa., March 25, 1917. Educated at the Univ. of Washington, Seattle. Made his N.Y. debut in "Catherine Was Great," and since has played in "Sleep, My Pretty One," "Many Happy Returns," "Clover Ring," "Oh, Brother," and "Love Goes to Press."

GIELGUD, JOHN. Born April 14, 1904 in London, where he studied for the stage at Lady Benson's School and the Royal Academy of Dramatic Arts. Since his London debut in 1921 at the Old Vic,

Dorothy Gish

Ernest Graves

Lillian Gish

he has achieved great success on the British stage. He was first seen on Broadway in 1928 in "The Patriot," and in 1936 returned here to play "Hamlet." This season he has been seen in "The Importance of Being Earnest," and "Love for Love."

GILBERT, BILLY. Was reared in the theatre, of theatrical parents, and has worked in almost every form of theatrical entertainment from burlesque to television. His most recent Broadway appearances were in "The Red Mill," and the current revival of "The Chocolate Soldier."

GILBERT, JODY. Born in Ft. Worth, Texas, on March 18, 1916. Spent three years with the Pasadena Playhouse, and made Broadway debut in 1938 in "Who's Who." After appearing in many films, she returned to the N.Y. stage this season in "If The Shoe Fits."

GILLMORE, MARGALO. Born London, May 31, 1897. Studied for the stage at American Academy of Dramatic Arts, and made first N.Y. stage appearance in 1917 in "The Scrap of Paper." Appeared in "The Famous Mrs. Fair," "He Who Gets Slapped," "Outward Bound," "The Green Hat," "Berkeley Square," "The Barretts of Wimpole Street," "Flowers of the Forest," and "Valley Forge." More recently she has played in "The Women," "No Time for Comedy," and "State of the Union."

GILMORE, VIRGINIA. Born in El Monte, Calif., July 26, 1919. Made her Broadway debut, 1943, in "Those Endearing Young Charms." Since then had leading roles in "The World's Full of Girls," "Dear Ruth," and "Truckline Cafe."

GISH, DOROTHY. Born Massillon, Ohio, March 11, 1898. Made her first stage appearance as a child actress in 1903 in "East Lynne." After an eminent career in the films, she returned to the stage in 1928 in "Young Love." Since then she has appeared in "The Inspector-General," "Getting Married," "The Streets of New York," "Pillars of Society," "The Bride the Sun Shines On," "Foreign Affairs," "Mainly for Lovers," "Brittle Heaven," "Missouri Legend," "Life With Father," "The Great Big Doorstep," "The Magnificent Yankee," and "The Story of Mary Suratt."

GISH, LILLIAN. Born Springfield, Ohio, Oct. 14, 1896. First appeared on the stage as a child of six, and in 1913 was seen in "The Good Little Devil." After a long and successful screen career, returned to the N.Y. stage in 1930 in "Uncle Vanya." Since then she has played in "Camille," "Nine Pine Street," "The Joyous Season," "Within the Gates," "Hamlet," "The Star Wagon," "Dear Octopus," "Life With Father," and "Mr. Sycamore."

GIVNEY, KATHRYN. Born in Rhinelander, Wis. Has appeared in N.Y. in "The Behavior of Mrs. Crane," "Lost Horizons," "Fulton of Oak Falls," "If This Be Treason," "Little Dark Horse," "Somewhere in France," "Flowers of the Forest," "Among the Married," "Wallflower," "Good Night Ladies," "The Happiest Years," and "This, Too, Shall Pass."

GOODNER, CAROL. Born in N.Y.C., 1904. Has appeared on Broadway in "They Walk Alone," "Let's Face It," "Blithe Spirit," "The Man Who Came to Dinner," "The Wookey," "The Family," "Lovers and Friends," and "Deep are the Roots."

GORDON, PAMELA. Born May 28, 1918 in London. Went to school in England, Switzerland and the U.S. and studied for the theatre at the Royal Academy of Dramatic Arts. First appeared on the English stage, and made Broadway debut as a walk-on in "Winged Victory." Appeared this season in "John Loves Mary."

GORDON, RUTH. Born in Wollaston, Mass., Oct. 30, 1896. Educated at Quincy High School, and received her dramatic training at American Academy of Dramatic Arts. Made her stage debut at the Empire Theatre, N.Y.C., with Maude Adams in "Peter Pan," in 1915. Since then has played in "Seventeen," "Fall of Eve," "Saturday's Children," "Here Today," "Ethan Frome," "The Country Wife," "Serena Blandish," "A Doll's House," "The Strings, My Lord, Are False," and "Over 21." Wrote the current success "Years Ago."

GOUGH, LLOYD. Has appeared on Broadway in "Yellow Jack," "The Ghost of Yankee Doodle," "Shadow and Substance," "My Dear Children," "Tanyard Street," "Golden Wings," "Heart of a City," and "Deep Are the Roots."

GRAHAM, RONALD. Born in Hamilton, Scotland, 1913. Made his Broadway bow in "Virginia." Since then played leading roles in "The Boys from Syracuse," "DuBarry was a Lady," "By Jupiter," and "Dream With Music."

GRAVES, ERNEST. Born May 5, 1919 in Chicago, Ill. Received stage training at the Goodman Theatre. Made Broadway debut in 1941 in "Macbeth." More recently appeared in "The Russian People" and "Cyrano de Bergerac."

GRAY, DOLORES. Born in Hollywood, Calif., June 7, 1924. Made her Broadway debut in "Seven Lively Arts," followed by "Are You With It?"

GREAZA, WALTER. Born St. Paul, Minn., 1900. Educated at Univ. of Minn. In 1927 made Broadway bow in "Love in the Tropics." Since then he has played in "Remote Control," "Wednesday's Child," "Ceiling Zero," "To Quito and Back," "Room Service," "A New Life," "Wallflower," "The Visitor," "The Overtons," and "Temper the Wind."

GREEN, MITZI. Born N.Y.C., Oct. 22, 1920. Made N.Y. debut in 1927 in vaudeville at Keith and Proctor's. First appearance on N.Y. legitimate stage in "Babes in Arms" in 1937 after a successful film career as a child star. More recently appeared in "Billion Dollar Baby."

Russell Hardie

Julie Haydon

Richard Hart

GRIFFITH, PETER. Born Oct. 23, 1933 in Baltimore. Appeared in summer stock before making his N.Y. stage debut in 1943 in "Kiss and Tell." Since then has been seen in "Harriet," "Strange Fruit," and "Street Scene."

GWENN, EDMUND. Born London, Sept. 28, 1875. First appeared on stage in England in 1895 and had a long career in that country. In 1935 he made Broadway bow in "Laburnum Grove." Since then has been seen in "The Wookey," "Sheppey," and "You Touched Me."

HAGEN, UTA. Born June 12, 1919 in Goettingen, Germany. Educated abroad and at the Univ. of Wis. Studied for the theatre for one term at the Royal Academy of Dramatic Arts in London, and made N.Y. debut March 28, 1938 with the Lunts in "The Sea Gull." Since then has been seen in "The Happiest Days," "Key Largo," "Vickie," "Othello" and "The Whole World Over."

HAJOS, MITZI. Born Budapest, Hungary, April 27, 1891. Among her famous starring roles are "Sari," "Pom-Pom," "Head Over Heels," "Lady Billy," "The Magic Ring," "Naughty Riquette" and "The Madcap." More recently she appeared in "You Can't Take It With You" and "Mr. Big."

HALEY, JACK. Born Aug. 10, 1902 in Boston. First N.Y. stage appearance at Century Roof, May 21, 1924 in "Around the Town." Since then has been seen in "Gay Paree," "Follow Thru," "Free for All," "Take a Chance," "Higher and Higher" and "Show Time."

HALL, GEORGE. Born in Toronto, Canada, Nov. 19, 1916. Received his stage training at the Neighborhood Playhouse. Formerly a member of the Martha Graham dance group, he made his Broadway debut in "Call Me Mister."

HALLIDAY, HILDEGARDE. Born in Nutley, N.J., Sept. 12, 1907. Educated at the Hartridge School for Girls, Plainfield, N.J. Her first Broadway show was "Garrick Gaieties" for the Theatre Guild. Since then has played in "New Faces," "Walk Into My Parlor," "Crazy With the Heat," and "The Odds on Mrs. Oakley." Has appeared in many N.Y. night clubs and on many radio programs.

HAMILTON, NEIL. Born in Lynn, Mass., Sept. 9, 1897. Educated at West Haven High School, Conn. After modelling for many prominent artists, he began his stage career in 1919. Appeared on the road with the Coburns in "The Better 'Ole," "The 'Ruined' Lady" with Grace George, "Artist's Life" with Peggy Wood, and had a season with the Toledo Stock Company in 1921 and the Cecil Spooner Stock Company in Brooklyn in 1922. That year D. W. Griffith discovered him and he played the lead in his first film "The White Rose." He remained in the pictures until 1944. Returned to stage for "Many Happy Returns." This was followed by "The Deep Mrs. Sykes," and "State of the Union" on the road.

HAMMOND, RUTH. Has appeared on Broadway in "Saturday's Children," "The Good Fairy," "Winterset," "The Women," "Three Waltzes" and "Life With Father."

HAMPDEN, WALTER. Born Brooklyn, June 30, 1879. Educated at Brooklyn Polytechnic Institute and Harvard. Made his stage debut in 1901 as a walk-on in F. R. Benson's Shakespearian Company. Since then has appeared in most of Shakespeare's and Ibsen's plays, also "Caponsacchi" and "Cyrano de Bergerac." More recently he had roles in "Seven Keys to Baldpate," "The Heel of Achilles," "The Rivals," "The Strings, My Lord, Are False," "The Patriots" and "And Be My Love." This season he re-appeared on Broadway as a leading player with the American Repertory Theatre.

HANLEY, ELLEN. Born in Lorain, Ohio on May 15, 1926. Attended the Juilliard Institute of Music for two years, and made Broadway debut in the chorus of "Annie Get Your Gun." Played ingenue lead this season in "Barefoot Boy With Cheek."

HANSEN, WILLIAM. Born March 2, 1911 in Tacoma, Wash. Graduated from Univ. of Washington, and studied for the theatre with Maria Ouspenskaya, and at Group Theatre School. Made his N.Y. debut in "My Heart's in the Highlands." Since then has appeared in "I Know What I Like," "Night Music," "Medicine Show," the Hayes-Evans' "Twelfth Night," the Evans' "Macbeth," "The Assassin" and "Brigadoon."

HARDIE, RUSSELL. Born in Griffin Mills, N.Y., May 20, 1906. Educated at St. Mary's College. After training with the Buffalo stock company, made his Broadway bow in "The Criminal Code." Since then has appeared in "Pagan Lady," "The Constant Sinner," "Happy Landing," "Remember the Day," "Sun Kissed," "Society Girl," "Saint Wench," "Roosty," "The Ghost of Yankee Doodle," "Primrose Path," "Under This Roof," "Snafu," and "Foxhole in the Parlor." On tour he was seen in "The Doughgirls" and "My Sister Eileen." Recently he played in "Home of the Brave" and "The Bees and the Flowers."

HARDWICKE, SIR CEDRIC. Born in Lye, England, Feb. 19, 1893. Recent N.Y. appearances include "Promise," "The Amazing Dr. Clitterhouse," "Shadow and Substance," "Antigone" and the 1946 revival of "Candida."

HARE, WILL. Born in Elkins, W. Va., March 30, 1919. Received his stage training with the American Actors Theatre. His N.Y. appearances include "The Eternal Road," "The Moon is Down," "Suds in Your Eye," "Only the Heart," and "The Visitor."

HARENS, DEAN. Born in South Bend, Ind., June

George Hayes

Mary Healy

Thomas Heaphy

30, 1921. Studied at the Goodman Memorial Theatre in Chicago, and had stock experience before making his N.Y. debut in 1941 in "The Talley Method." Since then has been seen in "Papa Is All," "Men in Shadow," "Those Endearing Young Charms" and "Tenting Tonight."

HARRIGAN, WILLIAM. Born in N.Y.C., March 27, 1893. Educated at N.Y. Military Academy. Among the many plays he has been featured in are "The Acquittal," "Polly Preferred," "The Dove," "The Great God Brown," "Moon in the Yellow River," "Criminal at Large," "Paths of Glory," "Portrait of Gilbert," "Among Those Sailing," "Roosty," "The Happiest Days," "In Time to Come," "Pick-Up Girl" and the Chicago company of "Dear Ruth."

HARRIS, LENORE. Born in N.Y.C. where she began her stage career under the management of Charles Frohman. She appeared in London as leading woman for Sir Charles Hawtrey. Among the many plays in which she has appeared on Broadway are "The Girl From Kay's," "The Whip," "Our Betters" (original production), "Bluebeard's Eighth Wife," "Dodsworth" and "The Man Who Came to Dinner." This season she was seen in "Present Laughter."

HART, RICHARD. Born April 14, 1915 in Providence, R.I., and educated at Brown Univ. His first stage experience gained at the summer theatre at Tiverton, R.I. On Broadway he has been seen in "Pillar to Post" and "Dark of the Moon."

HAVOC, JUNE. Was a member of Anna Pavlowa's ballet troupe at three, and a veteran of Mack Sennett and Hal Roach comedies before she was six. For many years she was known as "Baby June, the Darling of Vaudeville." Her first Broadway show was "Forbidden Melody." This was followed by "Pal Joey," "Mexican Hayride," and "Sadie Thompson." More recently she has been seen in "The Ryan Girl," "Dunnigan's Daughter" and "Dream Girl."

HAYDON, JULIE. Born in Oak Park, Ill., June 10, 1910. Educated at the Gordon School for Girls in Hollywood. New Yorkers have seen her in "Bright Star," "Shadow and Substance," "Time of Your Life," "Magic," "Hello Out There," "The Glass Menagerie" and "Miracle in the Mountains."

HAYES, GEORGE. Born Nov. 13, 1888 in London, and educated in England. Early stage training with Sir Johnston Forbes-Robertson. Made Broadway debut in 1912 as Osric in "Hamlet," and later appeared in "The Merchant of Venice," "An Ideal Husband" and "The Queen of Spades." He was seen this season in "Love for Love."

HAYES, HELEN. Born in Washington, D.C., Oct. 10, 1900. Educated at Sacred Heart Academy, Washington. Made her first appearance on the stage in her native city at the National Theatre in 1908 in "The Babes in the Wood." The following year made her N.Y. debut with Lew Fields in "Old Dutch." As a child actress played in "The Summer Widowers," "The Never Homes," "The Prodigal Husband," "Pollyanna" (on tour), "Penrod," "Dear Brutus" and "Clarence." Her first real grown-up role was in "Bab." This was followed by "The Wren," "Golden Days," "To the Ladies," "We Moderns," "Dancing Mothers," "Quarantine," "Caesar and Cleopatra," "Young Blood," "What Every Woman Knows" and "Coquette." More recently she has appeared in "Mary of Scotland," "Victoria Regina," "Ladies and Gentlemen," "Twelfth Night," "Candle in the Wind," "Harriet" and "Happy Birthday."

HAYES, MARGARET. Born in Baltimore, Md. Engagements in two Broadway plays, "I Must Love Someone" and "Bright Rebel" preceded Hollywood, where she made several pictures. Returned to N.Y. stage in "Many Happy Returns," and was last seen in "Little Women."

HEALY, MARY. Born in New Orleans, La., April 14, 1920, and educated there at St. Mary's Parochial School and Redemptorist High School. First stage experience in New Orleans Little Theatre. Made Broadway debut in 1942 in "Count Me In," and since than has been seen in "Common Ground" and "Around the World."

HEAPHY, THOMAS M. Born Jan. 19, 1891 in N.Y.C. and educated at Villanova College. Began his theatrical career with the National Catholic Repertory Theatre, and later was a member of Abbey Theatre in Dublin. On Broadway he has been seen in "The Goose Hangs High," "The Perfect Alibi," "Captain Applejack," "The White Steed" and "Happy Birthday." He has also appeared extensively on the radio and television, and toured with the USO.

HEMING, VIOLET. Born Leeds, England, Jan. 27, 1895. Educated at Malvern House School. All her acting has been in this country. She made her stage debut as Wendy in Frohman's children's company of "Peter Pan." Among her N.Y. plays are "Three Faces East," "Spring Cleaning," "This Thing Called Love," "Ladies All," a revival of "The Jest," "The Rivals," and "Trelawney of the Wells," "Love for Love," "Yes, My Darling Daughter," "Beverly Hills" and "And Be My Love."

HEPBURN, KATHARINE. Born Hartford, Conn., Nov. 9, 1909. Educated at Bryn Mawr College. N.Y. debut made Sept. 12, 1928 at Martin Beck Theatre in "Night Hostess," under the name of Katherine Burns. This was followed by "These Days," "A Month in the Country," "Art and Mrs. Bottle," "The Warrior's Husband," "The Lake," "The Philadelphia Story" and "Without Love."

Louis Jean Heydt Michael Higgins John Hudson

HEYDT, LOUIS JEAN. Born in Montclair, N.J., in 1907 and educated at Worcester Academy and Dartmouth College. Made Broadway debut in 1927 in "The Trial of Mary Dugan." Since then has appeared in "Strictly Dishonorable," "Nikki," "When the Bough Breaks," "Housewarming," "All Rights Reserved," "Thunder on the Left," "Bright Star," "Calico Wedding" and "Happy Birthday." Also appeared in many Hollywood films.

HIGGINS, MICHAEL. Born Jan. 20, 1922 in Brooklyn. Educated at Manhattan College, and had his theatrical training at the American Theatre Wing School and in summer stock. Made Broadway debut with Katharine Cornell in "Antigone."

HOBBES, HALLIWELL. Born in Stratford-on-Avon, England, Nov. 16, 1877. Made his stage debut with F. R. Bensen's company in Glasgow in 1898. Made his London debut 1908 as Tybalt in "Romeo and Juliet" and his N.Y. bow in 1910 with Forbes Robertson in "Cleopatra." His next Broadway appearance was in 1923 in "The Swan." Went to Hollywood in 1929 where he played in films until 1940 when he returned to the theatre for Laurence Olivier's production of "Romeo and Juliet." More recently has been seen in "Ten Little Indians" and "Hidden Horizon."

HODGES, JOY. Born in Des Moines, Iowa. Made her Broadway debut in "I'd Rather Be Right." Since then played in "Best Foot Forward," "Something for the Boys," "Dream With Music," "The Odds on Mrs. Oakley" and "Nellie Bly."

HOLLAND, BETTY LOU. Born in N.Y.C., Dec. 25, 1926. Educated at St. Agatha and Spence High School. Received her stage training at American Academy of Dramatic Arts. Made her Broadway bow April 18, 1946 in "Call Me Mister."

HOLLIDAY, JUDY. Born in the Bronx, N.Y. in 1924. Spent several years with the Revuers, a night club act. Appeared in the films "Something for the Boys" and "Winged Victory." Made her Broadway debut in "Kiss Them for Me," and has since been seen in "Born Yesterday."

HOLM, CELESTE. Born in N.Y.C., and was educated in schools in Holland and France. Her N.Y. engagements include roles in "Time of Your Life," "Papa is All," "Return of the Vagabond," "Eight O'Clock Tuesday," "The Damask Cheek," "Oklahoma" and "Bloomer Girl."

HOLMAN, LIBBY. Born Cincinnati, Ohio, and educated at Univ. of Cincinnati. First N.Y. appearance on June 8, 1925 in "Garrick Gaieties." Since then appeared in "Greenwich Village Follies" (1926), "Marry-Go-Round," "Americana," "Rainbow," "Ned Wayburn's Gambols," "The Little Show," "Three's a Crowd," "Revenge With Music," "You Never Know" and "Mexican Mural."

HOLMES, TAYLOR. Born Newark, N.J., May 16, 1878. Made his first stage appearance in vaudeville in 1899. Among his outstanding plays were "The Midnight Sons," "The Commuters," "Marriage A La Carte," "The Million," "The Third Party," "His Majesty, Bunker Bean," "The Hotel Mouse," "Happy-Go-Lucky," "The Great Necker," "The Sap," "Your Uncle Dudley," "Salt Water," "That's Gratitude," "Riddle Me This," "Big Hearted Herbert" and "Say When." In 1936 he toured as Jeeter Lester in "Tobacco Road" and more recently has played in "I'd Rather Be Right," "Marinka," and "Woman Bites Dog."

HOMOLKA, OSCAR. Born Vienna, Aug. 12, 1898, and graduated from the Vienna Royal Academy. On tne continent he starred in "The Emperor Jones," "Loyalties," "The Doctor's Dilemma" and "King Lear." In London he was first seen supporting Flora Robson in "Close Quarters." He made his American debut in 1937 in the film "Ebb Tide." New York first saw him on the stage in "Grey Farms," which was followed by "The Innocent Voyage" and "I Remember Mama."

HOPKINS, MIRIAM. Born Bainbridge, Ga., Oct. 18, 1902. Educated at Goddard Seminary, Vt., and Syracuse Univ. Made her stage bow in the chorus of the first "Music Box Revue." Other N.Y. appearances include "Garrick Gaieties," "Excess Baggage," "The Camel Through the Needle's Eye," "Lysistrata," "Knife in the Wall" and "The Home Towners." For years she spent most of her time in Hollywood, although she came back to N.Y. to star in "Jezebel" and "The Perfect Marriage." She also took over the role of Sabina in "The Skin of Our Teeth," played in "St. Lazare's Pharmacy" on the road, and was seen this season in "Message for Margaret."

HORREY, FREDERICK. Born in Nottingham, England, June 27, 1921. Received stage training in London at the Old Vic Theatre School. After playing numerous roles on the British stage, he made his N.Y. debut on Feb. 18, 1947 with the Donald Wolfit Company.

HOWARD, WILLIE. Born N.Y.C., 1883. First stage appearance was in 1897 as a boy soprano in vaudeville. In 1903 he joined his brother, Eugene, in a vaudeville act and they played together for many years, appearing in various editions of "The Passing Show," "The Whirl of the World" and "The Show of Wonders." Later he was seen in "Sky High," "George White's Scandals," "Ballyhoo of 1932," "Ziegfeld Follies of 1934," "The Show is On," and "My Dear Public."

HUDSON, JOHN. Born in Gilroy, Calif., Jan. 24, 1921. Went to college on the West Coast and studied for theatre with Max Reinhardt. Made Broadway debut in 1941 in "Junior Miss." Since then has appeared in "The Eve of St. Mark," "January Thaw" and the revival of "Craig's Wife."

HULL, HENRY. Born Louisville, Ky., Oct. 3, 1890. Among his many Broadway plays are "The Man

Josephine Hull

Walter Huston

Dorothea Jackson

Who Came Back," "39 East," "The Cat and the "Canary," "Lulu Belle," "Ivory Door," "Michael and Mary," "Springtime for Henry," "The Youngest," "Tobacco Road," "Masque of Kings," "Plumes in the Dust" and "Foolish Notion."

HULL, JOSEPHINE. Born in Newton, Mass., Jan. 3, 1886. Educated at Radcliffe College. Made her professional debut in the Copley Square Stock Company of Boston. Among the many plays she has appeared in are "Fata Morgana," "Craig's Wife," "March Hares," "A Thousand Summers," "Fresh Fields," "Night in the House," "American Dream," "An International Incident," "You Can't Take It With You," "Arsenic and Old Lace" and "Harvey."

HUMPHREYS, CECIL. Born Juyl 21, 1883. First appeared on the stage in England in 1904. First N.Y. appearance was in 1924 in "Parasites." More recently he has been seen in "Tovarich," "Victoria Regina," "The Merchant of Venice," the revival of "The Circle," Katina Paxinou's revival of "Hedda Gabler," Katharine Cornell's revival of "The Doctor's Dilemma," "The Patriots," and the Gertrude Lawrence revival of "Pygmalion."

HUNNICUTT, ARTHUR. Born in Gravelly, Ark., New Yorkers have seen him in "Love's Old Sweet Song," "Time of Your Life," "Lower North," "Dark Hammock," "Too Hot for Maneuvers," "Beggars Are Coming to Town" and "Apple of His Eye."

HUSSEY, RUTH. Born Oct. 30, 1917 in Providence, R.I. Educated at Pembrook College and Univ. of Mich. Appeared in many motion pictures before making her Broadway debut in "State of the Union."

HUSTON, PHILIP. Born in Goshen, Va., March 14, 1910. Educated at Blair Academy, Blairstown, N.J. Made his Broadway bow in 1934 in "Strange Orchestra." Since then has played in "Whatever Possessed Her," "Window Shopping," Maurice Evans' "Macbeth," and "Twelfth Night," "Othello," "Catherine Was Great," "The Tempest," "School for Brides," "Make Yourself at Home," and "The Winter's Tale."

HUSTON, WALTER. Born Toronto, Canada, April 6, 1884. First N.Y. appearance in 1905 in "In Convict's Stripes." Spent considerable time in vaudeville. Among the many plays in which he has appeared are "Mr. Pitt," "Desire Under the Elms," "Kongo," "The Barker," "Elmer the Great," "The Commodore Marries" and "Dodsworth." More recently he has played in "Othello," "Knickerbocker Holiday," "Love's Old Sweet Song" and "Apple of His Eye."

IDEN, ROSALIND. Born in Manchester, England. Leading lady for the Wolfit Company since 1939. Made her Broadway debut with this company in repertory.

INESCORT, FRIEDA. Born in Hitchin, England, in 1905. Made her American debut in 1922 in "The Truth About Blayds." Many Broadway hits followed, among them "Trelawney of the Wells," "Springtime for Henry," "You and I," "Love in a Mist," "Pygmalion," "Major Barbara," "Escape," "When Ladies Meet," "False Dreams, Farewell," and she played Portia in George Arliss' production of "The Merchant of Venice." Spent ten years in Hollywood and returned to Broadway to appear in "Soldier's Wife" and "The Mermaids Singing."

INGRAM, REX. Born Oct. 20. 1896 aboard a Mississippi river boat. Educated at Aburn Military Academy. First N.Y. appearance in 1934 in "Theodora the Queen," and during the same year appeared in "Stevedore." More recently he was seen in "Marching Song," "Haiti," "Sing Out The News," "Cabin in the Sky" and "St. Louis Woman."

IVANS, ELAINE. Born in Brooklyn. N.Y., Feb. 10, 1900. Appeared on Broadway in "Mrs. Partridge Presents," "The Love Habit," "Headquarters," "Just Life," "Crime Marches On" and "Life With Father."

JACKSON, DOROTHEA. Born in Elizabeth, N.J. and educated at Asbury Park High School. Early stage experience in summer stock. and played ingenue lead in road company of "Three's A Family." Made Broadway debut in "Portrait in Black."

JACQUEMOT, RAY. Born in New Brunswick, N.J. Played leads in several St. Louis Municipal Opera Company productions. Made his Broadway debut in 1943 in a revival of "The Student Prince." Has been seen in the Theatre Guild's productions "Oklahoma" and "Carousel," and followed Alfred Drake in the leading role of "Sing Out, Sweet Land." Most recent N.Y. appearance was made in "Louisiana Lady."

JAFFE, SAM. Born N.Y.C., March 8, 1898. Stage debut in 1915 in "The Clod." Has appeared in "Samson and Delilah," "The God of Vengeance," "The Maine Line," "Izzy," "The Jazz Singer," "Grand Hotel," "The Eternal Road," "A Doll's House," "The Gentle People" and more recently "Thank You, Svoboda."

JAMES, MARY. Born in Washington, D.C., and educated at Sweet Briar College. Received stage training at Neighborhood Playhouse. Made her Broadway debut in "Apple of His Eye."

JEFFREYS, ANNE. Born in Goldboro, N.C., Jan. 26, 1923. Educated at Anderson College. First acting experience was in Hollywood where she appeared in many films. From the movies, she went on to Grand Opera and in 1946 sang the title role of "Tosca" at the Brooklyn Academy of Music. She made her Broadway debut on Jan. 9, 1947 singing the role of Rose Maurrant in "Street Scene."

Barbara Joyce

Whitford Kane

Jane Kean

JOHNSON, BILL. Born in Baltimore, Md., and educated at Univ. of Md. Appeared on Broadway in "Two for the Show," "All in Fun," "Banjo Eyes," "Something for the Boys" and "The Day Before Spring."

JOHNSON, CHIC (HAROLD J.) Born in Chiaco, Ill., in 1891. Met and teamed up with Ole Olsen in 1914 and since then have played in nearly every town in the U.S., as well as in England and Australia. Practically unknown to Broadway in 1938, they brought in their explosive "Hellzapoppin" and settled down for a three year run. They followed this with "Sons O' Fun" and "Laffing Room Only."

JOHNSON, FRED. Born in Ireland, Aug. 6, 1899, and had first acting experience with the Abbey Theatre, Dublin. Made his Broadway debut Oct. 26, 1946 in "Playboy of the Western World."

JOLSON, AL. Born in Russia May 26, 1886. First stage appearance was in 1899 as one of the mob in "Children of the Ghetto." For several seasons he played in minstrel companies and vaudeville. Among the many musical shows in which he has appeared are "The Whirl of Society," "Honeymoon Express," "Dancing Around," "Robinson Crusoe, Jr.," "Sinbad," "Bombo," "Big Boy" and "Wonder Bar." Recently he has scored great success on the radio.

JORDAN, JOHN. Born in N.Y.C., Oct. 15, 1923. Made his debut as an actor as Michael in Eva Le Gallienne's production of "Peter Pan." Since then has appeared in "Green Waters," "Sun-up to Sundown," "Gold Eagle Guy," "Hilda Cassidy," "Best Foot Forward" and with the Experimental Theatre this season in "The Wanhope Building."

JORY, VICTOR. Born in Dawson City, Alaska, Nov. 23, 1902. Educated at Pasadena Junior College and Univ. of Calif. Theatre apprenticeship was in stock in Denver, Milwaukee, Minneapolis, Los Angeles and San Francisco. For a number of years he appeared in movies, and acted in over a hundred films. Broadway debut was in 1943 in "The Two Mrs. Carrolls," followed by "The Perfect Marriage" and "Therese." This season he was a leading player with A.R.T. and was seen in "Henry VIII," "John Gabriel Borkman" and "Androcles and the Lion."

JOY, NICHOLAS. Born in Paris, France, 1892, and received early theatrical training in England. Made his American debut at the age of twenty in "A Butterfly on the Wheel." Since then made notable appearances in "Wings Over Europe," "Topaze," "Rain," "End of Summer," "Ode to Liberty," "The Bride the Sun Shines On," "Music in the Air," "The Cat and the Fiddle," "Yes, My Darling Daughter," "The Philadelphia Story," "This Rock," "Mrs. January and Mr. X," "Ten Little Indians," "A Joy Forever" and "The Iceman Cometh."

JOYCE, BARBARA. Born Aug. 2, in San Francisco, Calif. Educated at Univ. of Calif. and Mills College. Made Broadway debut in 1943 playing role of Ellie May in "Tobacco Road." Since then has been seen in "The Petrified Forest," "Lady Behave," "All for All," "Skydrift," "Dunnigan's Daughter" and "Hidden Horizon."

JUDELS, CHARLES. Born Aug. 17, 1881 in Amsterdam, Holland. Made Broadway debut in 1903 in "Mary, Mary." Among the many plays in which he has appeared are "Old Dutch," "The Girl Behind the Counter," "The Slim Princess" and "Mary." After a long session in Hollywood, he returned to Broadway in "Louisiana Lady."

KANE, WHITFORD. Born in Larne, Ireland, Jan. 30, 1882. Made his stage debut in Belfast in 1903 in "Ticket-of-Leave Man." His first London appearance was in 1910 in "Justice," and his Broadway bow was made in 1912 in "The Drone." Since then he has become one of America's most dependable character actors. Among the many plays he has appeared in are "Hindle Wakes," "The First Legion," the Cornell revival of "The Doctor's Dilemma," "Excursion," "The Moon is Down," "Boyd's Shop," "St. Helena," "Yellow Jack," "Tiger, Tiger," "The Pidgeon," "Shoemaker's Holiday," "A Passenger to Bali," the First Gravedigger in both the Barrymore and Evans productions of "Hamlet," "Lifeline," "Land of Fame," "Thank You, Svoboda," "Career Angel," "Meet A Body," "It's a Gift" and "The Winter's Tale."

KARLWEIS, OSCAR. Born in Austria. Made his Broadway debut in "Cue for Passion." Since then has appeared in "Rosalinda," "Jacobowsky and the Colonel" and "I Like It Here."

KEAN, JANE. Born in Hartford, Conn., April 10, 1924. Educated at Julia Richman High School, N.Y.C., and studied dramatics at Fay Compton School in London. Has appeared on Broadway in "Early to Bed," "The Girl from Nantucket," "Are You With It?" and "Call Me Mister."

KEANE, GEORGE. Born in Springfield, Mass., April 26, 1917. Educated at C.C.N.Y. Received his stage training at Maverick Playhouse, Woodstock and with Columbia Laboratory Players. Made Broadway debut in 1938 in Maurice Evans' "Hamlet." Since then has been seen in "Richard II," "Henry IV," "The Moon is Down," "Othello," "Lifeline," "Park Avenue" and "Brigadoon."

KEITH, ROBERT. Born Fowler, Ind., Feb. 10, 1898. First N.Y. appearance in 1921 in "The Triumph of X" Has appeared in "New Brooms," "The Great God Brown," "Gentle Grafters," "Beyond the Horizon," "Fog," "Under Glass," "Peace on Earth," "Yellow Jack," "Goodbye, Please," "The Children's Hour," "Othello," "Work is for Horses," "Tortilla Flat," "The Good" and "The Romantic Mr. Dickens." More recently he was seen in "Ladies and Gentlemen," "Spring Again," "Kiss and Tell" and "January Thaw."

KEITH-JOHNSON, COLIN. Born London, Oct. 8, 1896. First stage appearance was made in 1917 in

Jackie Kelk

Pamela Kellino

Alexander Kirkland

London. N.Y. debut in "Journey's End" in 1929. He has also been seen in this country in "Hamlet," "The Warrior's Husband," "Dangerous Corner," "Noah," "Pride and Prejudice," and more recently in Miss Cornell's revival of "The Doctor's Dilemma," "The Winter's Tale" and "The Dancer."

KELK, JACKIE. Born in Brooklyn, N.Y., Aug. 6, 1923. Went to the Professional Children's School, and made Broadway debut at age of nine in "Bridal Wise." Also appeared as a child actor in "Goodbye Again" and "Jubilee." Has had considerable radio experience, and his voice is known to millions as that of Homer in the "Aldrich Family." Returned to the Broadway stage this season in "Tenting Tonight."

KELLINO, PAMELA. Born in Westcliff, England, March 10, 1917. Educated in Paris and London. Studied for the theatre under Italia Conti, and appeared on the English stage and in English films before making her Broadway debut on March 26, 1947 in "Bathsheba."

KELLY, PAUL. Born Brooklyn, N.Y., Aug. 8, 1899. Appeared on stage as a child actor, and had varied experience in stock before he first appeared on Broadway in "Seventeen" in 1918. Also appeared in "Penrod," "Honors Are Even," "Up the Ladder," "Whispering Wires," "Chains," "The Lady Killer," "Nerves," "Houses of Sand," "The Sea Woman," "Nine-Fifteen Revue," "Find Daddy," "Bad Girl," "Hobo," "Just to Remind You," "Adam Had Two Sons" and "The Great Magoo." After a long session in Hollywood, returned to N.Y. stage in "The Beggars Are Coming To Town."

KENNEDY, ARTHUR. Began his theatre career as a Group Theatre apprentice. Appeared with Maurice Evans' in "Henry IV" and "Richard II," and in "Life and Death of an American" and "Madam, Will You Walk." After appearing in several films, he returned to Broadway this season in "All My Sons."

KERRIGAN, J. M. Made his debut at the Abbey Theatre, Dublin, in 1907 and played with that company for nine years, appearing in more than one hundred different roles. He acted in the first American production of "The Playboy of the Western World" in 1911, and was again seen in this season's revival of the same play.

KIEPURA, JAN. Born in Sosnowicz, Poland, May 16, 1906, and educated in Warsaw. Made operatic debut in "Tosca" at Warsaw Opera in 1926, and since then has been heard with leading opera companies in Milan, Vienna, Paris, Berlin, Buenos Aires and New York. Made his Broadway debut in the New Opera Company's production of "The Merry Widow," and since then has been seen in "Polonaise."

KILBRIDE, PERCY. Born in San Francisco, Calif. Appeared on Broadway in "Lily Turner," "Post Road," "Three Men on a Horse," "George Washington Slept Here," "Cuckoos on the Hearth" and more recently "Little Brown Jug."

KING, DENNIS. Born in Coventry, England, Nov. 2, 1897. Made his stage debut in 1916 with the Birmingham Repertory Company. His N.Y. bow was made in 1921 in "Claire de Lune." Played in the Jane Cowl productions of "Romeo and Juliet," and "Antony and Cleopatra." Other appearances include "The Vagabond King," "The Three Musketeers," "Frederika," "I Married an Angel," the Ruth Gordon revival of "A Doll's House," Katharine Cornell's revival of "The Three Sisters," the Chicago company of "Blithe Spirit," and "The Searching Wind." More recently he appeared in "Dunnigan's Daughter" and the revival of "He Who Gets Slapped."

KING, JR., DENNIS. Made his Broadway debut in "Lower North." Since then he has appeared in "Kiss Them for Me," "The Day Before Spring," "The Playboy of the Western World" and "Parlor Story."

KING, EDITH. Recently has appeared in the Theatre Guild productions of "The Taming of the Shrew," "The Sea Gull," "Amphitryon 38," "Battle of Angels," "Hope for a Harvest," "Othello," and "The Would-Be Gentleman."

KINGSFORD, WALTER. Born in England, Sept. 20, 1881. Recently New Yorkers have seen him in "The Criminal Code," "The Pursuit of Happiness," and "Song of Norway."

KIRKLAND, ALEXANDER. Born in Mexico City, Sept. 15, 1903. Educated at Taft School and the Univ. of Virginia. Had his stage training with Jasper Deeter. Plays on Broadway include "Wings Over Europe," "The Devil to Pay," "Men in White," "Gold Eagle Guy," "The Case of Clyde Griffiths," "Till the Day I Die," "Many Mansions," the revival of "Outward Bound," "Junior Miss," and "Lady in Danger."

KIRKLAND, PATRICIA. First acting experience was in summer stock, and she played in "Kiss and Tell" on the road, prior to her first Broadway appearance in "For Keeps." Since then she has been seen in "Snafu," "Round Trip" and "Years Ago."

KNIGHT, JUNE. Born Hollywood, Calif., Jan. 22, 1911. Began her career as a dancer and first played in N.Y. in 1929 in "Fifty Million Frenchmen." She has also been seen in "Girl Crazy," "The Nine O'Clock Revue," "Hot Cha!," "Take A Chance" and "Jubilee." More recently she appeared in "The Overtons," "The Would-Be Gentleman" and "Sweethearts."

KROEGER, BERRY. Born in San Antonio, Texas, Oct. 16, 1912. Educated at Univ. of Calif., and received stage training at the Pasadena Playhouse. Appeared on Broadway in "The World's Full of Girls," "The Tempest," "Therese" and "Joan of Lorraine."

Otto Kruger

Sylvia Lane

John Larson

KRUGER, OTTILIE. Born in N.Y.C., Nov. 20, 1926. Educated at Marlborough School for Girls. Played on Broadway in "I Remember Mama," "A Joy Forever" and "Little A"

KRUGER, OTTO. Born in Toledo, Ohio, Sept. 6, 1885. Educated at Univ. of Mich. and Columbia. First NY. appearance, after experience in stock and vaudeville, was in "The Natural Law" in April 1914. Among the many plays in which he has appeared are "Young America," "Seven Chances," "Captain Kidd, Jr.," "The Gypsy Trail," "Adam and Eva," "The Meanest Man in the World," "To the Ladies," "The Nervous Wreck," "The Royal Family," "Karl and Anna," "The Game of Life and Death," and more recently "The Moon is Down" and "Little A."

KRUMSCHMIDT, E. A. Born in Berlin, Aug. 3, 1904. After extensive experience on the European stage, he made his Broadway debut on Dec. 29, 1942 in "The Russian People," and was seen this season in "The Big Two."

LAHR, BERT. Born N.Y.C., Aug. 13, 1895, and first played in vaudeville and burlesque. First N.Y. appearance was in "Delmar's Revels." He has also appeared in "Hold Everything," "Flying High," "Hot-Cha," "George White's Music Hall Varieties," "Life Begins at 8:40," "George White's Scandals," "The Show is On," "Du Barry Was a Lady," and "The Seven Lively Arts." This season he appeared in a revival of "Burlesque."

LANCASTER, BURT. Born in N.Y.C., Nov. 2, 1913. Educated De Witt Clinton High School and N.Y. University. Spent five years with circuses and two years in vaudeville and fairs as an acrobat. Returned from 26 months overseas in the Army to make his Broadway debut in "A Sound of Hunting."

LANDIS, JESSIE ROYCE. Born Chicago, Nov. 25, 1904. Made N.Y. debut in 1926 revival of "The Honor of the Family." Among the many plays in which she has appeared are "The Furies," "The Command Performance," "Solid South," "Marriage for Three," "Merrily We Roll Along," "Love from a Stranger," "Miss Quis," "Where There's a Will," "Brown Danube," "Dame Nature," "Love's Old Sweet Song," "Papa is All," "Kiss and Tell," "The Winter's Tale" and "Little A."

LANE, RUSTY. Born in Chicago, Ill., May 31, 1899. Was professor of drama at Univ. of Wisconsin. Made Broadway debut in "Decision." Since then has appeared in "Lower North" and "Bathsheba."

LANE, SYLVIA. Born in Brooklyn, N.Y., March 2, 1934. Attended Children's Professional School, and made her Broadway debut in "The Bees and the Flowers."

LANG, CHARLES. Born in N.Y.C., Feb. 15, 1915. Received stage training at American Academy of Dramatic Arts. Made Broadway bow in "Pastoral." Since then has appeared in "The World's Full of Girls," "Down to Miami," "The Overtons," and many motion pictures.

LANG, HAROLD. Born Daly City, Calif., Dec. 21, 1920. Appeared with the Ballet Russe de Monte Carlo and Ballet Theatre before making his Broadway bow in "Mr. Strauss Goes to Boston." "Three to Make Ready" followed.

LARRIMORE, FRANCINE. Born Verdun, France, Aug. 22, 1898. Made N.Y. debut as a child actress in "A Fool There Was" in 1910. Among the plays in which she has appeared are "Over Night," "Some Baby," "Fair and Warmer," "Here Comes the Bride," "Parlor, Bedroom and Bath," "Scandal," "Nice People," "Nobody's Business," "Chicago" and "Let Us Be Gay." More recently she has played in "Brief Moment," "Shooting Star" and "Spring Song."

LARSON, JOHN. Born in Elroy, Wisc., Feb. 2, 1914. Educated at Univ. of Wisc. (B.S.), Syracuse University (M.A.) and Yale. Made Broadway bow in "The Fatal Weakness."

LAURENCE, PAULA. Born in Brooklyn, N.Y., Jan. 25, 1916. Began her stage career with Orson Welles in "Horse Eats Hat" and "Doctor Faustus." Since then, besides becoming one of New York's most popular night club entertainers, she has appeared in "Junior Miss," "Something for the Boys," "One Touch of Venus" and "Cyrano de Bergerac."

LAWRENCE, GERTRUDE. Born in London, England and educated at the Convent of the Sacred Heart, Streatham. She studied dancing under Mme. Espinosa and acting under Italia Conti. First stage appearance was as a child dancer in the pantomime of "Dick Whittington." First stage appearance in N.Y. was in "Charlot's Revue" in 1924. She has also played in "Oh, Kay!," "Treasure Girl," "Candlelight," "The International Revue" and "Private Lives." More recently she has played in "Tonight at 8:30," "Susan and God," "Skylark," "Lady in the Dark," and a revival of "Pygmalion."

LEDERER, FRANCIS. Born Karlin, Prague, Nov. 6, 1906. He studied for the stage in both Prague and Berlin, and appeared extensively on the Continent and in England before his N.Y. debut in 1932 in "Autumn Crocus." In 1939 he replaced Laurence Olivier in "No Time for Comedy."

LEE, CANADA. Born in N.Y.C., March 2, 1907. Received his education at Public School No. 5. Had his stage training with the WPA Negro Federal Theatre Unit. New Yorkers have seen him in "Macbeth," "Haiti," "Stevedore," "Mamba's Daughters," "Native Son," "Across the Board on Tomorrow Morning," "Talking to You," "South Pacific," "Anna Lucasta," "The Tempest," "On Whitman Avenue" and "The Duchess of Malfi."

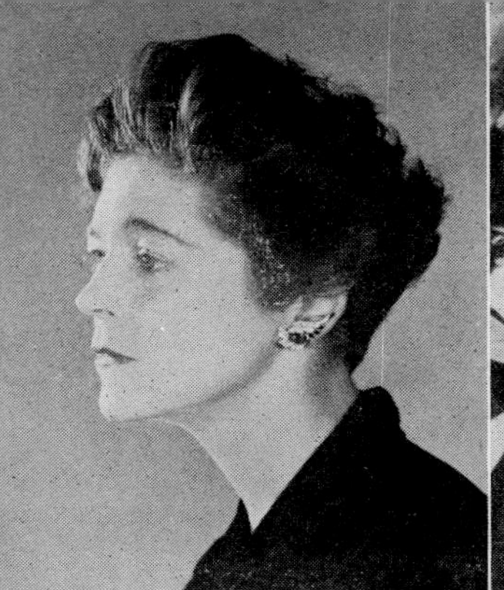

Eva Le Gallienne Marta Linden Pauline Lord

LEE, WILLIAM A. Born in Clatskanie, Ore., March 12, 1890. Has played in stock, vaudeville and radio. His recent appearance on the N.Y. stage were in "Mexican Hayride" and "Dream Girl."

LE GALLIENNE, EVA. Born in London on Jan. 11, 1899, and studied for the stage at the Royal Academy of Dramatic Art. Her first N.Y. appearance was in 1915 in "Mrs. Boltay's Daughters." Among the many plays in which she has appeared are "Bunny," "The Melody of Youth," "Mr. Lazarus," "Liliom," "The Swan," and "The Master Builder." In 1926 she started the Civic Repertory Company. Among the plays in this repertory were "Saturday Night," "Three Sisters," "The Master Builder," "John Gabriel Borkman," "La Locandiera," "Twelfth Night," "The Good Hope," "Hedda Gabler," "The Cherry Orchard," "Peter Pan," "The Sea Gull," "The Living Corpse" and "Alice in Wonderland." This company was disbanded in 1933. More recently she has appeared in a revival of "L'Aiglon," "Prelude to Exile," "Madame Capet," "Uncle Harry," a revival of "The Cherry Orchard" and "Theresa." This season she played leading roles with the American Repertory Company in such plays as "Henry VIII," "John Gabriel Borkman" and "What Every Woman Knows." She also appeared in a revival of "Alice in Wonderland."

LEONARD-BOYNE, EVA. Born in England in 1883, and first appeared on the stage there in 1906. Made N.Y. debut in 1912 in "Fanny's First Play," and later appeared in "The Man Who Married a Dumb Wife," "The Doctor's Dilemma," "The Apple Cart," "The Lake" and "Victoria Regina." Most recent appearance was in "Hidden Horizon."

LEONTOVITCH, EUGENIE. Born in Moscow in 1894, and first appeared on the stage in Russia. Later she appeared on the British stage, and first came to the attention of American audiences in 1928 in "And So To Bed," with the Chicago company. Her biggest Broadway success was made in "Grand Hotel" in 1930. More recently she has been seen in "Twentieth Century," "Dark Eyes," and "Obsession."

LEVENE, SAM. Born in N.Y.C., 1907. A graduate of the American Academy of Dramatic Arts, he has appeared on Broadway in "Dinner at Eight," "Three Men on a Horse," "Room Service," "Margin for Error," and more recently "A Sound of Hunting."

LEVEY, ETHEL. Born San Francisco, Nov. 22, 1881. Made her first stage appearance in 1897 in San Francisco, and later appeared at Koster and Bial's with Weber and Fields. From 1901 to 1907 she was associated with all the productions of George M. Cohan, playing in such shows as "Little Johnny Jones," and "George Washington, Jr." After this, she spent many years on the English stage. More recent Broadway appearances include "Sunny River" and "Marinka."

LINDEN, ERIC. Born N.Y.C., Sept. 15, 1909. Educated at Columbia University. His first N.Y. stage appearance was in "Marco Millions" in 1928. He also played in "One Way Street," "You Never Can Tell" and "Ladies' Money." Since 1931 he appeared in many motion pictures. Returned to the stage for "Trio" on the West Coast.

LINDEN, MARTA. Born in N.Y.C., Oct. 24, 1910. Stage apprenticeship at the Pasadena Playhouse, and appeared in several moving pictures before making Broadway debut on Oct. 26, 1946 in "Present Laughter."

LINN, BAMBI. Born in Brooklyn, N.Y., April 26, 1926. Educated at Professional Children's School. A student of Agnes de Mille, she has appeared in "Oklahoma" and "Carousel." This season she was seen in the title role in "Alice in Wonderland."

LOEB, PHILIP. Born Philadelphia, 1894. Received his stage training at the American Academy of Dramatic Arts. His N.Y. appearances include "Processional," "June Moon," "The Band Wagon," "Let 'Em Eat Cake," "Room Service," "My Sister Eileen," "Over 21," "Common Ground" and "Wonderful Journey."

LOGAN, ELLA. Born in Glasgow, Scotland, March 6, 1913. First stage appearances were in British and European music halls, and she later was seen in musical comedy. Made her Broadway debut in 1934 in "Calling All Stars." Since then she has been seen in "Scandals of 1939," "Hya, Gentlemen," "Sons O' Fun," "Show Time" and "Finian's Rainbow."

LONERGAN, LENORE. Born in Ohio, June 2, 1928. Educated at the Blessed Sacrament Seminary and Dominican Convent. Plays on Broadway include "Beyond the Blue," "Fields Beyond," "Mother Lode," "Crime Marches On," "The Philadelphia Story," "Junior Miss," "Dear Ruth," "Brighten the Corner" and "A Young Man's Fancy."

LONG, AVON. Born in Baltimore, Md. Had scholarship at Boston Conservatory of Music. Appeared on Broadway in "Porgy and Bess," "Very Warm for May," "Memphis Bound," "Carib Song" and "Beggar's Holiday."

LORD, PAULINE. Born Hanford, Calif., Aug. 13, 1890. Made her first stage appearance in stock in San Francisco and first played in N.Y. with Nat Goodwin's company in 1905. Her first hit was "The Talker" in 1912, and since then she has appeared in "On Trial," "Under Pressure," "Out There," "The Deluge," "April," "Our Pleasant Sins," "Night Lodging," "Samson and Delilah," "Anna Christie," "They Knew What They Wanted," "Mariners," "Spellbound" and "Distant Drums." More recently she appeared in "The Late Christopher Bean," "Ethan Frome," "Eight O'Clock Tuesday," "Suspect," "The Walrus and the Carpenter," "Sleep, My Pretty One," and toured in "The Glass Menagerie."

John Lund

Claire Luce

David Manners

LOVE, ELLEN. Born in Boston, Mass. Educated at Horace Mann School and Vassar College. Began theatre apprenticeship with the Jitney Players, Winter and Summer Stock. Broadway debut was in "Cape Cod Follies" in 1930. Other appearances include "Farewell Summer," "Tell Me, Pretty Maiden," "Cue for Passion," "Oklahoma" and "Sing Out, Sweet Land."

LOWE, EDMUND. Born San Jose, Calif., March 3, 1892. He was educated at Santa Clara Univ., and made his first stage appearance in 1911 in San Francisco. Made his N.Y. debut in 1918 in "The Brat." He also appeared in "The Walk-Offs," "Roads of Destiny," "The Son-Daughter," "The Right to Strike," a revival of "Trilby" and "Desert Sands." He made innumerable motion pictures, and recently returned to Broadway in "The Ryan Girl."

LUCE, CLAIRE. Born on a train going through Syracuse, N.Y. Made Broadway debut in "Little Jessie Jones," and was later seen in "Music Box Revue," "Ziegfeld Follies," "Society Girl," "Scarlet Pages," "The Gay Divorcee" and "Of Mice and Men." For several years she appeared with considerable success on the British stage, and returned to Broadway this season in "Portrait in Black."

LUND, JOHN. Born in Rochester, N.Y., Feb. 6, 1913. Began his stage career in the Railroad Pageant at the New York World's Fair. He understudied Alfred Drake in the revival of "As You Like It" in 1941. In 1942 he appeared on Broadway in "New Faces," and since then he has been in "Early to Bed" and "The Hasty Heart."

LUNT, ALFRED. Born Milwaukee, Wisc., 1893. Educated at Carroll College and Harvard. He made his first stage appearance in stock in Boston in 1913, and in 1914 he toured with Margaret Anglin, appearing in various roles. Following this, he supported Lily Langtry in a vaudeville playlet called "Ashes." In 1919 he made his first big hit in "Clarence." Among the plays which followed this were "The Intimate Strangers," "Banco," "Sweet Nell of Old Drury," "Outward Bound," "The Guardsman," "Arms and the Man," "Goat Song," "At Mrs. Beam's," "Juarez and Maxmilian," "Ned McCobb's Daughter," "The Brothers Karamazov," "The Second Man," "The Doctor's Dilemma," "Marco Millions," "Volpone," "Caprice," "Elizabeth the Queen," "Reunion in Vienna," "Design for Living," "Idiot's Delight," "The Taming of the Shrew," "Amphitryon 38," "The Sea Gull," "There Shall Be No Night," "The Pirate" and "O Mistress Mine."

LYON, FRANK. Born in Bridgeport, Conn., Jan. 19, 1905. Had first stage experience in stock, and made Broadway debut in "Love O' Mike." Since then he has been seen in "Loose Ankles," "Weather Clear, Track Fast," "Friendly Enemies," "Precious," "The Mermaids Singing" and "A Family Affair."

LYTELL, BERT. Born in N.Y.C., 1890. Made his Broadway bow in 1914 with Marie Dressler in "A Mix-Up." "If" and "Mary's Ankle" followed, then he had a long career in motion pictures. Returned to the stage in "Brothers." More recent appearances on Broadway include "The First Legion," "Margin for Error," "Lady in the Dark," "The Wind Is 90" and "I Like It Here."

MacDONALD, DONALD. Born Denison, Texas, March 13, 1898. Studied for the stage at the American Academy of Dramatic Arts, and first appeared in stock in Ottawa. Made N.Y. debut in 1913 in "When Dreams Come True." Among the plays in which he has appeared are "Have A Heart," "Getting Gertie's Garter," "Jack and Jill," "Processional," "Love 'Em and Leave 'Em," "White Wings," "The Second Man," "Paris Bound," "The Left Bank," "Forsaking All Others," "Little Shot," "On Stage," and more recently "Deep Are The Roots."

MacDONALD, JET. Born in Ashland, Kentucky, October 25, 1927. Attended Juilliard School of Music. Has appeared on Broadway in "Annie Get Your Gun" and "Beggar's Holiday."

Mac FARLAND, DOROTHEA. Born in Glendale, Calif. Made stage debut with Los Angeles Civic Light Opera Comany. Appeared as both Gertie Cummings and Ado Annie in N.Y. cast of "Oklahoma," and is now playing Ado Annie in the London company of the same play. Also appeared this season in the Experimental Theatre production, "As We Forgive Our Debtors."

MacKELLAR, HELEN. Born in Detroit, Feb. 13, 1895. First appeared on N.Y. stage in 1916 in "Seven Chances." Appeared in "A Tailor-Made Man," "The Unknown Purple," "The Storm," "Beyond The Horizon" and "The Mud Turtle." After a long session in Hollywood, returned to Broadway in "Dear Ruth." This past season has appeared on the road in "The Glass Menagerie."

MacMAHON, ALINE. Born in McKeesport, Pa., May 3, 1899. Educated at Barnard College, and made N.Y. debut in 1921 in "The Madras House." Appeared in "The Green Ring," "The Exciters," "Connie Comes Home," "The Grand Street Follies," "Beyond The Horizon," "Spread Eagle," "Maya" and "Once in a Lifetime." More recently appeared in "Heavenly Express" and "The Eve of St. Mark."

MADDERN, MERLE. Born in San Francisco, Nov. 3, 1887. Educated at Berkeley Univ. Made Broadway bow in 1909 with her aunt, Mrs. Fiske, in "Salvation Nell." Recent appearances include Cornell's production of "Romeo and Juliet," "L'Aiglon," "Decision," "A New Life," "Down To Miami" and "Antigone." Appeared this past season in "Land's End."

Eddy Manson

Lucille Marsh

Paul Marlin

MALDEN, KARL. Born in Gary, Ind. Appeared on Broadway in "Golden Boy," "Key Largo," "Flight To The West," "Missouri Legend," "Uncle Harry," "Counterattack," "Sons and Soldiers," "Winged Victory," "The Assassin," and "Truckline Cafe." Appearing this season in "All My Sons."

MALINA, LUBA. Born in Russia, daughter of Vitali Malina of the Moscow Art Theatre. Has appeared on Broadway in "Mexican Hayride," "Marinka" and "Lovely Me."

MANNERS, DAVID. Born in Halifax, Nova Scotia, April 30, 1900. Educated at Trinity School, N.Y. and Univ. of Toronto. Received stage training at Hart House Repertory Theatre, Toronto. Made Broadway debut in "Dancing Mothers." After a long session in Hollywood, returned to Broadway in "Truckline Cafe." Appeared this past season in "Lady Windermere's Fan."

MANNING, IRENE. Born in Cincinnati, Ohio, 1916. Educated at Eastman School of Music. Sang with St. Louis Municipal Opera Co. and Civic Light Opera Co. of Los Angeles, after which she appeared in the films. Made Broadway debut in "The Day Before Spring."

MANNING, JACK. Born June 3 in Cincinnati, Ohio. Graduate of Univ. of Cincinnati. Has played on the Broadway stage in "The Great Big Doorstep," "Junior Miss," "Harriet," "Othello," "The Streets Are Guarded," and "The Mermaids Singing." Appeared this past season in the Experimental Theatre Production of "O'Daniel," and in "Alice In Wonderland."

MANSON, EDDY. Born in N.Y.C., May 9, 1919. Attended Juilliard School of Music. Appeared on Broadway in "Tid-Bits of '46."

MARCH, FREDRIC. Born in Racine, Wisc., Aug. 31, 1897. Educated at Univ. of Wisc. On the road played in "Tarnish," "Zeno," "A Knife in the Wall," and the Theatre Guild productions of "The Guardsman," "The Silver Cord," "Arms and the Man," and "Mr. Pim Passes By." His Broadway debut was made in Belasco's production of "Deburau." In 1932 while appearing on the West Coast in "The Royal Family," he received picture offers and remained in Hollywood for ten years. Recent appearances in New York include "Your Obedient Husband," "The American Way," "Hope for a Harvest," "The Skin of Our Teeth," and "A Bell for Adano." Appeared this past season in "Years Ago."

MARCY, HELEN. Born June 3, 1920 in Worcester, Mass. Studied for the theatre at Yale Drama School. Has appeared on Broadway in "In Bed We Cry" and "Dream Girl."

MARGETSON, ARTHUR. Born in London, England, April 27, 1887. Made his first appearance in America in "The Passing Show of 1922." Since then New Yorkers have seen him in "Little Miss Bluebeard," "Paris," "Charley's Aunt," "Theatre," "Another Love Story," "Lovers and Friends," "Life With Father" and "Around The World." Appeared this past season in "Park Avenue."

MARINOFF, FANIA. Born in Odessa, Russia, March 30, 1890. Made first stage appearance at age of eight in stock in Denver. During her early career she supported such famous players as Henrietta Crosman, Mrs. Patrick Campbell and Arnold Daly. Among the many plays in which she has appeared are "The Man On The Box," "The House Next Door," "The Hero," "The Charlatan," "The Love Habit" and "Tarnish." More recently she appeared in revivals of "The Streets of New York," "The Pillars of Society," "Anthony and Cleopatra," and in "The Bride The Sun Shines On," "Christopher Comes Across," "Judgment Day," and "Times Have Changed."

MARKEY, ENID. Was a star in silent films before becoming a Broadway actress for A. H. Woods in "Up In Mabel's Room." Her more recent appearances on the N.Y. stage include "Barnum Was Right," "The Women," "Mornings at Seven," "Ah, Wilderness," "Mr. Sycamore," "Run, Sheep, Run," "Beverly Hills," "Last Stop" and "Snafu." Appeared this past season in "Happy Birthday."

MARKOVA, ALICIA. Born in London, England, December 1, 1910. At the age of thirteen she was accepted as a member of Diaghileff's famous troupe. Since then she has appeared in America with the Ballet Russe de Monte Carlo and the Ballet Theatre. She made her Broadway debut in "Seven Lively Arts."

MARLIN, PAUL. Born in Canton, Ohio, January 17, 1925. Received his stage training with the Hanna Stock Co. in Cleveland. Made his Broadway bow in "Round Trip," and more recently appeared in "Lovely Me."

MARLOWE, HUGH. Born in Philadelphia, Pa., January 30, 1914. Educated at Senn High School, Chicago. Received stage training at Pasadena Community Playhouse. Made Broadway debut in "Arrest That Woman." Other N.Y. appearances include "Young Couple Wanted," "Flight To The West," "Land So Bright," "Lady in the Dark" and "It Takes Two." Also played in Chicago company of "The Voice of the Turtle."

MARSH, LUCILLE. Born in Chicago, Ill., Aug. 17, 1921. Received her education at the Highland Park, Ill., Grammar and High School. Obtained her stage training at the Goodman Theatre, Chicago, and the Max Reinhardt Workshop in Hollywood. Made one picture, "Cover Girl," before making her stage debut playing the title role in the road company of "Janie." The road also saw her in "Abie's Irish Rose," "School for Brides," and "Set 'Em Up Tony." First N.Y. appearance was made in the Fred Stone revival of "You Can't Take It With You."

Mary Martin

James Mason

Jeanne Masky

MARSHALL, E. G. Born June 18, 1910 in Owatonna, Minn. Educated at Carlton College and Univ. of Minn. Appeared on Broadway in "Jason," "The Skin of Our Teeth," the revival of "The Petrified Forest," "Jacobowsky and the Colonel," "Beggars Are Coming To Town," and "Woman Bites Dog." Appeared this past season in "The Iceman Cometh."

MARSHALL, PATRICIA. Born in Minneapolis, Minn., and educated there at West High School. Has appeared on Broadway in "You'll See Stars," "Stars On Ice," "Hats Off To Ice," "What's Up" and "The Day Before Spring."

MARSTON, JOEL. Born March 30, 1922 in Washington, D.C. Received his theatrical training at Pasadena Playhouse. Made Broadway bow in 1944 in "Wallflower." Has appeared in "Good Morning, Corporal," "The Streets Are Guarded" and "Marriage Is For Single People." Appeared this past season in "A Family Affair."

MARTIN, LEWIS. Born in San Francisco, Nov. 1, 1888. Educated at Milton Academy, Milton, Mass. Played with the Alcazar Stock Co., San Francisco. Made Broadway debut in "Lucky Sam McCarver" (1925). Since then has played in many New York productions. More recent appearances include "Abe Lincoln in Illinois," "Mr. and Mrs. North," "The First Crocus" and "Joan of Lorraine."

MARTIN, MARY. Born in Wetherford, Texas, Dec. 1, 1914. Educated at Ward-Belmont School, Nashville, Tenn. Her first Broadway appearance was made in "Leave It To Me," and since then she has been starred in "One Touch of Venus" and "Lute Song." Recently appeared in London in Noel Coward's "Pacific 1860."

MASKY, JEANNE. Born in Chicago, Ill., June 11, 1926. Educated at Janesville, Wisc., High School and Barnum's Dramatic School. Made her Broadway debut in "Maid in the Ozarks."

MASON, JAMES. Born in Huddersfield, Yorkshire, England, May 15, 1909. Educated at Marlborough and Cambridge. Received his stage training at the Gate Theatre, Dublin and with the Old Vic Company in London. Has had great success in English films, his most popular being "The Seventh Veil" and "Odd Man Out." Made his debut on the N.Y. stage this season in "Bathsheba."

MASSEY, RAYMOND. Born in Toronto, Canada, Aug. 30, 1896. Educated at Toronto Univ. and Balliol College, Oxford. Made first professional stage appearance in England in 1922. Made his Broadway bow in 1931 in title role of "Hamlet." Since then has appeared in N.Y. in "The Shining Hour," "Ethan Frome," "Abe Lincoln in Illinois," the Cornell revival of "The Doctor's Dilemma," and the Lawrence revival of "Pygmalion."

MATHER, AUBREY. Born in Minchinhampton, England, Dec. 17, 1885. Educated at Charterhouse and Trinity College, Cambridge. Made his stage debut in 1905 as Bernardo in "Hamlet." Made his New York debut in 1919 in "The Luck of the Navy." Recent appearances include Polonius in Leslie Howard's "Hamlet," "Bachelor Born," "Good Hunting," "Hand In Glove" and "Foolish Notion."

MATHEWS, CARMEN. Born in Philadelphia, Pa., and had theatrical training at Royal Academy of Dramatic Art in London. Made Broadway debut in 1938 in Maurice Evans' production of "Henry IV." Was also seen with him in "Hamlet," and "Richard II." More recently she appeared in "Harriet," "The Cherry Orchard" and "The Assassin." Appeared this past season in "Made In Heaven."

MATHEWS, GEORGE. Born in N.Y.C., October 10, 1911 Started his stage career as an usher in the Mercury Theatre. Has played on Broadway in "Escape This Night," "Processional," "Retreat To Pleasure," "Life of Reilly," "They Should've Stood In Bed," "Cuckoos on the Hearth," "Eve of St. Mark," "The Streets Are Guarded," and "Kiss Them For Me." Appeared last season in "Beggars Are Coming To Town," and "Antigone," and this past season in "Temper The Wind."

MATHIESEN, JACK. Born in Chicago, Ill., May 19, 1924. Educated at Lane Tech. High School, Chicago. Made first N.Y. appearance in "Maid in the Ozarks."

MATTESON, RUTH. Born in San Jose, Calif. Has appeared on Broadway in "Parnell," "Wingless Victory," "Barchester Towers," "One For The Money," "The Male Animal," "The Merry Widow," "Tomorrow The World," "In Bed We Cry" and "Antigone." Appeared this past season in "Park Avenue."

MATTSON, ERIC. Born in Scranton, Pa. A leading man with the operetta companies of St. Louis, San Francisco, Los Angeles, Dallas and Detroit, he has sung in "New Moon," "Naughty Marietta," "The Chocolate Soldier," "The Desert Song," "Firefly," "Robin Hood," "The Bohemian Girl," and 'The Last Waltz." Recently appeared on Broadway in "Carousel."

MAUDE, MARGERY. Born April 29, 1889 in Wimbledon, Surrey, England. Made her American debut in 1913 with her father, Cyril Maude, in "Grumpy." Appeared in N.Y. in "Lady Windermere's Fan," "Paganini," "The Old Foolishness," and more recently in "Plan M," "The Two Mrs. Carrolls" and "O Mistress Mine."

McCANN, FRANCES. Has appeared on Broadway in "Rosalinda," "The Vagabond King," and "The Chocolate Soldier."

McCARTHY, KEVIN. Born Seattle, Wash., Feb. 15, 1914. Educated at Georgetown Univ. and Univ. of Minn. Made Broadway bow in "Abe Lincoln in Illinois." Also appeared in "Flight To The West,"

Jack Mathiesen

Ethel Merman

Burgess Meredith

"Winged Victory," and "Truckline Cafe." Appeared this past season in "Joan of Lorraine."

McCORMICK, MYRON. Born in Albandy, Ind., Feb. 8, 1907. His first professional engagement was with the University Players. In 1932 he made his first N.Y. stage appearance in "Carrie Nation." Since then he has played in "Goodbye Again," "Yellow Jack," "Small Miracle," "How To Get Tough About It," "Hell Freezes Over," "How Beautiful With Shoes," "Substitute For Murder," "Paths of Glory," "Winterset," "Wingless Victory," "Lily of the Valley," "The Damask Cheek," "Thunder Rock," "Storm Operation," and more recently in "Soldier's Wife" and "State of the Union."

McCRACKEN, JOAN. Born in Philadelphia, Pa., Dec. 31, 1922. Educated at West Philadelphia High School. Studied and appeared with the Catherine Littlefield Ballet. Toured with the Eugene Loring Dance Players. Appeared on Broadway in "Oklahoma," "Bloomer Girl" and "Billion Dollar Baby."

McDONALD, RAY. Born in Boston, Mass., June 27, 1922. Made Broadway debut in "Babes In Arms." Other appearances include "Crazy With The Heat," "Winged Victory" and "Park Avenue."

McGRATH, PAUL. Born in Chicago, Ill., and educated at Carnegie Tech. Made his stage debut in "The First Year." Since then New Yorkers have seen him in "Ned McCobb's Daughter," "John Ferguson," "The Good Fairy," "Here Today," "The Green Bay Tree," "Pigeons and People," "Ode To Liberty," "Susan and God," "Lady in the Dark," "Tomorrow The World" and "Common Ground."

McKAY, SCOTT (formerly CARL GOSE). Born Pleasantville, Iowa, May 28, 1917. Educated at Univ. of Colorado. Made Broadway debut in 1938 in "Good Hunting." Since then has been seen in "The American Way," "The Night Before Christmas," "Letters To Lucerne," "The Moon Is Down," "The Eve of St. Mark," "Dark Eyes," "Pillar To Post" and "Swan Song." Appeared this past season in "Another Part of the Forest."

MEADER, GEORGE. Born July 6, 1890 in Minneapolis, and graduated from Univ. of Minn. Sang in Opera at the Metropolitan and also in Europe. Appeared on Broadway in "The Cat and the Fiddle," "Champagne Sec," "Only Girl," and with the Lunts in "Taming of the Shrew," "Idiot's Delight," "Amphitryon 38," and "The Sea Gull." More recently he appeared in the revival of "The Red Mill."

MEADOWS, JAYNE (formerly known as JAYNE COTTER). Born in WuChang, China, Sept. 27, 1923. Educated at St. Margaret's School. Has appeared on Broadway in "Spring Again," "Another Love Story," "The Odds on Mrs. Oakley," "Many Happy Returns," and "Kiss Them for Me."

MEHAFFEY, HARRY. Born in Philadelphia. Educated at Univ. of Penn. Received stage training with Mae Desmond Stock Co. New Yorkers saw him first in "Good Earth." Since then played on Broadway in "Merrily We Roll Along," "Libel," "Pick-Up Girl" and "Little A."

MENDELSSOHN, ELEONORA. Born in Berlin, Germany, where she had a long and distinguished career. Has appeared on N.Y. stage in "Daughters of Atreus," "Flight To The West," "The Russian People" and "The Secret Room."

MENKEN, HELEN. Born in New York, Dec. 12, 1901, she first appeared on the stage in 1906 as one of the fairies in "A Midsummer Night's Dream." As a child actress she played with such stars as De Wolf Hopper, Eddie Foy, and Adeline Genee, after which she had considerable experience in stock. Among her Broadway successes are "Three Wise Fools," "Drifting," "Seventh Heaven," "The Captive" and "Congai." More recently she appeared in "Mary of Scotland," "The Old Maid" and "The Laughing Woman."

MERANDE, DORO. Has appeared on Broadway in "Our Town," "Love's Old Sweet Song," "The More The Merrier," "Junior Miss," "The Naked Genius," "Pick-Up Girl," "Violet" and "Hope For The Best."

MEREDITH, BURGESS. Born in Cleveland, Ohio, Nov. 16, 1908. Educated at Lincoln Grade School, Lakewood, Ohio, St. John the Divine Choir School, N.Y.C., Hoosac Prep School, Hoosik Falls, N.Y., and Amherst College. In 1930 was admitted to Eva Le Gallienne's Student Repertory Group. Played Peter in her production of "Romeo and Juliet," and other small parts in her company. Has appeared on Broadway in "Little Ol' Boy," "She Loves Me Not," "Hipper's Holiday," "Battle Ship Gertie," "Barretts of Wimpole Street," "Flowers of the Forest," "Winterset," "High Tor," "The Star Wagon," revivals of "Liliom" (with Ingrid Bergman), "Candida" (with Katharine Cornell), and more recently "The Playboy of the Western World."

MERMAN, ETHEL. Born in Astoria, L.I., N.Y., on Jan. 16, 1909. Her first stage appearance was in vaudeville with Clayton, Jackson and Durante. She scored her first Broadway hit in 1931 in "Girl Crazy." Among the musical shows in which she has appeared are "George White's Scandals," "Take A Chance," "Anything Goes," "Red, Hot, and Blue!," "Stars in Your Eyes," "Panama Hattie," "Something For The Boys" and more recently in "Annie Get Your Gun."

MERRILL, BETH. Appeared under Belasco's management in "Ladies of the Evening," "Lily Sue" and "Hidden." More recently has appeared on Broadway in "Autumn Hill," "The Lady Who Came To Stay" and "All My Sons."

Frank Milton

Mary Alice Moore

Arnold Moss

MERRILL, GARY. Born in Hartford, Conn. Educated at Trinity College. Appeared on Broadway in "Brother Rat," "Morning Star," "See My Lawyer," "This Is The Army," "Winged Victory" and "Born Yesterday."

MILLER, BENJAMIN. Born in New York City, May 3. 1923. Educated at Sayville High School, Long Island. N.Y. Made his Broadway bow in "Barefoot Boy With Cheek."

MILTON, FRANK. Born N.Y.C., August 2. 1918. Educated at Roxbury Prep School and Lafayette College. Has appeared on Broadway in "All in Fun," "Dream With Music," "On The Town" and "If The Shoe Fits"

MITCHELL, ESTHER. Born Newcastle. New South Wales. Australia. Made American debut in 1921 in "The Madras House" at Neighborhood Playhouse. More recently appeared on Broadway in "The Corn Is Green," "Call It A Day," "Within The Gates," "Miss Swan Expects" and "O Mistress Mine."

MITCHELL, JAMES. Born in Sacramento, Calif., Feb. 29, 1920. Graduated from Los Angeles City College. Studied dancing under Lester Horton. Made Broadway debut in "Bloomer Girl." Recently appeared in "Billion Dollar Baby" and "Brigadoon."

MITCHELL, MILLARD. He has appeared on Broadway in "Yellow Jack," "Three Men On A Horse," "Boy Meets Girl," "Mr. and Mrs. North," "See My Lawyer," "Kiss The Boys Goodbye," "Sons and Soldiers," "Storm Operations," "The Naked Genius" and "Love on Leave." Appeared this past season in "Lovely Me."

MONKS, JAMES. Born N.Y.C. Made Broadway debut in "Brother Rat." Since then has appeared in "Yesterday's Magic," "Eve of St. Mark," "Othello" and "The Story of Mary Surratt."

MOORE, MARY ALICE. Born in Florence, Arizona, Dec. 5. 1923. Educated at Northwestern Univ. Made Broadway bow in "School for Brides." Recently appeared with American Rep. Theatre in "Henry VIII," "What Every Woman Knows," "John Gabriel Borkman" and "Androcles and the Lion."

MOORE, VICTOR. Born in Hammonton, N.J., Feb. 24, 1876. Made his first appearance on any stage in "Babes in the Woods" at the Boston Theatre in 1893. Was with John Drew in "Rosemary" in 1896. Susequently played in "A Romance of Coon Hollow," "The Real Widow Brown," and "The Girl From Paris." For 25 years he toured the country in a vaudeville act, "Change Your Act, or Back To The Woods." This was followed by "The Talk of New York," "The Happiest Night of His Life," "Shorty McCabe," "Patsy on the Wing," "Easy Come, Easy Go," "Oh, Kay," and "Hold Everything." His recent starring roles include "Of Thee I Sing," "Let 'Em Eat Cake," "Anything Goes," "Leave It To Me," "Louisiana Purchase," "Hollywood Pinafore" and "Nellie Bly."

MORGAN, CLAUDIA. She was born in Brooklyn, N.Y., June 12, 1912, and is the daughter of Ralph Morgan. Her first Broadway role was in "Top O' The Hill." Since then she has appeared in "Wine of Choice," "Man Who Came To Dinner," "Accent On Youth," "On Stage," "Dancing Partners," "And Stars Remained," "Storm Over Patsy," "Masque of Kings," "In Clover," "Call It A Day," "Co-respondent Unknown," "The Sun Field" and "Ten Little Indians."

MORGAN, RALPH. Born in N.Y.C., July 6, 1888. Graduate of Columbia Univ. Made his N.Y. debut in 1908 in "Blue Grass." Among the many plays in which he has appeared on Broadway are "The Blue Mouse," "Under Cover," "A Full House," "Lightnin'," "The Five Million," "In Love With Love," "Cobra," "The Woman In Bronze" and "Strange Interlude." After several years in Hollywood he re-appeared on the N.Y. stage in "Fledgling," "The Moon Is Down" and "This Too Shall Pass."

MORRIS, McKAY. Born Houston, Texas, Dec. 22, 1891. Studied for the stage under David Belasco, and made N.Y. debut in 1912 in "The Governor's Lady." For several years he was with Stuart Walker's Portmanteau Theatre Company, and later appeared on Broadway in "Aphrodite," "Rose Bernd," "Romeo and Juliet," (Ethel Barrymore production). "The Laughing Lady," "The Shanghai Gesture," "Volpone," revivals of "Ghosts," and "Hedda Gabler" with Nazimova, and in "Retreat From Folly" and "Tovarich." Most recent appearance in "Lute Song."

MOSS, ARNOLD. Born in Brooklyn, January 28, 1910. Educated at C.C.N.Y. and Columbia. Received his stage training at Eva Le Gallienne's Civic Rep. Theatre. Appeared on Broadway in "Fifth Column," "Hold On To Your Hats," "Journey To Jerusalem," "Flight To The West," "The Land Is Bright" and "The Tempest." Appeared this past season in "The Front Page."

MUNSHIN, JULES. Born N.Y.C., Feb. 22, 1915. First appeared on Broadway in "The Army Play by Play," and more recently in "Call Me Mister."

MURPHY, DONALD. Born Jan. 29, 1920 in Chicago, Ill., and educated at Chicago Latin School and Florida's Rollins College. Faced his first New York audience in "The Moon Vine." Other Broadway appearances were made in "Janie," "Try and Get It," "For Keeps," "Signature" and "Common Ground." Appeared this past season in "Wonderful Journey."

MYRTIL, ODETTE. Born in Paris, June 28, 1898. Made first appearance as a violinist in Paris in 1911. Her Broadway debut was in "The Ziegfeld Follies of 1914." She has appeared on the N.Y.

Donald Murphy

Elisabeth Neumann

Richard Newton

stage in many musical shows which include "Vogues of 1924," "The Love Song," "Countess Maritza," "White Lilacs," "Broadway Nights," "The Cat and the Fiddle" and "Roberta." Most recent appearance was in revival of "The Red Mill."

NAGEL, CONRAD. Born Keokuk, Iowa, March 16, 1897. Made first appearance on Broadway with Alice Brady in "Forever After." Most of his acting career has been devoted to Hollywood picture making. In recent years returned to the stage, and has been seen in "The First Apple," "The Skin of Our Teeth," "Tomorrow the World," the City Center revival of "Susan and God," "A Goose for The Gander" and "State of the Union" on the road.

NATWICK, MILDRED. Born Baltimore, Md., June 19, 1908. Made N.Y. debut in 1932 in "Carrie Nation." Has appeared in "Amourette," "The Wind and the Rain," "The Distaff Side," "Night in the House," "End of Summer," "Love from a Stranger," the Cornell revival of "Candide," "The Star Wagon," "Missouri Legend," "Stars in Your Eyes," and more recently "Blithe Spirit" and "Playboy of the Western World."

NEAL, PATRICIA. Born in Kentucky, 1926. Educated at Northwestern Univ. Received her stage training at the Barter Theatre, Abington, Va. Understudied Sally and Olive in "The Voice of the Turtle" and played Olive for two weeks in N.Y. "Another Part of the Forest" marked her first important part on Broadway.

NEUMANN, ELISABETH. Born in Vienna, Austria, April 5, 1906. Made her Broadway debut in "From Vienna." Other N.Y. appearances include "Reunion in New York," "Claudia," "Tomorrow the World" and "The Whole World Over."

NEWTON RICHARD. Born in Vancouver, Canada, July 5, 1911. Educated at McGill Univ. Received his stage training at the Royal Academy of Dramatic Art, London. Made his Broadway debut in "The Duchess of Malfi."

NIESEN, GERTRUDE. Born at sea, July 8, 1910. Educated Brooklyn and N.Y. public schools. First regular stage appearance made at Hollywood Theatre, N.Y. Dec. 13, 1934 in "Calling All Stars." "Ziegfeld Follies" (1936) came next, and more recently "Follow the Girls."

NILLO, DAVID. Born July 13, 1918 in Goldsboro, N.C. Educated at Baltimore City College. First stage appearance with Ballet Theatre and American Ballet Caravan. Made Broadway bow in "Call Me Mister."

NORRIS, JAY. Born in Albany, Ga., on August 3, 1917. Appeared in several movies before making Broadway bow in "Strange Fruit."

NUGENT, EDDIE. Born in N.Y.C., Feb. 7, 1904, he comes from five generations of actors and his grandparents were the famous Flying Romein's of the Barnum and Bailey Circus. He began his career as a boy singer with the Metropolitan Opera Company. He appeared in vaudeville, and finally landed in Hollywood where he remained for nineteen years. Broadway has seen him recently in "See My Lawyer," "Brooklyn, U.S.A.," "Star Spangled Family" and "Round Trip."

NUGENT, ELLIOTT. Born in Dover, Ohio, Sept. 20, 1900, and educated at Ohio State Univ. Among the plays in which he has appeared are "Dulcy," "The Poor Nut," "Kempy," "The Wild Wescotts," "Hoosiers Abroad," "The Male Animal," "Without Love" and "The Voice of the Turtle."

OBER, PHILIP. Born in Fort Payne, Ala., March 23, 1902. Educated at Peddie School, Hightstown, N.J., and Princeton University. Made Broadway bow in 1932 in "The Animal Kingdom." Since then has appeared in "She Loves Me Not," "Personal Appearance," "Spring Dance," "Without Warning," "The Hill Between," "Kiss the Boys Goodbye," "Out from Under," "Mr. and Mrs. North," "Junior Miss," "The Two Mrs. Carrolls," "Doctor's Disagree" and "Craig's Wife."

OBER, ROBERT. Born Bunker Hill, Ill., March 10, 1889. Educated at Washington Univ., St. Louis. Broadway debut in "The Little Grey Lady." Has appeared in many plays, among which are "You Never Can Tell," "Ready Money," "The Bat," "The Cat and the Canary," and more recently "The Moon is Down" and "The Assassin."

O'BRIEN-MOORE, ERIN. Born May 2, 1908. Made N.Y. debut in 1926 in "The Makropoulos Secret." Since then has been seen on Broadway in "Skidding," "Street Scene," "Riddle Me This!," "Men Must Fight" and "Tortilla Flat." More recently she has appeared in "State of the Union" on tour.

O'CONNOR, UNA. Born Belfast, Ireland, Oct. 23, 1880. Studied for the stage at the Abbey Theatre School in Dublin, and made her debut in 1911 at the Abbey Theatre. During that same season she made her first appearance on Broadway in "The Shewing Up of Blanco Posnet." She re-appeared in N.Y. in 1924 in "The Fake," and later played here in "Autumn Fire." She is well known through her work in Hollywood. Returned to the Broadway stage in "The Ryan Girl."

OLIVIER, LAURENCE. Born Dorking, Surrey, England, May 22, 1907. Educated at St. Edward's School, Oxford, and studied for the stage under Elsie Fogerty. Made Broadway debut in 1929 in "Murder On The Second Floor." Later he was seen here in "Private Lives," "The Green Bay Tree," "No Time for Comedy" and his own production of "Romeo and Juliet." Has appeared with considerable success in both English and American films. Returned to Broadway in 1946 with the Old Vic Company.

Mary Orr

Warren Parker

Beatrice Pearson

OLSEN, OLE. Born 1892 in Chicago, Ill., and educated at Northwestern Univ. His first professional work was as a member of a quartet that played rathskellers in Chicago. In 1914 he met Chic Johnson, a ragtime pianist, and signed him on for the act. It was the beginning of a long and prosperous partnership. Together they have been brightening Broadway with "Hellzapoppin," "Sons O'Fun" and "Laffing Room Only."

O'MALLEY, REX. Born in London, Eng., Jan. 2, 1901. He received his stage training with the Birmingham repertory company. Among his many N.Y. appearances are "The Marquise," "Bachelor Father," "Lost Sheep," "The Apple Cart," "Wonder Bar," "The Mad Hopes," "Experience Unnecessary," "Revenge With Music," "You Never Know," "Matrimony, Pfd.," "The Simpleton of the Unexpected Isles," the Lunts' production of "The Taming of the Shrew," "No More Ladies," "Many Happy Returns" and "Lady Windermere's Fan."

O'NEILL, BARBARA. Educated at Sarah Lawrence College, she received her stage training with the University Players. Following a series of failures in New York, she went to Hollywood where she played in "Stella Dallas," "Gone With the Wind," "All This and Heaven Too" and "The Sun Never Sets." Returning to Broadway she has appeared in "When Doctors Disagree," "The Willow and I," "Counterattack" and "The Searching Wind."

ORR, MARY. Born in Brooklyn, N.Y., Dec. 21, 1918. Educated at Ward-Belmont School, Nashville, Tenn. Received her stage training at the American Academy of Dramatic Arts. Played on Broadway in "Three Men on a Horse," "Bachelor Born," "Jupiter Laughs," "Wallflower" and "Dark Hammock." On tour she had the leading feminine role in "Of Mice and Men."

OSATO, SONO. Born in Omaha, Neb., Aug. 29, 1919. Studied ballet with Adolph Bolm and Bernice Holmes in Chicago. Was with the Ballet Russe for eight years. Her first musical comedy appearance was in "One Touch of Venus," followed by "On The Town."

O'SHEA, KEVIN. Born Chicago, Ill., May 6, 1915. Studied for the theatre with Maria Ouspenskaya. Has been seen on Broadway in "The Eternal Road," "You Never Know," "Censored." "Lorelei," and more recently in "Dream Girl."

PAGENT, ROBERT. Born in Pittsburgh, Pa., Dec. 12. 1917. Educated at Univ. of Indiana. He received his ballet training in Paris under Egorova. Appeared with the Chicago Opera Ballet, Ballet Russe de Monte Carlo, and Col. de Basil's Ballet Russe. Has appeared on Broadway in "Oklahoma," "One Touch of Venus" and "Carousel."

PARKER, JEAN. Born in Deer Lodge, Montana, Aug. 11, 1918. After a successful career in Hollywood, made her Broadway debut this season in "Loco." This was followed by the revival of "Burlesque."

PARKER, LEW. Born Oct. 29, 1910 in Brooklyn. Has appeared on Broadway in "The Ramblers," "Girl Crazy," "Red, Hot and Blue," "Heads Up," and more recently in "Are You With It?," and "The Front Page."

PARKER, WARREN. Born in Alton, Ill., Feb. 25, 1909. Educated at Univ. of Michigan. Appeared recently on Broadway in "Swing Your Lady," "Lysistrata" and "Love Goes to Press."

PARKS, BERNICE. Got her first break in West Coast production of "Meet the People." Has been a headliner in many famous night clubs. "Beggar's Holiday" marked her Broadway debut.

PARNELL, JAMES. Born Oct. 9, 1923 in Minnesota. Studied for the theatre under Guy Bates Post. Played two years with U.S.O. camp shows, and made Broadway debut in "Oklahoma."

PATTERSON, ALBERT. Born in Bowling Green, Ky., Dec. 17, 1911. Educated at Polytech Institute and Columbia Univ. Made Broadway bow in "The American Way." More recently appeared in "Temper the Wind."

PAXINOU, KATINA. Born in Peiraeus, Greece, where with her husband, Alexis Minotis, she helped found the Greek National Theatre. Her greatest artistic triumph was in 1939, when she toured Great Britain and Europe in Sophocles' "Electra." New Yorkers have seen her in "Hedda Gabler" and "Sophie." She also had the role of Pilar in the film "For Whom the Bells Toll."

PEARSON, BEATRICE. She was born in Denison, Texas, July 27, 1920. She made her Broadway debut in the revival of "Liliom." Since then she has played in "Life With Father," "Free and Equal," "Get Away, Old Man," "Over 21," "The Mermaids Singing" and "The Voice of the Turtle."

PETINA, IRRA. Born 1900, in Leningrad, Russia, she began her musical studies in Philadelphia's Curtis Institute. Three years later she was singing with the Metropolitan Opera Company. On the West Coast she appeared in "The Chocolate Soldier," "Music in the Air," "The Gypsy Baron" and "The Waltz King." In 1944 she made her Broadway debut in "Song of Norway."

PETRIE, GEORGE. Born Nov. 16, 1915 in New Haven, Conn. Educated at Univ. of Southern Calif. In 1938 he made his Broadway bow in "The Girl from Wyoming." Has appeared in "The Army Play by Play," "Jeremiah," "Pastoral," "The Night Before Christmas," "Mr. Big," "Cafe Crown," "Winged Victory" and "Brighten the Corner."

PHILLIPS, MARGARET. She was born in Wales, July 6, 1923 and received her stage training at the Woodstock Summer Theatre and the Barter Theatre of Abington, Va. Has been seen on Broadway in "Cry Havoc," "The Late George Apley" and "Another Part of the Forest."

POST JR., WILLIAM. He attended Phillips-Exeter Academy and Yale, and made his Broadway bow

Margaret Phillips

William Prince

Olive Reeves-Smith

in "The Criminal Code." Has also been seen in "When the Bough Breaks," "Richard II," "Ah, Wilderness," "A Touch of Brimstone," the William Gillette revival of "Three Wise Fools," "My Sister Eileen," "Calico Wedding" and "Love Goes to Press."

POVAH, PHYLLIS. Her first important N.Y. assignments were in the Theatre Guild productions of "Mr. Pim Passes By" and "Windows." Since then she has played in "Minnick," "Blood Money," "The Tale of the Wolf," "Hotel Universe," "The Women," "The Naked Genius" and "Dear Ruth."

POWELL, BERTHA T. Born Aug. 25, 1895 in Atlantic City, N.J. Appeared on Broadway in "Show Boat," "Porgy and Bess," "Run, Lil Children," "Blue Holiday," "Carmen Jones" and "Louisiana Lady."

POWERS, TOM. Born July 7, 1890 in Owensboro, Ky. Studied for the stage at American Academy of Dramatic Arts. Made his Broadway debut in 1915 in "Mr. Lazarus." Among the many plays in which he has been seen on the N.Y. stage are "He," "The Apple Cart," "Strange Interlude," the Orson Welles' "Julius Caesar," and more recently in the Cornell revival of "Three Sisters," and in "Broken Journey."

PRINCE, WILLIAM. Born in Nicholas, N.Y., Jan. 26. 1913. Educated at Cornell. Made Broadway debut in Maurice Evans' production of "Richard II." This was followed by Evans' "Hamlet," and "Henry IV." Other appearances include revival of "Ah, Wilderness," "Guest in the House," "Across the Board on Tomorrow Morning," "Eve of St. Mark" and "John Loves Mary."

PRYOR, ROGER. Born in New York City in 1903. Had stage training in stock, and was seen on the New York stage in "Saturday's Children," "The Royal Family" and "See Naples and Die," after which he went to Hollywood and played in a number of films. Returned to Broadway in "Message for Margaret."

PURCELL, CHARLES. Born in Chattanooga, Tenn., 1883. Has appeared in many famous operettas such as "The Chocolate Soldier" and "Maytime." He has also been seen in "The Magic Melody," "Dearest Enemy," "Hit the Deck," and more recently "Park Avenue."

RAITT, JOHN. Born in Santa Ana, Calif., Jan. 29, 1917 and educated at Univ. of Redlands, Calif., where he received his A.B. Began his singing career with the Los Angeles Civic Light Opera Company. Sang the lead in the National Company of "Oklahoma," and made his Broadway bow in "Carousel."

RANDOLPH, DONALD. Born in British South Africa. Made his Broadway debut in "The Fatal Alibi." Other appearances include "Strange Gods," "Crime Marches On," "The Man from Cairo," "Errant Lady," "It's You I Want," "Reprise," "The Sun Field," "Lady in the Dark," "The Naked Genius," and with Maurice Evans in his full length "Hamlet," and "Richard II." More recently seen in "Life With Father."

RATHBONE, BASIL. Born June 13, 1892 in Johannesburg, Transvaal. Educated at Repton College, and first acting experience was with Sir Frank Benson's company in Shakespearian repertory. He made his American debut with this company in 1912, after which he returned to the London stage, where he achieved considerable success. In 1922 he appeared on Broadway in "The Czarina," and since then he has been seen in "R.U.R.", "The Swan," "The Grand Duchess and the Waiter," "The Captive," "The Command to Love," and opposite Katharine Cornell in "Romeo and Juliet." He has played in many motion pictures and is well known to radio listeners for his characterization of Sherlock Holmes. Returned to the Broadway stage this season in "Obsession."

REDFIELD, BILLY. Born in N.Y.C., Jan. 26, 1927. Made Broadway debut in 1936 in "Swing Your Lady" Since then has been seen in "Excursion," "Virginia," "Stop-Over," "Our Town," "Second Helping," "Junior Miss," "Snafu" and "Barefoot Boy With Cheek."

REDMAN, JOYCE. Born in 1919 in Ireland. Studied for the theatre at the Royal Academy of Dramatic Art, and made her London debut in 1935. Played a great variety of roles on the English stage. First Broadway appearance was with the Old Vic Company.

REED, FLORENCE. Born in Philadelphia, Pa., Jan. 10, 1883. Made her first appearance on the stage at the Fifth Avenue Theatre, N.Y. in 1901, appearing in a monologue. After several seasons of stock in New York, Providence, Worcester and Chicago, she joined E. H. Sothern's company and toured with him during the 1907-08 season. Among her many successes are "Seven Days," "The Painted Woman," "The Girl and the Pennant," "The Yellow Ticket," "A Celebrated Case," "The Wanderer," "Chu Chin Chow," "Roads of Destiny," "The Mirage," "East of Suez," "The Shanghai Gesture," and Lady Macbeth in "Macbeth." Recently New Yorkers have seen her as the nurse in the Cornell "Romeo and Juliet," the revival of "Outward Bound," "The Flying Gerardos," "The Skin of Our Teeth," "Rebecca" and "The Winter's Tale."

REEVES-SMITH, OLIVE. Born in Surrey, England. Broadway debut in 1916 in "The Better 'Ole." Has appeared in "Three Live Ghosts," "Aloma of the South Seas," "The Constant Nymph," "Jubilee," "Party," "Richard of Bordeaux," "Love from a Stranger," "Whiteoaks," "When We Are Married," "The Wookey," "The Doughgirls" and "Bloomer Girl."

Flora Robson

Donald Richards

Elizabeth Ross

REID, FRANCES. Born in Wichita Falls, Texas. Studied at the Pasadena Playhouse. Made stage debut in West Coast company of "Tovarich." Made Broadway debut in "Where There's A Will," followed by "The Rivals," "Bird in Hand," "The Patriots," "Listen, Professor," "A Highland Fling," "The Wind is Ninety," the G.I. "Hamlet" and "Cyrano de Bergerac."

RENNIE, JAMES. Born in Toronto in 1890, and educated at Collegiate Institute in that city. In 1916 he made his Broadway debut in "His Bridal Night." Has appeared in "Moonlight and Honeysuckle," "Spanish Love," "Shore Leave," "The Best People," "The Great Gatsby," "Young Love," "Alien Corn" and "Abide With Me." More recently he was seen in "One Man Show," and on the road in "State of the Union."

RICHARDS, DONALD. Born March 24, 1919 in N.Y.C. Educated at Theodore Roosevelt High School and Columbia University. In 1939 he sang leads with the St. Louis Grand Opera Company in "Pagliacci" and "Faust." First Broadway appearance was in 1940 in "Folies Bergere," followed by "Count Me In." This season he appeared in "Finian's Rainbow."

RICHARDSON, RALPH. Born in Cheltenham, Gloucestershire on Dec. 19, 1902. Made English debut in 1921 in "The Merchant of Venice." In 1935 he toured this country with Katharine Cornell, and was first seen on Broadway as Chorus and Mercutio in "Romeo and Juliet" in that year. He returned to N.Y.C. with the Old Vic Company.

RING, BLANCHE. Born Boston, Mass., April 24, 1877. She first appeared in support of such players as James N. Herne, Nat Goodwin, Chauncey Olcott and James T. Powers. Among her greatest successes were "The Jewel of Asia," "The Blonde in Black," "Sergeant Brue," "About Town," "The Great White Way," "The Midnight Sons," "The Yankee Girl" and "The Wall Street Girl." More recently she has been seen in "Strike Up the Band," "Stepping Sisters," "Madame Capet," "De Luxe" and "Right This Way."

ROACHE, VIOLA. Born Norfolk, Eng., Oct. 3, 1885. Studied for the stage at the Royal Academy of Dramatic Art. First appeared on Broadway in 1914 in "Panthea." Has been seen in "A Woman Disputed," "The Bachelor Father,," "The Distaff Side," "Pride and Prejudice," "Call it a Day" and more recently in "Bird in Hand," "Theatre," "No Way Out," "The Haven" and the revival of "Craig's Wife."

ROAD, MICHAEL. Born in Malden, Mass., March 18, 1915. Appeared on Broadway in "The Moon Vine," "Dear Ruth" and "Tenting Tonight."

ROBER, RICHARD. Born in Rochester, N.Y., May 14, 1906, and educated at Univ. of Rochester and Washington Univ. Received his stage training with the Lyceum Players at Rochester. He has appeared in "Berkeley Square," "East of the Sun," the Maurice Evans' productions of "Richard II" and "Henry IV," and the Lunt productions of "Amphitryon 38," "The Sea Gull" and "Idiot's Delight," as well as "Behind Red Lights," "Banjo Eyes," "Star and Garter," "Ramshackle Inn," "She Had to Say Yes" and "Oklahoma."

ROBERTS, JOAN. Born July 15, 1918 in N.Y.C. Made her Broadway debut in "Sunny River," and has since been seen in "Oklahoma," "Marinka" and "Are You With It?"

ROBERTS, STEPHEN. Born in Floral Park, N.Y., July 25, 1917. Educated at Rutgers College. Made Broadway debut in Orson Welles' Mercury Theatre in "Julius Caesar." Other appearances include "Danton's Death," "Native Son," "Summer Night," "Decision," "Catherine Was Great," "On Whitman Avenue" and "Joan of Lorraine."

ROBERTSON, GUY. Born Denver, Colo., Jan. 26, 1892. Originally planned to become an engineer, and made first stage appearance in a road company of "Head Over Heels." Made Broadway bow in 1919 in "See-Saw." Has appeared in "Wildflower," "Song of the Flame," "The Circus Princess," "White Lilacs," "The Street Singer," "Nina Rosa," "All the Kings Horses," "White Horse Inn," and "Right This Way."

ROBESON, PAUL. Born Princeton, N.J., April 9, 1898. Educated at Rutgers and Columbia Univ. Studied for the law and was admitted to the bar, but turned to the stage and made N.Y. debut in 1921 in "Simon the Cyrenian." Appeared in "Taboo," "All God's Chillun Got Wings," "The Emperor Jones," "Black Boy" and "Porgy." He played "Show Boat" in London, and afterwards appeared in the 1930 revival in N.Y. He is also known for his international song concerts, and his work in the films. Last Broadway appearance was in "Othello."

ROBINSON, BARTLETT. Born in N.Y.C., Dec. 9, 1912. Appeared on Broadway in "Sweet River," "Naughty Naught '00," "Fireman's Flame," "Merchant of Yonkers," "Dear Ruth" and "Another Part of the Forest."

ROBSON, FLORA. Born March 28, 1902 in South Shields, Durham, and studied for the stage at the Royal Academy of Dramatic Art. Made her English debut in 1921. Appeared on the N.Y. stage in "Ladies in Retirement" and "The Damask Cheek."

ROERICK, WILLIAM. Born N.Y.C., Dec. 17, 1912, and educated at Hamilton College. Broadway debut in 1935 in the Cornell production of "Romeo and Juliet." Has appeared in "Saint Joan," the Gielgud "Hamlet," "Our Town," "The Importance of Being Earnest," "The Land is Bright," "Autumn Hill," "This is the Army" and "The Magnificent Yankee."

Arthur L. Sachs

Fritzi Scheff

Jimmy Savo

ROGERS, EMMETT. Born Plainfield, N.J., Nov. 30, 1915. Has appeared on Broadway in "Growing Pains," "Her Man of Wax," "The First Legion," "Alice Takat," "Strip Girl," "Ethan Frome," "Richard II," "Henry IV," "Hamlet," "Papa is All," and the G.I. "Hamlet."

ROGIER, FRANK. Born in Patoka, Ill., July 14, 1918. Educated at James Milliken Univ. and Juilliard School. Made Broadway bow in "The Telephone" and "The Medium."

ROSS, ANTHONY. Born in N.Y.C., 1906, he graduated from Brown Univ. in 1932. His first appearance on Broadway was in "Whistling in the Dark." He has also played in "Bury the Dead," "Arsenic and Old Lace," "This Is the Army," "The Glass Menagerie" and "It Takes Two."

ROSS, ELIZABETH. Born Morristown, N.J., on Aug. 28. 1926. Studied for the theatre at Catholic University, Washington, D.C. Made Broadway bow in the leading role of 'The Song of Bernadette," and since then was seen in "The Story of Mary Suratt."

RUDY, MARTIN. Born in Hartford, Conn., Dec. 5, 1915. "Joan of Lorraine" marks his Broadway bow.

RUTHERFORD, MARGARET. Born in London, May 11, 1892. Educated at Wimbledon Hill School and Ravenscroft. She has had a long and varied career on the English stage, where she is a top ranking comedienne. Made her Broadway bow this season in "The Importance of Being Earnest."

RYDER, ALFRED. Made his N.Y. debut in Eva Le Gallienne's production of "Peter Pan." Since then has appeared in "Come What May," "All the Living," "Jeremiah," "Awake and Sing," "The Man with Blonde Hair," "Medicine Show," "Winged Victory," "Skydrift" and "Yellow Jack."

SACHS, ARTHUR L. Born N.Y.C., March 27, 1913. Educated at Yale. Made Broadway debut in 1933 in "Daughters of Atreus." Since then has appeared in "Howdy Stranger," "Without Warning," Maurice Evans' "Richard II," and "Henry IV," "Jeremiah," "Two on an Island," "Journey to Jerusalem," "As You Like It," "Johnny 2x4," "Swan Song" and "Joan of Lorraine."

SADLER, DUDLEY. Born in Muncie, Ind., Feb. 3, 1918. Made his stage debut on the West Coast with Gladys George in "Personal Appearance." Has played on Broadway in "The Man Who Had All the Luck," "Kiss Them for Me," "Woman Bites Dog" and "All My Sons."

SANDS, DOROTHY. Born March 5, 1900 in Cambridge, Mass. Educated at Radcliffe College. Stage training with the Neighborhood Playhouse and New York Repertory Company. Appeared in "The Grand Street Follies," (1927-28-29), "Many a Slip," "The Sea Gull," "The Stairs," "All the Comforts of Home" and "Papa Is All." More recently was seen in "Tomorrow the World" and "A Joy Forever."

SAVO, JIMMY. Born in N.Y.C., 1895. Was a prominent figure in vaudeville for many years before his first Broadway appearance in "Vanities of 1923." Has also been seen in "Vogues of 1924," "Hassard Short's Ritz Revue," "Murray Anderson's Almanac," "Earl Carroll's Vanities," "Parade" and more recently in "The Boys from Syracuse," "Wine, Women and Song" and "What's Up."

SAXTON, LUTHER. Born in Fairfax, S.C., July 12, 1916. Educated at Springfield, Mass., High School and Clark College, Atlanta, Ga. Made his Broadway bow in "Carmen Jones."

SCHEFF, FRITZI. Born Aug. 30, 1879 in Vienna. Studied music in Frankfort, and made operatic debut in title role of "Martha" in Munich in 1898. Later she sang at Covent Garden and the Metropolitan, and among her roles were Musetta in "La Boheme," Nedda in "Pagliacci," Zerlina in "Don Giovanni," and Cherubino in "Marriage of Figaro." In 1903 she made her light opera debut in "Babette." This was followed by "The Two Roses," "Fatiniza," "Girofle-Girofla," "Boccaccio," "Mlle. Modiste," "The Prima Donna," "The Mikado," "The Duchess," "The Love Wager," "Glorianna," "The O'Brien Girl" and "Bye-Bye Bonnie." In 1929 she appeared in a revival of "Mlle. Modiste," her greatest success. Recently she has been seen on the road in "I Am Different," "Ladies in Retirement," "Tonight or Never" and "The Circle."

SCHILDKRAUT, JOSEPH. Born in Vienna, March 22, 1895. Studied for the stage in Germany and at the American Academy of Dramatic Arts. Made his first N.Y. stage appearance in his father's company at the Irving Place Theatre in 1910. Made his first professional appearance in Germany in 1913 under Max Reinhardt. Reappeared on Broadway stage in 1921 in "Pagans." Was seen on Broadway in "Liliom," "Peer Gynt," "The Firebrand," "Anatole" and was also a member of the Civic Repertory Company. More recently he was seen on Broadway in "Uncle Harry" and a revival of "The Cherry Orchard."

SCHOLL, DANNY. Born July 2, 1921 in Cincinnati, Ohio. Made Broadway bow in "Call Me Mister."

SCHUNZEL, REINHOLD. Born in Hamburg, Germany, Nov. 7, 1886. Made Broadway debut in "Marinka." Since then has appeared in "He Who Gets Slapped" and "Temper the Wind."

SCOTT, MARTHA. Born in Jamesport, Mo., 1914, she came into prominence overnight in her first New York appearance in "Our Town." Following this success, she was seen briefly in "Foreigners," after which she went to Hollywood and made several pictures. Returning to the N.Y. stage she has been seen recently in "The Willow and I," "Soldier's Wife," "The Voice of the Turtle" and "It Takes Two."

Tonio Selwart

Joan Shepard

Joshua Shelley

SEGAL, VIVIENNE. Born in Philadelphia in 1897. Made her Broadway debut in 1915 in "The Blue Paradise." Appeared on the N.Y. stage in "Oh, Lady, Lady!," "The Yankee Princess," "Adrienne," "Castles in the Air," "The Desert Song," "The Three Musketeers," and more recently "I Married an Angel," "Pal Joey," and the revival of "A Connecticut Yankee."

SEIDEL, TOM. Born in Indianapolis, Ind., March 11. 1917. Educated at Carnegie Institute of Technology. Received his stage training at the Pasadena Community Playhouse. Broadway appearances include "Slightly Married," "Over 21" and "Harvey."

SELWART, TONIO. Born Wartenberg, Germany, June 9, 1906. Educated at Munich Univ., and studied for the stage at the Munich Dramatic School. Made his N.Y. debut in 1932 at the Civic Repertory Theatre, where he played small parts. His biggest success was in "The Pursuit of Happiness." Since then has appeared in "Laughing Woman," "Russian Bank," "Candle in the Wind" and "Temper the Wind."

SERGAVA, KATHARINE. Born in Russia, July 30, 1918, and educated at French College, Pulcheric. Has appeared with the Mordkin Ballet, the Original Ballet Russe and the Ballet Theatre. Made her Broadway bow in "Oklahoma."

SERVOSS, MARY. Born in Chicago where she first appeared on the stage playing small parts in stock. N.Y. debut in 1906 in "Bedford's Hope." Has appeared in "Upstairs and Down," as Portia in David Warfield's "The Merchant of Venice," "Tiger Cats," "Behold the Bridegroom," "Street Scene," "Counsellor-At-Law," "Dangerous Corner" and more recently in "Tortilla Flat," "Hamlet" with Leslie Howard, "Dance Night," "Suspect" and "Swan Song."

SHANNON, EFFIE. Born Cambridge, Mass., May 13, 1867. Made first stage appearance as a child in role of Little Eva in "Uncle Tom's Cabin." Her long and illustrious career has included the following plays: "Shenandoah," "Lady Bountiful," "The Moth and the Flame," "Taps," "Years of Discretion," "Pollyanna," "Under Orders," "Mama's Affairs," "Heartbreak House," and "The Fatal Alibi." More recently she has been seen in "The Bishop Misbehaves," "The Wingless Victory," "Barchester Towers," "Parnell" and "Jeremiah."

SHARPE, ALBERT. Born in Belfast, Ireland, April 15, 1885. Educated at Christian Brothers School, Belfast. Gained his first acting experience with Sir Frank Benson's Shakespearian Repertory Company. Played in vaudeville for over twenty years. "Finian's Rainbow" marks his Broadway debut.

SHELLEY, JOSHUA. Born in Brooklyn, Jan. 27, 1920. Educated at N.Y.U. Made his first N.Y. stage appearance in "Black Pit." Since then has been seen in "One Touch of Venus," "On The Town," "Tid-Bits of '46" and "Tenting Tonight."

SHEPARD, JOAN. Born in N.Y.C., Jan. 7, 1933, she was educated at the Professional Children's School. Her N.Y. appearances include "Romeo and Juliet," "Sunny River," "The Strings, My Lord, Are False," "This Rock" and "Foolish Notion." She toured in "Tomorrow the World" and her latest Broadway appearance was in "A Young Man's Fancy."

SHERMAN, HIRAM. Born in Springfield, Ill., Feb. 11, 1908. Has appeared on Broadway in Mercury Theatre's "Shoemaker's Holiday," "Sing Out the News," "Very Warm for May," "Boyd's Daughter," "The Talley Method" and "Cyrano de Bergerac."

SHOWALTER, MAX. Born in Caldwell, Kansas, June 2, 1917. Received his stage training at Pasadena Playhouse. Made Broadway bow in 1938 in "Knights of Song." Since then has been seen in "Very Warm for May," "My Sister Eileen," "Show Boat" and "John Loves Mary."

SIMMS, HILDA. Born in Minneapolis, Minn., she received her stage training with the Edith Bush Players and the Minneapolis Coach Players. She attended the Univ. of Minn., and after receiving her B.S. degree, she came East. Shortly after her arrival in N.Y. she joined the American Negro Theatre and was given a small part in their production of "Three's A Family." "Anna Lucasta" marked her Broadway debut.

SIMPSON, IVAN. Was born in England and came to this country with E.S. Willard, playing with him for several seasons in repertory. For many years he was in George Arliss' company in "Old English," "The Green Goddess" and other Arliss successes both on the stage and screen. Recent N.Y. appearances include "Bright Boy," "Sleep, My Pretty One," the revival of "The Barretts of Wimpole Street" and "The Haven."

SIVY, MICHAEL. Born in Leetsdale, Pa., Sept. 13, 1921. Educated at Carnegie Tech. "Temper the Wind" marked his Broadway debut.

SKINNER, CORNELIA OTIS. Born in Chicago, Ill., May 30, 1902, while her famous father, Otis Skinner, was playing an engagement there. She made her stage debut with her father in 1921 in "Blood and Sand." Engagements in "Will Shakespeare," "The Wild Wescotts" and "White Collars" followed. Then she became her own dramatist, director, costumer, and author in a series of character sketches in which she played all the parts. As a one-woman theatre, her success in these monodramas was so great that for fifteen years she played in them almost exclusively. Recently she has appeared in the Players Club revival of "Love for Love," "Theatre," "The Searching Wind" and "Lady Windermere's Fan."

SKIPPER, BILL. Born Feb. 28, 1922 in Mobile, Ala. First appeared on Broadway in "Higher and

Michael Sivy

Dick Smart

Howard St. John

Higher." Has also been seen in "Panama Hattie," "Banjo Eyes," "Star and Garter," "Tars and Spars" and more recently in "Billion Dollar Baby" and "Park Avenue."

SLEEPER, MARTHA. Born Lake Bluff, Ill., June 24, 1911. Made her Broadway bow in 1929 in "Stepping Out." Has appeared in "Good Men and True," "Russet Mantle," "Save Me the Waltz," "I Must Love Someone" and more recently "The Perfect Marriage," "The Rugged Path" and "Christopher Blake."

SMART, DICK. Born in Honolulu, Hawaii, May 21, 1915. Educated at Stanford Univ. Received stage training at the Pasadena Community Playhouse. Was in the chorus of "The Great Waltz" before embarking on a night club career. Recent Broadway appearances include "Two for the Show" and "Bloomer Girl."

SMITH, G. ALBERT. Born March 11, 1898 in Louisville, Ky. Made Broadway debut in "Rita Coventry." Has been seen in "Coquette," "The Animal Kingdom," "Of Mice and Men," "Ceiling Zero," "The Land Is Bright" and "State of the Union."

SMITH, HOWARD. Born in Attleboro, Mass., Aug. 12, 1895. He was educated at McGill Univ. On Broadway he has appeared in "The Eternal Magdalene," "Miss Quiss," "Solitaire," "The Life of Riley," "Decision," "Dear Ruth" and "Mr. Peebles and Mr. Hooker."

SMITH, KENT. Born N.Y.C., March 19, 1907. Educated at Lincoln School, Phillips Exeter Academy and Harvard. Made Broadway debut in 1934 in "Spring in Autumn." Since then has appeared on Broadway in "Dodsworth," "Candida," (Cornell revival) "Wingless Victory," "Saint Joan," "The Star Wagon," "Old Acquaintance," and "The Story of Mary Suratt."

SMITH, MILDRED. Born in Struthers, Ohio, May 16, 1923. Educated at Western Reserve Univ., Cleveland. Made Broadway bow in "Men to the Sea." Other appearances include "Blue Holiday," "Mamba's Daughters," "St. Louis Woman," "Lysistrata," and "Beggar's Holiday."

SMITH, MURIEL. Born in N.Y.C., Feb. 23, 1923, and educated at Roosevelt High School and the Curtis Institute, Philadelphia. Won a contest on the Major Bowes radio hour. "Carmen Jones" marked her Broadway debut.

SOREL, SONIA. Born in Milwaukee, Wisc., May 18, 1921. Received stage training at Pasadena Playhouse. Made first Broadway appearance in "The Duchess of Malfi."

SOTHERN, HARRY. Born in London, April 26, 1883, and educated at Cheltenham College. Has been in the theatre since 1906, first appearing in support of his uncle, E. H. Sothern. Among the many plays in which he has appeared on Broadway are "Kismet," "The Three of Us," "The Constant Nymph," "Lady of the Lamp," "Art and Mrs. Bottle," "Bird in Hand," and "Lean Harvest." More recently he was seen in "Shadow and Substance," "The Wookey," "Sheppey," "Devils Galore" and "Swan Song."

STARKEY, WALTER. Born May 3, 1921 in Texas. Educated at Univ. of Texas. First Broadway appearance was in "The Mermaids Singing." Has also been seen in "This, Too, Shall Pass."

STEPHENS, HARVEY. Born in Los Angeles, Calif., Aug. 21, 1902. Made his N.Y. bow with Walter Hampden in "Cyrano de Bergerac" after touring with the famous actor in Shakespearian repertory the previous year. Other Broadway engagements include "Dishonored Lady," "I Loved You Wednesday," "The Animal Kingdom," "The Party's Over," "Over 21," and "Violet."

STERLING, JAN. Born N.Y.C., April 3, 1923. Educated in Paris, London and Rio de Janeiro. Studied for the stage in Fay Compton's Dramatic School, London. Broadway debut in "Bachelor Born" was followed by roles in "When We Are Married," "Grey Farm," "This Rock," "The Rugged Path," "Dunnigan's Daughter" and "This, Too, Shall Pass."

STERLING, RICHARD. His eventful career includes roles in "A Successful Calamity," "Rolling Stones," "A Tailor Made Man," "It Pays to Advertise," "Fair and Warmer," "Expressing Willie," "Dulcy," "On Borrowed Time," "Ah, Wilderness!" "Alien Corn" and "Life With Father."

STICKNEY, DOROTHY. Born Dickinson, N.D., June 21, 1903. Educated at St. Catherine's College, St. Paul, Minn., and Northwestern Dramatic School, Minneapolis. Played several seasons in stock and toured in a variety of roles before she made her Broadway debut in "The Squall" in 1926. Has appeared in "Chicago," "March Hares," revival of "The Beuax Stratagem," "The Front Page," "Philip Goes Forth," "Another Language," "On Borrowed Time" and "Life With Father."

ST. JOHN, HOWARD. Born Chicago, Ill., Oct. 9, 1905. Educated at St. Ignatius and St. Boniface College and Univ. of Alabama. Made Broadway debut in 1925 in "12 Miles Out." Recent appearances include "Under This Roof," "Cuckoos on the Hearth," "Brooklyn, U.S.A.," "The Primrose Path," "Janie," "The Late George Apley," and "The Fatal Weakness."

STOCKWELL, HARRY. A native of Kansas City, Mo., he started in life as a newspaper man but switched to music when he received a scholarship at the Eastman Conservatory of Music. He has appeared on Broadway in "Broadway Nights," "As Thousands Cheer," the eighth and ninth editions of Earl Carroll's "Vanities," George White's "Scandals," "Oklahoma," "Marinka" and revival of "The Desert Song."

STODDARD, HAILA. Born Nov. 14, 1914 in Great Falls, Mont. Graduate of Univ. of Southern Calif.

Michael Strong — Ann Thomas — Elliott Sullivan

Broadway debut in 1938 in "Yes, My Darling Daughter." Also appeared in "Susanna and the Elders," "The Rivals," "Moonvine," "Blithe Spirit" and "Dream Girl."

STONE, DOROTHY. Born June 3, 1905 in Brooklyn. Made her Broadway debut in 1923 in "Stepping Stones." Has appeared on the N.Y. stage in "Criss-Cross," "Three Cheers," "Show Girl," "Smiling Faces," "The Gay Divorcee," "As Thousands Cheer," "Hooray for What!" and more recently with her father in a revival of "You Can't Take It with You" and in "The Red Mill."

STONE, FRED. Born near Denver, Colo., Aug. 19, 1873. His earliest years were spent with a travelling circus. Met Dave Montgomery and formed a partnership that lasted until Montgomery's death. Together they starred in "The Red Mill," "The Old Town," "The Lady of the Slipper," and "Chin Chin." Alone he starred in "Jack O' Lantern," "Tip Top," "Stepping Stones" and "Criss-Cross." In recent years Broadway has seen him in "Jayhawker," and revivals of "Lightnin'" and "You Can't Take It With You."

STRONG, MICHAEL. Born N.Y.C., Feb. 8, 1918, Educated at Brooklyn College. Received stage training at Neighborhood Playhouse. Has appeared on Broadway in "The American Way," "Spring Again," "The Russian People," "Counter Attack," "Eve of St. Mark," and "Thank You, Svoboda," "Men to the Sea," "It's a Gift" and "The Whole World Over."

STRUDWICK, SHEPPERD. Has appeared on Broadway in "Both Your Houses," "End of Summer," "Let Freedom Ring" and "Christopher Blake."

STUCKMANN, EUGENE. Born in N.Y.C., Nov. 16, 1917. Made his Broadway debut in George Coulouris' production of "Richard III." Since then has appeared in revival of "Counsellor-At-Law," "Othello," "The Tempest," "Foxhole in the Parlor," "Henry VIII," "Androcles and the Lion" and "Yellow Jack."

SULLIVAN, BRIAN. Born in Oakland, Calif., Aug. 9, 1919. Educated at Manual Arts High School, Los Angeles and Univ. of Southern Calif. Has appeared on Broadway in "Show Boat" and "Street Scene."

SULLIVAN, ELLIOTT. Born San Antonio, Texas, July 4, 1907. Educated at A&M College of Texas. Recent appearances on Broadway include "Winged Victory," "Skydrift" and "Brigadoon."

SULLY, ROBERT. Born N.Y.C., Nov. 20, 1918. Educated at Univ. of Penn. Appeared in several moving pictures before making his Broadway bow in "Marriage Is For Single People."

SUNDSTROM, FLORENCE. Born in N.Y.C., Feb. 9, 1919. Made debut on Broadway in "Parnell." Since then has appeared in "Petticoat Fever," "Bright Honor," "Brother Rat," "Johnny Belinda," "Mr. Strauss Goes to Boston," "Marriage Is For Single People" and "Happy Birthday."

SWEET, BLANCHE. Born in Chicago, Ill. Made her Broadway debut as a child actress. She appeared with great success for many years as a star in the silent films. Returned to the N.Y. stage for "The Petrified Forest," and has also been seen in "There's Always a Breeze," "Aries is Rising," and "Those Endearing Young Charms."

TABBERT, WILLIAM. Born in Chicago, Oct. 5, 1921. First Broadway appearance in "What's Up?" followed by "Follow the Girls," "Seven Lively Arts" and "Billion Dollar Baby."

TABER, RICHARD. Born N.Y.C., Oct. 31, 1891, Made Broadway debut in "Twin Beds" (1908). Other N.Y. appearances include "Is Zat So," "Three Live Ghosts," "Of Mice and Men," "Tomorrow the World" and "Wonderful Journey."

TALIAFERRO, MABEL. Born on a train nearing N.Y., May 21, 1889. Among the many plays in which she has appeared are "Polly of the Circus," "Mrs. Wiggs of the Cabbage Patch," "You Never Can Tell," "Claudia," "George Washington Slept Here," "Victory Belles" and more recently "Bloomer Girl."

TERRY, WILLIAM. Born Eugene, Ore., March 21, 1914. Educated at Univ. of Oregon, and studied for the stage at the Pasadena Community Playhouse. Made N.Y. debut in 1937 in "Straw Hat." Since then has appeared on Broadway in "Out of the Frying Pan," "Brother Cain" and "I Like It Here."

TEXAS, TEMPLE. Born Dallas, Texas, Oct. 7, 1925. Educated at Ward Belmont, Nashville, Tenn. Appeared on the N.Y. stage in "Seven Lively Arts," and "It Takes Two."

THOMAS, ANN. Born July 8, 1920 in Newport, R.I. Went to Professional Children's School and first appeared on stage as a child. Among the many plays in which she has appeared on Broadway are "Doctor's Disagree," "A New Life," "Having Wonderful Time," "The Man from Cairo," "Chicken Every Sunday," "The Would-Be Gentleman" and "Made in Heaven."

THOMAS, EVAN. Born Vancouver, Canada, Feb. 17, 1891. Educated at Charterhouse, England. Received stage training at the Royal Academy of Dramatic Arts, London. Recent Broadway appearances include "Golden Wings," "Rebecca" and "Lady Windermere's Fan."

THOMAS, FRANK M. Born July 13, 1890, in St. Joseph, Mo. Educated at Butler College. Made Broadway debut in 1912 in "Along Came Ruth." Among the many plays in which he has appeared are "The House of Glass," "Red Light Annie," "The National Anthem," "Remember the Day," and more recently "Chicken Every Sunday," "The Rich Full Life," "Jeb" and "Christopher Blake."

THOMPSON, CREIGHTON. Born Chicago, Jan. 7, 1889. Received stage training with Lafayette Stock Company. Recent Braodway appearances were made in "St. Louis Woman" and "Street Scene."

Sophie Tucker

Jerome Thor

Lenore Ulric

THOMSON, BARRY. Born N.Y.C. but educated abroad. Studied for the stage at the Royal Academy of Dramatic Arts in London. First played on Broadway in 1927 in "Immoral Isabella." Appeared with the Lunts in "The Taming of the Shrew," "Idiot's Delight," and "Amphitryon 38." More recently was seen in "Second Best Bed."

THOR, JEROME. Born Jan. 5, 1915 in N.Y.C. Studied for the stage at the Neighborhood Playhouse. Has appeared in "The Fabulous Invalid," "The American Way," "The World We Make," "Somewhere in France," "The Doughgirls," "My Sister Eileen," "Strip for Action," "Get Away, Old Man," "Calico Wedding," "No Way Out," "The French Touch" and the revival of "He Who Gets Slapped."

TONE, FRANCHOT. Born in Niagara Falls, N.Y., Feb. 27, 1906. Educated at Cornell Univ. Made his Broadway bow with Katharine Cornell in "The Age of Innocence." His next engagements found him in "Cross Roads," "Red Rust," "Hotel Universe," "Green Grow the Lilacs" and "Pagan Lady." One of the original members of the Group Theatre, he played with them in "The House of Connelly," "Night Over Taos," "Success Story" and "The Gentle People." His success in the theatre sent him to Hollywood where he appeared in many films. His most recent Broadway appearances were in "The Fifth Column," and "Hope for the Best."

TOZERE, FRERERIC. Born July 19, 1901 in Brookline, Mass. Made Broadway bow in 1924 in "Stepping Stones." Has appeared in "Journey's End," "Key Largo," "Watch on the Rhine," "Outrageous Fortune," "In Bed We Cry," "Signature" and "The Rich Full Life."

TRUEX, ERNEST. He was born in Red Hill, Mo., Sept. 19, 1890, and educated at the Whittier School, Denver, Colo. Made his first appearance on the stage in 1895 playing Little Lord Fauntleroy. Made his Broadway bow in 1908 with Lillian Russell in "Wildfire." Since then he appeared in "Rebecca of Sunnybrook Farm," "The Dummy," "Annie Dear," "The Fall Guy" and "Pomeroy's Past." After a session in Hollywood, he was again seen on the N.Y. stage in "Lysistrata," "Whistling in the Dark," "George Washington Slept Here," and "Helen Goes to Troy." This season he played in "Androcles and the Lion," "John Gabriel Borkman," "What Every Woman Knows," "Henry VIII" and "Pound on Demand."

TRUEX, PHILIP. Born Boston, Mass., Sept. 20, 1911. Educated at Haverford College. Made Broadway debut in 1933 in "The World Waits." Has since appeared in "Too Much Party," "The Hook-Up," "Battleship Gertie," "Mulatto," "Richard II," "The Fabulous Invalid," "Family Portrait," "The Man Who Came to Dinner" and "This Is The Army." More recently he was seen in "The Magnificent Yankee."

TUCKER, SOPHIE. Born Jan. 13, 1884 in Russia, but moved to Boston, Mass., when 3 months old. Educated at Parmenta Street School, Boston and Brown School, Hartford, Conn. First appeared as a singer in her father's cafe in Hartford in 1905, and shortly afterwards became well known in vaudeville. First Broadway appearance was in "Ziegfeld Follies of 1909." Since then she has appeared with outstanding success in vaudeville and night clubs and was also seen in N.Y. in "Town Topics," "Hello, Alexander," "Shubert Gaieties," "Earl Carroll's Vanities," and more recently in "Leave It To Me" and "High Kickers."

TURNER, MAIDEL. Born in Sherman, Texas. Trained for the theatre at Dramatic School of the Chicago Musical College. First stage appearance was as leading lady to Maclyn Arbuckle in "Welcome to Our City." Among the many plays in which she has appeared on Broadway are "Kick In," "The Varying Shore," "Spring Is Here," "What a Life," "By Jupiter" and more recently "Dark of the Moon" and "State of the Union."

TYLER, RICHARD. Born N.Y.C., Sept. 23, 1932. Educated at N.Y. Professional Children's School. Made Broadway debut with Maurice Evans in "Macbeth." Since then appeared in "The Moon Vine," "Tomorrow the World" and "Christopher Blake."

TYRRELL, DAVID. Born in New Jersey, Dec. 8, 1916. New York appearances include "It's Up to You," "The Overtons," "A Goose for a Gander" and "Love Goes to Press."

ULRIC, LENORE. Born New Ulm, Minn., July 21, 1894. Began her stage training with a Milwaukee stock company. As a famous Belasco star, appeared in such plays as "Tiger Rose," "The Son-Daughter," "Lulu Belle," "Kiki," "The Harem" and "Mima." More recent New York appearances include "Her Man of Wax" and "The Fifth Column." Also appeared in the Chicago company of "The Doughgirls."

VALENTINE, GRACE. Made her Broadway debut in 1914 in "The Yosemite." Among her earlier hits were "Johnny Get Your Gun" and "Lombardi, Ltd." More recently she appeared in "The Fabulous Invalid," "The American Way," "George Washington Slept Here" and "Happy Birthday."

VALENTINOFF, VAL. Born N.Y.C., March 23, 1919. Educated at P.S. 40, Wingate Junior High and Commercial High. Has danced with the Monte Carlo Ballet Russe, and the St. Louis and Detroit Opera Companies. Has appeared on Broadway in "Virginia," "Sons O' Fun," "Follow the Girls," and "Gypsy Lady."

VAN, GUS. Born in Brooklyn, N.Y., Aug. 12, 1887. Made his Broadway bow in "The Century Girl" (1916). Appeared in "Ziegfeld Follies" from 1918 to 1922, then played with William Collier and Sam Bernard in "Nifties of 1923." More recently was seen in "Toplitzky of Notre Dame."

Shirley Van

Raymond Van Sickle

Hilda Vaughn

VAN, SHIRLEY. Born in Mitchell, S.D., Aug. 12, 1927. Educated at Los Angeles High School. Made Broadway bow in "Billion Dollar Baby." Was seen this season in "Barefoot Boy With Cheek."

VAN PATTEN, DICK. Born N.Y.C., 1929. Has appeared on Broadway in "Tapestry in Grey," "The Eternal Road," "Home, Sweet Home," "The American Way," "The Woman Brown," "The Lady Who Came to Stay," "Run Sheep Run," "The Land Is Bright," "Kiss and Tell," "Decision," "The Skin of Our Teeth," "Too Hot for Maneuvers," "The Wind is Ninety" and "O Mistress Mine."

VAN PATTEN, JOYCE. Born March 9, 1934, Kew Gardens, L.I., N.Y. Made debut in 1941 in "Popsy," and has since been seen in "This Rock," "Tomorrow the World," "The Perfect Marriage" and "The Wind is Ninety."

VAN SICKLE, RAYMOND. Born in Frankfort, Indiana. Played with such stars as Mrs. Fiske, Margaret Anglin, Pauline Lord, Alice Brady and Marjorie Rambeau. Recent appearances include "Journeyman," "Chicken Every Sunday" and "Christopher Blake."

VARDEN, EVELYN. Born in Adair, Okla., June 12, 1893. Educated at Girls Collegiate School, Los Angeles. Received stage training in various stock companies. Made Broadway debut in "The Nest Egg" (1910). Recent N.Y. appearances include: "Alley Cat," "Life's Too Short," "Women of the Soil," "Weep for the Virgins," "Russet Mantle," "Prelude to Exile," "To Quito and Back," "Our Town," "Family Portrait," "Ladies and Gentlemen," "Grey Farm," "Return Engagement," "The Lady Who Came to Stay," "Candle in the Wind," "Dream Girl" and "Present Laughter."

VAUGHN, HILDA. Born Baltimore, Maryland. Educated at Girls' Latin School and Vassar College. Received stage training at American Academy of Dramatic Arts. Recent Broadway appearances include "Get Away, Old Man," "Jacobowsky and the Colonel" and "On Whitman Avenue."

VERMILYEA, HAROLD. Born N.Y.C., Oct. 10, 1889. Among the many plays in which he has appeared on Broadway are "It Pays to Advertise," "Get Rich Quick Wallingford," "The Enemy," "Sun-Up," "Loose Ankles," "The Alarm Clock," "Midnight" and "Madame Bovary." More recently he has been seen in "Jacobowsky and the Colonel" and "Deep Are the Roots."

von ZERNECK, PETER. Born in Budapest, Hungary, June 17, 1908, and educated at the University of Law in Budapest. He has appeared on Broadway in "Men in Shadow," "Land of Fame," "Common Ground" and "Hidden Horizon."

VYE, MURVYN. Born Quincy, Mass., July 15, 1913. Educated at Andover and Yale. Has appeared on Broadway in the Gielgud "Hamlet," "As You Like It," "Oklahoma," "One Touch of Venus" and "Carousel."

WALKER, JUNE. Born N.Y.C., 1904. First appeared on Broadway as a chorus girl in "Hitchy-Koo" in 1918. Has been seen in "Six Cylinder Love," "The Nervous Wreck," "Processional," "Gentlemen Prefer Blondes," "The Love Nest," "The Bachelor Father," "Waterloo Bridge," "Green Grow the Lilacs," "The Farmer Takes a Wife," "For Valor" and "The Merchant of Yonkers." More recently she appeared in "Round Trip" and "Truckline Cafe."

WALKER, NANCY. Born in Philadelphia, May 10, 1921. At the age of nineteen she scored an immediate success on Broadway in "Best Foot Forward" and was sent off to Hollywood where she made the films "Best Foot Forward," "Girl Crazy" and "Broadway Rhythm." Returning to N.Y. she scored another success in "On the Town," and since then has been seen in "Barefoot Boy With Cheek."

WANAMAKER, SAM. Born in Chicago, June 14, 1919. Educated at Drake University and received stage training at Goodman Theatre, Chicago. Made Broadway bow in "Cafe Crown," and has appeared in "Counterattack," "This, Too, Shall Pass" and "Joan of Lorraine."

WARAM, PERCY. Trained for the classic stage with the Ben Greet Players in his native England, he came to the United States more than thirty years ago. In recent years he has appeared in "R.U.R.," "Mary of Scotland," "Major Barbara," "Pride and Prejudice," "Life With Father," (the Chicago Co.), "The Late George Apley" and "Another Part of the Forest."

WARD, PENELOPE. Born in London, 1914. Made Broadway debut in 1937 in "French Without Tears." Since then, New Yorkers have seen her in "Set to Music" and "Lady Windermere's Fan."

WARING, RICHARD. Born Buckinghamshire, England, May 27, 1912. Received his stage training with Eva Le Gallienne's Civic Repertory Acting Company. Appeared opposite Miss Le Gallienne in "Romeo and Juliet," "Camille" and "Cradle Song." Other Broadway appearances include "Boy Meets Girl," "Come Across," "The Man Who Killed Lincoln," "The Corn is Green," "Henry VIII," "Androcles and the Lion," "What Every Woman Knows" and "Alice in Wonderland."

WARRE, MICHAEL. Born June 18, 1922 in London, and studied for the stage at the London Mask Theatre School. Made his initial appearance on Broadway in the Old Vic Company.

WATERS, ETHEL. Born Chester, Pa., Oct. 31, 1900. Commenced her career as a cabaret singer, and made Broadway debut in 1927 in "Africana." Appeared in Lew Leslie's "Blackbirds," "Rhapsody in Black," "As Thousands Cheer," "At Home Abroad" and made an outstanding success in a straight role in "Mamba's Daughters." More recent appearances include "Cabin in the Sky" and "Blue Holiday."

Peter von Zerneck

Billie Lou Watt

Sam Wanamaker

WATKINS, LINDA. Born Boston, Mass., May 23, 1914. Made Broadway debut in 1926 in "The Devil in the Cheese." Has appeared in "Ivory Door," "The Wild Duck," "Hedda Gabler," "Lady from the Sea," "June Moon," "Sweet Stranger," "Say When," "Penny Wise," "I Am My Youth" and more recently in "Janie."

WATSON, LUCILLE. Born Quebec, Canada, May 27, 1879. Studied for the stage at the American Academy of Dramatic Art, and first played in Ottawa in 1900. Made N.Y. debut in 1903 in "Hearts Aflame." Has appeared in "The Girl With the Green Eyes," "The Dictator," "The City," "Under Cover," "The Eternal Magdalene," "Heartbreak House," "You and I," "No More Ladies," "Pride and Prejudice" and "Yes, My Darling Daughter." More recently she was seen in "Dear Octopus," "Watch on the Rhine" and "The Family."

WATSON, MINOR. Born in Marianna, Ark., Dec. 22, 1889. Studied for the stage at the American Academy of Dramatic Arts. Played several seasons in stock before making his Broadway bow in 1922 in "Why Men Leave Home." Has appeared in "The Magnolia Lady," "Trigger," "This Thing Called Love," "It's A Wise Child," "Reunion in Vienna," "A Divine Drudge," "End of Summer" and most recently "State of the Union."

WATT, BILLIE LOU. Born St. Louis, Mo., June 20, 1924. Educated at Northwestern Univ. School of Speech. Played the lead in the Chicago company of "Kiss and Tell," and made Broadway bow in "Little Women," and since then appeared in "Barefoot Boy With Cheek."

WAYNE, DAVID. Born Traverse City, Mich., Jan. 21, 1916. Educated at Western State, Kalamazoo, Mich. Received stage training with the Eldred Players at Cleveland, Ohio. Made his Broadway debut April 25, 1938 as a walk-on in "Escape This Night." Since then has played in "Dance Night," "The American Way," "Scene of the Crime," "The Merry Widow," "Peepshow," "Park Avenue," and "Finian's Rainbow."

WEAVER, "DOODLES." Born in Los Angeles, May 11, 1914. Made N.Y. debut in 1941 in "Meet the People," and has since been seen in "Marinka."

WEBB, CLIFTON. Born in Indiana, 1891. First appeared on the stage as a child actor. Studied for Grand Opera, and had a brief operatic career in Boston before appearing on the regular stage. In 1913 he first played on Broadway in "The Purple Road." Among the many plays in which he has appeared are "Dancing Around," "Nobody Home," "Very Good, Eddie," "Listen Lester," "Meet the Wife," "Sunny," "She's My Baby," "Treasure Girl," "The Little Show," "Three's A Crowd," "Flying Colors," and "As Thousands Cheer." More recently he has been seen in a revival of "The Importance of Being Earnest," "Blithe Spirit" and "Present Laughter."

WEBER, WILLIAM. Born in Los Angeles, July 5, 1915. Educated at Univ. of Calif. and studied for the stage at Pasadena Playhouse. First Broadway appearance in revival of "Susan and God," and has been seen also in G.I. "Hamlet."

WEISSMULLER, DON. Born in Louisville, Ky., August 31, 1923. Has appeared on Broadway in "Keep Off the Grass," "Panama Hattie," "High Kickers," "Count Me In," "Ziegfeld Follies," "What's Up," "On the Town" and "Finian's Rainbow."

WELLES, ORSON. Born Kenosha, Wis., May 6, 1915. Made his first stage appearance in 1931 at the Gate Theatre in Dublin. Returning to this country, he toured with Katharine Cornell, and made his N.Y. debut as Chorus and Tybalt in her production of "Romeo and Juliet." Before this he had organized and managed the Woodstock Theatre Festival, and in 1937 was appointed a director of the Federal Theatre Project in N.Y. During this period he produced a Negro version of "Macbeth" and produced and acted in "Doctor Faustus." In 1937, with John Houseman, he founded the Mercury Theatre, which revived such plays as "Julius Caesar," "The Shoemaker's Holiday," "Heartbreak House," and "Danton's Death." He has achieved considerable fame in both films and radio, and returned to the Broadway stage in "Around the World."

WENGRAF, JOHN. Born April 23, 1907 in Vienna. Educated in Vienna, Paris and London. Made Broadway debut in "Candle in the Wind." More recently was seen in "The French Touch."

WEST, MAE. Born in Brooklyn, Aug. 17, 1892. Made her Broadway debut in "Folies Bergere." This was followed by appearances in "A La Broadway," "Vera Violetta," "The Winsome Widow," "Demi-Tasse" and "The Mimic World." It was as a writer-actress in "Sex" that she first came to the attention of N.Y. audiences. Greater success came to her in another play of her own authorship: "Diamond Lil." This led to a Hollywood contract where she made several movies. She returned to Broadway in another of her own plays: "Catherine Was Great," and since then toured this season in "Come On Up."

WESTMAN, NYDIA. Born in N.Y.C., Feb. 19, 1907. Educated at the Children's Professional School. As a child appeared in vaudeville with her father and mother and sisters in an act called "The Westmans." Made her legitimate debut in "Pigs." Since then has appeared in "Two Girls Wanted," "Buckaroo," "Jonesy," "Cooking Her Goose," "The Unsophisticates," "Ada Beats the Drum," "Lysistrata" and "The Merchant of Yonkers." Hollywood beckoned her and until recently she has been on the West Coast where she made numerous films. She returned to N.Y. to play "Life With Father."

Robert Willey

Eleanor Wilson

Lionel Wilson

WESTON, RUTH. Born in Boston, Mass., Aug. 31, 1908. Made her Broadway debut replacing Ina Claire in "Biography." Since then she has appeared in many plays among which are "No More Ladies," "The Red Cat," "Valley Forge," "The Dominant Sex," "There's Wisdom in Women," the Players Club revival of "Seven Keys to Baldpate," "Forbidden Melody," "The Country Wife," "Among Those Sailing," "Run, Sheep, Run," "The American Way," "Outward Bound," "Pastoral," "Out From Under," "George Washington Slept Here," "The Night Before Christmas," "The Lady Comes Across," "Western Union, Please," "The Sun Field," "What Big Ears," "Three's A Family" and "Oklahoma."

WHEELER, LOIS. Born in Stockton, Calif., July 12, 1922, she received her stage training with the Pacific Little Theatre and the Pasadena Playhouse. A scholarship with the Neighborhood Playhouse brought her to N.Y. and eventually to Broadway in "The Innocent Voyage." Other N.Y. appearances were in "Pick-Up Girl," "Trio" and "All My Sons."

WHITE, JANE. Born N.Y.C., Oct. 30, 1922. Educated at Ethical Culture School and Smith College. Had her theatre training with the New School for Social Research. Made her Broadway debut in "Strange Fruit."

WHITE, SAMMY. Born Providence, R.I., May 28, 1896. Broadway appearances include "The Girl Friend," "Yokel Boy," "Swing Your Lady," and the original production and revival of "Show Boat."

WHITE, WATSON. Born Cambridge, Mass., Jan. 3, 1888. Educated at Harvard. Trained for stage at American Academy of Dramatic Arts. Made his Broadway debut with David Warfield in "The Auctioneer" (1915). Recent N.Y. appearances include "Under the Roof," "Up in Central Park" and "Christopher Blake."

WHITING, JACK. Born Philadelphia, Penn., June 22, 1901. Educated at Univ. of Penn. Made Broadway bow in "Ziegfeld Follies of 1922." Has appeared in "Orange Blossoms," "Cinders," "Aren't We All?," "Stepping Stones," "Annie Dear," "The Ramblers," "Yes, Yes, Yvette," "She's My Baby," "Hold Everything," "Heads Up," "America's Sweetheart," "Take a Chance," "Calling All Stars," "Hooray for What," "Very Warm for May," "Hold On to Your Hats," and more recently in "The Overtons" and "The Red Mill."

WHITLEY, BERT. Born N.Y.C. Educated at Columbia Univ. Received his stage training at Neighborhood Playhouse. Broadway appearances include "The Wind and the Rain," "New Faces," "Fools Rush In," "Lady Precious Stream," "The American Way," "This is the Army" and "Cyrano de Bergerac."

WHITTY, DAME MAY. Born Liverpool, June 19, 1865. Made first stage appearance in England as a chorus girl in 1881. Her first American appearance was in 1895-6 when she toured this country with the Lyceum Company under Sir Henry Irving. In 1908 she played on Broadway in "Irene Wycherly," and did not return until 1932 when she appeared in "There's Always Juliet." She also played here in "Night Must Fall" and "Yr. Obedient Servant," and has made an eminent success in films. More recently she appeared on the N.Y. stage in "Therese."

WICKES, MARY. Born in St. Louis, Mo., and educated at Washington Univ. First played on Broadway in "The Farmer Takes a Wife." Has appeared in "One Good Year," "Spring Dance," "Stage Door," "Hitch Your Wagon," "Father Malachy's Miracle," "Stars in Your Eyes," "Danton's Death," "The Man Who Came to Dinner," "Jackpot," "Dark Hammock," "Hollywood Pinafore," "Apple of His Eye" and "Park Avenue."

WIDMARK, RICHARD. Born Dec. 26, 1915 in Minnesota, and educated at Lake Forest College, Ill. Has appeared on Broadway in "Kiss and Tell," "Get Away, Old Man," "Trio," "Kiss Them for Me," and "Dunnigan's Daughter."

WILLARD, CATHERINE. Born 1895 in Dayton, Ohio. Made stage debut in England with the Frank Benson Company. Later she played leading Shakespearian roles at the Old Vic in London. Her first American engagement was with the Henry Jewett Repertory Company in Boston. On Broadway she has played in "Simon Called Peter," "The Great Gatsby," "She Had To Know," "Young Love," "The Deep Mrs. Sykes" and "You Touched Me."

WILLEY, ROBERT. Born Pasadena, Calif., July 3, 1920. Educated at Pasadena Junior College. Stage training received at Pasadena Playhouse. Has appeared on the N.Y. stage in "Junior Miss," "Winged Victory" and "Little A."

WILLIAMS, RHYS. Born Clydach-cwm-Tawe, Wales, on Dec. 31, 1897. Made Broadway debut as an off stage singer in 1926 in "The Beaten Track." Has appeared in "Richard II," "Henry IV," "Hamlet," "The Corn Is Green," "Morning Star," "Lifeline," "Harriet," "Chicken Every Sunday," and "Mr. Peebles and Mr. Hooker."

WILSON, ELEANOR. Born Chester, Pa., and educated at Hollins College, Va. Received stage training at Pasadena Playhouse, and Cleveland Playhouse. "Eagle Has Two Heads" marked her Broadway debut.

WILSON, LIONEL. Born in N.Y.C., March 22, 1924, he won the annual Barter Theatre Award for being the most promising actor of the 1942 season. At nine, he made his stage debut in a suburban tour of "Dodsworth." The following year he joined the Ben Greet Players and had several minor Shakespearian roles with that troupe. He interrupted his career from 1940 to 1941 while he attended N.Y.U. He made his Broad-

William Windom

Estelle Winwood

Joseph Wiseman

way bow in "Janie," and followed this with "Good Morning, Corporal," "Kiss and Tell" and "Tenting Tonight."

WILSON, LOIS. Born Pittsburgh, Pa., June 28, 1900. Played in stock on West Coast, and was very successful as a silent picture star, appearing in over 300 films. In 1937 she made her Broadway debut in "Farewell Summer." More recently she has appeared in "Chicken Every Sunday" and "The Mermaids Singing."

WILSON, PERRY. She was born in Bound Brook, N.J., and attended the Kent Place School and later Tamara Daykarkanova's School for the Stage. Her first N.Y. appearance was made in "Cream in the Well" in 1940. Since then she has been seen in "Village Green," "The First Crocus," "Mexican Mural," "The Corn is Green," "The Stranger" and "On Whitman Avenue."

WINDOM, WILLIAM. Born N.Y.C., Sept. 28, 1923. Educated at Admiral Billard Academy and Williams College. Made Broadway debut in "Henry VIII." Other appearances include "What Every Woman Knows," "John Gabriel Borkman," "Androcles and the Lion," "Yellow Jack" and "Alice in Wonderland."

WINTERS, LAWRENCE. Born Kings Creek, S.C., Nov. 12, 1915. Educated at Howard Univ. Made N.Y. debut in 1942 in "Porgy and Bess," and more recently appeared in "Call Me Mister."

WINWOOD, ESTELLE. Born in Kent, England, Jan. 24, 1883, she studied for the stage at the Lyric Stage Academy. Made her first appearance on any stage at the Theatre Royal, Manchester, Eng., 1898 in "School." Made her American debut at the Little Theatre, N.Y. in 1916 in "Hush." Since then she has been seen in "A Successful Calamity," "Why Marry?," "Helen With the High Hand," "A Little Journey," "Moliere," "Too Many Husbands," "The Tyranny of Love," "The Circle," "Madame Pierre," "Go Easy, Mabel," "The Red Poppy," "Anything Might Happen," "Spring Cleaning," "The Buccaneer," "A Weak Woman," "The Chief Thing," "Beau-Strings," "Head or Tail," "Trelawney of the Wells," "Fallen Angels," "We Never Learn" and "The Furies." More recently New Yorkers have seen her in "The Distaff Side," "I Want a Policeman," "The Importance of Being Earnest," "When We Are Married," "Ladies in Retirement," "Ten Little Indians" and "Lady Windermere's Fan." Her only movie was "Quality Street," with Katharine Hepburn.

WISEMAN, JOSEPH. Born Montreal, Canada, May 15, 1919. Made Broadway bow in "Abe Lincoln of Illinois" (1938). Other appearances include "Journey to Jerusalem," "Candle in the Wind," "The Barber Has Two Sons," "The Three Sisters" (Cornell production), "Storm Operation" and "Joan of Lorraine."

WOLFIT, DONALD. Born Newark-on-Trent, England, April 20, 1902. Educated at Magnus. Made Broadway debut this season, appearing in "King Lear," "Volpone," "Hamlet," "The Merchant of Venice," and "As You Like It."

WOOD, PEGGY. Born Brooklyn, N.Y., Feb. 9, 1894. Studied singing with Mme. Calve, and made her N.Y. debut in 1910 in "Naughty Marietta." Has appeared in "The Lady of the Slipper," "Love O' Mike," "Maytime," "Buddies," "Marjolaine," "The Clinging Vine," "The Bride," in revivals of "Candida," "Trelawney of the Wells," and as Portia with George Arliss in "The Merchant of Venice." In London she appeared with remarkable success in "Bitter Sweet." More recently she has been seen on Broadway in "Old Acquaintance" and "Blithe Spirit."

WYCHERLY, MARGARET. Born London, Eng., Oct. 26, 1881. First stage appearance was in 1898 in "What Dreams May Come," after which she acted in stock and toured with Richard Mansfield. Among the many plays in which she has appeared are "Everywoman," "Cashel Byron's Profession," "The Nazarene," "The Blue Bird," "Damaged Goods," "The Thirteenth Chair," "Jane Clegg," "Back to Methuselah," "Six Characters in Search of an Author," and "The Adding Machine." More recently she has played in "Another Language," "Tobacco Road," and revivals of "Hedda Gabler" and "Liliom."

WYNN, ED. Born Philadelphia, Nov. 9, 1886. Made first stage appearance at age of fifteen, and continued for many years in vaudeville. His first Broadway show was "The Deacon and the Lady" in 1910. Has been seen in "Ziegfeld Follies" (1914-15), "Sometime," "The Shubert Gaieties of 1919," "The Ed Wynn Carnival," "The Perfect Fool," "The Grab Bag," "Manhattan Mary," "Simple Simon," "The Laugh Parade," "Hooray for What!" and "Laugh, Town, Laugh!"

WYNYARD, JOHN. Born London, England, Jan. 4, 1915. Educated at schools in Surrey, Eng. Made Broadway bow with Donald Wolfit Company, appearing in "King Lear," "Volpone," "Hamlet," and "The Merchant of Venice."

YURKA, BLANCHE. Born in Bohemia, June 19, 1893. Started her acting career in 1907 as understudy to Charlotte Walker in "The Warrens of Virginia." Since then has had a long and varied career. Her most recent N.Y. appearances were made in "The Wind is Ninety" and "Temper the Wind."

ZORINA, VERA. Born in Germany, Jan. 2, 1918. Educated in Norway and Germany. Made first professional appearance in Berlin in Max Reinhardt's production of "A Midsummer Night's Dream." Coming to this country, she toured several seasons with the Russian Ballet. Her first Broadway engagement was in "I Married an Angel." Since then she has played in "Louisiana Purchase," "Dream With Music," and "The Tempest."

PRODUCERS, DIRECTORS, DESIGNERS AND CHOREOGRAPHERS

ABBOTT, GEORGE. Producer, Director, Author, Actor. Born in Forestville, New York, June 25, 1887. Graduated from Rochester University and studied playwriting with Professor G. P. Baker at Harvard. Made his first appearance as an actor in "The Misleading Lady," 1913. Produced such plays as: "Chicago," 1926; "Coquette," 1927; "Twentieth Century," 1932; "Small Miracle," 1934; "Three Men On A Horse" and "Boy Meets Girl," 1935; "Brother Rat," 1936; "Room Service," 1937; "What A Life," 1938; "Too Many Girls," 1940; "Pal Joey," 1941; "Best Foot Forward," 1942; "Kiss And Tell," 1943; "Snafu," 1945; "Barefoot Boy With Cheek, 1947—many of these he co-authored. Directed "On The Town" and "Billion Dollar Baby." Has also produced and directed movies.

ALDRICH, RICHARD. Producer, Manager. Born in Boston, Mass., August 17, 1903. Married to Gertrude Lawrence. Graduated from Harvard, 1925; member of Professor G. P. Baker's "47 Workshop." From 1926 to 1928 was General Manager for Richard Boleslovsky's American Laboratory Theatre. Has either produced alone or co-produced: "La Gringa," 1928; "Art and Mrs. Bottle," 1930; "Twelfth Night," 1931; "Springtime for Henry," 1932; "Three Cornered Moon," 1933; "Petticoat Fever," 1935; "Fresh Fields" and "Aged 26," 1936; "Tide Rising," 1937; "My Dear Children" and "Margin for Error," 1939; "It Takes Two," 1947. Lieutenant-Commander in the U.S.-N.R., 1941-45. Operates the Cape Playhouse, Summer Theatre in Dennis, Mass. For the past two seasons has been Managing Director of Theatre Incorporated.

ALSWANG, RALPH. Scenic Designer. Born in Chicago, Illinois, April 12, 1916. Received training at Art Institute and Goodman Theatre in Chicago. As an apprentice, worked for leading designers including Robert Edmond Jones. First Broadway production was "Comes The Revelation" in 1942. Others were "Home of the Brave," 1945; "I Like It Here," "Swan Song," and "Lysistrata," 1946; "The Whole World Over" and "A Young Man's Fancy," 1947.

AMERICAN REPERTORY THEATRE, Cheryl Crawford, Eva Le Gallienne and Margaret Webster, founders, opened its first New York season on November 6, 1946 at the International Theatre with Shakespeare's "Henry VIII." Productions that followed (the first four bills alternating in repertory fashion) were Barrie's "What Every Woman Knows," Ibsen's "John Gabriel Borkman," and a double bill of O'Casey's "Pound on Demand" and Shaw's "Androcles and the Lion," Sidney Howard's "Yellow Jack" and the Eva Le Gallienne-Florida Friebus adaptation of Lewis Carroll's "Alice in Wonderland." This last was produced in conjunction with Rita Hassan. Stars of the American Repertory Company were Eva Le Gallienne, Victory Jory, Walter Hampden, June Duprez, Ernest Truex, Richard Waring, Margaret Webster and Philip Bourneuf. Bambi Linn joined the company to play Alice in the Lewis Carroll classic.

ANDERSON, JOHN MURRAY. Director, Producer. Born September 20, 1886 in St. Johns, Newfoundland. Educated at Edinburgh Academy, Scotland and Lausanne University, Switzerland. Began theatre apprenticeship at Sir Herbert Tree's School of the Theatre in London. Made New York debut as director of "Greenwich Village Follies" in 1919. Among the musicals he has staged are: "Music Box Revue," 1924; "Dearest Enemy," 1925; "Murray Anderson's Almanac," 1929; "Ziegfeld Follies," 1933; "Life Begins at 8:40," 1934; "Jumbo," 1935; "Ziegfeld Follies," 1936; "One For The Money," 1939; "Two For The Show," 1940; "Ziegfeld Follies," 1943; "Laffing Room Only," 1944; "Three To Make Ready," 1946. Motion pictures include "The King Of Jazz" in 1930 and "Bathing Beauty," 1943. Also staged the "Acquacades" at the New York World's Fair and at the San Francisco Exposition, all the "Diamond Horseshoe" Revues in New York, and in 1942 and 1943, The Ringling Bros. Barnum & Bailey Circus.

AYRES, LEMUEL. Scenic and Costume Designer. Born in New York City, January 22, 1915. Educated at Princeton and Iowa University. Broadway debut was the revivals of "Journey's End," and "They Knew What They Wanted," in 1939. Other plays include: "Angel Street," 1941; "The Pirate," "Lifeline," "The Willow and I," 1942; "Harriet," "Oklahoma," 1943; "Song Of Norway," "Bloomer Girl," 1944; "St. Louis Woman," and "Cyrano de Bergerac," 1946.

BALANCHINE, GEORGE. Choreographer. Born in Russia in 1904. Graduated from the State Dancing Academy in Leningrad. In 1925 became ballet-master for Serge de Diaghilev's Company. He introduced classic dancing to the Broadway Musical in his Slaughter On 10th Ave., number in "On Your Toes." Other Musicals include: "I Married An Angel," 1938; "Keep Off The Grass," "Louisiana Purchase," 1940; "Rosalinda," 1942; "Song Of Norway," 1944; "Chocolate Soldier," 1947. Has also choreographed for American Ballet Caravan, Ballet Russe de Monte Carlo, and Ballet Theatre.

BALLARD, LUCINDA. Costume and Scenic Designer. Born in New Orleans, La., April 3, 1908. Studied at Art Students League in New York, Fontainbleu Academy and in Paris. Worked as assistant to Norman Bel Geddes, Claude Bragdon etc. Broadway debut was "As You Like It" in 1937. Designed the costumes for "American Jubilee" at the World's Fair in 1939; the scenery and costumes for "The Moon Vine," 1943. Also costumes for "I Remember Mama," 1944; "Show Boat," 1945; "Annie Get Your Gun," "Happy Birthday," and "Another Part of the Forest," 1946; "Street Scene," "John Loves Mary," and "Chocolate Soldier," 1947.

BARRATT, WATSON. Scenic Designer. Born in Salt Lake City, Utah, June 27, 1884. Educated at Chase School of Art in New York, and Howard Pyle Illustration School, Wilmington, Delaware. First Broadway play was Al Jolson's "Sinbad" in 1918. He is the designer of the original "Student Prince" and "Blossom Time." For nine years has been Art Director and Assistant Manager of St. Louis Muncipal Outdoor Opera. A few of the hundreds of productions he has designed settings for in New York are: All Winter Garden Shows from 1918 to 1928; "Scarlet Sister Mary," "Artists and Models," 1930; "Three Waltzes," 1937; "Bachelor Born," "The White Steed," 1938; "The Time Of Your Life," "The Importance Of Being Earnest," 1939; "Love's Old Sweet Song," 1940; "Magic" and "Hello, Out There," 1942; "Ziegfeld Follies," 1943; "Rebecca," 1945; "Flamingo Road," "January Thaw," 1946; "Little A," 1947.

BERNSTEIN, ALINE FRANKAU. Costume and Scenic Designer. Born in New York City, December 22, 1880. Educated at New York public school and New York School of Applied Design. Learned her profession at the Neighborhood Playhouse on Grand St. Has designed costumes for a great number of Broadway productions including "The Willow and I," 1942; "Harriet," 1943; "Clover Ring" (also scenery), 1945; "The Eagle Has Two Heads," 1947. Also designed "Last Days of Pompeii," and "She" for R.K.O.

CHANEY, STEWART. Scenic Designer. Born in Kansas City, Missouri. Studied at Yale. Has been one of the busiest designers in the Theatre since he scored with his sets for "The Old Maid" during the season of 1934-35, which marked his Broadway debut. Among his hits are: "Life With

Father," 1939; "Blithe Spirit," 1941; "The Voice Of The Turtle," 1943; "Jacobowsky And The Colonel," "The Late George Apley," "Laffing Room Only," 1944; "The Winter's Tale," 1946. This season he designed "Obsession," "Craigs' Wife," and "Bathsheba."

CLURMAN, HAROLD. Producer and Director. Born September 18, 1901 in New York City. Educated at Columbia University and University of Paris. After brief career as actor, worked for Theatre Guild, Jed Harris, John Golden, Rodgers and Hart on production. In 1931 joined Lee Strasberg and Cheryl Crawford in founding Group Theatre. Became close friend of Clifford Odets and has staged all of his plays but one. Has written a book, "The Fervent Years" covering the Group's history. On Broadway has directed: "Awake and Sing," "Waiting For Lefty," "Golden Boy," 1937; "The Russian People," 1942; "Beggars Are Coming To Town," 1945. Co-produced and directed "Truckline Cafe," 1946. Co-produced "All My Sons," and directed "The Whole World Over," this season. He has also directed movies.

CRAWFORD, CHERYL. Producer, Manager. Born September 24, 1902 in Akron, Ohio. Graduated from Smith College, 1925. Broadway debut was as assistant stage manager and bit player in "Juarez and Maximilian" in 1926. At one time was casting director for the Theatre Guild. Also one of the founders and directors of the Group Theatre. Produced "All The Living," 1928; "Family Portrait," 1939; "Porgy and Bess," revival, 1942; "One Touch of Venus," 1943; "The Perfect Marriage," 1944; "The Tempest," 1945; "Brigadoon," 1947. Managing Director of the American Repertory Theatre.

CROUSE, RUSSEL. Producer, Author. Born February 20, 1893 in Findlay, Ohio. Served as press agent for the Theatre Guild for five years, during which time he wrote "The Gangs All Here" and "Hold Your Horses" which were produced in 1930 and 1933 respectively. In 1934 teamed up with Howard Lindsay on the book for the musical, "Anything Goes." Since then they have written "Red Hot and Blue," 1936; "Hooray For What," 1937; "Life With Father," 1939; "Strip For Action," 1943; and Pulitzer Prize Play, "State of the Union," 1945. As producers Lindsay and Crouse have been represented by "Arsenic and Old Lace," 1941 and "The Hasty Heart," 1944.

CZETTEL, LADISLAS. Costume and Fashion Designer. Born in Budapest, Hungary, on March 12, 1904. Studied at the Academy of Art in Munich, at the age of 16 went to Paris and became the only pupil of Leon Bakst. For twelve years he was head designer for Vienna State Opera. Came to America in 1936 after having designed costumes for theatres in Berlin, Vienna, Salzburg, Paris and London. Has designed many Metropolitan Opera Productions, including "The Masked Ball." "Rosalinda," "Helen Goes to Troy" and "La Vie Parisienne" are his Broadway Plays. Costumed Movie version of Shaw's "Pygmalion."

DALRYMPLE, JEAN. Producer, Publicity Director. Born September 2, 1910 in Morristown, New Jersey. Started in vaudeville in an act with the late Dan Jarret. Joined John Golden's staff when he produced "Salt Water," and succeeded in establishing herself as a crack publicist. Opened her own publicity office in 1940 and has since handled many Broadway plays and such personalities as the late Grace Moore, Lily Pons, Vera Zorina, Andre Kostelanetz, Tito Guizar, Nathan Milstein. Is a Latin American concert tour manager and has accompanied both Grace Moore and Jose Iturbi on numerous lengthy trips south of the border. Represents the New York City Center, which she helped organize with then Mayor LaGuardia and Newbold Morris. "Hope for the Best" starring Franchot Tone in 1945, marked her debut as a Broadway producer. This was followed by "Brighten the Corner" with the late Charles Butterworth and "Burlesque" starring Bert Lahr.

DAVISON, ROBERT. Scenic and Costume Designer. Born in Los Angeles, California July 17, 1922. Attended Los Angeles City College. Began Broadway career designing costumes for "Song Of Norway" and "Embezzeled Heaven" in 1944. He designed sets for "Day Before Spring" and "Oh Mistress Mine," 1945; "Around The World," "A Flag is Born," 1946; "Miracle in the Mountains," 1947.

DE LIAGRE, ALFRED JR. Producer and Director. Born in Passaic, N. J., October 6, 1904. Graduated from Yale in 1926. Began his theatrical career at the Woodstock Playhouse in 1930. Served as assistant stage manager for Jane Cowl's "Twelfth Night" 1931, and stage manager for "Springtime For Henry," in 1932. Made his Broadway debut as director and co-producer of "Three Cornered Moon, 1933. Other plays which he has produced and directed are: "By Your Leave," "The Pure In Heart," 1934; "Petticoat Fever," 1935; "Fresh Fields," 1936; "Yes, My Darling Daughter," 1937; "I Am My Youth," 1938; "The Walrus And The Carpenter," 1940; "Mr. And Mrs. North," 1941. The last few seasons he has produced "Voice Of The Turtle," 1943, and "The Mermaids Singing," 1945.

DE MILLE, AGNES. Choreographer. Born in New York City. Attended the University of California. Began as a choreographer for the Joos Ballet, The Ballet Theatre, and the Ballet Russe De Monte Carlo. In 1942, she did "Rodeo" for the Ballet Russe, which led to her being chosen in 1943 to choreograph "Oklahoma." This was followed by "One Touch of Venus," 1943; "Bloomer Girl," 1944; and "Carousel," 1945. This past season did the choreography for "Brigadoon."

DENHAM, REGINALD. Director, Author. Born in London, England, January 10, 1894. Received scholarship at Guildhall School of Music in London. In 1913, joined Beerbohm Tree's Company at His Majesty's Theatre, London; also acted with Benson's Shakespearean Company. Came to America in 1929 to direct production of "Rope's End," followed by "Jew Suss" and "Suspense," 1930. He then went back to London, returning again in 1940 to stage "Ladies in Retirement," which he co-authored. Then followed "Play With Fire," 1941; "Guest in the House" and "Yesterday's Magic," 1942; "Nine Girls" and "The Two Mrs. Carrolls," 1943; "Wallflower," "Dark Hammock," 1944. The latter two he co-authored with Mary Orr. Also directed "A Joy Forever," "Obsession," "Temper The Wind," 1946; "Portrait In Black," 1947. Co-authored "Dog's Delight" which was produced in London last year.

EISELE, LOU. Costume Designer. Born February 12, 1912 in New York City. Studied at the Art Student's League, Art Institute of California, and assisted well known designers on the Circus, nightclubs and legitimate plays. Broadway debut was "Follow The Girls," 1944. Other shows include "The Lady Says Yes," "The Girl From Nantucket," 1945; and "Ice Capades of 1947." During the 1946-47 season, designed the costumes for "Icetime," "Icetime of 1948," and "A Young Man's Fancy."

ELLIOTT, JAMES S. Producer, Director, Actor. Born in New York City, January 15, 1924. Made his debut as a producer in 1942 when he presented and directed "Arlene." Other plays include "The First Million," 1943; "Too Hot For Maneuvers," 1945; "Accidentally Yours," 1947.

FEIGAY, PAUL. Producer. Born in New York City, March 14, 1918. Educated at Pratt University and Yale School of Fine Arts. Received theatre apprenticeship as assistant stage manager and assistant director for the New Opera Company. In association with Oliver Smith produced "On The Town," 1944 and "Billion Dollar Baby," 1945. This season he presented "Land's End."

FFOLKES, DAVID. Scenery and Costume Designer. Born in Hagley, Worcestershire, England, October 12, 1912. Educated at Sebrights and Birmingham School of Architecture. Served theatre apprenticeship at Cambridge Festival Theatre. Broadway debut in January, 1937 with sets and costumes for Maurice Evans' "Richard II." Designed sets and costumes for "Young Mr. Disraeli," 1937; full-length version of "Hamlet," 1938; and "Henry IV," (Part I), 1939. Also designed the costumes for the World's Fair productions of "Taming of the Shrew," "As You Like It," "Comedy of Errors," and "Midsummer Night's Dream," 1939. Most recent productions: G.I. "Hamlet," 1945; "Henry VIII," "What Every Woman Knows," 1946; costumes for "Brigadoon," 1947.

FOX, FREDERICK. Scenery Designer. Born in New York City, July 10, 1910. Educated at Storm King School, Phillips Exeter Academy, Yale University, and the National Academy of Design. Theatre apprenticeship at Ward and Harvey Scenic Studios, and Ivoryton Playhouse, Ivoryton, Conn. Broadway debut with "Farewell Summer" in 1937. Has designed the sets for over 75 plays including "Johnny Belinda," 1940; "Brooklyn Biarritz," "Junior Miss," 1941; "Men in Shadow," "The Doughgirls," 1942; "The Two Mrs. Carrolls," "Those Endearing Young Charms," 1943; "Ramshackle Inn," "Decision," "Dear Ruth," "Anna Lucasta," 1944; "Good Night Ladies," "A Goose For The Gander," "Kiss Them For Me," 1945; "Little Brown Jug," 1946; and "John Loves Mary," 1947.

FREEDLEY, VINTON. Producer. Born in Philadelphia, Pa. November 5, 1891. Educated at Groton School, Harvard College, University of Pennsylvania Law School. Made Broadway debut in "L'Elevation" on November 4, 1917. Acted in various plays and musical comedies from 1917-1923. Among the plays produced from 1923 to date are: "The New Poor," "Lady Be Good," "Tiptoes," "Oh, Kay," "Funny Face," "Hold Everything," "Girl Crazy," "Spring Is Here," "Red, Hot and Blue," "Anything Goes," "Leave It To Me," "Liliom," (revival with Ingrid Bergman and Burgess Meredith), 1940; "Let's Face It," 1941; and "Jackpot."

FRIED, WALTER. Producer. Born in New York City. Educated at New York City schools and Columbia University. Made Broadway debut as a producer this season with "All My Sons" and "The Whole World Over." Has been general manager for such plays as "Golden Boy," "Awake and Sing," "Life With Father," and "Truckline Cafe."

GOLDEN, JOHN. Producer. Born in New York City on June 27, 1875. Educated at New York University. Made his theatrical bow as an actor at the Harrigan Theatre in 1890. After fifty years, Mr. Golden looks back, with nostalgia, on such hits as: "Lightnin'"; "Three Wise Fools"; "The First Year," 1920; "Seventh Heaven"; "The Wisdom Tooth," 1926; "Let Us Be Gay," 1928; "As Husbands Go," 1930; "When Ladies Meet," 1932; "Divine Drudge," 1933; "The Bishop Misbehaves"; "Susan and God," 1937; "Skylark," 1939; "Claudia," 1941; "Theatre"; "Counsellor-At-Law," revival, 1942; "Three is a Family," 1943; "Made In Heaven," 1946. The last few seasons has devoted his time to the annual auditions, and Equity-Library Theatre.

GORDON, MAX. Producer. Born in New York City, June 28, 1892. Began as a partner with Albert Lewis in the firm of Lewis and Gordon. His firm was associated with Sam H. Harris in production of "The Family Upstairs," "The Jazz-Singer," and "Easy Come, Easy Go," 1925. Commenced independent productions in 1930 with "Three's A Crowd"; "The Band Wagon," "The Cat And The Fiddle," 1931; "Design For Living," "Roberta," 1933; "Dodsworth," "The Great Waltz," 1934; "Jubilee," 1935; "The Women," 1936; "The American Way," 1939; "The Doughgirls," 1942; "The Late George Apley," 1944; "Born Yesterday," "Years Ago," 1946.

GORELIK, MORDECAI. Scenery Designer. Born August 25, 1899. Educated at Pratt Institute. Brooklyn, N. Y. Studied under Robert Edmond Jones, Norman Bel Geddes, Serge Soudeikine. Worked at Neighborhood Playhouse and Provincetown Players, N. Y. Studied stage production abroad at various times since 1922. Broadway debut with "Processional" for the Theatre Guild in 1925. Other plays on Broadway: "Loudspeaker," 1927; "Success Story," 1932; "Men In White" and "All Good Americans," 1933; "Sailors of Cattaro," 1934; "Let Freedom Ring," "Mother," 1935; "Golden Boy," 1937; "Tortilla Flat," "Casey Jones," "Rocket To the Moon," and "Thunder Rock," 1938; "Night Music," 1940; and "All My Sons," 1947. Motion Pictures include "Days of Glory," and "None But The Lonely Heart," both for R.K.O.

HAMMERSTEIN, OSCAR, 2nd. Author, Producer. Born in New York, July 12, 1895. Graduated from Columbia University. Began theatre career as assistant stage manager of "You're In Love," 1917. "Always You," 1919, was the first musical to be produced for which he wrote the book and lyrics. In 1944, he and Richard Rodgers, after extremely successful careers as author and composer respectively, turned producer, presenting "I Remember Mama," "Show Boat," "Annie Get Your Gun," "Happy Birthday," 1946; "John Loves Mary," 1947. He was also represented this season as author of "Show Boat," "Carousel," and "Oklahoma."

HARRIS, HERBERT H. Producer. Born in New York City, fifty years ago. Is president of Charbert. Broadway debut with "The Man Who Had All The Luck," 1944. Other plays on Broadway include: "The French Touch," 1945 and "All My Sons" which he co-produced this past season.

HARRIS, JED (Horowitz). Producer, Director. Born in Newark, N. J. 1899. Attended Yale University. Has produced in New York: "Weak Sisters," 1925," "Broadway," 1926; "Coquette," "The Royal Family," 1927; "The Front Page," 1928; "The Green Bay Tree," 1933; "A Doll's House," 1937; "Our Town," 1938; "Dark Eyes," 1943; "One Man Show," 1945; "Apple of His Eye," and the London production of "Our Town," 1946. This past season, he produced "Loco."

HART, BERNARD. Producer. Born April 21, 1911 in New York. Began as production assistant and stage manager. In 1944 he and Joseph M. Hyman formed a partnership and produced "Dear Ruth," followed by "The Secret Room," 1945, "Christopher Blake," 1946. All were directed by his brother, Moss Hart.

HAYWARD, LELAND. Producer. Born in Nebraska City, Nebraska, September 13, 1902. Attended Princeton University. Husband of Margaret Sullavan. After establishing successful talent agency in Hollywood and New York turned producer in 1944 and presented "A Bell For Adano," followed by the Pulitzer Prize Play "State Of The Union."

HELBURN, THERESA. Producer, Administrative Director, Playwright. Born in New York City. Studied at Bryn Mawr, Radcliffe, (Professor Baker's 47 Workshop) and Sorbonne, Paris. Began theatre career as playwright with Washington Square Players. One of the original founders of the Theatre Guild. Became Executive Director, 1920. Co-director since 1939. Has actively supervised all Guild productions. Directed "Chrysalis," 1932 and "Mary of Scotland," 1933.

HOPKINS, ARTHUR. Producer, Director. Born in Cleveland, Ohio, October 4, 1878. His first production was "The Poor Little Rich Girl," 1912. Since then has been responsible for "A Successful Calamity"; "Redemption," "Richard III," and "Hamlet" with John Barrymore; "Anna Christie";

"The Hairy Ape"; "What Price Glory?"; "Burlesque"; "Paris Bound"; "The Petrified Forest" and many more. Author of the books: "How's Your Second Act," "The Glory Road," "To A Lonely Boy." Recently he produced and directed "The Magnificent Yankee," and "Hear That Trumpet." Also directed the 1947 revival of "Burlesque."

HORNER, HARRY. Scenic Designer. Born Holic, Czechoslovakia, July 24, 1910. Graduated from University of Vienna. Attended Max Reinhardt's Seminary for Theatrical Arts. Came to America as assistant to Max Reinhardt on "The Eternal Road" in 1935. Designed his first Broadway production "All The Living" in 1937. Followed by: "The World We Make," 1937; "Family Portrait," 1938; "Banjo Eyes," 1939; "Let's Face It," "Lady in the Dark," 1940; "Star and Garter," 1941; "Winged Victory," 1943; and "Christopher Blake," 1946. Has also designed many motion pictures.

HOUSTON, GRACE, Costume Designer. Born in New Bedford, Massachusetts, October 25, 1916. Began theatre career as a dancer with the Rockettes at Radio City Music Hall. After serving as assistant to Irene Sharaff on "Boys And Girls Together," 1940, and Billy Livingston on "Something For The Boys," 1942, she designed her first show "The Two Mrs. Carrolls," in 1943. "What's Up," 1943; "Hats Off To Ice," 1944; "Up In Central Park," "Live Life Again," 1945; "Call Me Mister," 1946; and the revival of "Burlesque," followed.

HYMAN, JOSEPH M. Producer. Born in Cripple Creek, Colorado, on September 30, 1901. Educated at the University of Washington. "There's Always a Breeze," 1937, marked his Broadway debut. Co-produced with Bernard Hart "Dear Ruth," 1944; "The Secret Room," 1945; "Christopher Blake," 1946. Presented "Mr. Peebles and Mr. Hooker" this season on his own.

JONES, MARGO. Director. Born in Livingston, Texas, December 12, 1913. Graduated from Texas State College for Women. Her Broadway debut was as assistant director on "The Glass Menagerie," 1945. "On Whitman Avenue" and "Joan of Lorraine" followed in 1946.

JONES, ROBERT EDMOND, Stage Designer. Born in Milton, New Hampshire December 12, 1887. Graduated from Harvard. Began designing in 1911. Has designed such productions as "Man Who Married a Dumb Wife," 1915; "The Jest"; "Desire Under The Elms"; "The Green Pastures." 1929; "Mourning Becomes Electra," 1931; "Ah Wilderness," "Mary Of Scotland," 1933; "Sea Gull," 1938; "Without Love," 1942; "Helen Goes To Troy," 1944; "Lute Song," 1946.

KANIN, GARSON, Director, Producer, Playwright. Born November 24, 1912 in Rochester, New York. Studied at the American Academy of Dramatic Arts. Married to Ruth Gordon. Began Theatre career as assistant to George Abbott. Broadway debut was as understudy to Burgess Meredith in "Little Ol' Boy," 1933. Turned from acting to directing and from Broadway to Hollywood in 1938. Broadway plays he directed: "Hitch Your Wagon"; "Too Many Heroes," 1937; "The Rugged Path," 1945. Wrote and directed "Born Yesterday," 1946. Directed "Years Ago" this season.

KAZAN, ELIA. Director, Actor. Born September 7, 1909 in Constantinople, Turkey. Received A. B. at Williams in 1930 and had two years graduate work at Yale Drama School. Began theatre work as an apprentice with the Group Theatre in 1932. In 1933 made his debut as an actor in "Chrysalis." This was followed by appearances in many Group Theatre plays. In 1938, interrupted his acting career to direct "Casey Jones." 1941 found him staging "Cafe Crown" and "Skin Of Our Teeth" and turning all his time to directing. "Harriet," "One Touch of Venus," 1942; "Jacobowsky And The Colonel," 1943; "Deep Are the Roots," 1945. Co-produced "Truckline Cafe," 1946 and "All My Sons." Motion pictures include "Tree Grows in Brooklyn," 1944; "Sea of Grass," 1946; "Boomerang," 1947.

KENNEDY, JOHN. Director. Born in New York City, May 9, 1902. Attended Fordham University. Represents the fourth generation in the theatre. After much experience in stock, vaudeville and New York productions, became a stage manager. Made his Broadway debut as a director with "The First Million" in 1943. Followed by: "Artists and Models," "Mexican Hayride," 1943; "Up In Central Park," 1944; "The Would-Be-Gentleman," 1945; "Sweethearts," 1946. Since 1944 General Production Manager of St. Louis Municipal Opera.

KENT, CARL. Designer. Born in New York City, January 28, 1918. Studied at National Academy of Design and Art Students League. Began as a technical supervisor and associate designer. In 1940 he created the sets and costumes for "The New Yorker," a ballet presented by the Ballet Russe. His first Broadway show was "Tis of Thee," 1940. Followed by: "Career Angel," 1944; "Brief Holiday," "Interplay," ballet from "Concert Varieties," 1945; "As We Forgive Our Debtors," 1947. Also wrote music for "Crazy With The Heat."

LANGNER, LAWRENCE, Producer, Administrative Director, and Author. Born in Swansea, Wales. Married to Armina Marshall. Attended Birkbeck College, London and Polytechnic Institute. Began Theatre work with J. Bannister Howard, in London and the Washington Square Players in New York. Has actively supervised all plays produced by the Theatre Guild of which he is the founder. Authored "The Family Exit," 1932, and other one act plays; "Pursuit of Happiness," "The School For Husbands," which he also directed, 1933; "Susanna And The Elders," 1941. Founded and operates Westport Country Playhouse.

LEVE, SAMUEL. Scenic Designer. Born, Yanowa, in the Pripet Marshes, near Pinsk, Russia-Poland, December 7, 1910. Came to America in 1920. In 1935 graduated from Yale University. Began theatre career in summer theatres. Broadway debut was Mercury Theatre productions of "Julius Caesar" and "Shoemakers' Holiday," 1937. Other plays include: "Big Blow" for Federal Theatre, 1938; "Medicine Show," 1939; "Beautiful People," 1940; Maurice Evans' "Macbeth," 1941; "Beat the Band," 1942; "Mr. Sycamore," 1943; "Wallflower," 1944; "Hand in Glove," 1945; "A Sound of Hunting," 1946; "The Story of Mary Surratt," 1947.

LEWIS, ROBERT. Director, Actor. Born in New York City, March 16, 1909. Attended City College and Julliard School of Music. Worked with the Civic Repertory Theatre and the Group Theatre. Made his directorial debut with "My Heart's in the Highlands" in 1939. Followed by: "Heavenly Express," 1940 and "Brigadoon," 1947. Has acted in many movies at Fox and M.G.M., currently appearing in "Monsieur Verdoux."

LEWIS, RUSSELL. Producer. Born in Hollywood, California, July 19, 1908. Was educated in Europe. Served his theatre apprenticeship under Robert Edmond Jones. "Under This Roof" marked his New York debut in 1941. In 1946 he joined Howard Young in presenting a revival of "The Desert Song." This season they presented "Obsession," "Lady Windermere's Fan," and "The Story of Mary Surratt," all of which were produced on the West Coast and brought East.

LINDSAY, HOWARD. Producer, Author. Born in Waterford, New York, March 29, 1899. Attended Harvard before he enrolled at the American Academy of Dramatic Arts. Married to Dorothy Stickney. Began as an actor in 1909. His first success as an actor and director came in 1920 with "Dulcy." In 1933 he wrote "She Loves Me Not." Entered the ranks of producers in 1935 with "A Slight Case of Murder" which he co-authored with Damon Runyon. Followed by "Arsenic and Old Lace," 1941 and "The Hasty Heart," 1944. Created the role of 'father' in "Life With Father" in 1939. Co-author with Russel Crouse of "Life With Father," 1939 and "State of The Union," awarded Pulitzer Prize as best play of 1946.

LOGAN, JOSHUA, Director. Has staged many plays and musicals including: "On Borrowed Time," "I Married An Angel," "Knickerbocker Holiday," 1938; "Mornings At Seven," 1939; "Two For The Show," "Higher And Higher," "Charley's Aunt," 1940; "Annie Get Your Gun," "Happy Birthday," 1946; and "John Loves Mary," 1947.

LOWE, DAVID. Producer, Director. Born in New York City, February 28, 1913. Attended Ohio State University, Harvard Law School and Harvard Graduate School of Business Administration. Began his theatrical career as director-manager of Millpond Playhouse, Roslyn, L. I. Broadway productions are: "South Pacific," 1943; "Lovely Me," 1946; "Portrait in Black," 1947. Directed filming of Atom Bomb explosions at Bikini in 1946 for the Army Air Forces.

MAMOULIAN, ROUBEN. Director. Born in Tiflis, Caucasus, Russia, October 8, 1897. Studied at Lycee Montaigne, Paris, and Moscow University. His first Broadway production was "Porgy" for the Theatre Guild in 1927. "Marco Millions," "These Modern Women," "Cafe Tomaza," "Women," "Congai," "Wings Over Europe," 1928; "R. U. R.," "Game of Love and Death," 1929; "Month in the Country," "Die Gluchliche Hant" (The Hand of Fate), "Solid South," "Farewell To Arms," 1930; "Porgy and Bess," 1935; "Oklahoma!" 1943; "Sadie Thompson," 1944; "Carousel," 1945; "St. Louis Woman," 1946. Has done a great deal of work in Hollywood.

McCLINTIC, GUTHRIE, Producer, Director. Born in Seattle, Washington, August 6, 1893. Attended University of Washington and American Academy of Dramatic Arts. Married to Katharine Cornell. Began in 1913 as assistant stage manager. 1914 saw him serving in the triple capacity of stage manager, casting director and actor in Winthrop Ames' production of "The Truth." In 1921 he became a producer on his own. He then staged and produced, "The Dover Road," 1921; "Mrs. Partridge Presents," 1925; "The Shanghai Gesture," 1926. Directed "Saturday's Children" for the Actors Theatre Incorporated in 1927. "The Letter," 1927; "The Barretts Of Wimpole Street," 1931; "Criminal At Large," 1932; "Alien Corn," 1933; "Yellow Jack," and "Romeo And Juliet," 1934; "The Old Maid," "Winterset," and "Parnell," 1935; "Key Largo," 1939; "Mamba's Daughter," 1940; "The Morning Star" which introduced Gregory Peck to Broadway, 1942; "The Three Sisters," 1942. Recent productions are revival of "The Barretts," "You Touched Me," 1945; "Antigone," revival of "Candida," 1946.

MIELZINER, JO. Scenic Designer. Born March 19, 1901 in Paris, France. Studied at the National Academy of Design, Pennsylvania Academy of Fine Arts, Philadelphia and the Art Students League. As a scenic artist, he made his Broadway debut as the designer of the Lunts' production of "The Guardsman" in 1924. "Strange Interlude," 1927; "The Barretts of Wimpole Street," 1931; "Dodsworth," 1932; Cornell's "Romeo and Juliet," 1934; "Winterset," 1935; "Ethan Frome," "Saint Joan," Gielgud's "Hamlet," "On Your Toes," 1936; "Abe Lincoln in Illinois," "Knickerbocker Holiday," 1938; "Pal Joey," 1940; "Watch on the Rhine," 1941; "Pillar of Fire" for Ballet Theatre, 1942; "The Glass Menagerie," 1944; "Carousel," 1945; "The Rugged Path," "Dream Girl," "Annie Get Your Gun," "Another Part of the Forest," "Happy Birthday," 1946; "Street Scene," "Finian's Rainbow," 1947.

MILLER, GILBERT HERON, Producer. Born July 3, 1884 in New York. Son of Henry Miller. Educated at De LaSalle Institute, New York, Freres des Ecoles Chretiennes-Passy, Paris; Muller-Gelenick Realschule, Dresden; Bedford County School, Bedford, England. Began in the theatre as stock actor, stage manager and company manager. In 1922 he presented Doris Keane in "The Czarina," his debut as a Broadway producer. Other plays include: "The Swan," 1923; "The Play's The Thing," 1926; "Journey's End," "Berkeley Square," 1929; "Petticoat Influence," 1930; "The Good Fairy," 1931; "The Animal Kingdom," "The Late Christopher Bean," 1932; "The Petrified Forest," 1934; "Victoria Regina," 1935; "Tovarich," 1936; "Ladies In Retirement," 1940; and "Harriet," 1943; co-produced with Cornell "Antigone" and "Candida," 1946.

MOTLEY—Trade name for **ELIZABETH MONTGOMERY, PERCY AND SOPHIA HARRIS.** Scenic and Costume Designers. A British firm that is represented in London by the Harris Sisters, and in America by Elizabeth Montgomery. Miss Montgomery was born February 15, 1909. First Broadway production was Olivier-Leigh. "Romeo And Juliet," 1940. "The Doctor's Dilemma," 1941; "Lovers And Friends," 1943; "A Highland Fling," "The Cherry Orchard," "A Bell For Adano," 1944; "The Tempest," "Hope For The Best," "You Touched Me," 1945; "Skydrift," "He Who Gets Slapped," 1946. Also did costumes for "Pygmalion," and "Carib Song," 1946. This season "The Importance of Being Earnest."

NUGENT, ELLIOTT. Producer, Director, Author, Actor. Born in Dover, Ohio, September 20, 1900. Son of the late J. C. Nugent. Began career at age of 4 in vaudeville. Made Broadway debut in 1921 as actor, followed in 1922 by "Kempy," which he co-authored with his father. Co-produced with Robert Montgomery "All In Favor," 1942; "A Place of Our Own," 1945; "The Big Two," 1947. Directed "Tomorrow the World," 1943; "A Place of Our Own," 1945 and "Message for Margaret," 1947. Has directed many movies, most recent of which is "Welcome Stranger."

OENSLAGER, DONALD. Scenic Designer. Born in Harrisburg, Penna., March 7, 1902. Attended Phillips Exeter Academy; graduated from Harvard, 1923, (worked with Baker's 47 Workshop). First Broadway production was "A Bit O' Love." in 1925. "Good News," 1927; "Follow Thru'," 1928; "Girl Crazy," 1930; "Whistling in the Dark," 1932; "Anything Goes," "Gold Eagle Guy," 1934; "I'd Rather Be Right," "Of Mice and Men," 1937; "The Circle," 1938; "The Man Who Came To Dinner," "Skylark," "Margin For Error," 1939; "The American Way," 1940; "My Sister Eileen," "Claudia," 1941; "Pygmalion," "Three To Make Ready," "Born Yesterday," "Years Ago," "The Fatal Weakness," "Present Laughter," "Park Avenue," 1946; "The Eagle Has Two Heads," 1947.

PEMBERTON, BROCK. Producer. Born Leavenworth, Kan., December 14, 1885. Attended the College of Emporia, and graduated from the University of Kansas. Served as general manager for Arthur Hopkins from 1917 to 1920. On August 16, 1920, he made his debut on Broadway as a producer with "Enter Madame." In the past twenty-five years he has produced: "Miss Lulu Bett," 1920; "Six Characters in Search of an Author," 1922; "White Desert," 1923; "The Living Mask," "Mister Pitt," 1924; "Goin' Home," 1928; "Strictly Dishonorable," 1929; "Personal Appearance," 1934; "Ceiling Zero," 1935; "Kiss the Boys Goodbye," 1938; "Janie," 1942, and "Harvey," 1944.

PLAYWRIGHTS' COMPANY. Founded in 1938 by Maxwell Anderson, S. N. Behrman, Sidney Howard, Elmer Rice, Robert E. Sherwood and John F. Wharton. Banded together to present their own plays; broke this policy once, when they produced Sidney Kingsley's "The Patriots." This year finds them less two members, due to the death of Mr. Howard and the resignation of Mr. Behrman, and augmented by Kurt Weill. Their initial offering was "Abe Lincoln in Illinois," followed by "Knickerbocker Holiday" and "American Landscape," in 1938. "No Time for Comedy," "Key Largo," 1939; "Two on an Island,"

"There Shall Be No Night," "Journey to Jerusalem," "Flight to the West," 1940; "The Talley Method," "Candle in the Wind," 1941; "The Eve of St. Mark," "The Pirate," 1942; "The Patriots," "A New Life," 1943; "Storm Operation," 1944; "The Rugged Path" and "Dream Girl," 1945; "Joan of Lorraine," 1946.

ROBBINS, JEROME. Choreographer. Born, New York, N. Y., October 11, 1918. Attended New York University which he left to take up dancing. Worked with the Dance Centre, Theatre Workshop, W.P.A. Classes and Summer Theatres. Danced in such musicals as "Great Lady," "Stars in Your Eyes," and "Keep Off the Grass." Made his debut as choreographer for the Ballet Theatre with "Fancy Free." Made his Broadway debut as choreographer of "On the Town," 1944; "Concert Varieties," "Billion Dollar Baby," 1945.

RODGERS, RICHARD. Producer, Composer. Born June 28, 1902, in New York City. Studied at Columbia University, where he met the late Lorenz Hart. They teamed up and wrote "Garrick Gaieties," in 1925, and followed it with many hits. Collaborated with Oscar Hammerstein II, in 1943, on "Oklahoma" and "Carousel" in 1945. In 1944 they turned producers and presented "I Remember Mama," followed by "Annie Get Your Gun," "Happy Birthday," 1946; "John Loves Mary," 1947. Wrote the music for motion picture "State Fair" in 1945.

ROSE, BILLY (William Samuel Rosenberg). Producer. Born in Bronx, New York, on September 6, 1899. Divorced from Fanny Brice. Married to Eleanor Holm. At 18 was shorthand king of the world, averaging 350 words a minute. Entered the world of Arts as a song writer, authoring such hits as "Barney Google," "Mmmmm, Would You Like to Take a Walk?" "Don't Bring Lulu" and others. In 1931 he made his debut as a Broadway producer with the revue, "Sweet and Low"; it was not a hit. He changed the name to "Billy Rose's Crazy Quilt," cut it down to tabloid size, and sent it on the vaudeville circuit; it became a smash hit. Produced the "Casa Manana" show at the Ft. Worth Centennial, and the "Aquacade" Shows at the Golden Gate International Exposition, San Francisco, and the New York World's Fair. Is owner of the successful "Diamond Horseshoe," Manhattan Night Club. Other Broadway productions: "The Great Magoo," 1932; "Jumbo," 1935; "Clash by Night," 1941; "Carmen Jones," 1942; "Seven Lively Arts," 1944; "Concert Varieties," 1945. Writes a syndicated column entitled "Pitching Horseshoes" which reaches approximately 12 million readers daily.

ROTH, WOLFGANG. Designer. Born in Berlin, Germany, February 25, 1910. Studied at the Academy of Art in Berlin. Served his theatre apprenticeship with the Piscator Theatre, Berlin. Came to the United States in 1938. Made Broadway debut with "The First Million" in 1942. Other plays on Broadway include: "Too Hot For Maneuvers," 1945; "Androcles and the Lion," 1946; "Yellow Jack," and "The Wanhope Building," 1947.

SABINSON, LEE, Producer. Born, New York City, November 11, 1911. Attended City College of New York. Made his debut as Broadway producer with "Counter Attack," 1943. Followed by "Trio," 1944; "Home Of The Brave," 1945; "Finian's Rainbow," 1947.

SERLIN, OSCAR. Producer, Director, Author. Born Yalowka (Grodnow), Russia, January 30, 1901. Educated at De Paul Academy and University in Chicago, Ill. Began career by writing vaudeville and musical comedy acts, and working in New York as stage manager and assistant director. In 1929 co-produced and managed "The Guinea Pig," and produced "Broken Dishes." Other plays produced include: "Lost Sheep," 1930; "Life With Father," 1939; "The King's Maid" (also adapted and directed), 1941; "The Moon Is Down," "Strip for Action," 1942; "The Family," 1943; "Beggars Are Coming to Town," 1945; "Washington Square," 1947.

SHORT, HASSARD, Director, Actor. Born in Lincolnshire, England. Educated at Charterhouse, Surrey. Made his debut as an actor in "Cheer Boys Cheer" at the Drury Lane Theatre, London, playing opposite Fannie Ward. After a very successful career in London, he was brought to this country by Charles Frohman in 1901. He continued his career as actor until 1920, when he retired from acting and turned to directing. Among the productions he has staged are: "Her Family Tree," with Nora Bayes, 1920; "The Music Box Revues," of 1921-22-23; "Greenwich Village Follies," "Cradle Snatchers," "Sunny," 1925; "Three's a Crowd," 1930; "The Band Wagon," 1931; "Roberta," "Wild Violets," "As Thousands Cheer," 1933; "The Great Waltz," 1934; "Jubilee," 1935; "The American Way," "The Hot Mikado," 1939; "Lady in the Dark," "Banjo Eyes," 1941; "Carmen Jones," "Something for the Boys," "Star and Garter," 1943; "Mexican Hayride," 1944; "Show Boat," 1946.

SHUBERT, J. J., born in Syracuse, N. Y., August 15, 1880.

SHUBERT, LEE, born in Syracuse, N. Y., March 15, 1875.

SHUBERT, MESSRS., Theatre Managers and Producers. A Corporation formed by the late **Sam S. Shubert.** Began by operating a stock company in Syracuse, and sending small companies on tour. Moved to New York in 1900 and took over the management of the Herald Square Theatre. When Sam Shubert met with a fatal accident in 1905, his two brothers, Lee and Jacob J. Shubert, took over what had become one of the larger theatrical interests in New York. Today as the **Select Theatre Corp.** they manage three-fourths of the legitimate houses in New York and innumerable throughout the United States. As Messrs. Shubert they produce or are financially interested in from ten to twenty productions each season.

SHUMLIN, HERMAN ELLIOTT. Producer, Director. Born December 6, 1898, in Atwood, Col. Began as reporter on a theatrical trade publication, then turned press agent. In 1927, presented his first production, "Celebrity." This was followed by "The Last Mile," 1929; "Grand Hotel," 1930; "The Children's Hour," 1934; "The Little Foxes," 1939; "The Male Animal" and "The Corn Is Green," 1940; "Watch on the Rhine," 1941; and "Jeb," 1946.

SIMONSON, LEE, Designer. Born New York City, June 26, 1888. Graduated from Harvard in 1909. Worked with the Washington Square Players. One of the original directors of the Theatre Guild; he made his Broadway debut under their banner in 1919 as the designer of "The Faithful." Followed by "Heartbreak House," 1920; "Liliom," 1921; "He Who Gets Slapped," "Back To Methuselah," 1922; "Peer Gynt," "As You Like It," 1923; "Goat Song," 1926; "Road to Rome," 1927; "Dynamo," 1929; "Elizabeth The Queen," 1930; "Idiot's Delight," 1936; "Amphitryon '38," 1937; "Joan of Lorraine," 1946.

SMITH, OLIVER. Scenic Designer, Producer. Born in Hawpawn, Wisconsin, February 13, 1918. Graduated from Pennsylvania State College. In 1941 designed settings for the Ballet Russe de Monte Carlo. Made his Broadway debut in 1942 as designer of the scenery for "Rosalinda." Followed by "Perfect Marriage," 1944; "Beggar's Holiday," 1946; "Brigadoon," 1947. He joined Paul Feigay as co-producer and designer of "On The Town," 1944 and "Billion Dollar Baby," 1941. This season he presented "No Exit."

SOREL, FELICIA. Choreographer. Born in New York City. Received her training at the Dalcroze and Chalif Schools and with Michel Fokine in New York, Escudero and Uday Shan-Kar in Paris, and Wigwan in Berlin. Had own ballet theatre and company with Gluck-Sandor. Made Broadway debut in solo concerts. Did choreography for "The Two Bouquets," "Jeremiah," "The Pirate," "Run Little Chillun'," "Trojan Women," "Henry VIII," "Lysistrata."

SOVEY, RAYMOND. Scenic Designer. Born 1897 in Torrington, Conn. Left Columbia University, where he was studying, to teach Art at the Maryland Institute in Baltimore. Made his Broadway debut as designer of the costumes for Walter Hampden's "George Washington." Other productions include: "Little Accident," 1928; "Strictly Dishonorable," 1929; "Strike Up the Band," "The Vinegar Tree," 1930; "The Petrified Forest," "Fly Away Home," 1935; "Tovarich," "Libel," 1936; "Yes My Darling Daughter," "Our Town," "French Without Tears," 1937; "Ladies in Retirement," 1940; "Jason," "The Damask Cheek," 1942; "Tomorrow the World," 1943; "The Hasty Heart," "State Of The Union," 1945; "Apple of His Eye," 1946.

STROOCK, BIANCA. Costume Designer, Fashion Consultant. Born in New York City. Attended Hunter College. Married to James Stroock of Brooks Costume Co. Mother of Warner Bros. new starlet, Geraldine Brooks. Made her Broadway debut with "The Gay Divorce" in 1932. Other plays on Broadway include: "She Loves Me Not," 1933; "Philadelphia Story," 1939; "Claudia," 1941; "The Doughgirls," 1942; "The Voice of the Turtle," 1943; "Dear Ruth," "Soldier's Wife," 1944. Has dressed such famous stars as Tallulah Bankhead, Margaret Sullavan and Martha Scott. This past season she supervised the costumes for "The Fatal Weakness," "Christopher Blake," "Wonderful Journey," "The Big Two" and "Parlor Story."

TAMIRIS, HELEN. Choreographer. Born in New York City, April 24, 1905. Made her debut as a concert dancer in 1927. She had her own company for many years. Entered the musical comedy field as choreographer of "Marianne" and "Stove Pipe Hat." Represented on Broadway by "Up in Central Park," 1945; "Show Boat," "Annie Get Your Gun," and "Park Avenue," 1946.

THEATRE GUILD, THE. A producing organization founded in 1919 by some of the members of what had been the Washington Square Players. Original board of managers were Theresa Helburn, Lawrence Langner, Philip Moeller, Lee Simonson, Maurice Wertheim and Helen Westley. Its present directors are Lawrence Langner and Theresa Helburn. Since its inception it has been a subscription theatre; and today it has almost 100,000 subscribers throughout the country. On April 19, 1919, the Guild raised the curtain on its first production "Bonds of Interest." In the intervening years the Guild has presented nearly a hundred and sixty productions. Its first hit was "John Ferguson," which was also presented during its initial season. Among the Guild successes are: "Liliom," 1921; "Back to Methuselah," 1922; "Peer Gynt," "Saint Joan," 1923; "The Guardsman," 1924," "Strange Interlude," 1928; "Mourning Becomes Electra," 1931; "Mary of Scotland," 1933; "Porgy and Bess," 1935; "Philadelphia Story," 1938; "Time of Your Life," 1939; "Oklahoma," 1943; "Jacobowsky and the Colonel," 1944; "Carousel," 1945; "The Winter's Tale," "O Mistress Mine," "Merry Wives of Windsor," "The Iceman Cometh," "The Fatal Weakness," 1946.

THEATRE INCORPORATED, a non-profit, tax-exempt producing organization founded in 1945. Richard Aldrich, Managing Director. Committed to a sustained program of great plays of the past and outstanding plays of the present. Its income is devoted to building and maintaining a New York Repertory Theatre; to establishing an experimental theatre to encourage young playwrights, directors, and actors; to conducting bi-weekly auditions for actors; to holding a playwrights' seminar for young playwrights with periodic readings of their plays; and to the promotion and the utilization of the stage as an educational force. Last season produced "Pygmalion" and imported the Old Vic Theatre Company from London. This season produced "The Playboy of the Western World" and toured "Pygmalion" to Mexico, Canada and throughout the United States. Also produced "The Wanhope Building," the first production of Experimental Theatre, Inc.

TODD, MICHAEL (Goldbogen). Producer. Born in Minneapolis, Minn., June 22, 1907. Began theatrical career at Chicago World's Fair in 1933. Broadway debut was "Call Me Ziggy," 1936. Other shows include: "Man From Cairo," 1938; "The Hot Mikado," 1939; "Star and Garter," 1942; "Something for the Boys," "The Naked Genius," 1943; "Mexican Hayride," "Pick-Up Girl," "Catherine Was Great," 1944; "Up in Central Park," "Hamlet," "The Would-Be Gentleman," 1945, and "January Thaw," 1946.

WEBSTER, MARGARET. Director, Actress. Born in New York City, March 15, 1905. Educated in England at Queen Anne's School and London University. Became a successful actress in London before coming back to New York. Made her Broadway debut as director of Evans' "Richard II" in 1937. Other productions which she has staged include: full length "Hamlet," 1938; "Family Portrait," 1939; "Twelfth Night," 1940; "Macbeth," 1941; "Flare Path," 1942; "Counterattack," "Othello," 1943; "The Tempest," 1945; "Three To Make Ready," 1946. Founder-Director American Repertory Theatre, Inc., 1946. During season directed "Henry VIII," "What Every Woman Knows," "Androcles And The Lion."

WHITE, MILES. Costume Designer. Born in Oakland, California, July 27, 1914. Educated at University of California, California School of Arts and Crafts and New York Art Students League. Made Broadway debut with "Best Foot Forward," 1941. Other plays on Broadway include: "The Pirate," 1942; "Oklahoma!," "Ziegfeld Follies," 1943; "Bloomer Girl," 1944; "Carousel," 1945; and this past season, "Duchess of Malfi," and "Gypsy Lady." Motion pictures include "Up In Arms" and "Kid From Brooklyn."

WILSON, JOHN C. Producer, Director. Born Lawrenceville, N. J., August 19, 1899. Graduated from Yale University. First theatrical association was with the production of "Easy Virtue" in 1925. Became Noel Coward's manager. In 1935 joined the Lunts in presenting "Point Valaine" and "The Taming of the Shrew." Other plays include: "George and Margaret," 1937; "Blithe Spirit," 1941; "Bloomer Girl," 1944; "The Day Before Spring," 1945. Helped Alfred Lunt stage "The Pirate," 1942, and directed "Foolish Notion," 1945; "Present Laughter," 1946.

WIMAN, DWIGHT DEERE. Producer. Born in Moline, Illinois, August 8, 1895. Educated at Yale University. Gave up a business carer in 1921 to join Frank Tuttle in forming the Film Guild which made movies in Astoria, L. I. Made debut on Broadway as co-producer with Wm. A. Brady, Jr. of "Ostriches," 1925. Other plays on Broadway include "Road To Rome," 1927; "First Little Show," "Vinegar Tree," "Gay Divorce," 1932; "She Loves Me Not," 1933; "On Your Toes," 1936; "On Borrowed Time," 1937; "I Married An Angel," 1938; "Old Acquaintance," "Higher and Higher," 1940; "By Jupiter," 1942; plus some forty others. This past season produced the musical version of "Street Scene."

WINDUST, BRETAIGNE. Director, Actor. Born Paris, France, January 20, 1906. Graduated from Princeton University, 1929. Began his career as an actor with the University Players Inc. Joined the Lunts' Company of "The Taming of the Shrew" in 1935. He was retained by them to direct "Idiot's Delight," 1936, and "Amphitryon '38," 1937. Other plays include: revival of "The Circle," 1938; "Life With Father," 1939; "Arsenic and Old Lace," 1941; "Strip for Action," 1942; "The Family," 1943; "Hasty Heart," "State of the Union," 1945; "Finian's Rainbow," 1947.

YOUNG, HOWARD L. Producer. Born in Chicago, Illinois, July 16, 1911. Graduated from the University of California at Los Angeles. Served as general manager for Homer Curran for many seasons. Made Broadway debut as co-producer with Russell Lewis of "Desert Song" (revival) in 1946. Other plays include: "Obsession," "Lady Windermere's Fan," 1946; and "Story of Mary Surratt," 1947.

John Barton

Charles Butterworth

OBITUARIES

ADRIENNE AMES, 39, film actress and radio commentator, died in N.Y.C. on May 31, 1947. She was a Hollywood star for nine years. More recently she had considerable success with her own radio program. Her only stage appearance was in 1945 in "The Beggars Are Coming To Town."

JOHN BARTON, 69, veteran actor, died in N.Y.C. on Dec. 23, 1946. He played the role of Jeeter Lester in "Tobacco Road" for a period of nine years, both in N.Y. and on the road, following his nephew, James Barton, who had earlier played the same role. Prior to this long engagement, he had appeared in vaudeville for many years, both in this country and in England.

HERMAN BING, 58, movie comic, died by his own hand in Hollywood on Jan. 9, 1947. In 1926 he came to America, and made a brief success as a comedian with a stuttering German accent. In recent years he had been unable to secure work, and depression caused by his failure to make a comeback was considered the reason for his suicide.

ROLAND BOTTOMLEY, veteran actor, died Jan. 6, 1947 in N.Y.C. He went on the stage as a child in England, and first achieved fame in this country in silent motion pictures. Among the plays in which he later appeared were "Death Takes A Holiday," "The Gay Divorcee," "The White Steed," "The Wookey" and a revival of "A Kiss for Cinderella."

MAJOR EDWARD BOWES, 71, radio personality, died in Rumson, N.J. on June 13, 1946. He will be best remembered for his "Original Amateur Hour" on the radio, from which program many young hopefuls went on to fame.

EGON BRECHER, 66, veteran actor, died in Los Angeles, Calif., on Aug. 13, 1946. For eighteen years he was well known in the Viennese theatre both as actor and producer. His first role in N.Y.C. was that of Sparrow in the original production of "Liliom." Later he was associated with the Civic Repertory Theatre. Since 1933 he had been acting in moving pictures.

CHARLES BUTTERWORTH, 49, stage and screen actor, died on June 14, 1946 in Los Angeles as a result of an auto accident. First N.Y. appearance was in "Americana," which was followed by "Allez-Oop," "Good Boy," "Sweet Adeline," "Flying Colors," and "Count Me In." He went to Hollywood where he appeared in many movies, and was also active on the radio. His last stage appearance was in "Brighten the Corner."

ALEXANDER CARR, 68, stage and film comedian, died in Hollywood on Sept. 20, 1946. His greatest stage success was in the role of Mawruss Perlmutter in the "Potash and Perlmutter" series. Other stage appearances were in "Mendel, Inc.," "The Guinea Pig" and "The Wooden Soldier." He also played comedy roles in many moving pictures.

Alexander Carr

Herbert Corthell

Minnie Dupree

W. C. Fields

Walter Gilbert

JOHN COLTON, 60, playwright, died after long illness in Gainesville, Tex., on Dec. 28, 1946. His most celebrated play was "Rain," and he was also the author of "The Shanghai Gesture," "Drifting" and "Saint Wench."

HERBERT CORTHELL, 69, veteran of 50 years on stage and screen, died in Hollywood on Jan. 23, 1947. He appeared in scores of musical comedies, such as "Canary Cottage," "Tumble Inn" and "The Vagabond King." His last appearance on Broadway was in "Arsenic and Old Lace."

EDITH CRAIG, 77, daughter of Dame Ellen Terry and sister of Gordon Craig, died near London on March 27, 1947. For many years was connected with the theatre as actress, producer and designer.

MARIE LOUISE DANA, 70, veteran actress, died in N.Y.C. on Dec. 10, 1946. She appeared in "The Climbers," "Honeymooning," "The Return of the Vagabond" and "The Naked Genius." In "I'd Rather Be Right" she played the role of Roosevelt's mother.

J. MALCOLM DUNN, 70, character actor, died in Beechurst, L.I., N.Y., on Oct. 10, 1946. Among the many plays in which he appeared were "White Cargo," "The Devil Passes," "Men Must Fight" and "This Rock."

MINNIE DUPREE, 72, veteran actress, died May 23, 1947 in N.Y.C. Made her N.Y. debut in 1888 and had a long and illustrious career. Among her earlier plays were "Don Juan" (opposite Richard Mansfield), "The Climbers," "Hedda Gabler" and "The Road to Yesterday" In England she scored in "The Heart of Maryland" and "Way Down East." Later she was seen on Broadway in "The Charm School," "The Old Soak," "The Eldest" and "Arsenic and Old Lace." In 1938 she went to Hollywood and appeared in the film "The Young in Heart." More recently she appeared on the stage in "Dark Eyes," "Last Stop," and made her final appearance this season in "Land's End."

W. C. FIELDS, 66, comedian of stage, screen and radio, died in Pasadena, Calif., Dec. 25, 1946. First appeared on the stage as a juggler in vaudeville. For a period of ten years, he appeared in various editions of the "Ziegfeld Follies" and achieved great success as a comedian. One of his biggest hits was "Poppy," and this led to Hollywood where he became familiar to millions in both silent and talking pictures. He also made frequent radio appearances.

RICHARD FOY, 42, son of the late Eddie Foy, Sr., died of a heart ailment in Dallas, Texas on April 4, 1947. He was a member of the Seven Little Foys, a vaudeville team made up of the five sons and two daughters of Eddie Foy. In recent years, he was a theatre manager in Dallas, Texas.

WALTER GILBERT, 60, well known actor, died of a heart attack in Brooklyn on Jan. 13, 1947. Originally a lawyer, his dramatic power in court led to a stage career. Was seen in "Cobra," "Aloma of the South Seas," "Scarlet Sister Mary," "Mourning Becomes Electra," "Wednesday's Child," and "Skylark."

LUCILLE WEBSTER GLEASON, 59, veteran trouper, died in Hollywood on May 18, 1947. She was the wife of James Gleason, and together they were seen in such shows as "Is Zat So?" "The Fall Guy" and "The Shannons of Broadway." In 1929 they went to Hollywood, where they appeared in a score of pictures.

JOHN HALE, 88, retired actor and theatrical manager, died in Englewood, N.J., May 4, 1947. He was an actor and stage manager for Daniel Frohman and William A. Brady, and company manager for many successful plays until his retirement in 1941.

WILLIAM HARRIS, Jr., 62, well known producer, died in N.Y.C. on Sept. 3, 1946. Among the many plays he produced on Broadway were "The Yellow Jacket," (with Edgar Selwyn) "Arms and the Girl," "East Is West," "Abraham Lincoln," "The Bad Man," "In Love With Love," "Bluebeard's Eighth Wife," "Outward Bound," and "The Greeks Had a Word for It." His last production was "Miss Swan Expects" in 1939.

WILLIAM S. HART, 76, veteran star of stage and screen, died in Los Angeles on June 23, 1946, after a long illness. Made stage debut in 1889, and among his stage hits were "Ben Hur" and "The Virginian." His greatest fame came as a star in

Western pictures, and he became one of the highest paid and best known actors in the world. His movie career lasted from 1914 to 1926. Among his best remembered films are "The Disciple," "The Toll Gate," "Hell's Hinges," "The Square Deal Man," "Blue Blaxes Rawden," "Square Deal Sanderson," "Travelin' On," "Wagon Tracks," "Wild Bill Hickok" and "Tumbleweeds."

LUCIUS HENDERSON, 86, retired actor, producer and film director, died after long illness in N.Y.C. on Feb. 19, 1947. In his early years he played with Booth, Modjeska and Salvini. In 1910 he became interested in films, and directed such early stars as James Cruze, Marguerite Snow and Valentino. His last stage role was in 1929 in "My Maryland."

HENRY HERBERT, 68, Shakespearian actor, died in N.Y.C. Feb. 21, 1947. Associated with Ben Greet and F. R Benson, he appeared extensively in Shakespearian roles, and toured the British Isles and South Africa with his own company. In the American theatre he was seen in "The Lady of the Lamp," "The Man Who Changed His Name," and "Damaged Goods." Last stage appearance was in 1937 in "Arsenic and Old Lace."

LOUISE HOMER, 76, noted contralto, died of a heart ailment May 6, 1947 in Winter Park, Fla. For nineteen years she was one of the leading singers at the Metropolitan Opera, where she was heard in an extensive repertoire including "Aida," "Orfeo," "Le Prophete," "Samson and Dalila," as well as Wagnerian roles. She was also internationally famous as a concert artist.

BRIAN HOOKER, 66, author, playwright and composer, died in New London, Conn., on Dec. 28, 1946. He was the author of or collaborator on "June Love," "Marjorlaine," "The Vagabond King" and "Through the Years." He was also the translator of the acting version of "Cyrano de Bergerac."

SYDNEY HOWARD, 61, British comedian, died in London June 12, 1946. He appeared on the London stage for more than thirty five years, and was one of England's most popular entertainers.

ETHEL INTROPODI, veteran actress, died in N.Y.C. Dec. 18, 1946. A member of a theatrical family, she had been on the stage since she was 14. She was seen in "East is West," "The Trial of Mary Dugan," "Dinner at Eight" and many other plays. Her last Broadway appearance was in 1943 in "Doctors Disagree."

A. P. KAYE, 68, veteran of both British and American stage, died Sept. 7, 1946 in Washingtonville, N. Y. Among his Broadway successes were "Man and Superman," "A Tailor Made Man," "The Green Hat," "Rosalie," "Major Barbara," "Wings Over Europe" and "Plan M."

VINCENT LAWRENCE, 56, playwright, died in Corpus Christi, Tex., on Nov. 25, 1946. Among his plays were "Spring Fever," "Two Fellows and a Girl," "In Love With Love," "Sour Grapes" and "Among the Married." During the past ten years he worked mostly in Hollywood. His last Broadway play was "The Overtons."

CAROLINA LAZZARI, 57, former contralto for the Metropolitan Opera Company died in Stony Creek, Conn., Oct. 17, 1946. During her operatic career she had also appeared with Chicago Civic Opera and as a soloist with St. Louis Philharmonic Orchestra.

ALEXANDER LEFTWICH, 63, stage director and producer, died in Hollywood, Jan. 13, 1947. Associated with the theatre for nearly fifty years, he directed the following hits: "Hit the Deck," "Strike Up the Band," "Connecticut Yankee," "Present Arms" and "Rain or Shine." In his later years, he was a Hollywood film producer.

PAUL LEYSSAC, noted Danish actor, died in Copenhagen on Aug. 20, 1947. He was well known as an actor in London, Paris and Brussels, and in N.Y.C. was a member of the Civic Repertory Theatre for seven years. He was also known for his excellent English translation of Hans Christian Anderson.

CARLETON MACY, 85, veteran character actor, died at the Percy Williams Home, East Islip, on Oct. 17, 1946. He was well known in vaudeville and stock, and appeared in many Broadway plays including "Seven Keys to Baldpate," "Girl Crazy" and "Don't Look Now."

Lucille Webster Gleason

William S. Hart

Louise Homer

Grace Moore

J. C. Nugent

Raimu

F. J. Mc CORMICK, leading member of the Abbey Theatre, died in Dublin on April 24, 1947. Although never starred at the Abbey, he was considered Ireland's greatest actor. Associated with the Abbey since 1918, he played with this company on their five visits to the U.S. He also acted in the films, and made a great hit in the role of Shell in "Odd Man Out."

DONALD MEEK, 66, veteran stage and film actor, died in Hollywood on Nov. 18, 1946. He appeared in character roles in films. He first appeared on the stage as a child actor, and was seen in many Broadway plays, such as "Six Cylinder Love," "Tweedles" and "Broken Dishes."

ROSE MELVILLE, 68, stage star, died in Lake George, N.Y. on Oct. 8, 1946. Her most famous role was that of Sis Hopkins, and she played this part more than 5000 times during the period of 1900 to 1918.

GRACE MOORE, 45, operatic and screen star, was killed in an airplane crash near Copenhagen on Jan. 26, 1947. Appeared on Broadway in "Hitchy-Koo," "Above the Clouds" and "Music Box Revue." In 1928 she made her debut as Mimi in "La Boheme" at the Metropolitan, and sang there for many seasons in such roles as Tosca, Louise, Juliette, Manon and Marguerite. In 1930 she first appeared on the screen, and her most outstanding success was "One Night of Love." In France she made a film version of "Louise" under the supervision of the composer. She also appeared extensively on the radio and on the concert stage.

J. C. NUGENT, 79, well known actor and playwright, died in N.Y.C. April 21, 1947. His theatrical career began in 1900, and he became well known as a stage star and film actor. He was the father of Elliott Nugent, and together they wrote "Kempy" and "The Poor Nut." Later he played on Broadway in "That's Gratitude," "Big Hearted Herbert," "That Old Devil" and "A Place of Our Own." His last appearance on the stage was in "The Playboy of the Western World."

ROBERT O'CONNOR, veteran stage actor, died in Chicago on March 5, 1947. He appeared in the original casts of "The Prince of Pilsen," "Sweethearts" "The Student Prince," "Blossom Time," "Circus Princess" and "The City Chap."

ANTOINETTE PERRY, 58, noted stage director, died in N.Y.C. on June 29, 1946. Her first stage experience was as an actress, and she was seen in "The Music Master," "A Grand Army Man," "The Dunce Boy" and "The Ladder." In 1927 she became associated with Brock Pemberton, and from then on gained recognition as a director of such plays as "Strictly Dishonorable," "Personal Appearance," "Kiss the Boys Goodbye" and "Harvey."

CHANNING POLLOCK, 66, noted playwright, died in Shoreham, L.I. on Aug. 17, 1946. His most famous play was "The Fool." He also wrote "The Sign on the Door," "The Enemy" and "The House Beautiful."

VICTOR POTEL, 57, veteran slapstick comedian, died in Hollywood March 9, 1947. He was one of the original Keystone Cops, and acted in the movies for a period of 37 years.

'RAGS' RAGLAND, 40, stage and screen comedian, died in Hollywood on Aug. 20, 1946. He appeared in burlesque and vaudeville, and was seen on Broadway in "Who's Who" and "Panama Hattie." This latter show led to a screen contract, and his last work was in the movies.

RAIMU, 63, French stage and screen star, died in Paris on Sept. 20, 1946. Well known on the Parisian stage, he went into films in 1930. Best known to American audiences for his screen characterizations in "The Baker's Wife," "Un Carnet du Bal" and "The Well-Digger's Daughter."

ARTHUR RANKIN, 51, stage and screen actor, died March 22, 1947 of cerebral hemorrhage. His father was Harry Davenport, his mother Phyllis Rankin, and his family had been in the theatre for eight generations. In 1923 he went into moving pictures, and after his discharge from the Marines in the last war he started a theatrical agency.

BETTY CLARK ROSS, 67, early silent picture actress, died of a heart attack in Hollywood on Feb. 2, 1947. She played opposite Tom Mix in Western pictures.

IVY SCOTT, 61, musical comedy and operatic star, died in N.Y.C. on Feb. 4, 1947. She made her debut at the age of five, and among the many plays in which she has appeared were "The Merry Widow," "Robin Hood," "Music in the Air" and "Sunny River." Her last appearance was in "Song of Norway."

LEO SLEZAK, 71, leading member of the Vienna State Opera, and father of Walter Slezak, died in Bavaria on June 6, 1946. From 1909 to 1913 he was a leading singer with the Metropolitan Opera Company in N.Y. In the thirties he appeared successfully in many German and Viennese films, including "Two Hearts in Three Quarters Time."

SERGE SOUDEIKINE, 60, distinguished stage designer, died in Nyack, N.Y. on Aug. 12, 1946. Educated in Moscow and Paris, he first designed sets for Maeterlinck's plays, and these gained him immediate recognition. He designed sets for the Metropolitan Opera Company, for "Chauve Souris," for numerous ballets, and for "Porgy and Bess."

EVA TANGUAY, 68, personality songstress and vaudeville headliner, died as a result of a stroke in Hollywood on Jan. 11, 1947. She had been in poor health for many years, was nearly blind and suffered from arthritis. In 1910 she played the lead in the "Ziegfeld Follies," but her greatest fame came in vaudeville. Her best known number was "I Don't Care."

LAURETTE TAYLOR, 62, beloved actress, died in N.Y. on Dec. 7, 1946. First appeared on stage as a child in vaudeville, where she was billed as "La Belle Laurette." Made N.Y. debut in 1903 in "From Rags to Riches." After several years in stock, she returned to N.Y. and established herself as one of Broadway's foremost actresses. Among the many plays in which she appeared are "Alias Jimmy Valentine," "Seven Sisters," "The Bird of Paradise," "Peg O' My Heart" (her most famous role), "Just As Well," "Happiness," "The Harp of Life," "Out There," "The Wooing of Eve," "One Night in Rome," "The National Anthem," "Humoresque," "In a Garden," "The Comedienne," "The Furies," and the revival of "Outward Bound." After a period of retirement, she returned to Broadway in her last triumph, "The Glass Menagerie."

SIDNEY TOLER, 72, veteran stage and screen actor, died in Hollywood Feb. 12, 1947. He had his own company at the age of nineteen, and later toured with Julia Marlowe. He was the author of several plays, including "The Dancing Master" and "Ritzy." Among his stage successes were "Tommy" and "It's a Wise Child." In 1929 he went to Hollywood, where he scored his greatest film success in the role of Charlie Chan.

FLORENCE TURNER, 59, one of America's first film stars, died in Hollywood on August 28, 1946. She was known as "The Vitagraph Girl" and was one of the top screen stars of 1910. After the first world war, she made an unsuccessful attempt to start her own company and lost all her money. During the twenties she appeared in extra roles, and was scheduled for a part in a new movie at the time of her death.

BEN WEBSTER, 82, veteran actor and husband of Dame May Whitty, died in Hollywood Feb. 26, 1947. He began his acting career in 1887 as a protege of Sir Henry Irving, and toured with him and also with Ellen Terry, Dion Boucicault and Mrs. Patrick Campbell. His first American appearance was in 1905 in "The Marriage of William Ashe." He was leading man to Mrs. Campbell in "The Second Mrs. Tanqueray" and "Hedda Gabler." After a long career on the stage, he devoted his later years to films, and was last seen in "Lassie Come Home."

DALLAS WELFORD, 74, retired actor, died in Santa Monica, Calif., Sept. 28, 1946. In 1900 he came here from England as the star of "Mr. Hopkinson." He remained in this country and was later seen in "The Girl from Rectors," "Madame Sherry," "The Were-Wolf," "Blossom Time" and "The Student Prince."

Eva Tanguay

Laurette Taylor

Sidney Toler

FAMOUS PLAYERS OF YESTERDAY

Born Died	
	A
1855-1926	Adler, Jacob
1859-1940	Anderson, Mary
1866-1931	Arbuckle, Maclyn
1868-1946	Arliss, George
1885-1946	Atwill, Lionel
	B
1864-1922	Bacon, Frank
1882-1912	Barrison, Mabel
1882-1942	Barrymore, John
1848-1905	Barymore, Maurice
1873-1941	Bates, Blanche
1880-1928	Bayes, Nora
1854-1931	Belasco, David
1855-1911	Bellew, Kyrle
1873-1944	Bennett, Richard
1863-1927	Bernard, Sam
1845-1923	Bernhardt, Sarah
1869-1927	Bingham, Amelia
1872-1928	Blinn, Holbrook
1833-1893	Booth, Edwin
1893-1939	Brady, Alice
1871-1936	Breese, Edmund
1863-1915	Bunny, John
1872-1943	Byron, Arthur
	C
1900-1938	Cabot, Eliot
1874-1933	Cahill, Marie
1865-1940	Campbell, Mrs. Patrick
1871-1941	Carle, Richard
1886-1936	Carlisle, Alexandra
1862-1937	Carter, Mrs. Leslie
1879-1927	Carus, Emma
1887-1918	Castle, Vernon
1883-1930	Chaney, Lon
1872-1931	Cherry, Charles
1887-1940	Clark, Marguerite
1851-1932	Coghlan, Rose
1878-1942	Cohan, George M.
1876-1916	Cohan, Josephine
1866-1943	Collier, William
1875-1933	Courtney, William
1847-1924	Crabtree, Lotta
1845-1928	Crane, William H.
1875-1945	Craven, Frank
1865-1944	Crosman, Henrietta
1888-1943	Crumit, Frank
	D
1875-1927	Daly, Arnold
1860-1935	Daniels, Frank
1850-1898	Davenport, Fanny
1859-1933	De Angelis, Jefferson
1865-1928	Ditrichstein, Leo
1865-1943	Dixey, Henry E.
1856-1924	Dockstader, Lew
1898-1941	Dolly, Jennie
1869-1934	Dressler, Marie
1853-1927	Drew, John
1870-1920	Drew, Sidney
1877-1927	Duncan, Isadora
1859-1924	Duse, Eleonora
	E
1894-1929	Eagels, Jeanne
1875-1937	Earle, Virginia
1881-1929	Eddinger, Wallace
1868-1931	Edeson, Robert
1871-1940	Elliot, Maxine
1883-1941	Eltinge, Julian
	F
1884-1939	Fairbanks, Douglas
1876-1929	Farnum, Dustin
1881-1910	Faust, Lotta
1868-1940	Faversham, William
1861-1939	Fawcett, George
1887-1936	Fenwick, Irene
1867-1941	Fields, Lew
1865-1932	Fisk, Minnie Maddern
1853-1932	Forbes-Robertson, Sir J.
1872-1913	Fox, Della
1854-1928	Foy, Eddie
1876-1941	Franklin, Irene
1885-1939	Frederick, Pauline
1860-1915	Frohman, Charles
1851-1940	Frohman, Daniel
	G
1717-1779	Garrick, David
1897-1936	Gilbert, John
1855-1937	Gillette, William
1867-1943	Gillmore, Frank
1884-1936	Glendinning, Ernest
1859-1919	Goodwin, Nat C.
1884-1933	Guinan, Texas
	H
1869-1926	Hackett, James K.
1883-1942	Hamilton, Hale
1911-1937	Harlow, Jean
1872-1946	Harned, Virginia
1884-1911	Harringan, Edward
1896-1937	Healy, Ted
1853-1938	Heath, Thomas K.
1879-1936	Heggie, O. P.
1873-1918	Held, Anna
1878-1921	Herz, Ralph
1857-1927	Hilliard, Robert
1870-1929	Hitchcock, Raymond
1885-1912	Hite, Mabel
1874-1932	Hodge, William
1858-1935	Hopper, DeWolf
1873-1926	Houdini, Harry
1893-1943	Howard, Leslie
1880-1936	Howland, Jobyna
1893-1945	Hunter, Glenn
	I
1881-1934	Illington, Margaret
1838-1905	Irving, Sir Henry
1859-1930	Irwin, Flo
1862-1938	Irwin, May
	J
1829-1905	Jefferson, Joseph
1889-1942	Jones, Buck
	K
1874-1939	Kalich, Bertha
1882-1945	Keane, Doris
1858-1929	Keenan, Frank
1809-1893	Kemble, Fannie
1894-1944	King, Charles
	L
1862-1932	Lackaye, Wilton
1856-1929	Langtry, Lily
1888-1938	Lawrence, Florence
1890-1929	Lawrence, Margaret
1878-1935	Lean, Cecil
1870-1941	Leonard, Eddie
1875-1925	Lewis, Ada
1876-1943	Loftus, Cissie
1909-1942	Lombard, Carole
1876-1935	Loraine, Robert
	M
1863-1931	Mack Andrew
1878-1934	Mack, Willard
1865-1931	Mann, Louis
1857-1907	Mansfield, Richard
1854-1928	Mantell, Robert B.
1864-1943	Marshall, Tully
1857-1919	Mason, John
1886-1927	Maurice
1853-1944	Mayhew, Kate
1875-1934	Mayhew, Stella
1888-1931	McCoy, Bessie
1883-1936	McCullough, Paul
1857-1937	McIntyre, James
1867-1927	McRae, Bruce
1879-1936	Meighan, Thomas
1882-1939	Mercer, Beryl
1886-1946	Merivale, Philip
1860-1926	Miller, Henry
1898-1936	Miller, Marilyn
1880-1940	Mix, Tom
1845-1909	Modjeska, Helena
1886-1935	Moore, Florence
1886-1939	Moore, Owen
1900-1941	Morgan, Helen
1894-1925	Morris, Clara
	N
1879-1945	Nazimova, Alla
1898-1930	Normand, Mabel
	O
1880-1938	Oland, Warner
1860-1932	Olcott, Chauncey
1885-1942	Oliver, Edna May
1847-1920	O'Neill, James
1871-1921	Opp, Julie
1902-1939	Osterman, Jack
1887-1943	Overman, Lynne
	P
1860-1941	Paderewski, Ignace
1885-1931	Pavlowa, Anna
1892-1937	Perkins, Osgood
1869-1931	Power, Tyrone
1862-1943	Powers, James T.
1873-1943	Price, Kate
	R
1820-1858	Rachel, Mme.
1860-1916	Rehan, Ada
1870-1940	Richman, Charles
1874-1930	Ritchie, Adele
1861-1928	Roberts, Theodore
1865-1942	Robson, May
1879-1935	Rogers, Will
1864-1936	Russell, Annie
1861-1922	Russell, Lillian
	S
1885-1936	Sale, Chic
1865-1930	Schildkraut, Rudolph
1873-1935	Sears, Zelda
1860-1929	Shaw, Mary
1885-1934	Sherman, Lowell
1755-1831	Siddons, Mrs. Sarah
1882-1930	Sills, Milton
1867-1943	Sitgreaves, Beverly
1891-1934	Skelly, Hal
1858-1942	Skinner, Otis
1859-1933	Sothern, Edward H.
1873-1937	Standing, Guy
1882-1928	Stevens, Emily
	T
1899-1934	Tashman, Lilyan
1878-1938	Tearle, Conway
1892-1937	Tell, Alma
1881-1934	Tellegen, Lou
1864-1942	Tempest, Marie
1865-1939	Templeton, Fay
1848-1928	Terry, Dame Ellen
1834-1911	Thompson, Denman
1887-1940	Tinney, Frank
1853-1917	Tree, Sir Beerbohm
1874-1940	Turpin, Ben
	V
1885-1926	Valentino, Rudolph
1882-1927	Valli, Valli
1894-1943	Veidt, Conrad
	W
1873-1915	Walsh, Blanche
1877-1939	Ware, Helen
1867-1942	Weber, Joe
1879-1942	Westley, Helen
1845-1936	Whiffen, Mrs. Thomas
1889-1938	White, Pearl
1869-1942	Whiteside, Walker
1853-1914	Willard, E. S.
1872-1942	Williams, Hattie
1854-1935	Wilson, Francis
1865-1928	Wise, Thomas A.
1881-1931	Wolheim, Louis
1869-1916	Woodruff, Harry

INDEX

PHOTO CREDITS

Gail Miller—Sketch on page 5; Acme—page 13b.L.; Arthur-Kufeld—Pages 80, 81; Barry—page 99t.; Cecil Beaton—pages 25, 26b.r.&b.L.; Marcus Blechman—pages 15t.r., 151; Stanley Conley—page 126; Cosmo-Sileo—pages 12, 111, 139r.; Engstead—page 134r.; Fred Fehl—pages 119t.L., 128, 130r., 131, 135; Leo Freedman—pages 15t.L.&b.L., 24, 63b.r., 139L.; Peter Gibbons—pages 42, 121; Globe—page 108; Bob Golby—pages 52, 102L., 103r.; Graphic House—pages 9, 31, 37c., 41, 48, 49, 50, 68, 71, 72, 73, 77, 78, 79, 98, 100, 101, 105, 113t.L., 119b.L.&t.r., 124t., 140c., 143, 145; Harcourt, Paris—page 127b.; Hiller-Washburn—page 82; Hugelmeyer—pages 53, 54, 55; International News—page 13b.r.; George Karger—page 8, 22c.r., 124b.; Kolling, Lehker & Toy, Inc.—page 124b.; James J. Kriegsmann—pages 21t.r., 29; Labatt-Simon—page 130L.; Lucas-Pritchard—pages 6, 10, 30, 36, 74, 106; Louis Melancon—page 57b.; John E. Reed—page 26t.r.; William Riethof—pages 16, 97; Otto Rothschild—pages 14, 17; Alex Siodmak—page 13t.r.; Talbot—page 11, 19, 20, 21b.r., 51, 56, 59, 83, 107, 146; Toland. Detroit—pages 60, 61; Richard Tucker—page 63t.&b.L.; Truofsky—pages 84, 86; Valente—pages 57t.r., 62, 109, 122, 137; Vandamm—pages 3, 7, 18, 22t.&b.r., 23, 27, 28, 32, 33, 34, 35, 37t.&b., 38, 39, 40, 43, 44, 45, 46, 47, 58, 64, 65, 67, 69, 70b.L., 75, 76, 89, 90, 91, 92, 93, 94, 95, 96, 102r., 103L., 104, 110, 112, 113b.L.&t.c.r., 114, 116, 117, 118, 120, 123, 127t., 138, 144, 148, 149, 150.

Key (t.) top; (b.) bottom; (c.) center; (r.) right; (L.) left.